Also by Bob

Praise for *Whe*

"Bob Bergin has woven historical fact about the AVG into a thrilling novel. It will grab your interest and hold it to the very end." – **Bob Layher**, Flight Leader, 2nd Squadron "Panda Bears," AVG Flying Tigers

"Old Asia hands love Bob Bergin's novels because the author's adventures help stir up memories of their own. The sights, sounds, smells, and feel of the Far East come alive on his pages. In *When Tigers Fly*, Bergin works another element into his exciting storytelling: expertise in aviation and its role in winning the Pacific War. Buffs of history and fiction will have an equally hard time putting down the book." – **Brett M. Decker**, former Editorial Writer and Books Editor, *The Asian Wall Street Journal,* Hong Kong

"Bob Bergin has made good use of his long experience in Southeast Asia and his knowledge of the Flying Tigers. He has written an exciting warbird adventure – full of details that put you right into the middle of the action." – **Group Captain Veerayuth Didyasarin**, RTAF (Retd.), President, Foundation for the Preservation and Development of Thai Aircraft

"A story that shows great imagination. It's set in exotic places that are remarkably well-described. The characters are fascinating, the plot moves quickly and leads to a surprising climax. The AVG background is a great touch. In my opinion the details are very accurate. A very interesting book." – **Ken Jernstedt**, Flight Leader, 3rd Squadron "Hell's Angels," AVG Flying Tigers

"The plausibility of finding original AVG P-40s was handled well. To me, as a historian of the AVG, the plot at first seemed farfetched. But Bergin even had me going at times: 'Hmmm, maybe it is possible! Aww, come on!' I really enjoyed it." – **Frank Boring**, Co-producer of "Fei Hu," The Story of the Flying Tigers documentary

Praise for *Stone Gods, Wooden Elephants*

"A fast-paced page-turner by an old Asia hand with an insider's knowledge of the intricacies of the antiquities trade. A good read for the armchair adventurer." – **Sylvia Fraser-Lu**, author of numerous books on Asian arts and antiquities, including *Silverware of South-East Asia and Splendor in Wood: The Buddhist Monasteries of Burma.*

"An adventure story with a delightful twist. Bergin leads you through the jungles of Thailand and the world of antiquities with a steady hand and a sharp eye. A good read." – **Richard Rashke**, author of *Escape from Sobibor* and *The Killing of Karen Silkwood*

"A great story that captures the total sensual package of being in Southeast Asia – negotiating the complexities of social relations, colliding with street-level life, peering down the small side streets shrouded with ancient patinas, and stumbling into the riot of everyday adventures, some soft and quiet, others loud and threatening, but all of them worth the price of a return ticket." – **Lew Stern**, Department of Defense Southeast Asia Affairs Specialist and author of many books and articles on Asia

"A surprise at every turn. A pleasant surprise to find that Bob Bergin has written a fascinating mystery in an area where he has a wealth of knowledge. He has been traveling in Asia for many years searching out art and antiques. Weaving his expertise in this area into an incredible story of rare art, smuggling, and deception – while keeping the vision of the lush jungles and klongs of Thailand – proves a rapid pace of intrigue, rushing waters, elephant trails, and mystery." **Dick Rossi**, President, Flying Tigers Association

"Stone Gods, Wooden Elephants has most everything a reader could want – quirky characters, an exotic locale, and an interesting story. I was familiar with Bob Bergin's nonfiction writing, as he is a valued contributor to some of Primedia's historical magazines, so I expected a novel by him to be well worth reading. But I was impressed by this engaging and well-imagined tale." – **Nan Siegel**, Primedia History Group

SPIES *In The* GARDEN

A NOVEL OF WAR AND ESPIONAGE

BOB BERGIN

IMPACT PUBLICATIONS
MANASSAS PARK, VA

Spies in the Garden

ISBNs: 978-1-57023-306-7 (13 digit), 1-57023-306-3 (10 digit)

Library of Congress: 2009932694

Publisher: For information on Impact Publications, including current and forthcoming publications, authors, press kits, online bookstore, and submission requirements, visit the left navigation bar on the front page of our main company website: www.impactpublications.com.

Publicity/Rights: For information on publicity, author interviews, and subsidiary rights, contact the Media Relations Department: Tel. 703-361-7300, Fax 703-335-9486, or email: query@impactpublications.com.

Sales/Distribution: All U.S. bookstore sales are handled through Impact's trade distributor: National Book Network, 15200 NBN Way, Blue Ridge Summit, PA 17214, Tel. 1-800-462-6420. All special sales and distribution inquiries should be directed to the publisher: Sales Department, IMPACT PUBLICATIONS, 9104 Manassas Drive, Suite N, Manassas Park, VA 20111-5211 USA, Tel. 703-361-7300, Fax 703-335-9486, or email: query@impactpublications.com

For those who served

Chungking
CHINA
Kunming
Salween R.
Irrawaddy R.
Hanoi
Mandalay
FRENCH INDO-CHINA
BURMA
Chiang Mai
Toungoo
Sittang R.
THAILAND
RANGOON
Mekong R.
Moulmein
Bangkok

HISTORIC CHARACTERS

American Volunteer Group (AVG) – One hundred American pilots and 200 ground personnel serving under the command of Claire Lee Chennault as a unit of the Nationalist Chinese Air Force. Also known as the "Flying Tigers", this was a U.S. covert action operation before there was a name for it.

Bureau of Investigation and Statistics – The official name of what was really the Chinese Secret Intelligence Service. Aimed primarily at Chiang Kai-shek's political enemies, it carried out "all kinds of espionage and intelligence work". Its leader was Tai Li.

John Birch – An American missionary.

Charles R. Bond – Pilot in the AVG First Pursuit Squadron, the "Adam and Eves." Former U.S. Army Air Corps pilot.

Gregory Boyington – Pilot in the AVG First Pursuit Squadron. Former U.S. Marine Corps pilot.

Claire Lee Chennault – Commander of the AVG "Flying Tigers". A retired U.S. Army Air Corps captain, he came to China in 1937 to be the aviation advisor to Generalissimo Chiang Kai-shek. Also called the "Colonel" and the "Old Man."

Chiang Kai-shek – Head of the Kuomintang (KMT), the Chinese Nationalist Party, and of the Chinese Nationalist Government. Also "the Generalissimo."

Madame Chiang Kai-skek – Wife of the Generalissimo.

Allen Bert Christman – Pilot in AVG Second Squadron. Former U.S. navy pilot and cartoonist.

Chou En-lai – Head of the Chinese Communist liaison office in Chungking.

William "Wild Bill" Donovan – Became President Roosevelt's "Coordinator of Information" in 1941. Later established the Office of Strategic Services (OSS). Awarded the Congressional Medal of Honor for actions in World War I.

James Doolittle – Lt. Col. U.S. Army Air Corps. Legendary barnstormer and air racer.

Harvey Greenlaw – AVG Executive officer. Former U.S. Army officer and aircraft salesman.

Olga Greenlaw – Wife of Harvey, the AVG Executive officer. Appointed by Chennault to keep the AVG's War Diary.

David Lee "Tex" Hill – Deputy Squadron Leader of the AVG Second Squadron "Panda Bears". Former U.S. Navy pilot.

Paul Frillman – An American missionary in China, Chaplain of the AVG.

Flying Tigers – See American Volunteer Group (AVG).

Eddie Liu – Interpreter for Tai Li.

John Van Kuren "Jack" Newkirk – Squadron leader of the AVG Second Squadron Panda Bears. Also known as "Scarsdale Jack" and "Newquack". Former U.S. Navy pilot.

Office of Strategic Services (OSS) – America's strategic intelligence service during World War II. Forerunner of the CIA.

Arvid "Oley" Olson – Squadron leader of the AVG Third Squadron "Hell's Angels".

Edward Rector – Pilot in the AVG Second Squadron Panda Bears. Former U.S. Navy dive bomber pilot.

RAF – British Royal Air Force.

Joseph W. Stilwell – Lieutenant General, U.S. Army. Commanding General of U.S. forces in the China-Burma-India theater. Also known as "Vinegar Joe".

Tai Li – Head of the Bureau of Investigation and Statistics. Chiang Kai-shek's Spymaster. He was called "the most feared man in China."

CHAPTER 1

Kyedaw Airdrome
Toungoo, Burma
November 5, 1941

The morning air was crisp, the sky clear and a brilliant blue. Harry stood by the side of the runway and watched four of the long-nosed airplanes in the distance, maneuvering over the jungle. After a while Charlie, the pilot who had brought him from the railroad station, found him there. "The Colonel will see you shortly," he said. As if in explanation he added, "The Old Man is still pissed off. About 'Circus Day'."

Harry nodded. He kept his eyes on the four airplanes – they were chasing each other now – but the words stuck in his mind. Finally, he had to ask, "Circus Day?"

"Monday," Charlie said, and laughed. "A bunch of airplanes got busted up. It was a goddamn shambles, a circus, one broken airplane after another." He shook his head as if he still found it hard to believe, then looked around. No one was near, so he went on.

"We had some new pilots arrive last week. Monday we started checking them out. Good pilots, most of them, but they never flew anything like our P-40s. One guy – a Navy pilot named Conant – he commanded a flying boat before coming out here. That's a big airplane. It sits high off the water. It was what he was used to. He did fine with the P-40, until he tried to land it. His approach was good, and then he just landed it – thirty feet above the runway. The P-40 stalled and dropped like a brick. Tore off the landing gear, busted the prop, bent the wings. It was a total write-off. And that was just the first busted airplane of the day."

Harry listened while he kept his eyes on the four airplanes. They were in single file now and had slowed down and let the distance between each other grow. The first of them was lined up with the runway, close enough that Harry could see the landing gear when it was extended.

"I think it was six airplanes that got damaged on Monday," Charlie said, his eyes too on the approaching airplane. It was over the end of the runway now, coming in fast and high, maybe too high. Harry had not been up close to modern pursuit airplanes like this P-40, but he had spent time hanging around airports when he was a kid. "Is he trying to land that thing?" he asked.

"Yeah," Charlie said, but there was no conviction in his voice.

The airplane passed over them, still high. It leveled off, and the sound of the engine changed as the pilot powered it down. "Oh, shit," Charlie said. "Here we go again."

The airplane floated toward the far end of the runway. He'll go around for another try, Harry thought. And then the airplane just dropped out of the air. A puff of smoke blossomed where the right wheel touched first and the tire burst with a distant "pop." The airplane bounced back up into the air, then dropped again and landed hard on the same side where the tire had burst. This time the entire landing gear gave way, collapsing up into the wing. The airplane slid down the runway lopsided until the landing gear on the other side folded under, and then the craft slid flat on its belly down the rest of the runway and off into the brush.

A chorus of cheers came from the hangars behind them. "Way to go, Conant!' somebody yelled. There was laughter and someone else shouted, "We don't need any Jap Aces. Conant's here!" There were more cheers.

Men emerged from the hangars and other small buildings that faced the runway, some already running toward the airplane. There was a nurse in the center of one group of runners. It was the first woman Harry had seen here, all starchy white, from shoes and stockings to a small cap perched on her hair that was flaming red. Charlie saw her too. "Hey, Red," he called. "You don't need to run. It's only Conant."

She gave a little wave, slowed to a walk and turned toward them. "You're right, Charlie," she said when she was closer, "I doubt he'll need me." She stopped, a little breathless, and offered her hand to Harry, while Charlie said the unnecessary: "Red's our nurse." She smiled, and Harry saw the concern on her face.

There was a screech of metal and they turned to look at the runway. The fastest runners had reached the airplane and slid the canopy back. The pilot rose slowly from his seat and stepped down on the twisted wing. He stood there for a moment, surveying his broken airplane. They could see him shake his head, and watched as he turned in their direction and waved. The audience by the hangars cheered and laughed. There was a single lingering laugh, and then total silence.

Harry could feel it behind him, a presence like pressure on his neck. He turned to where all the eyes were. In the doorway of one of the shacks, under a sign that said "Operations" stood Colonel Claire Lee Chennault, the "Old Man" himself. He looked like a soldier standing there, in khaki uniform with a shiny leather belt across his chest. All eyes were fixed on him. His eyes were fixed on the broken airplane, his stare so intense that it seemed he could burn a hole through the twisted metal. His jaw was tight with trying not to say something. Time stood still, until – finally – the Old Man turned to go back inside. Before he went in, he spoke. Harry thought he heard a sigh just before the Old Man's words: "Christ on a crutch!"

When he was out of sight, motion began to return to the airfield. In a voice that was smaller now, Charlie said, "Tomorrow's pilot lecture is going to be a doozy. Does that make it seven for the week, Red?"

Red raised her eyebrows. "Seven crashes in three days," she said. "And all I've used so far is a small bottle of mercurochrome."

They had not noticed the man approaching until he stood right alongside them. Moments before he had been standing in the doorway behind Chennault. He was younger than Chennault, but older than the pilots Harry had seen, and looked different from them. It was probably his clothes. Like Chennault, he wore a uniform, but one that made him look British: a khaki bush jacket, but with shorts instead of the long trousers the Old Man wore. Centered on his head was a peaked officer's hat.

"Mr. Ross," he said, offering his hand. "I'm Lieutenant Colonel Greenlaw, the Executive Officer of the American Volunteer Group." The way he said it made it sound important. He gave Harry a moment to digest it, then added, "Colonel Chennault asks that you join him for lunch."

"Well, thank you, Colonel...," Harry said, and turned to Charlie, who winked, and said, "See you later, chum," and hooked his arm through Red's. The two ambled off. They could have been on a stroll in Central Park. Harry and Greenlaw watched them go until Greenlaw said, "Well, Mr. Ross, come follow me."

He led Harry to a dusty sedan, a gray Studebaker parked in the shade of a hangar. They stood by the car and while they waited they could feel the day getting warmer. Greenlaw seemed preoccupied. He stared off across the airfield, not even looking as another of the long-nosed airplanes came in for a landing. Then as if suddenly aware of Harry, he turned to him and said, "The Old Man has a full plate. We have more pilots arriving next week, and we have our hands full with the ones already here." With the smallest trace of a smile he added, "As you may have noticed." Just then they saw the Colonel walking toward them. Greenlaw said, "I'm driving, Mr. Ross. You get in back with the Colonel."

The Colonel shook hands with Harry and looked at him for a long appraising moment. "Pleased to meet you, Ross," he said, and he looked as if he meant it. Up close the Old Man was smaller than he seemed when everyone was looking at him. He was compact, rugged-looking, in his mid-fifties probably, but his hair was still black. His face was tanned and weathered. Deep lines and a square jaw gave him a rough and determined look. This was not a man to have as an enemy.

Greenlaw held the door as the Old Man slid into the back seat, while Harry trotted around the back of the car to use the door on the other side. The Colonel looked quietly out the window as they drove across the airfield and out the gate. It was only when they were on the road heading toward town that he seemed to relax.

"Well, Mister Ross," he said looking over at Harry, "you're not seeing us at our best." He turned to look out the window again before he added, "But it is a better day than Monday." He looked toward Greenlaw and raised his voice to direct his next comment to him. "Did you know, Harvey, that the boys are calling Monday 'Circus Day'?" Greenlaw shook his head, but said nothing. The Colonel leaned back in his seat. He thought for a moment, then said, "You know, Harvey, I think we need to paint a white line across the runway, maybe a third of the way down. If a pilot doesn't have his airplane on the ground when he passes that line, he goes around. And he pays a fine."

"Good idea, Colonel," Greenlaw said. "I'll see to it." The Old Man leaned back in the seat and said nothing more for the rest of the drive.

As they neared the town, Greenlaw caught Harry's eyes in the rear-view mirror and said, "My house is here in Toungoo. The Colonel thought it would be better to have your talk there." He brought the car to a stop before turning on to Toungoo's main street. They sat there for a time and watched lines of trucks roll by. When Greenlaw said, "They're all going to China," Harry suddenly understood. Toungoo's main street was Steel Road. It came all the way from Rangoon, passed through Toungoo town, and headed north to Mandalay, and then kept going north until it reached Lashio. There it became the Burma Road, and crossed rivers and mountains and went on into China, up to Kunming and finally to Chiang Kai-shek's capital, Chungking. With the Japanese controlling China's coast, the Burma Road was China's lifeline. It was the main road into China, the only road. It was always crowded with trucks rolling north, their heavy cargoes, loaded in Rangoon, bulging under roped canvas covers.

When Greenlaw saw his chance, he pulled out, maneuvered around a half-dozen slow-moving trucks, and turned sharply into the courtyard of a two-story wooden house, where two banyan trees stood like sentinels. As the Studebaker rolled to a stop, a turbaned servant waiting on the veranda raced to open the front door. The Colonel led the way in. "Olga!" he shouted. "You have a guest."

The woman who emerged from the back of the house was much younger than the Colonel or Greenlaw, and startlingly attractive. Her black silk slacks and high-collared Chinese blouse were tight and set off a good figure. Her hair was short and dark; her eyes made mysterious with make-up. In the soft light that filtered through bamboo blinds she looked exotic. For a moment Harry thought she was Chinese. "Well, Colonel Chennault," she said. "good morning to you, sir." Her voice was American.

"Olga,' Chennault said, "I'd like you to meet a friend, Harry Ross, up from Rangoon. Harry, this is Olga, Mrs. Greenlaw." Olga offered Harry her hand and looked closely at him as he took it. "Are you one of the Colonel's new pilots?" she asked.

"Harry's not with the group," Chennault answered for him. "He's destined for other things. He's going back to Rangoon this afternoon."

"Well, Harry, welcome to Toungoo – and to the 'New Greenlaw Hotel'." So he did not misunderstand, she added quickly, "This is our home – Harvey's and mine – but we call it the Greenlaw Hotel because it's always open to the group. The boys come at all hours for coffee or for a drink, or just to relax. I hope you will too when you're in Toungoo. You don't have to be one of the Colonel's pilots to come see us."

"Olga, if it's no great imposition, we'll have lunch out on the veranda," the Colonel said, already pushing on the door with open louvers that led outside. He paused halfway out. "Oh, and Olga, could you try to keep the servants away?" Harry saw Harvey Greenlaw catch Olga's eye and raise an eyebrow.

"Why, sure, Colonel," she said. "You just get comfortable. I'll have your drinks out to you in a minute."

"Just coffee, Olga," Chennault said.

"I know, Colonel. No bourbon 'til the sun goes down."

Harry sat down across from Chennault in one of the big teak and rattan chairs. It was comfortable out here, cool and shady under the trees, and very quiet. Olga appeared with cups and saucers, and Harvey Greenlaw came behind her, carrying a silver coffee pot. He poured for both of them, then set the pot near Harry. "Excuse me, gentlemen," he said and went back inside to leave them alone.

Harry and the Colonel sat quietly for a time, sipping at their coffee. When Harry felt the Old Man's eyes on him, he turned to him and the Old Man said, "Son, who are you reporting to?" The question was unexpected and so direct that it took Harry a moment to find his voice.

"Mister Donovan," he said finally, "Colonel Donovan."

"'Wild Bill' Donovan," the Old Man said. "Recipient of the Congressional Medal of Honor."

"Yes sir, Colonel 'Wild Bill' Donovan."

"I understand he has a new title now. Besides 'Wild Bill', I mean."

"I guess you must mean the job President Roosevelt gave him. In July, the President named him the Director of the COI – that's the Coordinator of Information. It's a new office under the White House."

"Now that is a fancy title for 'Wild Bill'." After a moment, the Old Man added, "I understand you call him 'Uncle'."

"I do, sir. But he's not my uncle, just a good friend of my father."

"You must be from New York, like Donovan."

"Yes, sir, I am."

"And Colonel Donovan brought you into the COI and personally dispatched you out here to the East."

"Yes, sir. I had just finished school. I studied Asian History at Columbia and I really wanted to come out here to the East, to see China and Japan. My father wanted me to join him in the law. Uncle Bill – Colonel Donovan – rescued me. He made it possible for me to come out here."

The Old Man smiled, but he looked satisfied. He nodded and set his coffee cup down. "A good man, Donovan," he said. "I know what he's trying to do, and he has a hard road ahead of him – out here in the East anyway. You will learn that out here too, I suppose."

Harry was not sure what to say, and a long silence followed. The Old Man leaned back in his chair and lit a cigarette. He was relaxed now. He exhaled a great stream of smoke at the tree limbs hanging overhead before he went on.

"Donovan sent me a letter. He said you would be coming. He spoke very highly of you. He said you would be representing yourself out here as a journalist." The Old Man looked up at the trees and smiled at that; he said, "Maybe misrepresenting yourself is more accurate. But 'Wild Bill' said I could be completely open with you. And if there is anything I needed, I should just let you know. I appreciate that. There are always things we need out here, even if it's just a bottle of bourbon. Colonel Donovan said you would keep him informed of the progress of our group – and that you would keep both him and me informed of what the Japs are up to here in Burma. I appreciate all that." His black eyes met Harry's. "Frankly, son, I don't see how you will find out what the Japanese are doing. They are way ahead of Donovan and anything he can do. They are way ahead of everybody else out here. The Jap is on the march. He is everywhere. His influence is very wide."

"But the British, sir...."

"Ah, the British,' the Colonel said. He blew more smoke and watched it rise into the trees. "The British have been here for a century, son. But the British are blinded by their arrogance, by their feelings of superiority. They don't see what's happening. They can't see it because they can't believe that any Asian is capable of subverting their colony. They can't believe that the Jap is capable of creating a network of spies in a British colony. Or capable of flying an airplane over it. But the Jap is very good at both, and at many other things besides."

Olga pushed through the door, balancing a steaming bowl of rice on a tray, and put it on the table where two places had been set. Harvey Greenlaw came behind her again, carrying a tray with curry and other dishes that Harry did not recognize. "Why, Olga, you have cooked up a feast," the Colonel said, getting to his feet.

"Well, thank you, Colonel, but it's really the doing of our kitchen help," she replied, causing Chennault to ask, "Does that mean you, Greenlaw?" More good-naturedly than Harry expected, Greenlaw said with a straight face, "One of my many qualifications, Colonel, one of my better ones."

For Harry's benefit, Olga explained about the food, that some of the dishes were Indian, some Burmese, but all were spicy. Harry looked as if he was taking it all in, but his mind was busy with what the Colonel had just said. As soon as Olga and Greenlaw left them to their lunch, Harry turned to the Old Man.

"Sir, Colonel Donovan said that we would have to depend on the British if things turn out badly here. They know the land, and we Americans have no presence here, no capability. We have no means to gather information that would help us evaluate the situation in Burma, or in other parts of Asia."

"What you say is correct, son, more or less. In actual fact, America is here now. We are here, the AVG, the American Volunteer Group. And you are here. You, son, are the point of the spear, the beginning of the intelligence organization that Donovan intends to have in Asia. The American Volunteer Group is a first step in America standing up to Japan's ambitions.

For now, we can not do that directly – we are not yet at war with Japan – but we can do it by helping the Chinese. And now you are here, alone, or almost alone, I take it. It may not seem like much to you, Ross, but your presence here means that back in Washington, at least Colonel Donovan has a sense of the real situation out here. In time, others back home will start to focus on China, on Burma, on other parts of Asia. They will start to understand what's happening here. Then others like you will come here. In time we will not have to depend on anyone else. For I assure you, son, if we do have to depend on the British, we will all be greatly disappointed."

The Old Man lit up another cigarette from the one he had been smoking, and went on. "Our group, the AVG, won't be in Burma for long. Our work is in China, and by the end of this month, I hope to have the boys up there. You can tell Colonel Donovan that – in fact, I ask that you pass that on to him. By the end of this month, we will have all our airplanes assembled and the boys will be flying them as if they know how. You can tell Donovan that we have our problems. You saw one today. But our problems are all part of the process of turning a group of young men into an effective fighting force. By the end of the month they will be ready."

The Colonel put aside his cigarette. He spooned some curry on Harry's plate, then served himself. "Come on, son, you eat heartily," he said. "You'll learn to love this food." He took a spoonful of curry and tasted it before going on. "There is one other thing I would like you to tell Colonel Donovan. Tell him the Japanese have started to look us over. We've had Jap airplanes flying over the airfield recently. They're up high and by the time we get one of our airplanes up there, they are already too far away to intercept. It seems they may be coming from Thailand next door. If they are, I think I know where from. We're planning on flying our own reconnaissance into Thailand shortly. Mind you, son, that's a very sensitive subject. It's not for anyone's ears but Donovan's."

"I also want you to tell the Colonel that if the situation goes downhill, our biggest need will be a warning net, something I have not been able to convince the British that we will need. I have a warning net in China. It's very effective. The Japanese can not approach any of our cities without us knowing exactly where they are and how many airplanes they have."

Suddenly the big louvered door swung open and a tall, lanky young man in khaki shirt and trousers stepped out on the veranda. "Well, if it ain't 'Smilin' Jack' himself," the Colonel said. "I hope you're not here to bring me more bad news, Mr. Newkirk."

"The RAF has landed, Colonel." Newkirk said. He pronounced it "raff," like a word, and it took Harry a moment to recognize it as the acronym for the British Royal Air Force.

"They bring any rank with them?" the Old Man asked.

"Two Wing Commanders and a Group Captain, sir. The Group Captain threatens not to leave Toungoo until he's talked with you. I have a few of the boys chatting them up and serving them tea. Once they taste the tea, the RAF will be eager to get back to their officers' club in Rangoon." He glanced at Harry then, and acknowledged his presence with a nod. "I'm sorry, Colonel, I didn't mean to interrupt your lunch with your guest."

"Young Ross here is a writer, Jack. He's a journalist, but a good man, a friend of the AVG." The Colonel looked right at Harry as he said that, the first time Harry heard himself introduced under his "cover".

"Harry, this is Jack Newkirk. Jack's from your neck of the woods, Scarsdale, New York. He's the leader of our Second Pursuit Squadron, the ones we call the 'water boys,' because the Second is mostly Navy pilots. It's Jack's boys you saw flying out there this morning. They're good pilots mostly, but they can't seem to land an airplane like a normal person. They either land them in the air or try to drive them through the runway."

"It comes from landing on aircraft carriers," Newkirk said, trying to explain as he extended his hand to Harry. "You have to set those airplanes down hard on a ship. And from flying the P-boats, the big seaplanes where the pilot sits 20 feet above the ground."

"Jack, you sit down and keep Ross company. We'll have Olga bring you a plate. Greenlaw will drive me back to the field. You stay with Ross and get him to the four o'clock train. You can say what you want to him. He knows that what we tell him here is not for publication. It's for his edification only. I want him to understand what the local situation is. I also want him to know how our group is progressing. I've told him a few of the things that are going on. Maybe you can fill in any background he needs, and answer his questions."

He turned to Harry. "Sorry I won't be able to join you over dessert. It was a pleasure meeting you, Ross. I'll look forward to seeing you back here again. Give my best to 'Wild Bill'. I will go and thank Olga for this fine meal."

They started getting out of their chairs, but the Colonel was through the door before they could manage it. Newkirk looked at Harry and shrugged. "The Old Man is a pistol. They sure keep him busy." As they sat back down, he asked. "What can I help you with, Mr. Ross? I suppose you know how we're organized and what our mission is."

"What I know is probably a bit sketchy. I know the AVG has a hundred airplanes and about three hundred men, and that a hundred of those men are pilots. I understand you all came from the U.S. Army, Navy and Marines, but you had to resign your commissions. So that makes you civilians now. I know you have all signed contracts, but I don't know with whom. And I didn't know there were any women involved with the AVG, but I met a nurse out at the airfield."

"You have most of it," Newkirk said. "As far as the ladies go, we have two of them, Red and Jo. They're both nurses. Both very good, they fit right in. And, of course, there's Olga. She's not an official part of the AVG, but she's been a good friend to all of us. As far as how many of us there are, I don't know the exact number of people we have right now. When we're all together we should have about 300, or maybe a few less than that. Not everybody is here yet, and in the last couple of months we've lost a few. We lost three pilots to accidents, and a few more pilots, and some ground crew to resignations. And we are all civilians. Our contracts are for one year with a Chinese-American company named CAMCO – the Central Aircraft and Manufacturing Company. The company handles projects for the Chinese government. As far as our mission goes, that's to protect the Burma Road."

Newkirk paused here, looked directly at Harry for a long moment. With a small smile he added, "And to perform other duties that are assigned to the AVG. Our basic job, Mr. Ross, is to help the Chinese defend themselves from the Japanese. As I'm sure you know, the AVG is a unit of the Chinese Army Air Force."

Harry did not respond immediately. Newkirk's openness made it easy to talk with him, and his comments brought home the significance of what Harry was seeing here. He found it easy enough to accept it all when Colonel Donovan had first explained the AVG to him in Washington. Talking with Chennault had impressed it deeper. But now, listening to Newkirk, it suddenly became very real. He shrugged. It was an unconscious gesture of his acceptance of what it all meant, and he summed it up:

"A secret group to fight a secret war."

"That's what it is, Mr. Ross." Newkirk was smiling.

It was a long moment before Harry found his next question. "Your airplanes are going to be very important. How are they? Is the P-40 a good airplane?"

"It's as good an airplane as most of us have flown. The P-40 is not the hottest thing in the sky. The British call it the Tomahawk, and they're not particularly impressed with it. The big question is, is it a match for Japanese airplanes? The Colonel is the one who could best tell you that. He's watched the Jap airplanes in the skies over China for years. He's seen them bomb Chinese cities and shoot the Chinese Air Force out of the sky. I think we can handle the Jap bombers all right, but their pursuit airplanes are something else. They are lighter than ours, and they're quicker and more agile. The Old Man has strong ideas about what we will do when we meet them. He was a teacher, you know, somewhere back in civilian life. Every morning here in Toungoo he lectures the pilots on Jap airplanes and the tactics they use. He calls it his kindergarten. He believes that if we do as he says, we'll lick the Japs in the air. I think he's right."

"It sounds like the Colonel will have the AVG prepared to stand up to the Japanese Air Force. But the AVG is going up to China. What about Burma? Do you think the Japanese will come this way? Will there be war with the Japanese here?"

"Oh, there will be war here, Mr. Ross. The Japanese are coming. It won't be long."

It struck Harry that Jack Newkirk from Scarsdale, New York, was very confident in what he said.

CHAPTER 2

Rangoon, Burma
November 7, 1941

Harry would never have seen the girl that second time had it not been for the obnoxious "brrraaap" of her little red roadster. Even so, he got only a glimpse. She went by so fast that he could not be certain that it was her.

He was in the back seat of the hotel's big black Buick, on his way to meet Doyle at the Gymkhanna Club, craning his neck, trying to see both sides of the street at once. They were passing through a high–class part of Rangoon he had not seen before, and he wanted to see it all. He had all the Buick's windows rolled down so he would not miss anything. That made it breezy, but the breeze felt good.

The driver was a fussy little Burmese with the instincts of a schoolmaster. He seemed determined to teach Harry the name of the owner of every house they passed. "And here, sir," he said as they moved along the front of another mansion at the pace of a leisurely walk, "is the Rangoon residence of Sir Geoffrey Blather-on – or some such worthy – the representative of Woolsey Motors, sir. He has lived in Burma since 1926."

Harry politely looked interested, but was not really listening. The names were all British and totally meaningless. Looking at the houses and imagining what they were like inside was much more interesting. The houses were huge, set well apart from one another, and stood amidst lawns and gardens and groves of trees that were remarkably well tended. When the houses could actually be seen, that is. Too often hedges, trees and walls obscured the view of any passerby. At times the only sign of habitation was a driveway that led toward a distant glade of trees, or stone pillars and iron gates that guarded an entrance. But for the glaring sun and the brilliance of the tropical flowers that spilled over walls, Harry might have been driving through a suburb of any of the more civilized towns of England.

Not that there was any sign of English life – or of any but an abundant plant life. Occasionally, he might glimpse a Burmese gardener, working quietly, the only sound a faint clicking of shears. Once past that, there remained only the drone of the driver's voice and the rustle of the Buick's tires on the road. If Harry listened carefully, he could hear the buzz of a thousand insects, the usual background noise, steady, normal, almost comforting.

It was suburban tranquility at its finest, and to have it shattered by the obnoxious crackle of the car overtaking them was like a daydreaming schoolboy having his ear boxed by the teacher who crept up on him. Harry whirled around to see what was going on – and brrraaap – just like that – the girl in the red car went by. Her eyes met his for the briefest of instants, and he was left watching the sassy rear end of the roadster get smaller and smaller in the windscreen. The girl was beautiful, as beautiful as he had remembered. If it was the same girl. But it had to be – there could be no two like her. On impulse, he asked the driver, "Who was that lady?" .

"The lady, sir, the lady driving the car? I'm afraid I do not know, sir. She is not British, is she? She is probably a Chinese." The last said with a measure of disdain. "And she should not be speeding on this road in any case. Children will be playing here on school holidays."

Harry was quick to come to her defense. "I don't see any children. It's not a school holiday, is it?"

"No, sir. The children are all in England now." After a pause: "And there they will certainly be safer." As if the German bombs falling on England every day now had no meaning in this garden of suburban tranquility.

"The children don't live here." Harry said, stating the fact. .

"The ones of school age, sir. It is better that they attend schools in England than the schools that are here."

"Yes," Harry mumbled, "I'm sure." He stopped listening, and regarded the image of the girl as he had first seen her. It was only three days ago. It was at his hotel, The Strand, the best Rangoon had to offer. He was standing outside the main entrance, on the topmost of the half-dozen or so steps that led to the street. The girl was at the curb, her back to him. He could see nothing of her face, but her proportions, stylish dress, and flowing black hair caught his attention. He was barely conscious of someone joining him on the top step, but the movement must have caught the girl's attention. She looked back and her eyes touched his for an instant before moving on. They stopped somewhere next to him and her face, lovely as it was, lit up then with a smile that took Harry's breath away. He looked to see what had caused this transformation. Next to him was a man, blond, about his age, with the smooth, regular features that Harry thought rather conventional, but that he knew most women would find handsome.

When he looked back to the girl, she was disappearing into the back of a sparkling black limousine that had appeared at the curb. It was a brand new Cadillac. A little wave of her hand and she was gone. It was only as the car disappeared down Strand Road, that Harry was struck by the fact that the girl was not English. She was not Western at all, but probably Burmese or Chinese, or maybe some kind of Indian. Harry had not yet the experience to distinguish between all the races represented in this corner of the Empire. But was it peculiar, he wondered, that her race did not make a bigger impression on him? He had not been in the East long. Perhaps it was that he found her a pleasant contrast to the rather washed-out looking British ladies he was more accustomed to seeing here, with pale skins, bland faces, and looking totally uncomfortable in this lush tropical setting. The girl who had disappeared in the Cadillac looked like she belonged here.

She was still on Harry's mind when the Buick stopped under the canopy at the entrance to the Gymkhana Club. A turbaned Sikh held the car door for him as he bounded up the steps and into the shaded interior of the club, full of energy. He strode right into the dining room, on his left, just as he remembered. It was only a week ago that he had first come here. Doyle had brought him on the very day he arrived in Rangoon. That seemed so long ago, and he was looking forward to seeing Doyle again. They had met just that once, and Harry decided that he liked the man. Which was fortunate: his future here would be closely linked to Doyle. Doyle was his contact in Rangoon, his lifeline, his only link to Uncle Wild Bill Donovan and Donovan's organization.

Ceiling fans turned lazily overhead. Across the room a long row of doors stood open on the garden, making the room fresh and bright. It was well past the formal lunch hour, and few diners remained. Doyle sat at a corner table, almost hidden by a small grove of potted palms.

"Harry. Over here," Doyle spotted him and slid his chair back to stand up. He was tall and healthy-looking, if not particularly good-looking. His face was too angular for that, and horn-rimmed glasses made him look studious. A year or two older than Harry, he seemed much more mature, a young man in a hurry to be finished with his youth. But wise beyond his years, Donovan had said, and told Harry to listen to him. He smiled as Harry came up to him. "Ah, you survived your encounter with Colonel

Chennault, I see. Come, sit, tell me about it." Then as they shook hands, he looked at Harry's face and experienced a brief doubt. "Or did you get to see him?"

Harry could not keep a smile off his face as he slid into the chair across from Doyle. "Of course I did. We had lunch."

"Lunch! Good show! Did he actually talk about what he's doing up there? Did you see what he's accomplishing? Our British friends tell me he's having nothing but problems, that he's been losing airplanes – and men."

Harry looked at Doyle for a long moment, not sure what to say. He was not expecting questions about Chennault's secret operation, not so openly. He looked around the room and confirmed what he already knew, that it was practically deserted. In their corner there was no one to hear, unless a waiter wandered by. Doyle read his mind. "I asked the waiter to leave the menus," he said, "and to come back when we're ready. He won't bother us." He pushed a white card towards Harry. "There's good old roast beef, usually overcooked, but edible."

Harry nodded and looked down at the menu. After a few moments he looked up again and said, "Chennault is having problems. He's lost some airplanes and a couple of pilots in accidents. He said that was normal, part of putting a fighting force together."

Harry picked up the four-day-old *New York Times* that he had carried in with him. He resisted the temptation to look around the room first, but simply pointed at the headline. What he quietly said to Doyle had nothing to do with what the headline said. "My report to Colonel Donovan is taped to the back page. It's in his code. They said you would know what to do with it."

Doyle nodded and a small smile came to his face. He took the paper and glanced at the lead article. "Okay," he said, "I'll get it transmitted to Donovan." He put the paper down on the table and picked up his water glass. He raised it to Harry. "That was well done, Harry, for a new man. Anybody watching us would not give that newspaper a second thought – except maybe a spy. Or a spy-catcher, I suppose."

He grinned then and leaned in. "Look, Harry," he said, quietly, "I know Chennault's operation is sensitive, but the fact is, everyone in Rangoon is talking about Chennault's Air Corps, Chennault's Irregulars. The only ones who don't seem to know what's happening up at Toungoo are the American Consul here in Rangoon and the bigwigs back in Washington." He tapped the *New York Times*. "I hope your encoded insights will bring Washington up to date." He finished by jerking his chin at the far side of the room. "I just saw the waiter. Let's get our ordering over with and we can talk freely."

Ordering was quick and easy. Harry followed Doyle's recommendation and it was roast beef, the trimmings, and gin and tonic all around. Harry was glad for the distraction of dealing with the waiter. It gave him time to recompose his thoughts. When they had their drinks in hand, Harry raised his to Doyle. "Cheers," he said. "Thanks for lunch."

Doyle raised his glass. "Cheers, Harry." They drank and Doyle said, "Today's a week, Harry. It was just last week you arrived. Today you're practically a veteran. How do you like it so far?"

"I like it fine. But it doesn't feel like a week, more like months." He raised his glass for another swallow and added, "I feel totally overwhelmed."

"Overwhelmed by what?"

Harry put his glass down on the table, carefully. "By what's going on," he said. "Or by trying to understand what's going on. It looked so simple back in Washington. There, I was confident that I knew what I was getting into. Now I'm here and I feel I don't have a clue."

Doyle shrugged. "You did have time to prepare, didn't you? You read your assigned reading, listened to your tutors?"

"I actually did that. I read everything from Lao Tzu to Rudyard Kipling. I actually did listen to my tutors. They were quite good. One was a professor of East Asian history, another a former diplomat who spent his life out here. We drank a lot of coffee and talked a lot about Burma, the British, the Japanese, the whole business. It was all simple enough. Then I got here and talked with Chennault, and since then a few others. Now I'm sure I don't know what's going on."

"Ah, the 'mysterious East'." Doyle smiled. "I wouldn't get too concerned, Harry. Not yet. It's early days, as the Brits say. Once you've been here a while, some of the mystery will drop away."

"It's not the 'mysterious East' that bothers me, it's the British Empire. I don't understand how they deal with the Japanese. In Washington there was a lot of concern about Japan being on the march. From what I see here, the British look on the Japanese as a petty annoyance, hardly worth bothering about."

"The British have a need to appear unconcerned when things get serious. I don't know why that is, and I can't say that normal British nonchalance accounts for their lack of urgency in dealing with the Japanese. Things do get complicated out here. It's not just the British and the Japanese. There are also the Burmese, and they're not just a single ethnic group. They're tremendously diverse: Burmans, Karen, Shan, and a half-dozen others. And probably not one of them is enamored with being part of the British Empire. Then there are the Chinese – who are becoming much more aggressive all the time. And next door are the Thai. And then the Indians. Did you know, Harry, that the population here in Rangoon is more than fifty percent Indian? How do you think the Burmese feel about that?"

Harry raised his eyebrows at the number of resident Indians and started to say, "I'm not sure…," but Doyle talked right over him. .

"The Burmese, the Indians and all the rest are a British problem. That's the way I see it. The only problem you and I need to be concerned with is the Japanese. Maybe that's a gross oversimplification, but I don't think we have to understand all of what's going on. We certainly don't have the luxury of time to figure it all out."

"Tell me about the British then," Harry said. "Chennault didn't inspire my confidence in them. According to him, the British are blinded by feelings of superiority. But one of the last things Colonel Donovan said to me was that we owe the British a lot, and that in the bad times that are coming out here, we will have to count on them."

"I'm not sure that I can explain it for you, Harry. I've been in Burma longer than you have, but not by much. I've been here seven, almost eight months now. I know that most of the Americans at our Consulate stay close to the British. This is a British colony after all. The British are in charge, and they know what's going on. Or at least that's the assumption. Most of my friends here – and I don't have many – are British. They're all smart people. They certainly seem to know what's going on. Are their views prejudiced? I don't know if that's the right word for how they look on the Asians. Does that affect how they see the situation out here? I'm sure it does, but I'm not sure it means they don't see things clearly when it comes to the Japanese. Frankly, I really don't know. I don't have enough experience with what's happening here. I don't know of any American who does."

Doyle went on. "I know Donovan expects me, as an officer of the U.S. Consulate, to stay close to our British friends. There's a lot they can teach us about Asia. There's a hell of a lot they can teach us about spying. America hasn't got many spies. You and I will have to teach ourselves how to go about it."

He let Harry think about this for a while, then added, "I think we can learn a lot from the British, but that doesn't mean that we accept as gospel everything the British tell us. God help us if we do. What the British see, and what they tell us they see, is a starting point. You and I will have to work from there. Look at you. You're here, and not declared to the British as a member of the Donovan organization. I take that as a sign that great value is set on our independence in espionage. You, Harry, and others like you will be the core of our espionage efforts here, the core of our future intelligence service – independent of the British and everyone else."

Then lunch arrived, and while the waiter served them they talked about the weather, which was quite nice. The rainy season had ended, and before it got really hot there would be a couple of months of cool nights and mornings. When the waiter left, Doyle turned back to the British. "They have done a lot for us here. Even for Chennault. The airfield he's on is British. Granted, the rent is paid by the Chinese government with American money."

He shrugged his shoulders and, after thinking about it, Harry shrugged his. "You'll see after you've been here a while," Doyle said. "You'll meet some very good Brits, bright and knowledgeable. Some will think like you do; some won't. You'll have to sort that out for yourself."

Harry had said nothing for a long while. He had heard Doyle out and sat thinking. Finally he said, "Spying. Espionage. You used the words, and that's what we're here for. The few days I've been here, I've been all caught up with Chennault and what he's doing. But monitoring Chennault – checking in with him really – is just a friendly gesture toward a man Donovan greatly respects. What I'm really supposed to be doing is finding out what the Japs are up to. How the hell do I do that?"

"I don't know, Harry. You and I are breaking new ground. I know the chaps in Washington expect me to guide you into areas where you can be effective at collecting information. I've given a lot of thought to that, but I can't say I know what those areas are. I don't even know where to begin. Let me tell you what I've been thinking, how I see things breaking down for us. There are just the two of us from the Donovan organization out here, you and me. I'm a member of the American consulate, ostensibly a commercial attaché, and I've been declared to the British as an American intelligence officer. I won't be declared to anyone else, but just by being an embassy officer, I will be suspected of being an American spy by everybody I meet, Burmese, Indians, Chinese and Japanese – and everyone else."

He leaned in closer to Harry. "Now, as for you, you're a journalist. For now at least, you're not a spy to the British or anyone else. So, between us there is a natural division of labor. I will handle all our dealings with the British and talk to all who will want to talk with me simply because I am a U.S. official – and who they will assume has intelligence connections and hence a direct line back to the powers in Washington.

"Your job will be considerably different from mine. You will deal with those who may not want to talk with an American official. You can even go after the Japanese if you like, although I don't think you will be able to do that directly. You might get some idea of what they are doing through the sympathizers, the Burmese and, god help us, the Indians. You might do better going through their enemies – the Chinese. A good Chinese connection could be very lucrative. They know a lot about the Japanese that they will never tell us. In any case, my job will be to point you toward some of those people that I could never talk to as an official."

"I'd love to get at the Japanese. Where would I start? How would I start?"

"Well, you won't have to go far to find a Jap. They're everywhere in Burma. They've been coming here for years and settling down, going into business. Walk down any street in downtown Rangoon. Take a look at the nicer shops – the clean ones, the bright ones, the ones that are not so full of clutter – those are the Japanese shops. It can be a toy shop or a silk shop. It can be a barber shop or a camera shop or a travel agency. Camera shops seem to have a particular appeal to the Japanese. Think about it. It puts them in direct contact with the British soldier. Sell the Tommy his film, and then develop it. Give him a discount so he brings in his friends. Doesn't it strike you how useful developing a soldier's film can be?"

"I get your point, but surely the British know this."

"I'm sure they know it. But I'm not sure they find it terribly upsetting. The British seem to find it terribly difficult to feel threatened by Asians."

"Maybe the Brits are right. What any one Japanese barber or photographer can do may not be very significant."

"I'm sure that's right, Harry. Maybe there's only so much one Jap can do – but isn't intelligence the piecing together of bits of information like a jigsaw puzzle or a mosaic? Even if each Jap brings in only one piece, when you fit together enough pieces, a picture starts to emerge. How much of the picture you see depends on how many pieces you can fit together."

Both of them sat and stared at their drinks and thought about this for a time. "And besides barbers and photographers, there are Japanese here in positions where they could do even more harm," Doyle said. After thinking about this, he added, "All things considered, Harry, you would do better chasing the Chinese for information."

Which reminded Harry. "Do you know a Chinese lady, or at least I think she's Chinese.... She drives a little red English car, an MG, I think. And she also gets chauffeured around in a big black Cadillac."

"How young a lady are we talking about?"

"Early twenties, maybe."

"Sounds like some rich man's daughter – or kept woman. Whoever owns the Cadillac probably is Chinese. Any rich and proper British subject would own a Rolls Royce or Daimler."

"How would I meet someone like that?"

"I don't know, Harry. Join a Chinese temple society, maybe. If she's Chinese, she won't be at any of the usual places. Ladies of color aren't generally acceptable in polite British society. She can't go to many of the places you or I would go to. She could not come here, for example. It just isn't done."

"But I did see her at the Strand."

"That's probably not unusual. The Strand has an international clientele and a lot of business goes on there. I would think that if her daddy or her sugar daddy is rich enough, getting in the Strand would not be a big problem."

"Would an English boyfriend take her there?"

Doyle thought about it. "A daring one might, but I don't think there are that many socially daring Brits." He thought a bit more and added, "Just had a thought. If you want to meet a Chinese girl, you might want to try the Silver Grill. Sooner or later, everybody turns up there."

"The Silver Grill, huh?"

CHAPTER 3

"Are you one of those American pilots then?" The girl was quite pretty. Her English was good, her skin was dark. She was Burmese, maybe, or Indian, but there had to be some English in her too. She had delivered the sandwich he had ordered from the barman, and now stood next to his booth, leaning in toward him.

"No, I'm not," Harry said.

"Oh, you're not American?"

"Not a pilot."

"Oh," she said and straightened up. She smiled, a little sadly it seemed, and turned away. Harry watched her go, disappointed. He was having no luck with the ladies. This was the second night he had come here, and last night had been the same. He had seen women approach other men, chat them up, then leave and reappear with a drink and join them. He had tried the bar and tried the booths. It made no difference. None of the girls had asked to sit with him, or even to buy a drink. A deficiency in his technique? Perhaps he would have to talk to Doyle about that.

He looked around the big room that was the Silver Grill. He was early tonight. His watch was just going on 7 pm, or 1900 hours by the military clock he was trying to get accustomed to. There were few guests so far, just three men sitting at the long bar – every place in British Asia worth its salt had a long bar – and a few more guests in the booths, chatting, or drinking, or having an early meal. It was hard to see who was in the booths. Their high backs made them a good place for a tryst. But, alas, there were no females to tryst with, except two cleaning ladies, ancient crones to Harry, at least half-a-dozen years older than he. Perhaps it was the early hour. Perhaps unescorted ladies appeared only when there was no chance of offending local British gentry who might be present. Even his sandwich girl had dropped out of sight.

Harry sighed. The Silver Grill was a disappointment. He had heard much about it, even before his arrival in Rangoon. Aboard ship, someone said the Silver Grill was "the" place in Rangoon, renowned for friendly women, excellent food and exotic atmosphere. On his first visit he thought he must be in the wrong place. There were few women, and those were not particularly friendly. The food was ordinary and the atmosphere what one would expect in an English pub, a mildly exotic one, perhaps, as one of the barmen did wear a turban.

He chewed his ham sandwich and watched individuals come and go. By the time he finished, arrivals outnumbered departures. It did not make a crowd, but at least the Silver Grill was starting to feel occupied. He stepped up to the bar to order a drink. He had not had the beer he wanted with his sandwich. From his observations of life in Rangoon, it seemed gin and tonic was what one drank while the sun was up, and scotch once the sun went down. He asked for a scotch and, because he did not much care for the taste of scotch, asked that soda be dumped in it. When it came, he took a healthy swallow. It was lukewarm and unpleasant. He did not intend it, but he made a face as he put the glass back on the bar.

"Off, is it?" said the man next to him. A decade or more older than Harry, he had a tanned face, a bushy ginger mustache, and a blazer with a crest on the breast pocket. "No, not off," Harry said as casually as he could. "Just not my usual." He hoped the man would not ask what his "usual" was.

"Pity," the man said, then tipped his glass to Harry. "Cheers." He drank, then turned full-face to Harry, for a good look. "Are you one of the American volunteer pilots?" he asked.

"No," Harry said, "American journalist. And you?"

"Pilot. Royal Air Force. Here to write about the American volunteers, are you?"

"Not just now," Harry said. The Brit nodded. He looked at Harry as if expecting more. "A project for the future, perhaps," Harry added, and then in self-defense asked, "What does the Royal Air Force think of the American volunteers?"

The man's mustache tilted up. "Good chaps," he said. "The ones I've had the pleasure of meeting. Experienced fliers – a good thing, of course." He took another pull at his drink. "What does the RAF think?" He said it "raff," the way Harry heard it pronounced before. "I can't say I know what the RAF thinks. Our leaders don't share such thoughts with a simple Wing Commander. Actually, the idea of a volunteer air corps, a civilian air corps, does seem a bit odd, doesn't it? An air corps needs discipline, military discipline." His mustache twitched. "Believe me, I know of what I speak."

"Wouldn't the American volunteers be helpful out here if the Japanese do come this way?"

The man seemed to need time to think about that. Finally he said, "Don't know, really. I would think we don't need much help. We have good men out here, good airplanes. Some of our chaps fought the Germans during the Battle of Britain. That taught us a bit. It is a different kind of show out here, of course. But there's not much to fear from the Japanese." Perhaps seeing a trace of skepticism on Harry's face, he went on. "The Japanese don't make good airmen. They're runty little devils with poor eyesight. Can't fly at night or in bad weather. Get disoriented very easily. Their airplanes aren't very good either. Nothing like our Spitfires or Hurricanes."

"You have Spitfires here?" Harry asked.

"Well, unfortunately, no. All our Spitfires are needed at home to fend off the Hun and his Messerschmitts. We do have Hurricanes in Singapore, but it's Brewsters here. Do you know the Brewster Buffalo?"

Harry nodded. He remembered photos of the aircraft, fat and round like a barrel, ungainly looking. "That's an American airplane," he said, a little surprised. "That's what you fly?"

"Yes, I fly the Brewster. Fine aircraft, first rate. The Spitfire is magnificent, but our Hurricanes and Buffaloes are as good as anything the Jap has. Jap airplanes are all small, like their pilots, small guns and no armor. Our Buffaloes have two .50 caliber guns in the nose and two in the wing. One good burst from those fellows and the Jap aircraft will just blow apart."

The Brit looked toward the door. "Well, speaking of runty devils, here's your chance to meet the American irregulars. Chennault's Air Corps has just arrived."

Harry turned toward the door where three young men stood looking around, maybe trying to find a friendly face. They were hardly runty; they looked more like athletes. The tallest one was in khaki trousers and shirt, the one next to him wore a civilian shirt and khaki trousers, and the third was totally in mufti, a blazer over blue shirt and gray trousers.

"The three musketeers," the Wing Commander said. "They come here from time to time. They're among the good chaps. The tall one is called 'Tex', which I suppose means he's from the state of Texas. The one wearing the coat is Eddie, the other Bert."

As though hearing them talk about him, the one in the blazer turned toward them and walked over. "Good evening, Wing Commander," he said. There was a trace of the American south in his voice, the courtly south.

"Evening, Flight Leader," the Brit said, and put his drink on the bar to shake hands. "Flight Leader, I would like you to meet one of your countrymen." The Brit turned to Harry and said, "Sorry, but...."

"The name's Harry, Harry Ross. Good to meet you, Flight Leader."

"Ed Rector," the Flight Leader introduced himself. "Just Ed. Nobody calls me 'Flight Leader' but this rank-conscious Brit."

"Now, now, Flight Leader, it must be your need of a drink. Here, let me see to that," he said and turned to the bar. "Boy," he shouted, "Whiskey me, boy. One here for the Flight Leader, and one for his Yank journalist friend here."

While the Brit was dealing with the barman, Ed leaned toward Harry, said quietly, "Didn't I see you up at Toungoo last week? Up at the airfield?"

"I was there on Wednesday, just for the day."

Ed's eyes narrowed. "You know the Old Man," he said. It was not a question.

"Not really. I met him for the first time that day."

Ed nodded. "And you met Newquack."

Harry rolled the name through his mind. It sounded familiar, but not right.

"Newquack," Ed repeated, "Our beloved Squadron leader." When Harry still looked unsure, he added, "Oh well, he probably introduced himself to you as Newkirk. We let him call himself that, except for times when Newquack is more appropriate. It helps him keep things in perspective. Anyway, Jack Newquack said you were a writer of some kind. But he said you were okay, so I guess I can talk with you. Ah, thanks for the drink, Wing Commander," he said, taking a large scotch. Harry took the drink offered him and nodded his thanks.

"Eddie, have you been tormenting poor Newkirk, again?" the Wing Commander asked. Turning to Harry he said, "There, now you see what I meant about the need for military discipline. I don't see how poor Squadron Leader Newkirk puts up with these chaps." Then turning to Ed, he said, "Tell me, Flight Leader, how are things going at Kyedaw," using the name for the AVG's airfield at Toungoo. "If you chaps are demolishing aircraft at your regular rate, you must have used up all your allotment by now."

Rector stuck his nose in the air. In his best Englishman's voice, he said, "Doing quite well, actually. Our side has no need to ration things like dear old England. We have ample supplies of everything." He sniffed at the air. "And I personally haven't destroyed an aircraft in two or three hours."

The Wing Commander narrowed his eyes and pulled back his upper lip to show large front teeth under the ginger mustache. Like Colonel Blimp, he wheezed a bit before saying, "Good show, old chap. It does appear you are ready to take on the Hun, or the Jap. If the Jap does come this way, and should he bring his airplanes, the RAF will try to spare a specimen or two for you civilian chaps."

"Most generous of you, Wing Commander. I'll be sure to pass that on to Squadron Leader Newquack, and to Tex and Bert. They will be most gratified."

Reverting to his normal voice, the Wing Commander said, "As a matter of fact, old boy, I'll be happy to tell them myself. There's something I need to talk to you chaps about." He looked around the room. "Do you happen to know where Tex and Bert have gone off to?"

Rector looked over his shoulder and shrugged. "Don't see them, but they're here somewhere. Come on, we'll find them. See you later, Ross." The Wing Commander looked at Harry, nodded, and with drink in hand, turned to follow Rector across the room.

Harry turned back to his scotch. He had two glasses now, his original, and the one the Wing Commander had brought him. It was going to be a long night. Just then Rector came back. "Harry," he said, "how would you like to see a real swinging joint?" Before Harry could say yes, Ed explained: "Tex and Bert are going with the Wing Commander. The RAF is having some kind of fete over at the officers' club at Mingaladon. That's the RAF aerodrome on the north side of town. Some sort of semi-official party. There won't be any ladies except RAF wives. Not my kind of thing." As an afterthought he added, "Tex is taking the jeep. We can hire a rickshaw. Come on, let's go."

Harry put down his drink and hurried after Ed, who was already striding toward the door. When he caught up, Rector said, "They call it Wallaby's, where we're going. That's the Australian influence. It's really run by a half-caste fellow named Willowby, I think, Ernest Willowby, who's more English than the English. You'll like the place. It's a mixed crowd, some Brits, but everybody else too, Burmese, Indians, half-castes, Chinese even. All the rich ones."

Over Ed's objections, they hired two rickshaws instead of just one. Each could comfortably seat one large American. Where the streets were wide, they rode side by side. Where they were narrow, Ed went first and Harry behind. There was no traffic, and Harry found himself enjoying the slow, steady pace. There was a lot to take in, and the light to see it was good. It came from street lamps here and there, but mostly it spilled from the open fronts of shop houses, or from oil lamps set on sidewalks where small tables had been set, miniature restaurants, hundreds of them it seemed, where whole families sat on tiny stools eating foods from large pots that steamed behind them. Those not dining, stood about in small groups or squatted on the ground and talked about the day or planned the next. There was a babble of voices and laughter, good natured and loud, a mix of smells that came from the food, and from other things, some like fine perfume, some rancid or sickly sweet. When people noticed them, they waved and shouted greetings. Young ladies tittered. The rickshaw boys moved slowly enough to exchange words or make a joke. It was all very pleasant, very happy.

They turned off the main streets and plunged into a warm and humid darkness on a narrow road lined by low-growing trees. Light was sparse here, and only glimmers showed when they passed a cottage, before plunging again into long stretches of dark road. Then, as if a switch had been thrown, there was bright light. They entered the courtyard of a cottage where automobiles were haphazardly parked. The quiet of the night was replaced by voices, laughter, and music. A young man dressed in white ran toward the rickshaws. "Hey, boy! Scotch!" Ed shouted. "Big ones. Chop, chop"

"Chop, chop?" Harry asked. Ed shrugged. "Some of the guys say it means 'hurry up'. I don't know"

They walked through the front door and into a hallway, a room to each side, each like an old lady's parlor. There were lounge chairs and small tables, and little framed pictures on the wall. There were a few women, but mostly it was young men who sat there, legs crossed, looking relaxed, holding glasses. The smoke of a hundred cigarettes hung in the air. Ed took off his blazer and looked around. "Let me throw my coat over the chair and reserve our place. It's mostly Asians here tonight. Ah, here come our drinks. Grab one and we'll go for a walk. There's a cozy little bar in one of the rooms back here. It's got a Victrola. Somebody's usually dancing."

And there was dancing, shoulder to shoulder, a small crowd packed tightly together, the Victrola playing something new by one of the big bands so popular back in the States now. All of the women dancing, and most of the men, were Asian., Ed started into the room, but stopped halfway through the doorway. "It's too crowded," he said. "Let's go back outside."

"Wait a minute." Harry stopped him. "That girl, the one in the red dress. Do you know her?"

Ed turned back to look. "The pretty one? I've seen her before, but I can't say I know her. There, you see the fellow cutting in on her partner just now? That's Flight Officer Collins. He's a RAF pilot. We can ask him."

They waited until the music stopped, but before the floor could empty, the Victrola started playing "Sentimental Journey." Three couples stayed on the small dance floor, swaying to the music. Collins and the girl in red were among them. "Well, Harry," Ed said, sounding resigned, "I think we are fated to have our first drink standing in this doorway." When Harry suggested they could always come back, Ed said, "No, no, now you have me curious too. We'll wait here until the music stops." They stood and sipped their drinks, watched the dancers.

As the music died, Collins and the girl broke apart. Collins headed their way, while the girl turned toward a door on the side. "Hey Collins," Ed said as he came up to them, "I want you to meet my friend, Harry. Come have a drink with us."

He greeted them both and shook hands. "I'll be happy to join you gentlemen. I'll be there in a moment. I need to check in with some friends."

They walked back to the parlor where Ed had left his blazer and found a third chair to pull up to their little table. Collins came along in a minute and sat down.

Ed did not waste time. "Hey, Peter, who was the pretty girl I saw you dancing with?"

Collins smiled. "That's Lucy," he said.

"Lucy," Ed repeated. "The Oriental girl, her name is Lucy?"

"Short for Lucifer, I think."

"Lucifer!" Ed laughed. "A temptress, is she?"

"More of a full-fledged devil, I'd say. Actually, Lucy is a good substitute for her proper Chinese name. That starts with a 'Lu', and then becomes something quite unpronounceable."

"Known her a long time?" Harry asked.

Collins turned to him. "Yes, actually. I met her in London."

"London?" Ed said. "You're full of surprises, Peter Collins. Chinese ladies from London. Whatever next?"

"Lucy was a student there. Many of us here tonight are old boys from schools in England. Or should I say old boys and old girls? Not many of the latter, though. In any case, Lucy did her schooling in England. You might say we became old boys together."

"Well, my goodness," Ed said. And just then Harry saw Lucy walking toward them. Peter saw her too. "And speaking of the devil," Peter said. Harry watched Lucy brush her fingers lightly over Peter's shoulder as she walked around behind him. "Lucy, I'd like you to meet some Yank friends," he said. "They spotted you on the dance floor. You see, I told you so, everybody does notice Lucy."

She took the hand Harry offered, and their eyes met briefly, as they had on two other recent occasions. Harry more than half expected some sign of recognition, a small interested tilt of her head, a glance that lingered and meant, "Ah, it's you." But her glance did not linger, nor did her head tilt in a way that signaled the least interest. Or even recognition. Harry felt himself deflate and become smaller.

He could not help but watch her. He liked the way she looked, the way she moved; he liked everything about her. Her dark eyes lit up when she smiled, bright with life and intelligence. After a while he felt bolder. He leaned toward her and asked, "Did I see you driving a little red car?"

An easy smile came to her lips and totally disarmed him. "It is quite possible. I do have an MG, and it is painted red."

Peter heard some of this. "Chinese red. It's Lucy's heritage"

"I was on my way to lunch...." Harry stared to tell her, but then realized that she was no longer listening to him, but to something Collins was saying. Ah well, he thought, if she was spoken for, maybe she would matter less to him.

"You're a journalist, Mr. Ross?" her voice broke into his thoughts. It surprised him that she knew anything about him. "Yes," he said, "I'm a writer. But please call me Harry."

Her eyes stayed on him, and he saw interest in them. He glanced at Flight Officer Collins, who was in deep discussion with Rector, hands moving in front of his face like banking airplanes. "What kind of things are you writing?" she asked.

"Well," he said, a little uncertainly, "not very much of anything since I've been in Rangoon. I'm still settling in. I hope to write about what's going on here, in Rangoon, in Burma. Back in America right now, people are keen to learn what the Japanese are up to. I hope to be able to tell them a little about that...once I can figure it out. "

"You're employed by a newspaper? In New York?"

New York, the big time. The idea that she would think him involved with that almost made him giddy. "I'm a free lance, actually," he told her. "There are newspapers in New York and in Washington that have promised to publish what I write – if it's good enough." He was not sure what more to say. It was only his cover, after all. He had rehearsed the story numerous times, but found it hard to talk about what he only pretended to be.

Lucy waited expectantly, and when it seemed he would say no more, she asked, "I wonder if you could tell me...," but just then Flying Officer Collins interrupted to see if everyone was doing all right on the drinks. When she turned back to him, Harry asked a question before she could: "What do you do, Lucy?"

"It's why I asked you about writing. It's been my dream to write, but I can't get started."

"If there is something that interests me greatly, I can write about it," Harry offered a little lamely.

"It's really not that," she said. "It's time and other things. Like you, I'm a newcomer here. I got to Rangoon only this summer."

"You came from London?"

She nodded. "By way of China. I was back in China for over a year. The Japanese are making it difficult for us there, and my father wanted me to join his firm. Whatever dreams I might have, my father's dream has always been to have his daughter work in his company."

"What kind of a company?"

"A trading company. Imports, exports, goods of all kinds, but now mostly things to help the war effort in China. The goods come through the Port of Rangoon, but most go to China. You've probably seen the trucks. They're everywhere these days. It makes my father feel virtuous, finding the things that China needs."

"And you work with him. What do you do?"

"A little of everything. He wants me to know everything about the company. I do accounting, invoices and shipping documents, I deal with the problems the British customs office brings us. Sometimes I even supervise the coolies unloading at the docks."

"You work on the docks...."

"That's where our godown is, our warehouse. You must come by sometime. My office is pleasant for morning tea."

Real invitation or not, Harry noted it. "And in your free time you drive a flaming red MG. That must make up for some things."

Just then Collins interrupted them, putting one hand on Lucy's shoulder and holding the other out where Harry could see his watch. "Have to get Lucy home," he said, "before her dad turns me into a pumpkin."

"Flight Officer Collins," Rector said, "you're leaving before the serious drinking even starts." Then he looked at Harry and added, "I guess Harry will have to serve in your stead," and Harry did not like the sound of that at all.

CHAPTER 4

Rangoon, Burma
November 14, 1941

"Congratulations," Doyle said. "You've been noticed." Harry looked at Doyle uncertainly. He was not sure whether this was going to be good or bad. They were sitting in Doyle's secret tea garden, a few unmatched tables and chairs set among the trees and bushes at the end of a small lane where no one ever went. Harry reached for the teapot, and poured himself a cup of tea, which he sorely needed. Last night was not so long ago, and under Rector's influence he had drunk more scotch than he thought possible.

"What have I done?" he asked when he looked up.

"You've scored, old man. You've won yourself a trip to Toungoo."

Harry sighed. "Doyle," he said, "I feel really crappy this morning. Maybe that's why I can't follow you."

"Bad night at the Silver Grill, Harry? Well, you should be pleased. Your very first report, where Chennault said that the Japs have been looking over Kyedaw, the AVG airdrome, Donovan wants all the details. You'll have to get to Toungoo as soon as you can. This morning if possible."

Harry took a long drink of tea. "That's a long way to go. Can't they send us something from Toungoo?"

"They can't, I'm afraid. There's no secure communications. The Brits don't allow Chennault to use their system, and they won't let him set up his own net. The only communication he has is commercial telegraph. The Burmese run that, and I'm sure they would be fascinated with anything the Americans in Toungoo send out. Sorry, Harry, you're going to have to go up there. And then you'll have to come right back to send off your report to Washington."

"Christ, it gets complicated. I'll need somebody to pick me up at the railway station." He remembered that Ed Rector was flying one of the P-40s up to Toungoo this morning, or was it tomorrow? He'd send a telegram. Newkirk had said to use his name.

* * *

Newkirk was waiting with a Studebaker staff car at the Toungoo railroad station and drove him to meet Chennault in the Ops shack out by the runway. It was early afternoon, and hot. The pilots and ground crew had dispersed to shady places.

It was hot and sticky in the little room with just a small fan struggling to move the heavy air. Chennault sat behind the desk, looking comfortable enough. He skipped the pleasantries and started right in. "I've invited Jack to sit in on this, Harry. I told him you're our connection to the intelligence people back in Washington. I won't always be available, and Jack can serve in my stead."

Harry nodded. "The reason I'm here, sir, is that Colonel Donovan wants to know more about the Japanese airplanes that have been looking you over. As you had asked, I sent him your comments about that."

"I don't know if there's much more to tell him," Chennault said. "Well, let me give you some background. The whole business started a few weeks ago, the latter part of October. The Japs were leaving us alone in Kunming. We had no air raids on the city in almost a month. Before that they were bombing Kunming regularly. It was so unusual – leaving us alone like that – that I figured they were up to something. One possibility was that they were repositioning their bombers. The logical place for the Japs to hit us is right here, in Burma. Here we have no warning net, no way to know that they are coming until their bombs start to fall. They would catch all our airplanes on the ground."

"So towards the end of the month…." The Old Man looked at Newkirk. "When was it, Jack, about the 24th?" Newkirk nodded. "So on 24 October, I sent our three squadron leaders into Thailand, Jack here, Olson and Sandell. Thailand is a neutral country, but I thought there was a good chance the Jap was already there. We needed to look. The British don't want us to do that, they don't want to upset anyone. Newkirk and the boys flew over north Thailand. They went as far as Chiang Mai. That's a big city, the biggest in the north. It's a railhead. It's got a nice airfield, it's the place the Jap would be. But Newkirk and company saw nothing. They stayed up high, but they would have seen the airplanes had they been there."

"Two days later, a silver airplane came over Kyedaw. He was up at about 6,000 feet. We sent some P-40s after him, but they could not catch him. Next day, he was back and brought some friends. Again, we couldn't catch them. One of our boys counted five of them. And he confirmed that these airplanes are silver."

"Could these silver airplanes have been British?"

"No, son, all the British airplanes, in Burma and in Malaya, are painted in RAF camouflage. These were not friendly airplanes."

"And you think they're coming from Thailand?"

The Colonel's shoulders moved, just a bit, a small shrug. "That's what I thought. But Jack went there and found nothing."

"If not Thailand, where would they be coming from?"

Newkirk turned to the Colonel, who said, "Go ahead, Jack"

"Indo-China is the other possibility," Newkirk said. "That would be a round trip of over a thousand miles. That's a long haul. Our planes can't do it; maybe theirs can."

Chennault frowned. "Jack's right. If you look at the map – over there on the wall – you can see that east of Thailand is French Indo-China. The French still govern there, but since the fall of France, the government of Indo-China is Vichy French. They are Nazi collaborators, part of the Nazi-Jap Axis. That makes them allies of the Japanese. And that allows the Japanese to base their airplanes in the northern part of French Indo-China."

"Are the British aware of this?"

"You would think so," Chennault said, his jaw tight.

"But it changes nothing for them?"

Chennault sat quietly and did not answer at first. Then he said, "I had asked the Brits for help here at Kyedaw. They've just sent us some Gurkhas. That's a big step forward. Heretofore, they would not let us use American guards or hire Burmese. The natives could wander freely around the airfield day and night."

Newkirk started getting to his feet as Chennault said, "Well, son, I hope that fills 'Wild Bill's' needs. I wish I had more for him. You can tell him that I think it's starting. It won't be long before the Japanese make their move here. Jack will take care of whatever else you need. Jack or one of his pilots will get you to the train."

Newkirk excused himself to stay and talk with Chennault, and Harry walked outside. One of the P-40s was taxiing back up the runway toward the end of a row of a half dozen airplanes. It started turning toward Harry. On the tip of the airplane's wing Harry saw what he had not noticed before, the twelve-pointed white star in a blue circle that he recognized as the insignia of the Chinese Air Force. The P-40 was coming right at him now, and as he wondered whether he should get concerned, it lurched to a stop. With a final roar, the engine was shut down. The propeller slowly wound down and finally stopped. It was very quiet now, only ticking noises coming from the hot engine. The pilot slid back his canopy.

"Hey, Harry!" The pilot waved, then shucked off his goggles and leather flying helmet. It was Ed Rector. "Harry, what are you doing here? How did you get up here so quick?" Not so quick, Harry thought; it was the day before yesterday they had been together in Rangoon. Ed was not waiting for an answer.

"How long are you going to be here?" he asked, after he hopped off the wing.

"I go back this afternoon."

"Ah, too bad," Rector said, and really looked disappointed. "You should stay over. I could have showed you our fine town of Toungoo, and the railroad station hotel – the China Hotel they call it. It's not really very nice, but it's got a restaurant we call the Savoy, and that's fun – if you like your fun a little on the wild side. Hey, if you're going back this afternoon, I'll drive you back to the station. We'll have time for a drink anyway. Come on, walk along with me. I have to change clothes, and there's something I want you to see on the way."

They walked toward an open-sided shed, mostly a roof covering an airplane. When they reached it, Ed jerked his head back over his shoulder and said, "That airplane back there that I was flying, that's not my airplane. I was just doing an engine check. This is my airplane here, Number 36. How do you like her?"

"Impressive," Harry said, and he meant it. He took a step back to see it better. "Scary," he said, looking up, into the gaping mouth of a shark.

"We're painting that on all the airplanes," Ed said. They stood side by side and looked up into the shark's mouth painted on the front of the airplane. The plane's long, pointy nose was perfect for the open mouth with its massive white teeth, red tongue and blue lips. Above the mouth, an eye looked at them, a dull blue pupil in a dead white ball, the vacant stare of a killer. Harry felt a small shiver go down his spine.

"Those Japs are a superstitious bunch," Ed said. "When they see this, God knows what they'll make of it." He reached up and patted the airplane's nose. "If we can scare them to death, we won't have to shoot them."

Ed explained more as they walked. "It was Erik's idea, Erik and Charlie Bond. They saw a photo in the newspapers. A British RAF outfit fighting the Germans in North Africa painted the snouts of their P-40s with shark teeth like that. Erik thought it would be a great squadron insignia. He talked with the Old Man, and the Old Man liked it. He said to Erik, 'You paint all the airplanes like that, the whole AVG.' And so here we are, the 'Sharks of the Sky'." Ed laughed when he said that, and so did Harry. It reminded Ed of something else. "Hey, Harry, not only am I now a flying shark, but I'm a Panda Bear, too. Come over here, I have to show you this." They walked over to another airplane.

"This is Bert's airplane," Ed said. "Bert's an artist, so he painted his own airplane first, for practice."

It was on the side of the airplane, just behind the rear of the canopy, a black and white Panda Bear waving a paint brush. "Isn't that neat?" Ed said, "Bert was a cartoonist before he joined the Navy. He's going to paint Pandas on all the Second Squadron airplanes. Each Panda will be different. Tex's Panda will have cowboy boots and a six gun. There's one of a Panda riding a bicycle – that will go on Pete Pietach's airplane. I don't know what Bert is going to paint on mine."

"How did you guys get to be Panda Bears?" Harry asked.

"Newquack," Ed said, "In his wisdom, Squadron Leader Newquack decided that the Second Pursuit Squadron will be Panda Bears. Heretofore we were known to all and sundry as the 'Water Boys' - because we all came from the Navy." Ed's voice turned more serious. "What actually happened, Harry, is that the AVG has been formally divided into three squadrons. Once that happened, each squadron needed a name and its own insignia. It's a traditional thing. The Third Pursuit Squadron was the first to actually pick a name for themselves. I'll show you. A couple of their airplanes are parked over here."

They walked over to another line of airplanes while Ed explained how the Panda Bears came into being. "Some of us in the Second wanted an insignia with a Chinese theme. Once we finish training here, our job will be to protect China. Newquack came up with this idea of a Panda Bear. That's pretty Chinese, I guess, but some of the squadron didn't like it. A Panda is a cuddly thing, like a kid's Teddy Bear. That's not the image that a pursuit pilot wants to project. But Newkirk is the squadron leader, so he got to choose the name. But look at this, Harry." They stopped under the nose of one of the airplanes. "This is a Third Squadron airplane. Look up there on the side, right under the front of the canopy."

It was not easy to miss. A naked lady sitting there, pert breasts, legs stretched out in front of her. A pair of white wings grew out of her shoulders. The rest of her was brilliant red, including the small halo over her head that made her an angel.

"Did you see the movie, Harry? It was famous a couple of years ago, 'Hell's Angels'. It was about the war in the sky during the Great War. You must have seen it."

"I did see it," Harry said.

"Well, here you are, the 'Hell's Angels', the real ones, brought to life. The Third Pursuit Squadron is now the Hell's Angels."

He gave Harry time to admire the red lady, then they walked on, past more airplanes with red ladies, all different; some sitting, some standing. "I like that one," Ed said, pointing at a red lady looking back over her shoulder, showing off a nicely rounded bottom.

"I like that one too," Harry admitted. It made him think of Lucy. "That's a great insignia."

"Well, it's better than a Panda Bear. But I think the First Squadron is the best. Their art needs some work, but I really like the idea of it."

They walked over to another line of airplanes. Harry knew what to look for now without being told. It was behind the cockpit this time, on the left side of the airplane, farther back toward the tail, a great green ball. He studied it for a moment and it still looked like a great green ball, and that's what he told Ed.

"Well, it's not perfect," Ed said, "They're still working on it. It's supposed to be an apple." He sounded almost disappointed with Harry. "You see, all three of our squadrons are pursuit squadrons, so the First Squadron is the 'First Pursuit'. Got that?" He looked Harry right in the eye. "Okay, maybe it's not that subtle. One of the guys, Dick Rossi, pointed out that the first pursuit had to be Eve chasing Adam through the Garden of Eden. As soon as he said it, everybody knew he was right. And that gave Charlie Bond his idea. He painted a big red apple on his airplane, and on it drew a cartoon of Eve chasing Adam. It looked pretty good. With a little work it would have been fine. But then the Old Man saw it. He said a red apple would never do; it looked too much like the big red ball the Japs paint on their airplanes and call a sun. Charlie had to think about that one. But, hell, there are green apples, so that's what Charlie did – he made the apples green and everybody was happy. Maybe even the Japs?"

Now Harry could make out the ball as an apple. He could even see the stem. And now he saw the stick figures painted on the apple: a running Eve pursuing a running Adam.

"Great idea," he agreed, "but the apple needs work – and Adam and Eve too."

"Well, Charlie's no artist, but his idea is great."

From where Harry stood, he could see maybe a couple of dozen P-40s. About half were wearing their shark teeth, and in the shade of a hangar, another was having the shark mouth painted on. "Your war paint is almost ready," he said. "Then all you need is the war. Is it coming?"

"It's coming," Ed said. "It won't be long now."

"Are you guys ready?"

"We're ready. Most of us are looking forward to it." When he said that, Ed saw something in Harry's eyes that made him add, "Civilian," and throw a punch at Harry's shoulder.

Harry tried to twist out of the way, but was not quick enough. "Hey, Flight Leader," he said, "watch who you accuse. You're a civilian now too. All of you are."

"Yeah, I forget that sometimes. It's all that Navy training coming out."

They walked toward the billets and Ed was quiet, thoughtful. "You know," he said, "that's something I don't think a full-time civilian like you could understand. First, the Navy trains you, then they measure you every way they can. I got pretty high marks. A lot of the pilots in training with me got an 'E' for excellence in dive-bombing. Only two of us – Bert Christman and I – also got an 'E' in aerial gunnery. When I heard about the AVG, I saw an opportunity to find out if I was as good as I thought I was. And, my goodness, Harry, it was a chance to come here to Asia."

He stopped walking then, and just stood, looking off into the distance. "You can't imagine what that meant for me. I had read twice over everything Rudyard Kipling had written, and here was my chance, to come to Burma, to fly these beautiful P-40s, and to fight. And on top of it all, they would pay me this fabulous salary." He feinted another light jab at Harry's shoulder. "Harry, it was an opportunity that was heaven-sent."

"Well, Flight Leader, I am pleased to find a man who's happy in his work."

"I am that. And how about you? Aren't you happy in your work, sir?"

"I guess I am. I am certainly happy to be in Asia. I read a little bit of Kipling too, and some Conrad, and I've wanted to come here ever since I can remember. But I can't say I'm as taken as you are with the idea of getting in the middle of a war."

"It's different for you, Harry. You're a civilian. You're a writer, a watcher, not a doer."

"The two aren't opposed. I'd like to think I can be involved in the action, and also write about it."

"Well, maybe you can…but you don't have that Navy training, Harry. You are not prepared. You haven't been tested."

And this time Harry threw a punch at Rector's shoulder. It was not a particularly light one.

CHAPTER 5

A few days after he returned from Toungoo, Harry decided to find the warehouse where Lucy worked. However casual her invitation to visit her had been, she had invited him, hadn't she? Morning tea, she had said. Well, it was a nice morning, a good time to find her and have that tea.

He was well wheeled now, having negotiated the rental of a blue Ford roadster from a member of the Gymkhanna Club going off on an extended leave. His plan was to drive along the river until he spotted the red MG parked by a warehouse. That was simple enough, but he had not factored in the length of the river nor the number of warehouses built along it. He was hot, sticky and frustrated when he finally glimpsed a flash of red among the industrial grays and browns and jungle greens that filled his windscreen as he drove slowly along the road that followed the river. There was little to be seen of the river itself, just the buildings, and the patches of jungle that surrounded them.

It was Lucy's MG, and it was parked by itself in front of a large wooden building that seemed bigger than most of its neighbors. Harry pulled his roadster alongside the red car. Although there was a high double door right before him, there seemed to be something going on around the side of the building, and that was where he headed.

He turned the corner and saw Lucy. A line of trucks was being loaded, and a group of what he took to be their Chinese drivers stood in a semi-circle with Lucy in the middle, her back to him. She was speaking in Chinese and the drivers watched her intently. She wore loose black trousers and a black collarless shirt, a coolie outfit, but no coolie Harry had ever seen looked so good. She finished whatever she had been saying to the drivers, and turned to a tough-looking Burmese who stood alongside her. Him she addressed in Burmese. The man listened and nodded. She turned away from him and found herself looking right at Harry. If she was surprised by his presence she failed to show it.

"Just passing by," he said. "You look busy. I can stop on my way back."

"I'm finished now. Come in for tea."

They walked to the godown's front entrance. Without breaking stride she said, "You have a car." It surprised him that she had noticed. Inside the warehouse, instead of the gloom he expected, there was light, a lot of it, spilling down from long windows set near the tops of the walls. The interior of the building was all teak, and unpainted. The wood glowed in the shower of sunlight.

"I watched you brief the drivers," he said as they walked. "It was quite impressive. They hung on your every word."

She laughed. "If they listened, it was because I was speaking of their year-end bonuses. I told them there would not be any if they kept losing our goods."

The aisle narrowed as they got farther back in the warehouse. In places they had to squeeze through. The floor was crammed with goods, even vehicles. Parked in rows were small open trucks they called "jeeps", and the noses of two new Buick sedans poked out from under tarpaulins. There was a lot of machinery, engines, generators, water pumps, huge things. There were rows of rubber tires for trucks and automobiles and maybe even airplanes. Mostly there were crates, wooden crates everywhere, and cardboard boxes, row after row of them, all sizes and stacked high, some almost touching the ceiling.

"My office is up there," she said, and Harry's eyes followed a steep, narrow stairway up to a platform built under the roof. Lucy started up and Harry let her get a little way ahead before he went after. At the top he saw the platform was much larger than it had seemed from below, and that it was partitioned by half-walls into little rooms. Where they arrived were four desks, manned by young clerks, all standing now and bowing, big smiles on their faces. They were near the windows here, which were all open. A light breeze flowed in and ruffled the papers on the desks.

Lucy led him into an adjoining room where there were two large desks, and a table set directly under a window. "My office," she said. "This is my desk. Sit by the table, Harry. Tea is on its way. It's pleasant here in the mornings, when the river breeze is fresh. By noon it won't be so nice."

Harry sat and looked out on the river where there was great activity. Ocean-going vessels were anchored in mid-stream, and others were tied up alongside the docks where the arms of great cranes swung back and forth over them. Rice barges drifted downriver with the current and small motorized ferries putted across it from one bank to the other. Directly below the window was the quay fronting the warehouse. A gang of coolies worked there, unloading wooden boxes from a barge.

"Great view," he said. "Must be a nice place to work, even if only in the mornings." He looked at the second desk and asked, "Your father's?"

"Yes, when he's here. He doesn't like offices particularly. He's out on the Burma Road today. Having a good time, I'm sure."

Harry was curious. "What's he doing out there? Not driving a truck, I would think."

"No, not driving a truck," she said, "He's fixing a problem." She leaned forward and looked out the window, down at the quay. "You see the coolies down there, Harry? The boxes they're carrying are whiskey. Whiskey is always a problem. A couple of weeks ago, whiskey started disappearing on the way north, so at first Father simply threatened the drivers. But it still disappeared, and he added guards to the trucks." She shrugged. "But whiskey kept disappearing. He felt he had to act. "

Harry thought about it. "Is it really a problem he can fix?"

"Oh, I think he'll fix it. He's very good at that. He's thought about it a good bit. He said that when small amounts of whiskey are lost – a few bottles or a case or two at a time – there are many small hands involved. But, he said, when whole truckloads go missing, you can be sure there is only one big hand involved. So, all he needs to do is find the one big hand, the one man along the Burma Road who deals in large quantities of whiskey. It shouldn't be too difficult."

"Well, good luck to him. Your father sounds quite clever. Problems aside, whiskey must be good trade. "

"It's very good trade. We send a lot to China. Most of our shipments still go to the British here, but the market for scotch whiskey in China is growing. The generals have acquired the taste."

"So your father is going up the Burma Road. It's a long way to go to fix a whiskey problem. Will he be doing anything else up north?"

"There are many other things. There are people in China he needs to see."

"Is he going as far as Kunming?"

"Yes, he will go to Kunming, and then beyond, to Chungking."

"Ah, Chungking, the city on two rivers. It must be a great city. It's one of the places I want to see. Is Chungking your home?"

"Chungking is where our government is. It's where Chiang Kai-shek is."

"Ah, the Generalissimo! So, I guess your father will see him, have tea with him, eh?" Harry said it lightly, expecting, at most, a smile from

Lucy. Instead, she quite matter-of-factly said, "Yes, he will see General Chiang."

"Oh," Harry said, not quite sure what to say. "He knows the Generalissimo, then. Will he deal with other members of the government as well?"

"I expect so. The business he does is quite important to the government. My father is the agent for many of the things that China needs. Because of that he knows many Chinese officials and they know him. He even knows your Colonel Chennault."

"He knows Chennault!" Harry was surprised again..

"He's been talking with the Colonel and his staff about aircraft parts, radios and telephone systems, all for the Chinese Air Force. As an advisor to General Chiang, Chennault is someone my father would know."

"Of course," Harry said. "Your father certainly seems well connected"

"When it comes to people around General Chiang, he is – especially those responsible for keeping the supply line open. He's been very busy since China lost Shanghai."

The mention of Shanghai brought Harry back to an earlier question. "You didn't say where your home is in China. It's not in Chungking, is it?"

She turned to look out the window. It was only after some time that she said, "My home was in Nanking."

Harry felt a little shiver. He knew what had happened in Nanking – everyone did. "I'm so sorry," he said. "It was a great tragedy."

She did not look at him. "You know what happened in Nanking, Harry, but many people don't. I have English friends who know nothing about what happens in China. I don't think they want to. China is big and far away. News from there makes no impression on them."

"It's hard to believe anyone doesn't know what happened in Nanking. The newspapers were full of it," he remembered. "It started about this time of year, didn't it?"

"It started in October. It's four years ago now, in 1937. It was October when the Japanese attacked Shanghai. Then they went after General Chiang and the government in Nanking. Nanking was so beautiful. It was a city of trees and temples, and the Japanese smashed it all. They came into Nanking in December, and their soldiers ran wild. They killed hundreds of thousands of Chinese – men, women, children – and they did it all in one month. The lucky ones were the ones they shot. They burned people, buried them alive. They used Chinese for bayonet practice. Chiang and the government fled to Chungking then, beyond the reach of the Japanese. Nanking was lost to us, as Shanghai was. With Shanghai lost, everything China needs has to come into the country by land. "

"The reason for the Burma Road," Harry said. "You know, when I started reading about China, I thought the Burma Road was always there, a highway between ancient kingdoms."

Lucy looked at him now, the trace of a smile on her lips. "It hasn't always been there, Harry. It's only been a couple of years."

"And now it keeps China alive."

"It's all China has. Our lifeline is that single road that two hundred thousand Chinese coolies built with their hands." She turned back inside now to look at him. "I'm afraid for China, Harry. I don't know how long we can survive. Japan has taken almost everything from us. Now they even control Indo-China – and they're trying to close the Burma Road."

"Close the Burma Road? The Japanese are in no position to do that."

"Perhaps not," she said, "but they are negotiating with the British. They're trying to do just that."

"I can't believe that the British would even talk with the Japanese about it."

"The British may not have much choice. They're feeling pressure from the Japanese now. They're in for a lot of trouble here, and in India. While the British fight for their survival at home, the Japanese stir up trouble here in the colonies. The Japanese are talking with anti-British insurgents, the secret national armies in Burma and India, and in Malaya and Singapore as well."

"You sound as if there is no loyalty to the British in the colonies."

"There's not, and why should there be? The British are colonialists, the masters of the colonies. Why should the people they've subjugated have any love for them? Haven't you noticed, Harry? The Burmese greet the British with smiles, but most Burmese hate them. The Japanese are taking advantage of it. At this very moment there are Japanese Army officers in Burma. They're here to talk with Burmese nationalist leaders and with Burmese students."

"Surely the British wouldn't allow that."

"Allow what, Harry? They come here posing as journalists." A hard look at him went with that.

He had to think this through. "I know you're right about the way the Burmese look on the British, but I tend to forget that. And I see what the British have done here. Rangoon is a beautiful city, the economy is vibrant, the lives of the Burmese…."

"Harry, do you feel the Burmese should be grateful for being given huge brick buildings which are poor copies of some second-rate palace in London, and which a Burmese can enter only if he works there as a tea boy?"

Harry had to smile. "You make your point well, Lucy. I'll accept everything you say about the British – your experience is far greater than mine – but what I still question is how you know what the Japanese are up to here?"

"If you are not Burmese, Rangoon is not a very big place. You will learn that, Harry. If you're an outsider here, you deal with other outsiders – a group that's very select and very small. You deal with businessmen and diplomats. You meet the journalists and the colonels and the generals. You get to know people at the top of things. People like that are engaged in affairs that require them to know what's going on. Not one will have a complete picture of what's happening, but each will have an important piece. Talk with enough of them, Harry, ask the right questions, and soon you will have a very good idea of what's going on."

"Then maybe you can tell me," he said, "why are the British here so unconcerned with what's going on around them?"

"Maybe because Britain's real concerns are elsewhere. They're fighting for their survival at home. In Asia they're stretched thin and face threats from the Japanese and from the people of their own colonies. The British realize all that."

"Maybe they do, Lucy, but it seems to give them no fear of the Japanese. You know what the Japanese can do. Do you think they're coming here?"

"They're coming," she said.

At least there was no disagreement there. "When they come," he said, "what will you do?"

"What everyone else will – start up the road that leads north."

"You'll go to China?"

"I'll go to China if it's possible. If not, I'll go to India with the British."

Harry left the warehouse and his meeting with Lucy in an uncertain frame of mind. He had certainly enjoyed seeing her again. She was as lovely as he remembered, and very pleasant to be with. He thought that once they talked, he would find her to be very bright, and she was bright, but how did she become so knowledgeable, and knowledgeable about some of the very things that he was supposed to know? She was obviously a well-connected young lady – or least her father was, which was probably the same thing – and she struck him as very competent. But it was other things about her that troubled him. He was surprised by how much more there was to her than he expected, more dimension than he would have credited to any Asian woman. She had opinions, strong ones that it seemed she had formed herself, and she was not afraid to voice them. He was sure that she would be quick to defend what she thought. And she was quick to contradict him, to tell him when he was wrong. It was not at all what he expected from an Asian woman.

* * *

"It's because she's Chinese," Doyle told him when they met that evening. "Chinese women are more opinionated than Burmese or Indians or other Asians. It's the way they're brought up. Haven't you noticed, Harry? Put two Chinese together are they're always louder than anyone else. Other Asians speak softly, but Chinese shout. That's what their women learn from. And the Chinese are not as polite as other Asians. They're not polite enough to let a man have his opinions, right or wrong, without fear of contradiction. A good non-Chinese Asian woman will never contradict a man or tell him he's wrong. She's too polite to do that. Particularly if he's a Westerner."

"Christ, Doyle, you're spending too much time with the local Brits. You're starting to think like them."

"You think so, Harry? You'll see. Once you meet more Asian women, you'll see."

"But how does she know these things? How does she know the Japanese are meeting nationalists? How does she know that the Japs are negotiating with the British to close down the Burma Road? Is this what all the important 'outsiders' are talking about at the Gymkhanna Club?"

"Lucky guess, I'd say."

"Lucky guess? Then it's true."

"Well, some of it is. The British aren't telling me what they are talking to the Japanese about. But it seems to be pretty well known – at least among my British Embassy friends – that visitors from Japanese intelligence have been poking about here, and upcountry, and meeting with some pretty strange Burmese."

"The British allow this?"

"Well, they're journalists, Harry. The Japanese intelligence officers come here as journalists." He shrugged. "What can the British do?"

"So Lucy's right. She does know."

"She's partially right, Harry. Yes, I'll agree with that."

"Then why is she telling me this?"

Doyle smiled. "She's set her cap for you. She sees you as a good catch."

"I doubt that. I doubt she sees me as a good catch. Not even a catch. When I suggested we might get together some evening, she said she would have to defer to Flight Lieutenant Collins' schedule."

Doyle looked at Harry for a long moment. "Look, Harry. There is something there with Lucy. I don't know what it is, but I think it's worth you keeping after her. I suspect you will not find it very difficult to stay in touch with her. I think she will always be there when you want her."

Something serious in Doyle's tone made Harry start listening carefully. "What's happening, do you think?"

Doyle shrugged again and smiled. "Not the hoped-for romance of your life, probably. What I think is more likely is that Lucy has been set on to you." He looked toward the ceiling as if lost in thought. "Her father perhaps? If not her father, perhaps an uncle?" He thought some more and finally said, "Someone does see you as a catch, Harry, I'm sure of it. Someone with a link to Tai Li, I would say."

"A link to what?"

"A link not to what, Harry, a link to whom. Tai Li. You haven't heard of him? Nasty fellow, Tai Li. He's the chap who runs the Generalissimo's intelligence service. I think it may be Tai Li trying to get a hook into you. He wants to use you, I would say."

"Why me?"

"Why you, a succulent young journalist? Well, I can't say I know for sure, Harry, but I would think that a young impressionable American journalist would be of great use to the schemes of Tai Li and the Generalissimo."

CHAPTER 6

Rangoon, Burma
December 8, 1941

The telephone rang and rang. It stopped and started again. Harry pulled his head back under the covers. He had had few calls since he moved into his newly rented bungalow on a wooded hill not far from the center of Rangoon. Few people had his number, but Doyle was one. Maybe he better answer it. In case it was Doyle.

" 'Arry? Philippe here." The voice was strange, the accent French. A Frenchman with a cold? "I would like to buy you a cup of tea."

"Tea?" Something niggled at the back of Harry's mind. He sat up. "Philippe?" he asked.

"Yes, it is Philippe, 'Arry. It is late. I want to buy you that cup of tea. Yes?" There was a fine note of urgency in the voice now. Harry glanced at the alarm clock. Oh, lord, no wonder. It was almost 9:30 in the morning. He was awake enough now to recognize that he was botching it up. "Yeah, Philippe," he said, trying to sound in charge of himself. "Let's do tea, eh?"

"Very good, 'Arry. I will see you, eh?"

"Yes… I look forward to it."

Jesus. It had been Doyle, and Doyle was using their new coded procedure. They had just worked it out, and here he was, already botching it up. "Philippe" was Doyle, and "a cup of tea" was a meeting at Doyle's secret tea garden. "Philippe" had not specified a time, thank God, which meant "come now, right away." If he had given a time, Harry would have to add hours to the time stated, depending on what day of the week it was, and Harry was not completely sure. He looked at the clock again. Even if he skipped shaving, it would take him at least a half hour to get to Doyle. It was a good thing he had the roadster.

Harry parked on the main street, a little beyond the lane that led to Doyle's secret tea garden, and walked the rest of the way. It was good place to meet. The heavy growth of shrubs gave no view of the garden from the street, and suggested no reason to suppose that two foreigners might want to meet there.

The old woman who ran the place recognized him. She gave him a jerky bow and looked to where Doyle sat, half hidden in the bushes. Harry expected to be greeted with some smart-aleck comment. Instead, he found Doyle unusually subdued.

"Sorry to get you out of bed, Harry," Doyle said and handed him a sheet of paper folded in three, like a letter. "It's an early summary. There's more coming over the newswires now."

Harry sat down and read it. Then he looked up at Doyle and said, "Jesus Christ."

Doyle nodded. "Yeah, it's bad." He picked up the larger of the two pots on the table and poured for Harry. "I had the old lady bring some coffee," he said. "I know you're not crazy about tea in the morning."

Harry stared dumbly at Doyle. Here was Doyle being gracious, while he was numb, stunned by what he read. As if he had been hit in the middle of his forehead with a hammer. "This is incredible. It's unbelievable. We're at war. The Japanese have sunk our fleet."

They sat and just looked at one another. Then Doyle said, "It's even worse than that. From what the Embassy is getting now from the wire services and radio broadcasts, the Japs are running wild. They've bombed Singapore. They've bombed Manila and Hong Kong. They're landing troops in Malaya and Thailand."

"Christ! When did it start?"

"The early morning hours. It was about 2:00 a.m. in Malaya. Singapore was bombed at 4:00 a.m. Pearl Harbor was attacked about 3:00 a.m. our time. I heard about Hong Kong on the radio just as I was leaving the Embassy. Hong Kong was bombed after 8:00 a.m. this morning."

"I can't believe the Japs were able to get near Singapore. How bad is it?"

"I don't know. At this point I don't think anyone does." Doyle picked up his tea cup, then set it back down again without drinking from it. "There was a message from Washington. You're going to have to go up to Toungoo again. Donovan wants to know what Chennault is doing and what he's seeing, what he expects to happen. You can wait a couple of days before going up there. Chennault probably has his hands full right now."

* * *

It was Ed Rector who came to the station to meet him. He had one of the small open jeeps. He looked tired.

"We can't stop for a beer. Toungoo town is off limits right now. I'll buy you a drink up at the airdrome. The Old Man wants you to stay over in the barracks tonight."

"That's fine," Harry said, "What's been happening at the airdrome?"

"It's quiet now, but everybody's on edge. We're all blacked out. Even here in town they're trying." He looked toward the windows of the restaurant in the railway station. "The Savoy is using candles. The rest of the town...." He shrugged. "You can't get the natives to turn out their lights. Most of them don't have any real lighting anyway."

Very little light showed from the jeep, its headlights painted over. Once they turned on to the road leading to the airfield, Ed turned them off and they drove in darkness. "Your eyes will get used to it," he said. "There's starlight, and the moon will be up before long. It's kind of nice driving this way. It rests the eyes. We spend the daylight hours staring at the sky, waiting for the Japs to come. It wears you out."

"What do you think is going to happen?"

"We were ready to move up to our home base at Kunming, and maybe this will speed it up. We're too vulnerable sitting here."

With the airfield just ahead, Rector said, "We have Gurkhas guarding us now, on loan from the British. Sharp troops, but maybe they've worked for the Brits too long." As they neared the gate, Rector slowed the jeep to a crawl. "Watch this," he said.

A figure loomed out of the darkness, a black silhouette against the lighter star-flecked sky. Harry could make out the oval of a wide brimmed hat and the dark line of the rifle extended across his chest. "Halt!" an Asian voice shouted. "Who goes there?"

"Enemy officers," Rector responded.

There was a moment of silence, and then: "Pass, enemy officers." The Gurkha stood aside. Rector saluted him as they drove by. "That's war, Harry," Rector said.

Rector drove past the dark hulk of the barracks and headed for the runway. They stopped at what Rector called the "ready shack," a thatch roof held up by a teak post on each corner. "It keeps the sun off during the day, and lets the breeze through. At night, I like to think of it as our tropical veranda bar." Rector reached behind the jeep's seat and brought out a bottle of scotch. "There are glasses behind your seat. I hope you don't need anything to mix this with."

They sat and sipped at their scotch. It was peaceful, and the bugs had not found them yet. "I thought some of the guys would be out here," Rector said, and eventually they were joined by two other pilots. Rector introduced them, but Harry could not see their faces. "Everybody's asleep," one of them said. "Bad news is tiring."

Everybody was tired, and after a while Harry and Rector walked to the barracks. It was dark inside, but Rector led him to a bunk, one among many, and showed him how to tuck in the mosquito net. He fell asleep quickly, listening to something scratching in the ceiling. In the morning Rector was there to take him to breakfast in the pilots' mess. They ate alone. The pilots, Rector said, were out by their airplanes, watching the sky. The Old Man was busy, but Squadron Leader Newquack would brief him. Rector went off to sit by his airplane.

It was early afternoon before Newkirk sent for him. They met in the operations shack by the runway.

"I'll try to bring you up to date, Harry. We're on a war footing. Everybody's at the airfield now, all leaves have been canceled. We're keeping our engines warm. Since Monday we've had airplanes gassed and armed, sitting on the end of the runway, ready to take off. We've been expecting to be hit from the start, and we've had a number of alerts. So far there's no sign of the Japs. At night we're blacked out. We sit around in the dark and get to our bunks pretty early. We have airplanes ready to go up at night if we have to. We had an alert at 3:30 Wednesday morning. Everybody ran around in the dark and it was a damn mess. It's a wonder nobody got killed. We had six airplanes on alert that night. They took off and flew around the area for about an hour. They saw nothing and came back. It was still dark, and one of them got wrecked on landing. The pilot was all right. At daybreak, we sent our photo reconnaissance airplane to have a look at Chiang Mai in Thailand. We got good photos, but they showed nothing at the airfield there. On Thursday, we sent three airplanes to Bangkok. Ed Shilling flew the photo airplane. Bert Christman and your pal Ed Rector went along as escorts. It was a good mission. The photos showed more than 80 airplanes at Bangkok's airport. A few may have been Thai airplanes, but most of them were Japs. And that's where it stands. The Japs are in Thailand, but there's been no sign of them here. But that's just a matter of time."

"What will happen to the AVG now, Jack?"

"Well, the Old Man would like to move all of us up to Kunming. We're really not prepared for combat down here. We're here in Burma to get everybody trained, and that's finished now. We were getting ready to move to Kunming when this happened. We would be on our way if it weren't for Brooke-Popham."

Harry knew the name, but he could not resist. "What's a 'brook pop 'em'?"

"Better get your 'Sir' in there, Harry. It's Air Chief Marshal Sir Robert Brooke-Popham, the British Commander-in-Chief of the Far East. He's based in Singapore. I'm sure you know who he is."

Oh, that Brooke-Popham," Harry mumbled, and felt a little foolish for being smart-assed. He let Newkirk continue, undisturbed.

"Sir Robert has finally noticed what's going on in Asia, and he's worried. He wants the AVG to stay in Burma and help the RAF defend Rangoon. He's put in a request with the Generalissimo, Chiang Kai-shek, our boss. The upshot is, the Old Man is sending the Third Squadron down to Mingaladon airdrome at Rangoon. The Third will be on loan to the RAF, but still under the Old Man's command. Most of the Third's ground crew will be going down to Rangoon on the train tonight. The pilots will fly their airplanes to Rangoon tomorrow. The Brits are going to need all the help they can get."

"What about the First and Second Squadrons?"

"I expect we'll move up to Kunming very shortly. It's just a matter of the Old Man saying when."

"Now that we're officially at war, Jack, will the status of the AVG change?"

"It hasn't yet, although the U.S. Army wants all of us back in uniform. That's pretty evident. I know the Old Man has gotten a couple of telegrams. But it involves a lot of politics. The AVG is part of the Chinese Air Force and all the personnel signed one-year contracts. I'm not sure how this will all play out, but it's something only the Old Man can deal with."

Harry left Newkirk in the Ops shack and started back toward the barracks. P-40s were everywhere, scattered all over the field, dispersed so that a surprise attack would not catch them all bunched together. Six airplanes were on the end of the runway. Harry could see pilots sitting in the cockpits. Those were probably the alert ships, ready to go into the air as soon as the alarm sounded. Harry squinted, trying to make out fuselage numbers. On an airplane not far from him he saw it, number 36. He walked over to where Rector was sitting in a rounded rectangle of shade under the wing, engrossed in a book. Harry stood alongside before he was even noticed. "Kipling?" he asked when Rector looked up.

Rector chuckled. "Actually, it's a romance, set in the American Deep South during the Civil War. A ladies' book, I think. They don't have much to read in the alert shack."

"Your squadron leader tells me you've been down to Bangkok. I'm disappointed that you never told me that."

"If that's what Newquack said, then it must be." Rector stood up then so it would be easier to talk. "Yeah, we did go to Bangkok, Bert and Erik and I. It was great – I felt I was committing an act of war. We flew right over Bangkok's Jap-infested airport. I don't know if they even saw us or not. We stayed at 20,000 feet, so they couldn't have seen much of us. I didn't even know the Japs were down there until they developed the film. That's war, Harry."

A pilot came out of one of the small buildings near the runway, and was walking across the grass in their direction. "Why, that's Charlie Bond," Rector said. "He came back from Thailand an hour ago. Hey, Charlie!" he yelled. "Come on over here," and the man turned toward them. When he was closer, Rector said, "I got somebody here for you to meet. He wants to hear all about Chiang Mai."

"Not much to tell," Charlie said, and turned to Harry. "I went over there today with Bob Little. We did a visual reconnaissance of the airfield. We went there at 20,000 feet. Bob went down for a close look, while I stayed on top watching for Japs. Bob Neale brought a flight of four that rendezvoused with us midway back, just in case. But wouldn't you know it, we never got chased."

"There were no Japs there?"

"Nope, not a one that we saw." Charlie looked at Harry closely now. "You with the Group?"

"He came up here to talk with the Old Man," Rector said.

Bond kept looking at Harry. "You with the Army? State Department?"

"He's a journalist, Charlie."

"Is that right? A reporter. Well…good meeting you. They treating you pretty well here? Better than Edgar Snow, I hope." With a small wave and a "See you around, boys," Bond resumed walking across the field.

"What was that about? What happened to Edgar Snow?"

"Well, some of the boys are suspicious of journalists. A lot of them have been sniffing around here lately. The AVG being here in Burma was supposed to be a secret, but the press somehow learned about it. A few weeks ago we had a crowd of journalists come here. You can't chase them away, and the Old Man even entertained some of them. A few of our pilots did interviews. But they drew the line at Edgar Snow. He wrote all those books about the Chinese Communists. He's been called a Communist sympathizer. Why, hell, the Chinese Communists are fighting the Nationalist Chinese, and the AVG is part of the Chinese Nationalist Air Force. So when Edgar came around, the boys were a little leery. He was pretty full of himself too. It got so that nobody would talk with him. At least one of the guys waved a beer bottle like he was going to smack him with it."

"Thanks for telling me. Wish you had warned me before."

"Don't be so sensitive, Harry, it doesn't apply to you. Newquack says you're all right, so you must be. Hey, have you talked with the Old Man yet?"

"I haven't, but I sure want to. I'm not going back to Rangoon until I do."

Early next morning Rector got him out of bed. "Hey, Harry, the Old Man's leaving. He wants you to get out to the runway right away."

Rector had a jeep waiting outside and they drove to where a twin-engined British Blenheim bomber stood at the end of the runway. A Studebaker staff car was pulled up alongside. Harvey Greenlaw was there, opening the back door for Chennault as they drove up. Rector saluted the Old Man, and Harry felt like he should.

"Mornin', boys," the Old Man greeted them. "Ross, I'm glad to see you here. I'm off to Rangoon to meet with some people. General Brett, the U.S. air commander for Southeast Asia and some British brass are passing through. Newkirk told you our Third Squadron will be with the RAF at Rangoon, and that our First and Second Squadrons are moving up to Kunming." The Old Man looked at Rector. "You'll be going up there tomorrow, Eddie." He turned away from Rector then, and moved closer to Harry. He spoke almost in his ear.

"You tell Donovan we're ready to fight the war and that he'll be hearing about the AVG very shortly. There's a lot of politics going on right now with the Brits and the Generalissimo, but that shouldn't interfere with our fighting the Japs. After I finish in Rangoon, I'll be going up to China. I hope to see you up in Kunming one day. In the meantime, Oley Olson, leader of our Third Squadron in Rangoon, will be in touch with you." With that, Chennault turned and walked to the open door of the Blenheim bomber. "See you, boys," he said before he climbed in.

The rest of the day was taken up with preparations for the move north to Kunming. A couple of transports from CNAC, the China National Aviation Corporation, landed at Kyedaw to move the headquarters staff and technicians up to Kunming. Another group of ground crew prepared for the long drive up there in a truck convoy along the Burma Road.

Harry was on the side of the runway, watching the takeoffs. The Adam and Eves were first. Eighteen of them were lined up, and one P-40 after another rose into the clear air, until one lost power as it was lifting off. The P-40 rolled off the end of the runway into the brush and tore off its landing gear.

Just before the Panda Bears started their takeoffs, Harry saw Jack Newkirk leave the Operations shack and start walking toward his airplane.

Harry met him halfway there to wish him a bon voyage. They shook hands and Newkirk said, "We just heard that Kunming was bombed this morning. There were a lot of civilians killed. There were ten Jap bombers. They'll be back tomorrow and we'll be there to catch them."

"Good luck, Jack. Get a Jap for me."

Harry waved his thumb in the air as Newkirk took off. He waited until he saw Rector's number 36 on the end of the runway, and waved his raised thumb as Rector went by. "Good luck, Ed," he said quietly.

CHAPTER 7

Kunming, China
December 20, 1941

Squadron Leader Jack Newkirk would be the first of the AVG pilots to meet the enemy; Flight Leader Ed Rector was probably the first of the AVG pilots to shoot down a Japanese aircraft. For neither man was the experience quite what he expected.

By air, Kunming was 700 miles from Toungoo, and at an altitude of 6,000 feet, a world away from Burma's tropical heat. It was an old city built on ancient trade routes, the capital of China's Yunnan Province and the northern terminus of the Burma Road. The airfield was just southeast of the city, on the edge of a great lake. Not very far from mountains often cloaked with threatening clouds.

When the AVG arrived, there was a single unfinished runway, and thousands of coolies hauling crushed rock to complete its hard surface. There were bomb shelters everywhere, and scars of old bomb craters. Kunming had long served the Japanese as a bombing range. They could bomb at their leisure. The Chinese no longer had airplanes or antiaircraft guns that could reach them. On the morning of the day that the AVG arrived, Japanese bombs had killed hundreds of Chinese in the city. That evening some of he pilots went into the city and saw for themselves the bodies of the unburied dead.

Chennault was back in Kunming. He expected the Japanese bombers to return the next day. They did not. But on the morning after that, on December 20, Chennault's warning net – Chinese watchers on the ground with telephones – reported ten Japanese bombers coming from a base in Vietnam and headed in the direction of Kunming.

Chennault ordered the First Squadron to intercept the bombers south of the city. The pilots manned their airplanes.

At 10:00 a.m., a red flare went up and 16 of the First Pursuit's P-40s took off. Moments later they were followed into the air by eight Second Squadron Panda Bears led by Squadron Leader Jack Newkirk. The Pandas were the backup. They were to stay close to the city and wait for any bombers that might get through. When the eight Panda Bears got to altitude, Newkirk took a flight of four to the northeast, while the other four stayed over the city.

Ed Rector was among those left on the ground, watching the takeoffs. His P-40 was undergoing routine maintenance, and he was not at all pleased with being left behind. If the maintenance had been scheduled 30 minutes earlier, he would be flying with his squadron mates. He watched until the last of the P-40s was in the air, and then trotted to the edge of the field, where his airplane stood. It looked naked without the cowling covering its engine. He was still a way off when he shouted at the three mechanics working on the airplane. "You're going to have to hurry. We can't have the Japs catching us on the ground. Get those spark plugs back in." He looked up at the sky where he could just make out the climbing Panda Bears. "Look at that," he said. "Lucky Jack Newkirk, right in the lead."

But it was not to be "Lucky Jack Newkirk" day. The Japanese were not aware of any other airplanes in the Chinese sky. The Japanese Air Force owned the sky and had grown accustomed to going about its deadly business unopposed. The ten Japanese bombers took off that morning from their airfield at Haiphong in Indo-China. Rather than bothering with the problems of navigation, the pilots leisurely followed the railroad tracks that led north into China and then turned east toward Kunming. When the bombers neared Kunming, instead of continuing straight on to the city and dropping their bombs, they turned to circle around the city, so they could approach it from the far side. There was no special reason for this – it was a tactic, one they often employed. By turning to circle around the city this morning, the Japanese unknowingly avoided the First Pursuit's P-40s waiting for them south of the city. But their circular course took them into that sector of the sky northeast of the city that was occupied by Jack Newkirk and his flight.

And that was how an incredulous Jack Newkirk came to be looking through his windscreen at ten Japanese bombers coming right at him. They were grouped in a large V formation, like huge geese, and in a part of the sky where they were not supposed to be. The incongruity of it all caused Jack Newkirk to pause. The three other Panda Bears in his flight were equally astounded. Radios crackled.

"Look there, the Japs!"

"Can't be Japs."

"They ain't P-40s."

"Look at the red balls."

"It's Japs!"

Newkirk's uncertainty was very brief; it cost him the advantage of surprise. The Japanese saw the P-40s – and they did not hesitate. They jettisoned their bombs, pointed their noses down, and banked away. Those at the airport, watching the sky, could not see what was happening, but heard distant explosions as the jettisoned bombs impacted in the rice fields. Newkirk turned his flight after the fleeing bombers, and fired while they were still far away. The four P-40s got in that one pass, and the bombers were gone, vanished somewhere among the clouds. All that Newkirk could see was empty sky. There was nothing more to do, but turn his flight back toward the airport.

Ed Rector watched Newkirk's four P-40s approach for landing. He looked at the mechanics who were almost finished with his airplane, "Goddamn it," he yelled, "get that cowling back on!" He grabbed his parachute, strapped himself in, and in minutes was in the air. He headed south.

The Japanese bombers were also headed south – in haste now. The glimpse their pilots had of the long-nosed airplanes evoked a great desire to see no more of them. They turned away from Kunming, but made a very serious mistake. Instead of heading southeast in a straight line that would take them directly home, they flew due south. Despite their hurry, the Japanese pilots had reverted to their old ways. By going directly south they would again intercept the railroad tracks that they could then follow all the way home. What they would not know for another few minutes was that they were now headed right for the piece of sky where the 16 P-40s of the First Squadron waited. The same spot to which Ed Rector was now racing.

For bombers, the Japanese airplanes were fast. They were Kawasaki Ki-48s. They had two engines, a crew of four, and a small tactical problem. They had nothing to protect them from pursuit airplanes like the P-40, but one rear-facing gun. It was manned by a gunner who lay prone on a platform that was dropped down from the belly of the airplane. It looked like a dustbin, and that's what it was called.

So it was that south of the city of Kunming, ten Japanese Air Force Ki-48s, 16 First Pursuit P-40s and Ed Rector converged in what would become a great free-for-all in the sky. As he neared, Rector saw the First Pursuit's P-40s harrying the Japanese bombers. The P-40s seemed to be attacking from every direction and their burning tracers criss-crossed the sky. To Rector it was a scene of total confusion, but he remembered what Chennault had taught him – what he had practiced at Toungoo.

He climbed to get well above the Japanese bombers and the other P-40s. There he paused for a moment, on a high perch, like a hunting falcon, and looked down on the scene. He tipped his airplane down and sent it in a long curve of pursuit toward the last bomber on the left of the large V. He knew he was too far away when he started shooting, but soon he saw his tracers striking the bomber and moving across it from wingtip to wingtip. He watched and wondered why it did not explode. So intent was he on seeing his bullets strike that he was unprepared when the bomber's tail suddenly filled his windscreen. In that same instant he saw the dustbin gunner shooting back at him, and instinctively shifted his aim. The bullets raked across the dustbin; the gunner's body jerked and slumped over the gun. At the last possible moment Rector shoved the stick forward, and his P-40 skimmed just below the bomber's belly – as Rector looked up into the face of the gunner and saw the gaping maw where his lower jaw had been. Years later he could close his eyes, see the scarred paint, and count the rivets on the belly of that Japanese bomber. And he could clearly see the shattered face of the man he had killed.

As Rector climbed away he looked back. A flame had started just behind the pilot's canopy and streamed back a good fifty feet beyond the bomber's tail. He watched and the bomber nosed over and dove toward the ground.

By then the First Pursuit's P-40s were all over the Japanese airplanes. The bombers had tightened their formation, but they were finding it hard to stay together. Several had been hit and two were falling behind, trailing smoke. The wing on one suddenly folded back and snapped off. The rest of the airplane started to tumble, but then exploded, and left nothing of itself but a shower of debris.

Rector had the altitude for another pass, but something was wrong with his guns. He pulled the trigger. A couple of rounds fired off, and the guns quit. With no guns, there was nothing more to do. He could leave the bombers to the First Pursuit. Later, when he told the Old Man, Chennault said that leaving the fight then was a mistake. Rector did not need guns; he should have stayed and feinted at the bombers, made false passes at them. That would have distracted them, drawn their fire to him, and made it easier for First Pursuit's P-40s to make their passes. "Good Christ!" Rector thought when Chennault said that, but he did not say that to the Old Man.

Back on the ground, Newkirk was not pleased with himself. He was angry, "black with anger," someone said. His squadron was the first to meet the Japanese, but it had not scored. Even worse, Newkirk had not even gotten in a good burst at the bombers. His guns had jammed, he said. "Buck fever," said the Old Man.

It was a while before the First Squadron airplanes returned. They had chased the bombers a long way from Kunming. Most of the airplanes came in together. A few stragglers were close behind. The pilots were excited, jubilant. Everybody had a story to tell and everybody wanted to tell it. It was agreed that four of the bombers had gone down for sure and several more had probably crashed. The ground crew found bullet holes in the P-40s that the pilots did know about, and they all felt lucky. They had come through their first combat victorious and not lost a man.

It was then that someone noted that Ed Rector had not landed.

Later, Chennault wrote that, in the AVG's first encounter with the Japanese Air Force, "The pilots for a few incredulous seconds could hardly believe the bombers were really Japs. It was strictly a case of buck fever with no team work – only a wild melee and sheer luck that kept P-40s from shooting each other."

CHAPTER 8

Harry let himself into the warehouse. It was almost dark, and the place looked deserted, although Lucy's MG was still parked in front. She said she would wait when he telephoned. Just inside the door, a young Burmese, one of Lucy's clerks on his way out, stepped aside to let Harry pass. He smiled and bowed, and Harry bobbed his head a few times, still not sure how to respond to such deference.

The office area at the top of the stairs was well lit, by lamps now, and Lucy was there to greet him. A single clerk was closing up, gathering papers into files. The clerk said good night as Harry followed Lucy into her office.

She turned and took a long look at him. "I haven't seen you since the war started."

Harry just nodded, although there was much he wanted to tell her. The tension at Toungoo and the excitement of the pilots had infected him. Coming back by himself on the train, he had time to think, and he felt his excitement grow as he drew closer to Rangoon. By the time he arrived he was exhilarated by thoughts of the coming war and the part he might play in it. It would be a great adventure, and he was ready. It was what he wanted to tell Lucy, but he felt awkward now.

"Have you been to the war?" she asked.

It was no secret where he had been. "I was up at Toungoo with the American volunteers. The war feels real up there. It was exciting." He sat down at the table while Lucy poured tea. "Did you hear?" he asked, and before she could respond, rushed to tell her. "The AVG was in combat. They intercepted Japanese bombers at Kunming and shot down a half dozen or more. I just heard this morning. It's been on news broadcasts."

"Were any of the AVG hurt?" she asked.

"I don't think so, but I don't really know. It's all war information now. Details the news services get are sparse. I'll know more when I see the AVG again." He took a big swallow of tea.

She studied his face. "Your trip has done you good. You look healthy, very alive. But you won't find many in Rangoon who share your excitement about the war. There's some dread of what's coming, but no sense of impending doom yet. The Japanese in Malaya still seem far from Rangoon."

"I thought there had been raid alerts here."

"Yes, there were. The sirens went off a number of times, but nothing happened. Once I watched a Japanese plane from this window. It was very high, just a silver spot in the sky, going about its own business."

"Then you've seen more of the enemy than most have." He leaned back and nibbled on a biscuit. "You know, I do find this very exciting. I guess it's because I can't believe my good fortune." He saw a smile start on her face and again rushed his words. "Back at school, and even as a kid, I was fascinated by Asia. And now I'm here. The great tide of war is rolling in and I'll be here to see it."

"I don't think it will be pleasant to watch," she said.

"Maybe not pleasant, but I will watch it. This will be my war – my generation's war. Instead of sitting in a law office in New York and reading about it in the *Times*, I'll be here to witness it."

She said nothing, waiting for him to go on, and that was encouragement enough. "I guess I'm trying to say that I feel fortunate to be given the chance to witness the great events of history instead of just reading about them. In a small way, I may even be part of what happens here."

She nodded. "I think I know what you mean, Harry," and then laughed and just briefly touched his arm. "You're like an excited schoolboy waiting for the circus to come to town. You look ready to celebrate."

"I am ready to celebrate," he said, then hesitantly added, "If you will come along."

And with no hesitation Lucy said what he was not expecting her to say, "Of course I will, Harry."

He stared at her for a long moment. He could not believe his luck. He thought immediately of the Silver Grill, but the dining room at the Strand was more elegant, and just along the river, not very far from here. "Let's go now," he said. "We'll have dinner. With wine, and drinks before. I do feel very fortunate. It is something to celebrate."

The Strand was a good choice. It was a slow night, with few guests in the dining room. "Japanese jitters," Lucy said. But the food was especially tasty, Harry thought, and the staff solicitous. Harry enjoyed it all, although he would have been as content at the Silver Grill or at any other Rangoon dining room that night. It was Lucy who made the evening wonderful. He had her all to himself. She was the most attractive woman in the room, and she was enjoying herself because of him. Her eyes were for him alone and gleamed with interest when he spoke. She knew the menu well, but still asked him to help her choose. And her smile when she took a sip of wine that he had ordered showed how well he had chosen. He sat back and felt fortunate.

"Tell me about your visit to Toungoo," she said, and he told her, but left out parts that might be "militarily sensitive". Her curiosity centered on the pilots. Was Ed Rector there? What about the others she had met? Were they ready for war? "They're ready," he assured her. "It's a test they are well prepared for."

"Did you see Colonel Chennault? Did you speak with him?"

He told her that he had seen "the Old Man", but only in passing, to exchange greetings. It could not hurt to let her know that he knew a man like Chennault, and that a man like Chennault knew him.

"Some of the American volunteers are at the airdrome here now," she said, "to help the Royal Air Force." A good thing, she thought. The Americans were not popular with Rangoon's British residents, who would never imagine that the RAF would need help from a ragtag group like the American irregulars. The RAF itself was quite grateful for the help. These days, anyone who owned a radio knew there was at least the possibility that by themselves the British might not be able to hold the Japanese. The Burmese and the Indians who worked for the British government seemed to understand that and were terrified.

"And if the Japanese take Rangoon," she said, "or just cut off the port, what will happen to China? How will China survive?" Her British friends had told her not to worry. The Japanese would be stopped in Malaya and before long pushed back into the sea. And they would be pushed out of Thailand – if indeed they were in Thailand.

"Oh, they are there," Harry said. "The Japanese are in Thailand," and he almost told her about the reconnaissance mission that Ed Rector had flow and the eighty Japanese airplanes captured on film.

"Peter told me that as well," she said. It was her first mention of Flight Officer Collins, who was standing alert at the airdrome. She had not seen him in days. "Poor Peter," she said, "he speaks so confidently, but in his eyes I see uncertainty. He lost friends in England during the Battle of Britain and, in the last two weeks, in Malaya and Singapore. The British pilots, the young ones, are all so casual about what's coming. Their senior officers are full of swagger, convinced that they can't possibly lose."

She picked up her wine glass and looked deeply into it. "The Japanese in town, the merchants, they've all disappeared, Harry."

"Wise of them, I'd say."

"It's a frightening thing. There's talk that they have gone to meet the Japanese Army, to lead it back to Rangoon." She shrugged. "I don't know if that's true, but I think if the Japanese merchants have left Rangoon, it won't be long before the Japanese Army attacks the city."

"There's a lot of talk now. Many are concerned that it's the Burmese quislings who will use lights to guide the Japanese bombers to their targets here in Rangoon." And as Harry said that, the war suddenly felt very close.

"Enough talk of doom," she said, and raised her glass. "Let's drink. Christmas is coming. It's just days away. My father hosts an annual Christmas dinner at the biggest Chinese restaurant in town. Everyone comes. This year you must join us. Father insists on having plum pudding and other English Christmas delights."

"I wouldn't miss it," Harry said. "My first Christmas in the tropics."

The tenor of their conversation had changed. They spoke only of the past now, happy things they remembered. They tried not to talk of the war, and it was mentioned again only once. It was Harry who brought it up. "You know what I would like to do?" he asked. "When the Japanese airplanes come to Rangoon, I would like to be on a roof from where I could see it all." Lucy looked surprised, even a little disconcerted. "Oh don't worry," he added then, "they'll go after the military targets, the airbase, the army compounds."

But as he thought about it, he started looking worried. "And maybe the ships and the docks," he said. "It would probably be smart to stay away from there once it starts."

* * *

Tuesday, December 23, 1941
Rangoon, Burma

The sirens started early and got many of Rangoon's British residents out of their beds. Most stayed indoors, feeling quite safe and not wanting to be bothered further. Some ambled out into their gardens and gazed up at the cloudless morning sky. It looked benign enough, and that caused many to go back inside, to find Cook and order an early breakfast. A few were like Harry, who rolled over in his bed and wondered if it was time to find a vantage point to watch the Battle of Rangoon. He fell asleep again before he could decide.

The noise stopped, and there was an unnatural silence, but not for long. The sirens started wailing a second time. For some reason this was more disconcerting than the first. Among many of the British it induced a sinking feeling, a sense of dread. But that passed quickly enough. "Nervous Nellie air raid wardens," they said. And laughed when wardens told them to go to shelters.

In the native quarters, decisions had been made. When the sirens wailed, the Burmese, the Chinese and the Indians herded their families into air raid shelters that had been hastily built when these troubles first started. They sat in the shelters in discomfort and waited. When nothing happened, they did not feel foolish, as the British might have done, but simply led wives and children back to the shops and houses, which often were the same thing. They knew for certain that one of these times the air raid alert would be real.

It was almost 11 o'clock when the sirens started again. This time they wailed on and on, much longer than they usually did. The native quarters were cleared quickly, and even the most blasé of British eyes turned to the sky. It was as clear up there as it had been in the early morning. There was neither cloud nor sign of enemy. Then a rumble, as Royal Air Force's airplanes took to the air in a long arc around the city as they climbed higher and higher. Normal procedure, some said, and not particularly alarming. A few thought there were more aircraft than usual. "Chasing a Jap observation airplane," someone said, and everyone relaxed.

Then came a new sound, a drone in the distance that grew louder and louder and became a roar of engines, an almost overwhelming din of many airplanes flying close together. Intermingled with this din were dull crumps of explosions diminished by distance, and sharp bangs in rapid series like the crackling of strings of firecrackers. "Anti-aircraft guns!" someone cried out, and even the most senior British bureaucrat stopped what he was doing, put down his pen, and went outside to stare at the sky.

They were silver dots against the blue sky, glinting in the sun. Those nearest the docks saw them first – grouped together in Vs of three. Six Vs, 18 Japanese bombers headed for the docks. Chasing behind came a swarm of smaller airplanes that merged with the bombers. Spectators stared open-mouthed as explosions flashed red through the Vs of airplanes and flame and long plumes of smoke trailed behind. Above all the other noise was the whine of a diving bomber that ceased when it struck the ground.

The action overhead was so thrilling, so like a movie projected against the distant sky, that even the most cautious observer came outdoors to watch. Despite the efforts of the small airplanes that tried to impede their progress, the bombers droned on. When they were precisely over the docks they dropped their bombs. From a distance, the falling projectiles were just specks that drifted across the sky and then downward toward the warehouses on the quay and the vessels moored alongside. Some drifted beyond the docks and into the city itself.

The fall of bombs seemed to last forever. Observers watched, mesmerized. Then they touched and geysers of smoke and flame erupted. Earth and wood, glass and flesh and metal were flung upwards, high above the exploding docks and warehouses. Where the bombs touched the city, fountains of debris rose high over office buildings and shop houses and showered burning shards into neighborhoods of wooden houses. Near the docks fires raged, smoke so thick that it became an impenetrable wall that sealed the area off from the living.

There was panic then, and people ran, everywhere, the natives and the British. On the quay, workers fleeing the first bombs ran into the exploding geysers of the ones that followed and became part of the debris that was flung high in the air. There were crippled and wounded now, screaming, crawling and dying. They were alone. Those who could run did not stop to help.

In the parts of the city distant from the docks, crowds still stood in open areas and watched the sky, tempting the Japanese pursuit airplanes. The pursuits dove down and flew low over the city and along the wide avenues and looked for targets on the ground.

* * *

The second alert got Harry out of bed. By the third, he was on his way, driving his roadster to the Strand, where he had an appointment for lunch. He drove on, ignoring the sirens and was quite near the railroad station when cars in front started pulling to the side of the road. He was still on high ground here and had a good view of the city and the river beyond. As good a vantage point as any, he thought, and followed the car in front. He pulled the roadster over and got out, just as the driver from the car in front pointed at the sky.

"There, there they are," the man said in a conversational tone. Harry saw the 18 dots high above the river.

"Ah, over there, the enemy." A cultured voice, a Burmese gentleman in white suit and horn spectacles that gave him the look of an intellectual. They looked where he pointed, and there were more airplanes, small ones, coming in from one side of the bombers and above them, trying to catch them. Harry stated what was obvious to him. "The enemy are the ones in front," he said. "The ones you called the enemy are the Royal Air Force's pursuit airplanes."

The man gave Harry a pleasant smile and little bow, "Ah, yes – as I said."

Whatever Harry might have answered was lost when the rippling sound of the bombs exploding on the docks reached them. They turned to the distant scene and watched in fascination. The view from where they stood on the hill was wide, and they could see behind the first 18 bombers another thirty or more. Although these passed near the docks, they saved their bombs until they were well over the city. Harry's thoughts were with Lucy. The bombs from this second wave would not be near her. From what he could see of the dock area, they were not needed. Everything there was already burning. He could not tell if Lucy's warehouse was within the bounds of the maelstrom of smoke and flame that engulfed sections of the riverfront. He hoped Lucy had not been watching the incoming bombers from her office window.

"They're killing people!" someone shouted. "There, in the market."

Harry turned with the others to look toward the open-air market down the hill from where they stood. Crowds of Burmese had gathered there, in the open areas to watch the spectacle in the sky. Two low-flying Japanese pursuit airplanes were diving on the market. At the last moment they pulled up to zoom over it, and the sound of their machine guns reached those on the hill.

"Bastards!" someone cried. As if it overheard, one Japanese airplane turned its nose in their direction and came up the hill toward them.

"Oh, shit," someone said then, and they all threw themselves on the ground and tried to make themselves small. The Japanese pursuit flew over, not seeing them or not caring. Harry stole a glance upward and saw the helmeted head of the pilot in an open cockpit.

Thoughts of Lucy flickered through his mind, but so much was happening that he was not thinking, only reacting. He looked back toward the river. The docks were an inferno of smoke and fire, but that was where he had to go. For a while they watched pursuits in the distance diving on parts of the city, and sometimes heard the distant rattle of their guns. Then suddenly there were no Japanese airplanes in the air at all, at least none that were near. They had done their work, were headed home. Twice he saw laggard Japanese pursuits dive on unseen targets, and then they too were gone.

He got back in his roadster and started for the river. He did not get far.

The roads were littered with debris and blocked by abandoned cars. He finally left the roadster in the shade of a tree, and started to walk. The bombs had left their mark everywhere, and the destruction got worse as he got closer to the river. Fronts of smashed shop houses spilled into the street near overturned vehicles. Small groups were frantically trying to dig survivors out of rubble with their hands, others were treating wounded. A row of bodies was laid out on a section of surviving sidewalk.

When he reached Strand Road where it paralleled the river he was stopped by a British soldier. There were hoses everywhere, and fire trucks, and men standing in small groups, looking toward the conflagration farther down the road.

"You can't go this way, sir," one of the soldiers stepped up to him and said. "The fires are too intense. There are unexploded bombs. The volunteers will deal with it."

"Can I help?" Harry said.

"There's nothing you can do, sir. The volunteers are trained. Some learned from the Blitz. Best you go home, sir, and care for your family."

Harry turned away, not sure where to go. Back to his car, he supposed. With the car he would at least be ready to move when it was possible again.

He walked through a neighborhood near the railroad station. There was a lot of damage here. One row of shop houses had been gutted by fire, another mashed flat into a long, low pile of rubble. He stopped to look at it, and a Burmese boy staring at it quietly said, "It was a Japanese bomber, sir. It came down here, killed everyone." Harry stepped closer. Now that he knew what happened, he started recognizing pieces of airplane. A scorched tail, or maybe it was a wingtip stuck up in the air, like a huge headstone, a blackened Japanese sun showing on the end.

There were others, mostly Burmese, but a few Westerners too, poking around in the mangled mess of metal and shards of glass that had intermingled with bricks and wood beams and colorful glazed tiles from the front of one of the shops. It must have been a fancy goods shop of some kind. Small perfume bottles were scattered about, colored bars of ladies' soap, and shiny things he did not recognize. As if on display, a large radio set stood on top of this heap of expensive trash. Torn from the aircraft, but it looked intact. Near it was a twisted machine gun barrel, and next to that, a small hand. It was not attached to anything, but looked like it was holding onto something. Harry leaned close to see it better.

"It's yours if you want it." An American voice; Harry turned. A young man, but older than Harry, in khaki shirt and shorts, and what they called "mosquito boots". He looked weary, his face dirty with smudges of oil. "I got this," he said, and shook a Japanese sword at Harry. "It was the pilot's. I think the hand was his too." He shook his head. "Fucker thought he was a samurai. Well, somebody samuraied his ass." He put the sword in his left hand and offered Harry his right. "I'm Olson, he said, "AVG Third Squadron. I saw you up at Toungoo. How you doing?"

"I'm doing fine," Harry said, feeling surreal, acting in a dream. He looked at the others, recognized faces from Toungoo. At least one was a pilot, the others AVG ground crew, here to view the remains of an enemy.

"We wanted to see what it was we shot down, what kind of equipment the Jap has. Well, there it is....You can't tell much about the airplane by what's left of that. One of the engines is over there. It's a nice piece of work, like something we would have. Japs probably copied it from us."

Olson kicked at something on the ground. "Part of the gunner," he said, but Harry did not want to look. As they got away from the others, Olson took Harry by the arm and quietly said, "The Old Man said I should bring you up to date when we had a chance to get together. There was not really much to say 'till now. We're heading back to the airdrome. Would you like to come along? I can't promise dinner will be much, but we've got a good supply of beer. We can talk on the way."

They had two jeeps and a Studebaker sedan. Olson led Harry to the sedan, then got in and drove. "There's room enough in the jeeps for the others," he said. After he maneuvered around the trash in the streets, he turned to look at Harry. "Did you see much of the fight?" he asked. Harry told him he had seen two waves of bombers dropping bombs on the docks and city, and RAF pursuits attack the bombers. "I guess some of them were your P-40s. I watched one airplane go all the way down, a bomber I guess. A couple of others seemed to be on fire in the air."

Olson nodded. "I wondered what it looked like from down here. We lost two of our guys. The RAF lost a bunch. But we made up for it, I think. We don't have a count yet, but between us and the RAF we got about a dozen Jap planes."

"From what I've seen, the city got hit hard."

"From the air it looked like all Rangoon was burning. There are fires all over town, but it was the docks that really got hit. Christ! And our airfield! First they bombed us, and then their goddamn pursuits came down and worked us over with their machine guns."

There were many people on the street, in little groups, all walking in the same direction. Olson slowed to a crawl until he was around them, and then went on.

"And it's only the first day of the war for us. We lost three airplanes today, and a half dozen more are damaged. We had only fifteen to start, and there's nothing to replace the ones we lose. The Japs will come back tomorrow. The ground crew will be working all night to get all the airplanes back up in the air."

By now, Olson was braking repeatedly for people on the street. They were mostly Indians, long lines of them, all heading north, all carrying bundles or suitcases or wooden boxes. Farther away from the city the crowds started to thin out. When the road was finally clear, Olson said, "It's happening, the exodus out of the city. The Brits were talking about it. They thought that the Indian coolie was born with the British stiff upper lip, that they would stay and work in Burma come hell or high water. It never dawned on the British: What the hell do the Indians have to hang around for once the Japs start dropping bombs on them? Nothing. The Indians have nothing here. It's not their home, not their country. They're all going to walk back to India." He swerved around a family that was carrying a bed. "Well, that bunch will be comfortable if they don't find accommodation on the road. Anyway," he continued, "it's going to be a goddamn mess with all the coolies gone. Who the hell is going to do all the work?"

British sentries at the entrance to the Mingaladon airdrome stood back and waved the AVG vehicles on. "They're finally getting to know us," Olson said. He drove to the end of one of the runways where a number of the long-nosed P-40s were parked. Others were under the large trees beyond, and what looked like a couple of burned-out hulks of airplanes. The only structure of any kind was a tent. As they drove past it, Olson said, "Our ready room," and, as he parked next to a P-40, "This is home. The Brit quarters are over there," and jerked his chin at a cluster of small wooden barracks-like buildings across the runway. "They have an officers' club. We'll walk over later. They got shot up pretty bad."

Harry followed Olson as he walked among the P-40s. "Some of the guys are feeling real lucky right now. After they landed they found bullet holes all over their airplanes. They never even knew there were any Japs near them."

One of the mechanics was furiously beating tin cans flat with a hammer. "He's making patches," Olson said, "to put over the bullet holes in the planes. We don't have anything else. Look at this." He ran his hand along a propeller blade until he stopped at a ragged notch in the edge. "A bullet hit the prop here. Nothing they can do about that, except file down the rough edges and hope it stays balanced. The blade should be replaced, but there are no spares. We have no spares for anything."

They stopped where a mechanic was kneeling on a little platform up near the engine. "Hey, Rudy," Olson said, "come down and tell our friend what happened to your man Paul. Tell him how these goddamn Jap samurais fight."

The mechanic jumped down and wiped his hands. "Our Paul Greene," he said. "It was something else." He looked at Harry and went on. "Paul nailed one of the Jap pursuits, and then the Jap's friends came after Paul. They shot his controls away. Paul had no choice. He parachuted, and goddamn if the Japs didn't chase him all the way to the ground. Shooting all the way. Paul just hung there in his parachute, trying to be small. The Japs flew around him in circles and took turns shooting at him. They put holes in his canopy, but they never touched him. Paul was trying so hard to climb up his own shroud lines to hide in the canopy that he almost collapsed his parachute. He hit the ground hard and knocked himself silly. But he's okay now."

"That's the Jap samurais for you," Olson said, "shooting our guys in their parachutes, machine-gunning civilians in the city. Fuck it. I need a drink. Let's go over to the Brit Officers' Club."

As they walked across the field Olson said, "The Japs hit every vital thing here, commo, anti-aircraft positions, the runways. The Brits figure that the Japs were so accurate because they had help from the locals who picked the targets."

They stepped into what looked like a wooden barracks building that had obviously suffered in the Japanese attack. Part of the roof was gone, and chunks of wood were torn from the side. "Goddamn mess," Olson said as they went through the door. Glass shards scattered over the floor sparkled in the setting sun. It was gloomy inside and Harry saw two men sitting at the bar. Another was walking toward them, on his way out. "Well, Flight Officer Collins," Olson said, "or is it Wing Commander Collins now?" He started introducing Harry.

"Oh, yes, Ross, we've met," Collins said, shaking Harry's hand. He looked very tired.

Left uncertain by what Olson had said, Harry asked, "Are congratulations in order?"

"Congratulations?" Collins repeated, looking puzzled. "Oh, the rank you mean. It's meant as a joke, I think. We lost five pilots today. Three were senior to me. I've moved up it seems."

The moment was awkward. Harry knew his next question could make it worse, but he risked it. "Have you heard anything of Lucy?"

"Yes," Collins said. He looked animated. "Yes, she called here. The telephones are working, oddly enough. She's fine. They never hit her warehouse. She was quite lucky. She's back hard at work. Ross, if you want to reach her, try the Strand hotel. She's using one of her father's rooms there. Ask for Lucy, or Miss Liu, they will know. Listen, Ross, I would love to buy you a drink, but I'm on alert tonight. I'm off at midnight, if you're still here. "

They shook hands, and Collins walked off.

CHAPTER 9

The Ambassador doesn't know what to do," Doyle said, "The workforce is gone, all of it. The Indian coolies from the docks started it. Then the Indian shopkeepers went. By nightfall, everybody was on the road – Indians, Chinese, Burmese. They all camped on the edge of the city last night. This morning they're back on the road, heading north again. The whole city is shut down. There's nothing to buy or eat."

Harry nodded as he watched Doyle butter a fragment of toast. Not every establishment in Rangoon was shut down on this first morning after the Japanese bombing. Doyle's secret tea garden was open for business. The old woman who ran it had obviously spent the night in her little wooden house at the back. But the city was almost as empty as Doyle suggested. It was 7:00 A.M. and Rangoon's streets, always full of people from the first glimmers of dawn, were all but deserted.

Harry felt numb, detached from himself. Yesterday had been a long day. It had been going on midnight when he broke off from Olson and the rest of the AVG holding down the British officers' club at the aerodrome. There had been a good stock of beer and the AVG pilots seemed to have an inexhaustible supply of scotch. "With the grace of God," one of them said, "there will be no early alerts," and they all drank to that.

When Harry had absorbed all he could of the day's actions, two of the pilots took a jeep to look for his roadster. They found it untouched, and Harry drove home through streets that were empty except for the volunteer crews clearing rubble and filling bomb craters in the roads. Once he saw them piling corpses into a truck. At his bungalow he made a pot of coffee and sat down to write a report on all that he had heard, and only then fell into bed.

"The worst part is the docks." Doyle, having finished his toast, turned back to the problem again. Harry tried to stay focused. "There's a mountain of materiel out there and there's nobody to handle it. The Ambassador was totally beside himself this morning. One of Chiang Kai-shek's people called on him last evening. The Chinese need the stuff on the docks. There are weapons out there. Ammunition, vehicles." Doyle paused, long enough to make Harry look directly at him to see what was coming. "How do we get the workers back?" Doyle asked then. "Do we plead? Cajole? Beg?"

"I don't know," Harry said after an appropriately thoughtful pause. "I never studied labor relations."

"We have to do something. I hoped you might have some ideas. There's an ammunition ship, the Tulsa, coming upriver today. It's loaded with lend-lease munitions for China. The Brits want some of that too. They need it. And they need it off the ship as soon as possible." Doyle shook his head. "It's sure a different world from yesterday."

Harry was only half listening. Something was working at the back of his mind. "You know, maybe I have an idea," he finally said, "about the docks."

"I'm listening."

"I'm not sure yet. Call it half an idea. It's something I need to work on."

Doyle sighed, loudly. "Just don't work too long. The Japs will probably be back by noon. I was on the streets watching the show, with everybody else yesterday. When the sirens go today, I'll be running for the shelters – with everybody else."

Harry started getting up. "Let me check something out. I'll get back to you in an hour."

Harry was halfway to the gate when Doyle called him. He turned, and Doyle said: "Merry Christmas, Harry." Harry's eyes were blank. "Tomorrow," Doyle said. "Tomorrow's Christmas."

"Wonderful," Harry said. "I don't have my shopping done."

It was turning into another brilliantly clear morning, and as Harry turned his roadster on to Strand Road and drove along the river, he saw that the cleanup crews had done an incredible job. There were still stacks of debris, but in most places it had already been hauled away. Among the volunteers were some who had experienced the London Blitz, and that probably accounted for it. As he drove, the landscape along the river looked different too. There were huge gaps in the jungle green now, areas that were all shades of black under the morning sun, burnt-out areas. Each time he passed a warehouse he looked at it carefully, and was surprised to see no obvious sign of damage. After a while it struck him. The warehouses were all wood. They were either untouched by the bombs, or they had disappeared. When a bomb struck, a fire started and the structure burned completely to the ground.

Lucy's warehouse looked no different than it had. There was no sign that a bomb had even come close. As he walked to the entrance, a convoy of a half dozen trucks pulled out of the yard, cargoes bulging under roped canvas.

"We were lucky," Lucy said, when she met him on the warehouse floor. "We stayed when the sirens went off. I wasn't expecting anything to happen. Nobody was." They embraced quickly, awkwardly, even though Harry felt as though he had known her for most of his life.

"You were lucky," he told her, looked around. "It looks like business as usual here. I saw coolies working and trucks rolling out. Are all your workers here?"

"Every one."

"Boy, we sure need to talk."

She suggested they go up to her office. There she spoke with a clerk while Harry stood by the open window, and looked out on smoking black ruins where warehouses had stood, and on twisted and smoldering metal on ships tied along the quay. Out on the river he could see only the funnel and masts of a ship that now rested on the river bottom. Two vessels nearby listed dangerously. "What a goddamn mess," he said as Lucy stepped up to him. He went on to tell her what Doyle had said about the exodus of workers and the growing concern of the British and American embassies. "The workers are mostly Indians," he finished. "They have no commitment to what happens here in Burma. How do we get the workers back?"

"We're dealing with the same problem here," she said, "but, as you see, our people are working, our trucks are leaving, fully loaded. We plan to have our warehouse completely cleared in two days."

"How do you do it?"

"Money, Harry. Coolies make very little money. You offer them a lot. If they see a chance to make a lot of money in a short time they'll take the risk."

"All we need is money?"

"Money is the start. Money will bring the coolies back. Then they will work until their fear of the Japanese outweighs their interest in money. To keep them working, there must be some provision for their safety. Everyone knows the Japanese airplanes will be back. There must be shelters, and the workers must be allowed to go there when the Jap airplanes come. Even with that, Japanese pressure on Rangoon will reach a point where no worker will stay. But right now it's possible to get them to work. I agreed to pay our workers three times their wages as long as there is a danger of the

Japanese airplanes returning."

"That sounds good, Lucy, but what I'm talking about is not a single warehouse, but the whole waterfront. How do we do that?"

"One warehouse or a hundred, it's all the same. The people who run the port – I don't mean the British officials, but the real bosses, the ones you don't see. The embassy calls them 'thugs'. They're the Chinese and Indian bosses who control the port workers. All of them are all still here. The port is their domain. They will be the last to leave. It all becomes a matter of contacting them and making an offer."

"How do we do that?"

"You need someone they will trust."

"Like who?"

"If my father were here...."

"You told me he's in Kunming." He looked at her for a long moment. This was what had been niggling at him. Now he would see if he was wrong. "Look, how about you?" he asked. "You work closely with your father. You must know these people. Can you do it?"

She spent no time thinking about it. "I can approach them," she said. "They know who I am. They would accept me as representing my father's interest. We must not tell them we are doing it for the Americans or the British. And you must stay out of it. Your face is the wrong color."

"That's no problem," he said. "They don't need to see me, and neither the Brits nor the Americans would want to show their hand. If you're willing to try, what would you need from me?"

"Money, cash money, a lot of it. British pounds and shillings. And gold. Gold for the bosses. If you really want this done, I can draw up a budget."

"You draw up a budget," he said. "And I'll get somebody to authorize it. The embassies are desperate. Unless they figure this out for themselves, I'm sure you have a deal." Harry stated getting up. "Let me get on my way and find us that pile of money. You know, I've never done anything like this, but it's kind of interesting. "

* * *

"It's so obvious," Doyle said, "that I think they're a little ashamed, the Brits and the Americans. Everybody agrees that money is the way to go, but they have no one they can trust as the bridge to the thugs who control the port. By default, you and Lucy will do that. At least get it started. Except for our Ambassador, no one in the embassy will know who the two of you are. Everything will go through me. Both our Ambassador and the Brits know that I'm Donovan's man. If anything goes wrong, I get blamed and Donovan gets blamed, and nobody in the embassy gets dirtied up. That's why they like it."

"That's the way the world works," Harry said. "Lucy's game for it. I'm ready. By the way, is this what spies do?"

"It seems like something spies should do." Then Doyle screwed his face into his most serious look. "Harry," he said, solemnly, "do you trust that girl? Are you sure she won't run off with all our money?"

"Of course I trust her," Harry said, not quite sure if Doyle's concern was real. "But if she does run off with the money, it's your ass, isn't it? You said nobody will even know who I am."

That brought what looked like genuine worry to Doyle's face. It made Harry want to reassure him. "Whatever happens, it's money well spent, Doyle. If we don't get all that stuff unloaded and away from the docks, the Japs will burn it up and there won't be anything for money to buy. We have to try."

"You're right," he said, "we have to try," but he still looked uncertain. "Look, Harry, I was trying to be funny with my comment about Lucy, but there is something you do need to know. Please don't take this the wrong way." He paused there for a long moment before continuing. "I found out who Lucy's father is. He's one of the bosses, a big man on the Chinese side, there's no question of that. His name is Liu Bo Nian. We don't know much about him, except that he's rich, influential, and very devious. He's been called Chiang Kai-shek's secret Foreign Minister and Chiang Kai-shek's bag-man. Both titles seem to fit, although it's generally agreed that whatever money is in the bag, it's mostly his. Thanks to his connections, he's a very successful businessman."

"Sounds mysterious."

"He is mysterious, dark and mysterious. He has contacts in the international community at a very high level, but otherwise he tries to blend into the background. Which probably explains why he's eager to have his pretty daughter up front. It's a given that he's linked to Tai Li and Chinese intelligence. He's probably an important part of the Chinese intelligence apparatus. He's nobody to fool with. If you ever get Lucy to talk about him, find out what you can. I don't think we even know what he looks like."

"Okay, Boss," Harry said. "It sounds like another spy job."

* * *

Harry never knew there was so much money in the world, or that it was so heavy. It was all in the small denomination bills that Lucy wanted, and packed in nicely wrapped boxes. The embassy could handle a flow of cash like this for a few days, but beyond that, currency would have to be flown in from Delhi. There was also the question of the gold that the embassy seemed more reluctant to give up than paper currency. "No problem," Lucy said. If she could find a Rangoon jeweler willing to go into his hidden stash, she could probably buy all the gold she needed with a portion of the cash. She would just budget more cash. Harry insisted they go by the book, and eventually the gold was forthcoming.

They loaded six boxes into Lucy's MG, and she asked Harry to turn the rest of the boxes over to the concierge at the Strand. Once she completed her first delivery, she could go to the concierge in the lobby to get more. The bellboys would even load it for her. When Harry said he was a little worried about getting others involved, she said, "It could be Christmas gifts, Harry. It's nothing to worry about. The concierge is used to handling luggage and boxes. All kinds of things. Nothing left at the Strand ever gets lost." Harry thought about what might happen during an air raid, but he said,"Fine." Then he hung around the lobby of the Strand and kept his eyes on the door of the room where the boxes were kept. Despite the casualness with money that he had shown to Doyle, he did feel responsible for it. If the sirens went off, he was sure the staff would scatter and God knows what would happen to all that cash. No one actually knew what was in those boxes, but if the sirens went off, he would spend the next bombing raid sitting in the lobby.

It was not very long before Lucy came back for her second load, and from behind a potted plant he watched the bellboys load six more boxes in her car. Then she was off again. As the afternoon went on, Harry relaxed, as did everyone else. The longer the Japanese bombers stayed away, the less likely it seemed they would return. But worried eyes kept glancing at the sky.

Lucy moved quickly. She had at least a half dozen places to go, and had most of the money disbursed by late afternoon. On her third trip, she saw Harry and smiled. "I know what you're doing," she said, "but you don't need to." He offered her lunch, but she said, no, she would prefer to complete her work. People were waiting for her. "And someone is waiting to meet you," she added. "My father came back from Kunming. He flew in this morning, and he would like to meet you."

"Fine," Harry said. His mouth was suddenly very dry.

"He's upstairs, in his room. I can't join you. I have another boss to meet. I'm late already."

The room she sent him to was in a rear corner on the top-most floor.

Harry knocked on the heavy door, and thought he heard a response from inside. He pushed gently and the door opened. Heavy drapes were drawn over the windows and the room was dimly lit, but as he entered it was evident that this was not a standard hotel room, at least not any more. It was an office, a very fancy one, that should have been in London maybe. It was all dark wood and brass and leather. Near the far wall was a large mahogany table that served as a desk. The green-shaded shiny brass lamp standing on it provided most of the room's light. To the side was a pair of leather chairs and a settee grouped around a coffee table. There were side tables and bookcases, all of dark wood, and on the walls exotic pictures in gilded frames that Harry recognized as 19th century prints of India. Only the fireplace was missing.

A youngish Asian man suddenly came into the room from a door on the side. He seemed not at all surprised to see Harry, who assumed this was probably the owner of the voice he thought he had heard through the door. As the man came closer he extended his hand and said, "Ah, you must be Ross. Good of you to come." If Harry had not been looking directly into the man's Asian face, he would have believed he was shaking hands with an Englishman. The accent was perfect English upper class. "I'm Liu Bo Nian," he said, "Lucy's father."

This was so unlike what Harry had expected, that it was all he could do just to mumble his own name. This was no Chinese patriarch, no stern old man in the robes of a mandarin. This was a young man – or at least young-looking – handsome, even elegant in a well-fitted, tweedy suit. Harry was not acquainted with bespoke suits and Saville Row tailors, but he knew that was what he was looking at.

"Or would you prefer 'Harry?'"

"Harry is fine, Mr. Liu," he somehow managed to say.

"Please, Harry, not 'mister.' My friends call me 'Louie.' I would be honored if you did the same."

Liu invited him to sit on the leather settee, and as they moved to sit down, Harry took a good look at him. He was certainly not old. He might have been in his mid-forties, but looked ten years younger. His eyes were alert and intelligent, his hair was stylishly slicked back. Nothing about him seemed Chinese. He moved and spoke like an English lord, a modern one, a member of a modern international set.

"I understand you and Lucy are now running the Port of Rangoon," he said, "That's a very impressive day's work"

"It's all Lucy's doing, sir. She's a real business woman."

"Not sir, Harry, Louie. I know Lucy is a first rate business woman, although she fights being that. I really have to thank you for nudging her in the right direction." He got to his feet. "I'm forgetting my manners," he said. "Let me fix you a drink. Whiskey?"

"Yes, thank you," Harry said. Whiskey was becoming familiar, a comfort at a time like this.

As Liu fixed their drinks at a small teak bar, he said, "Lucy tells me you're a journalist. Running the port is a long way from journalism."

"We're not really running the port, sir... ah, Louie. We're just doing a favor for friends at the embassy."

"Ah, the embassy, is it? Well, these are extraordinary times – times that create strange bedfellows. We will all find ourselves in roles that we never expected to play." He handed Harry a large glass of whiskey, raised his own to Harry and said, "To our new roles. Cheers." They both drank. To Harry the whiskey tasted very good indeed.

"Take my case," Liu said as he set his glass down. "I'm a businessman, a trader. My goal is to make money, and yet I find myself caught up with governments and politics. And that includes your government as well. A few days ago I met your Colonel Chennault. We were all in Chungking with General Chiang Kai-shek. Sir Archibald was there as well." Then, sensing that Harry did not have his familiarity with first names, he quickly added, "General Sir Archibald Wavell, the British Commander-in-Chief for India and now Burma. Everyone suddenly sees a compelling need for a coordination of effort, now that the Americans are in the war – which is a very good thing. The war was China's alone for too long."

"Will you be working with Chennault and with the British?"

"I'll be working with everyone, I suppose, the Allies as well as General Chiang, but doing the same thing I've always done. The difference will be that more of the goods I handle will be war materiel. I'm looking for radios for Colonel Chennault, and for airplane parts. With America in the war, there's some ambiguity about Chennault's role. For now, he and his volunteers are still part of the Chinese Air Force. Effectively they are the Chinese Air Force. I will be working with the British on General Chiang's behalf, negotiating for guns and ammunition right here in the Port of Rangoon. Which, of course, is another reason I was pleased to find that you and Lucy have things so well in hand here. It will make my work easier." Harry nodded and took another drink of his whiskey. He looked up to see Liu studying his face.

"There was an additional reason I wanted to meet you. Lucy has spoken of your journalistic endeavors. Telling readers in America the story of what's happening out here is very important to China. Now that America's in the war, it's important to your country as well. America must know what's happening out here. This serves both our interests. If there is any way I can help you with this, please, feel free to call on me, directly, or through Lucy. If you need information on military events or political background, I may be able to help. If you need photos, or if you need to travel to get your own, I may be able to arrange that. My company has vehicles, ships, and even an airplane or two. China needs all the help it can get, and our fight is your fight now."

They were interrupted by a man who came in through the side door carrying a tray of appetizers. As he served them, Liu said, "Harry, I don't know if you've thought much about the future – the near future, I mean. I don't know how long the British Army will be able to hold the Japanese, but not long, I would think. The British, of course will evacuate to India. Lucy and I will relocate our office to China. If you find yourself in China in the coming months, I would be pleased to help you settle in."

They talked for a time and Harry started to relax. He asked what Liu thought about the effect of the Japanese bombings on the viability of the Burma Road and possible alternatives to it. "All supply will be by aircraft," Liu said, "over the Himalayas. Very dangerous flying, but it's the only alternative." General Chiang had an airline, he said, CNAC, and pronounced as a word the letters that stood for the China National Aviation Corporation. "CNAC's pilots," Liu said, "there are Chinese and there are Americans, and they will pioneer the routes." In time the American Air Corps would probably join in, he thought. Harry was impressed by the depth of Liu's knowledge and the thought he had obviously given to the myriad problems that the Japanese push for conquest would bring.

"There is another matter," Liu said, "something entirely different. Lucy tells me you already have a good many contacts here – one expects that of a journalist, of course." He took an envelope from an inner pocket of his coat. "This may be useful to someone you know," he said as he handed it to Harry. "It's a list of names, nineteen in all, and all Burmese. They are individuals who helped the Japanese find their targets in their first bombing raid yesterday. They will continue to help the Japanese, of course. One curious thing is that they are all close to the British, socially in some cases, but most work for the British government in some way. They helped pinpoint British positions for the Japanese Air Force."

Harry took the envelope. "Where did the names come from?"

Liu smiled. "Like you, I have contacts."

"I'll see that it gets to our embassy," Harry said, "but I'm sure they will want to share it with the British."

Liu nodded. "The British are in the best position to deal with this. If there is any question about how the names were acquired, you may say they are individuals well known to General Chiang Kai-shek's security apparatus."

Harry folded the envelope and stuck it in a pocket. "Oh," Liu said as if he suddenly remembered something. "One thing I would ask, Harry, please do not mention the list to Lucy. I think it would disturb her if she thought the names were given to the British."

Harry just nodded. He had no experience in this, but he could imagine what would happen to the Burmese on the list once it was handed to the British. He had no compunctions about passing the list on. Yesterday there had been a lot of dead in the streets of the city. "I won't tell Lucy, sir," he said. "Thank you for all your help."

"Thank you for yours. What you and Lucy are doing is quite useful. Again, if there is anything I can do. I don't know how long I'll be in Rangoon. Much depends on the British of course. In any case, I will need to get back to Kunming before too long. I don't want Lucy to stay here past a certain point. She will follow me to Kunming. I expect you will eventually be there. If you are, please come see me. I'm sure we can be of mutual assistance."

Later, when he told Lucy about the meeting, and how impressed he was with her father, she smiled and said, "He is very seductive, isn't he?" She was quiet for a few moments, thinking. "I'm very lucky," she said, "particularly as a Chinese woman, to have so modern, so chic a father. He's very generous, and very open with people he likes. But even then, the most important things he keeps to himself."

He called a meeting with Doyle and excitedly told him about the meeting. By the time he finished, Doyle was as excited as he was. "Incredible. Not a bearded Fu Manchu, but a clean-shaven Sir Louie. He's got your number."

"Does he think I'm an intelligence officer?"

"Maybe, but I doubt it. Remember, America doesn't have an intelligence service that he could fit you in. No, I think he sees value in you as a journalist and as an activist. Someone who moves around and knows people can be very useful to a guy like Sir Louie. Then again, someone like Sir Louie, entangled in endless conspiracies, would naturally believe that any intelligent mortal would do things in a similar way. We'll see, Harry. Stay in touch with him. He'll be trying to get things from you. The idea is to get more from him."

"We were lucky today. I have bad feelings about tomorrow. Japanese radio says their Air Force will have Christmas presents for Rangoon tomorrow."

CHAPTER 10

Christmas Day 1941
Rangoon, Burma

Harry woke up early and felt doom hanging over him like a sword on a rapidly fraying cord. It was Christmas, but unlike years past, he lacked any interest in rushing down to see what the day would bring. He pulled himself from his bed reluctantly.

Seeing Lucy at the warehouse was the first order of business. He drove there on roads he had to himself. The city was cloaked in a stillness that had nothing to do with the holiday.

"Some of the docks are working," Lucy told him, "but not all. I thought the money would be enough to bring all the coolies back. But the bombs and the fires, and the Jap airplanes that came down to shoot crowds on the street left them terrified. It's not a merry Christmas."

Lucy had been in contact with the dock bosses since dawn. She found the numbers of returned coolies disappointing. "More will come today," she told Harry in between taking calls.

"We're doing fine, Lucy," he said. "We don't need to do it all."

Just after ten o'clock the sirens started. Lucy stood up, looked at the head clerk and nodded. Within minutes workers from the warehouse and from the quay in front of it were walking to trucks parked along the side. Harry stood back while Lucy directed the loading of the trucks that would take them to shelters. Then the two of them checked the warehouse to assure everybody was out, and locked the doors.

They drove their cars separately back along Strand Road and parked on a small street near the hotel. The streets were totally empty now. Not a vehicle moved, not a single person walked. Only a pair of mangy dogs sniffed at something in a gutter. Everyone was in the shelters. Harry knew of a shelter behind the hotel, but he had another idea.

"Let's take my car," he said, "and drive over to where I was on Tuesday. It's on high ground and from there we can see the river. There's nothing nearby, no targets to attract Jap bombs. We can watch from there, and we'll be safe."

Lucy shrugged. "It's better than a stuffy shelter," she said.

As they drove through the deserted streets they could see the pursuit aircraft that had taken off from Mingaladon airdrome, climbing over the city, a dozen long-nosed P-40s and 16 barrel-round Brewster Buffaloes. Lucy counted them. "Peter's airplanes," she said, "the fat ones."

They stood on the hill and looked toward the river, the city spread out before them. Harry pointed across the river to the section of sky where he had first seen the Japanese bombers coming two days ago. Just then a growing rumble of many engines made him turn around. "Christ!' he said, "they're coming from behind us."

He could not see them yet. A stand of tall trees nearby in a small patch of jungle blocked his view. He walked to one side of the trees so he might see that quarter of the sky. He was some distance from Lucy when he saw the first V of approaching Japanese aircraft. "Lucy," he called to her, "there they are," and pointed. More and more airplanes came into sight as he watched, fifty at least. They were bombers mostly, in stately formations. Their protecting pursuits flitted around them like angry gnats.

He could see the bombers being harried by the long-nosed pursuits, the AVG's P-40s. Fires flared and bombers started falling back. Several were burning. One, the unluckiest, was already spiraling down. The vast formation was crossing the sky directly over him now. With a hand to shade his eyes he watched a while longer, then turned to look out across the city toward the docks where the Japs must be headed. Suddenly he caught a movement in the corner of his eye, a black form hurtling down through the trees.

"My God," was all he managed to say as the little patch of jungle erupted into a fountain of debris and the thunder of the explosion engulfed him. Something rushed toward him and he knew he should duck. Before he could, it struck him in the face.

He was on the ground then, with no sense of falling. He tried to push himself up, but it was easier to just lie in the sun. He knew he had to find Lucy. He raised up on his elbows to look for her. Everything was totally still and quiet. He could not see Lucy anywhere, even though she was kneeling by him now, looking in his face. Her lips moved, but he heard nothing.

Then, from a great distance, he heard her saying his name.

He wanted to respond, but words would not come to his lips. He saw flecks of blood on her face and that made him say what he had wanted to tell her: "They're dropping their bombs early," he said, and his words came as from deep inside a barrel. "Fuckers," he said then, for the sake of saying it. This time his words sounded good. "You are feeling better," Lucy said, and looked relieved, although Harry was not aware of it.

From somewhere beyond Lucy came the crumps of bombs exploding farther away. Muddled though he was, he knew the Japs could not have waited to reach the docks. They were dropping their bombs on the city.

He started to get to his feet again, but the ground moved quicker than he could. Lucy steadied him with both hands. His dizziness passed, but now his head hurt. He looked at her and saw it again. "You have blood on your face," he said.

She touched her face. "I think it's yours."

"What the hell hit me?"

"A tree limb," she said, and 20 feet away he saw a piece of tree as big as he was. "I think it just grazed your head. Let me look at your face," she said, touching him.

He held still as Lucy examined him. In the sky above him now he saw another wave of bombers pass, this time surely headed for the docks. A half dozen AVG P-40s were among them, like dogs among a running herd of terrified deer. As though feeling the teeth snapping at their flanks, the bombers veered away from the docks and jettisoned their bombs. Harry watched the trajectory of the bombs as they fell harmlessly into the river or impacted in the rice fields on the other side. They missed the docks completely; on the river a single unlucky vessel took a hit. The Japanese had turned for home, the P-40s nipping at them, drawing blood.

Lucy's voice broke through the action. "I don't think you have any real damage. A few cuts and some nasty scrapes on your face and forehead, but nothing that looks serious."

"Here," he said, reaching for her hand, "steady me," and this time got to his feet. "We can't stay here. I need to get to the airport. Find out what's happening."

She studied his face for a long moment. "I'll drive you there. We have to clean you up a bit." He did not argue.

By the time they were on the road the raid was over. Groups of people were walking north again. There were no great numbers yet, but it was a sign of what would come before the day was over. "They're giving up on Rangoon," Lucy said.

Nearer the airdrome they started catching up with other cars going their way, moving as if in a convoy. All were civilians, British mainly, but there were a few Harry recognized as Americans. It seemed a happy bunch. There was much waving and shouting as they all turned off on the road leading to the airdrome. During the brief wait for the sentries to wave them through the gate, a portly British gentleman turned and waved his hand at them, two fingers extended in a "V" for victory.

Past the sentry Harry directed Lucy to drive along the runway to the area where Olson had taken him. The convoy of cars they had been with split up, some headed toward the AVG area, some to the British side of the field. There, smoke could still be seen coming from freshly damaged wooden buildings.

"I'll drop you," Lucy said. "But then I want to drive to the British side. I want to see if Peter is all right."

The AVG end of the runway looked festive. People were milling around two tables set up in the open, heaped with food. As Harry climbed out of the roadster, he heard laughter and shouts of "Merry Christmas!" A familiar AVG face waved him over. "You're just in time for Christmas dinner."

"Victory dinner," someone corrected him.

A lot of civilians had gathered by one of the P-40s. Drinks in hand, everyone was looking at the airplane, walking around it or standing back to see it better. More than one civilian shook his head in disbelief. The airplane looked lopsided. A large piece of its wing was missing. One British man looked uncertainly into Harry's face, then gestured at the airplane with his whiskey glass. "He ran into a Jap. Jap's wing just folded up. But these American airplanes are built of stouter stuff." He said that very approvingly.

Harry turned to where some of the AVG were setting up another table. A couple of pilots were helping with this one. It would be the bar. He saw a familiar face behind a case of scotch and asked, "Where did you get all the food?"

"Courtesy of Bill Pawley," the man said. When he saw no recognition on Harry's face he added, "The civilian airplane company rep. He said we did good today." There was more food than Harry had seen in days. Roast chicken, hams, and stacked crates of whiskey. "And there's beer, cold beer," the man added. "I don't know where he got cold beer."

From behind him, Harry caught snatches of conversation. "A great victory," a British voice said. "The Yanks accounted for 20 Japs today. And took no losses!"

"No," someone else said. "They lost two."

"Our chaps did poorly," said a third Brit, "The RAF lost six Buffalos."

It could have been a football game. The word "victory" was well used.

Harry heard it again and again. He looked for Olson then, and saw him just as he stepped up to the tables. "Oley," he said as he came from behind him, and Olson turned. His eyes widened as they fell on Harry's face. "Good Christ," he said, "who did you tangle with?"

Lucy had cleaned him up, but his face had deep scratches and was heavily bruised. "A tree," he said.

"A tree," Olson repeated. "Sure. I hope the tree looks as bad as you do."

"I saw some of what you guys did today. It looked good. What's the score?"

"Not sure yet," Olson said. "As of now, about 20 to two, our favor. Two of our guys are down. We're not sure about them. They may have gotten out."

"The AVG knocked down 20 Jap planes?"

"At least 20, maybe more. The count's not complete."

"Congratulations."

Olson nodded. He ran a hand through his hair. He looked beyond tired, weary. "The British didn't do so well," he said. "They got two, maybe three Japs, but they lost six airplanes at least. Four pilots for sure. The way we're losing Brits, the war will be over soon."

"How are the airplanes you still have?"

"Shot up. We still have a dozen, more or less. I don't think there's one without battle damage." He turned to look where the P-40s were parked. "Did you see Parker's airplane, the one-winged wonder? He ran into a Jap, knocked him down with his wing. Parker brought it back, but that P-40's probably a write-off." He looked away from Harry when he added, "I'm sending a telegram to the Old Man, telling him we need to get out of here. Or to get reinforcements here real quick." He looked out over the airfield. "Got to get back to work," he said. "Sir Archibald is here with us tonight, and General Brett. They're both coming to dinner."

That was a surprise. "You've got General Archibald here, the British Commander-in-Chief for India and Burma? They risk having him here during the Jap bombing?"

"It was sort of inadvertent," Olson said. "They blundered in here this morning in a DC-2 transport while the Japs were starting their bombing run. They had no idea what was going on. It was amazing they didn't get shot down by one side or the other. We got Sir Archibald out of his airplane and into a slit trench by the runway just as the bombs started to explode."

"My God," Harry said.

"A typical operation of your British high command," Olson added, and looked over his shoulder again. "They'll be here soon."

Harry could feel the tension in the man. "Thanks for the wrap-up, Oley," he said, now as eager as Olson to get to other things. He had just seen Lucy walk into the area. She looked disoriented, and that was unusual. "Lucy," he called to her.

She turned toward him. Before she even got near she started to tell him, "Peter has crash-landed. They think he's all right. He telephoned from somewhere outside the city. They told him to take an ox-cart back." She walked right into Harry's arms. He held her close and said, "Peter will be all right. He's a pilot. They're hard to keep down." Finally she drew back from him. "Yes, he'll be all right. Thank you, Harry."

"Come on," he said, "you must be as hungry as I am. Let's get near the food before all the pilots get here."

A small group of men in full uniform walked across the runway toward them. It was evident that the senior man was the one in the center of the group, and slightly in the lead. With a fancy hat and starched general's regalia it had to be General Sir Archibald Wavell. A half-step behind, a man wearing the three stars of a Lieutenant General of the U.S. Army Air Force, General George Brett. The two ranking Allied Commanders in Asia. A few hours ago they had just missed a hit by Japanese bombs. They never knew the Japanese were in the sky. "Remarkable," Harry said aloud and laughed. When Lucy looked at him, a question on her face, he said, "Later."

All the British present, civilian as well as military, fell silent and stood up straight. Few of the AVG reacted at all. Two pilots took advantage of the distraction to grab some ham from the table. Olson snapped a smart salute, said some words of welcome, and invited everyone to eat.

Harry was no longer aware of his head hurting, and now he had a big appetite. Once the worthies from the high command had been served, he grabbed a couple of plates embellished with the crest of the RAF officers' club. He handed one to Lucy and heaped his with ham and chicken. He was gratified to see Lucy do the same. They carried their plates away from the tables to enjoy their meal in quiet. While they ate, snatches of conversation came from behind them.

"Look at all these Brits," an American voice said. "Yesterday we were ruffians they wouldn't talk to; today we're heroes."

"Not heroes, winners. The Brits figure we'll keep the Japs away."

"They know the RAF won't. The RAF's all but gone."

"Rangoon sure knows it. The city's shutting down."

"The telephones still work."

"Did you see the crocodile? It was bigger than ever today."

Harry looked at Lucy. He knew the crocodile. "The refugees," he told her. It was what the AVG called the steady stream of refugees that moved north on the road past the airdrome. Thousands of them, moving like one big single-minded animal, a large one, a long one. A crocodile.

"Did you notice the taxis and the buses?" This voice sounded British.

"Nobody notices taxis and buses. Nobody here uses them."

"Exactly. That's why nobody knows there're gone. There are no more taxis and buses in Rangoon. They're all on their way to India."

"Jesus," said a British voice. Another said, "The restaurants are closed. There are no newspapers. Garbage collection has stopped. Christ, I saw bloated bodies on the street near my club."

"Dogs," someone else said. "That's normal."

"Not dogs," the first British voice said; "people." After a pause, "Well, they were Burmese."

"There you have it."

In the midst of this dark talk, one of the AVG pilots, standing behind them and listening, stepped to the head of the table. In a solemn tone he announced, "I have some really bad news." Everyone in earshot fell mute; everyone looked at him. "Well?" It was Olson who finally spoke up for them all.

"The Greek has closed down the Silver Grill!"

"Oh my God," somebody said. "Holy shit!" an American voice exclaimed. Faces fell and Olson looked more troubled. "The Silver Grill has closed!" somebody shouted. "Rangoon has fallen!"

There were many more words about the Silver Grill, some shouted and others passed quietly and in confidence. This had the makings of a real crisis. Harry looked at Lucy. "A job for us?" he said. "We could have a real impact on the war."

A small smile came to her face, the first that evening. "My father can do it. He gets the Greek his whiskey. You and I can help with the staffing problem."

"Talk with your father," Harry said. There was confidence in his voice. He was sure Wild Bill Donovan would approve of a move like that.

CHAPTER 11

The Japs have had enough!" "They've turned tail." "The Japs are running back to Malaya." "The bombers are not coming back!"

There were British, and even a few Americans in Rangoon who said things like that. It was wishful thinking. The Burmese did not talk about the Jap bombers, nor did the Indians and the Chinese who remained. They knew the bombers were coming back. It was a matter of time.

The AVG's Christmas Day victories had raised spirits. And hopes. For days there was no sign of the Jap bombers. A few Japanese airplanes did fly over the city during that time, but they dropped nothing more lethal than leaflets – which, for some, were as bad as bombs. They promised that the Japanese Army was coming. By land, by sea, by parachute.

The city was all but shut down now. Some things still worked, and some did not. There was still electricity, and telephones worked in most places. Garbage collection was a thing of the past and the sickly sweet smell of rot hung in the air.

Mingaladon aerodrome was the center of what was still going on. AVG mechanics toiled under the sun by day and under oil lamps by night. They plugged leaking fuel lines and hydraulic lines, spliced severed wires and covered bullet holes in wings, fuselages and tails often with patches beaten out of beer cans. They cursed the heat, the Japanese, and the lack of spare parts.

Meanwhile the pilots hung around near their airplanes and watched. They tried to look casual, but it was easy to see they were tense and weary. When they tired of watching the mechanics, the pilots napped, or played cards, or pitched baseballs to one another. Mostly they just sat and watched the clouds and waited. They knew that Squadron Leader Olson had radioed Kunming for reinforcements. The response from the Old Man was to "hang on."

Harry got out to the airfield at least twice a day, first in the morning to get briefed on what was expected to happen, and then in the early evening to review what did happen. With no Japs in the air, nothing much did, and there was little for Harry to report to Washington. It gave him time to think. It looked like a lot of the war was going to be boring.

Each time Harry visited the field, it was Oley Olsen who briefed him, and then they would have a beer. As they were drinking their beer one day, Olson asked, "Ed Rector is a friend of yours, isn't he, Harry? He'll be here on Sunday, coming down as a passenger on the CNAC airplane." He pronounced the acronym for China National Aviation Corporation, the Chinese airline, as a single word. "A couple of other Second Squadron pilots will be with him. Maybe some ground crew. Newkirk and the rest of the Pandas will fly the airplanes down here early in the week." He looked at Harry for a long moment, then with a tired smile added, "Fresh men, fresh airplanes. The Third Squadron is being relieved."

"That's great," Harry said, a little surprised. "You guys have done a hell of a job, Oley."

Olson nodded. "It's what they pay us for." A simple statement of fact, not false modesty. Seeing the question in Harry's eyes, he added, "Our airplanes aren't fit for combat anymore. Nor the guys. They're beat." He was smiling now. "They tell me that every two minutes of combat time is worth two months of hard labor on a chain gang. Everybody's looking forward to getting back to Kunming. We get fresh eggs there every day!"

* * *

28 December 1941
Mingaladon Airdrome
Rangoon, Burma

Harry watched the CNAC flight from Kunming land. It taxied to the apron where two trucks and a half dozen men waited to unload the cargo. A dozen or so passengers walked away from the transport. Among them, three men in khaki shirts and trousers, carrying leather jackets. AVG pilots.

"Ed!" Harry shouted. "Hey, shark! Ed Rector! Shark of the sky! Over here!"

"My goodness! Harry Ross, what brings you out here?"

"I'm here to welcome the Panda Bears to Rangoon."

"How did you know we were coming? I thought that was a military secret."

"Can't be much of a secret. My Japanese gardener told me. He said you would be on today's airplane, and that Squadron Leader Newkirk will bring the rest of the Pandas and the airplanes here tomorrow."

"Well, you're right about that, Harry. You do have a good source. Listen, we have to check into the billets and drop off our bags. After we do that, let's go find us a drink."

Harry gestured toward two AVG ground crew standing by a jeep. "Your check-in is taken care of. The guys here will take your bags. We can go over to the Silver Grill right now. Bring your friends. "

"Harry, that's very hospitable of you, but the Silver Grill is closed down. Everybody knows that. Oley said that in one of the messages he sent to the Old Man."

"The Silver Grill is closed all right, but only to the public. I have a key to the back door."

"Harry, you kidding me? You're not! Well, damn it, let's go. I'm thirsty."

They drove over in a jeep, Harry and Ed, and Pete and Lynn, the two Panda Bear pilots who had arrived with Ed. Harry pulled the jeep around the back of the Silver Grill and parked. He unlocked the back door and invited the three pilots to enter. The lights were on, and the big room seemed empty at first, but there were a half dozen young ladies – "the pretty ones" - as Harry thought of them, sitting in a couple of the high-backed booths. They jumped up when they saw their guests arrive. One of them walked up to Harry and said, "Your table is ready, Mr. Harry. Will it be whiskey for all?"

"Whiskey for all," Ed repeated, sounding just a bit awed by their reception. Although he tried not to show it, Harry felt the same way. How amazingly different this was from the previous times he had come here. No one had ever called him by name before, or remembered his drink. And then yesterday he stopped here, just briefly, with Louie. Everyone knew Louie, it turned out. The Greek who owned the Silver Grill was there. In Harry's experience, the Greek was a surly man, but he met Louie with smiles and great deference. "Yes, of course," he said to them, "Mr. Harry can entertain the American volunteers here." They were great heroes now, the Americans. The Silver Grill would not be open to the public yet, but Mr. Harry could have a key to the back door. Would that be satisfactory? There would be girls on duty, of course. "The pretty ones," he said.

A few of "the pretty ones" were there then, and they all knew Louie too. They stepped up to say hello to him, even while the Greek was standing there, and Louie knew all their names. "You take good care of Mr. Harry when he comes," he told them. "We will, we will," responded a chorus of tinkling voices. To the Greek Louie said, "Don't worry about whiskey. You'll get all you want." The Greek nodded and handed Harry the key. Louie said, "Have fun, Harry."

Ed rolled the full bottle of Black Label around in his hand. The second bottle, the one they were drinking from, had also been full before they had opened it. "You must be a great friend of the owner," Ed said.

Harry took a deep drink of his scotch; it went down easily now. "Better," he said. "I know his whiskey supplier."

"Now that's the man to know."

"It's not a big deal, really," Harry said, but he knew that it was a big deal. "The Silver Grill will be open to the public again starting tomorrow – if the Jap bombing raids don't start again, but that's a job for you sharks of the sky. You guys have to keep them away."

"Don't you worry about the Japs, Harry. You have the first team here now."

"How are things in Kunming?" Harry asked. "The radio talked all about the big raid. It seems like months ago now. When did all that happen? Was it just a week ago?"

"Eight days," Ed said. He looked reflective. "It does seem about a year ago. Twenty December was a memorable day. I don't think any of us in Kunming that day will ever forget it. Did you know I got the first one, Harry? The first Jap bomber the AVG knocked down?" His eyes narrowed and looked past Harry, at something far away. "I got up high and then came down just behind the last bomber. I can still see that gunner shooting at me. I shot his jaw away. Jesus, I can close my eyes and still see that."

"I heard you had a problem. Did you get yourself shot down?"

"No, sir, I did not get shot down!" He looked directly at Harry now, a little ruffled. "It was even more embarrassing than that. I took a wrong compass course when I turned to head back to Kunming. I flew dumb and happy right out into the boondocks. I had no idea where I was. Then I got caught in a blind canyon and ran out of fuel." He paused and made a show of looking around the room. "I don't tell too many people that, Harry. Anyway, I landed near a village. I didn't know if I was in Japanese-controlled territory or what. Turned out the villagers were quite hospitable. The only problem I had was that all that rice wine we quaffed. It gave me one hell of a headache."

They sat quietly for a while, watching Pete and Lynn, the two other two pilots engaged in some kind of drinking game in the next booth. Each was flanked by two of the girls, who cheered when their pilot won a roll of the dice.

"Your friends are having a good time," Harry noted.

"It's a nice change for them, from the Chinese girls in Kunming. The girls we get to meet up there may be sweet, but they're not very sophisticated. The Rangoon girls are something else, aren't they? Look at the ones here. They're sweet, they speak great English – and they can hold their own in a conversation."

"They're Anglo-Indian, most of them, or Anglo-Burmese. They're more British than the Brits."

Just then Pete came over and sat down next to Ed. "Ed," he said, "Lynn and I were just talking. The girls here are sure nice. The whiskey's not watered and there sure is a lot of it. We both thought that this would be a great place to have our New Year's Eve party."

Ed looked at Harry. Harry shrugged and said, "No problem. I think that can be arranged. If we're not getting bombed – or overrun by Jap parachute troops."

"We'll take care of that part of it." Ed said, "You just arrange things here."

"Not to worry. It will be taken care of." Harry said it with great confidence. For luck, he followed that with a big swallow of whiskey.

He found Louie early the next day and got right down to it. "Louie, I need some help," he said, and tried to explain how plans for the AVG New Year's Eve Party came about. "Then I agreed to make the arrangements. It was only later I thought that maybe the Greek has other plans for that night."

"If that's what the AVG wants.... Don't worry about the Greek. Tell your friends that the Silver Grill is theirs on New Year's Eve."

"Thanks, Louie. There's one other thing. I thought Lucy might be able to help me with the arrangements, supervise the decorations and such. The biggest thing, though, is that food is getting to be scarce in town, and...."

Louie was looking at him thoughtfully. "You know, Harry," he said, "I don't think you want to get Lucy involved with the Silver Grill, not directly. Invite her to the party, by all means. But if you ask her to get involved with the preparations, she would have to deal with the young ladies there. That's probably not a good idea."

Harry was about to object, but realized that it was best to say nothing. He had not thought of Louie as a protective father, but maybe it was himself he was protecting. He nodded, as if he understood.

"As for the food," Louie added, "I don't see any problem. You can certainly ask Lucy to have her chaps scour the docks for foie gras, cocktail onions and such. Meat is the difficult thing, but I can have some ducks flown in on CNAC. Some beef if you want it."

Incredible, Harry thought. "Let's do it! We'll need beef for hamburgers. We'll need some chicken too." He hoped Wild Bill Donovan would never hear about this.

* * *

Later the same day Harry asked Lucy to come with him to the New Year's party. "Peter Collins has already asked me," she said, "The AVG has invited some of the British pilots, the ones they call 'the good guys'. Peter had a terrible time on Christmas Day. He had to parachute from his Buffalo, you know. He got banged up a bit. I think I should have to go with him in any case."

"Sure," Harry said, "of course," and tried to hide his disappointment. What about me, he thought. I got banged up on the same day. His face still had the marks, but he did not want to show his feelings. "Do you think your guys on the docks could look for cans of foie gras, cocktail onions, things like that?"

"Of course, Harry," she said, and looked surprised.

* * *

Nothing much happened in the days leading up to the party. On the 30th, Harry was at the airfield to watch Newkirk lead in the Second Squadron airplanes, 17 fresh airplanes in all. The British community was also out in force to greet the AVG newcomers, as were the Americans and the gentlemen of the press. More journalists were arriving every day. Every newspaper and magazine in the English-speaking world seemed to have someone representing them in Rangoon, or someone on the way. The defense of Rangoon was becoming the big story, and the biggest part of that story was the American Volunteer Group.

The party at the Silver Grill was set for New Year's Eve, but early arrivals were banging on the door by mid-afternoon. Harry had expected as much, and left word that anyone who knew about the AVG party and looked more-or-less respectable was to be admitted. They could have all the whiskey they wanted – there was a mountain of whiskey stacked on the docks now – but no food. That would come later and be served under supervision.

By sundown, when Harry made his appearance, the party was well underway. The food was set out in great variety and abundance, thanks to

Louie, and the crowd grew even bigger, until it seemed that the walls would have to be pushed out to contain it all. Everyone in Rangoon was there, all of the military, the British, the Americans, and every diplomat, businessman and journalist in the city that day. And there were women, beautiful women, English and Indian, Burmese and Chinese, and every Anglo-mix under the sun. From this throng rose a cacophony of sound, like noise, but sweeter, a mixture of voices – chatting, shouting, yelling, laughing – and of music, just brief snatches of jazz that came from the Anglo-Indian quartet bunched together at the far edge of the dance floor. They played valiantly, trying to be heard.

It was a happy, carefree crowd. Standing in the corner of the bar, Harry felt good just watching it. He felt the excitement, the expectation. This aberration, this lull in the war made life seem possible again. Beyond the faces he could see, Harry knew there were others he could not see in the shadows of the high-backed booths – the perfect venue for the big deals he knew were going on. He got an occasional laugh or snatch of conversation, but he could not really make out what was happening.

"So if you shoot down a Jap – or you get yourself shot down – you come to me first. I'll make sure your story gets front-page play."

A half dozen pilots stood around the speaker's booth. "What's he saying?" one of them asked. "Who the hell is this guy?"

"Reporter from some Podunk newspaper in Ohio or Indiana. Some place like that."

"Hey, I'm from Ohio," another said. "Watch what you say."

"I can't pay for interviews," the reporter said. "You understand that? It wouldn't be ethical. But…." The pause was dramatic. "But I can get a couple of bottles of whiskey for anybody who gives me an exclusive."

"So what?" The pilot sitting across from the reporter rose to his feet, picked up his drink and walked away. Three of the four others turned and followed him.

"What the hell. What's he mean, 'so what'?" The reporter felt his generosity spurned. It took him aback. "I said whiskey, real whiskey, two bottles free."

"Hey, Mac," said the remaining pilot leaning over him. "You're in Rangoon now. Whiskey's free."

"What the hell's he mean, 'whiskey's free'?" the reporter said as the last pilot walked away. "What's he mean?"

In another booth nearby, negotiations proceeded between a burly British Army Sergeant in uniform and a weary-looking American in wrinkled khaki shirt and trousers.

"You call them what? Jeeps?" the Sergeant said. "We can see them lined up on your docks. Our officers are strict, very strict. Our orders are not to go over there. Otherwise I would just drive one away. There's hundreds more sitting on the docks. No one can possibly use them all. Nobody will miss one."

"Actually, Sergeant," the American said, confidentially, "they would be missed. They're all accounted for. Every single one. Very strictly. They belong to the American government, or maybe it's the Chinese government now." He shrugged, then looked around to assure no one else could hear. "The Chinese are sending drivers down here for them – even as we speak. There's a record of every truck. It would be my ass if we lost one."

"The Japs will have them," the sergeant said. "They'll have them in a week."

"But, for an acquaintance, a friend…," the American went on, not bothering to listen. He leaned across the table between them. "There is a price, you understand, Sergeant, there is a price. Just like there is on everything else. For $200 dollars I take my chances and you get your jeep."

"Two hundred dollars!" The Sergeant shouted it. Two British officers turned to look at him. He ignored them, shouted again, "I could buy one in London for that!"

"Go to London then," the American said. After a moment he added, "I'll throw in two cases of scotch whiskey."

"Five cases!"

"Sold!"

There was love in the air too, although some of it sounded more like business.

"Stockings, baby. How's silk stockings sound to you?"

"Sounds like shit, Yank," the pretty Anglo-Indian girl said. "Stockings! What do you think I am?" She started to get up.

"But…," the yank said.

She sat back down again. "Look, Yank," she leaned close before she continued, an edge in her voice now. "It's 20 dollars American for a short time. I should make it 25 for you. And there are no overnights. We do it upstairs."

"Upstairs! Twenty dollars! Christ, how about a bottle of whiskey – and a pair of stockings?"

The young lady got up and walked away.

* * *

Lucy sat in the corner booth across from Peter Collins. They had come into the Silver Grill soon after Harry did. They chatted with him briefly and then moved quickly to the corner booth when they saw it was empty. They sat there now, alternatively looking at each other and then quietly staring down into their drinks. Harry could not help but glance over at them from time to time. They look like lovers, he thought.

"Shilling for your thoughts," Doyle said as he came up behind Harry. Anticipating that Harry might not be pleased to be seen with him, he quickly added, "Everybody's here tonight, everyone's a friend." Harry just nodded. Watching Lucy and Collins had put him in a sour mood.

"You did a good thing, getting the Greek to give the Silver Grill to the AVG for their party. It's good for everybody."

"It wasn't me who did it," Harry said.

Doyle laughed. "Yes you did," he said, "but you just gave me the spy's perfect response, 'I didn't do it.' Uncle Wild Bill would be proud of you."

"Well, I didn't do it. And tonight's not a night to be philosophical."

"You're just being crabby, Harry, and I'm not being philosophical. It's just that we're seeing out the old year and seeing in the new. I'm reflecting on where things stand here at the end of 1941; where we're heading in 1942. That's why I think you did a good thing with the Silver Grill. It's great for morale."

"Morale," Harry said, "you need morale? The AVG chaplain's over there. He's a nice guy."

"Don't knock morale. It's what the war effort needs right now. This may be our darkest hour, Harry. I sure hope it doesn't get darker. Has it struck you that we're losing this war. Look at these people here," he said, and waved his glass of whiskey and ice in a wide, encompassing arc. "They know we're losing. At least the sane ones do."

Harry looked at the crowd, closely for the first time this evening. He recognized individual faces, a lot of them, although he did not know the names that went with them. And then something struck him, the difference, the incredible difference between the British in their dress uniforms and formal-looking civilian clothes, and the Americans in their khakis and shorts. It was not just the clothes. On a night like this, the Americans would have looked casual in tie and tails.

"You're wrong, Doyle," he said. "Maybe the British do know they're losing. Look at them. They're dressed for a surrender ceremony, not a party. Christ! They're all pale-faced and fragile-looking. Escapees from winter in England."

"Which they may well be," Doyle said.

"But now look at the Americans, look at the AVG. They're tanned, full of life, cocky, ready to go. The Brits are sitting in corners, quiet, just talking with each other. Look at the AVG. They're chasing the girls, shouting, drinking up everything in sight. They're having a hell of a time. They don't know they're losing the war. Because they're not."

Doyle looked around the room, and then he nodded. "You have a point, Harry, but maybe it's just a small one. The AVG is winning, but they're the only ones. Look at the rest of Asia. The Japs just have it all. We're going to have a hell of a time getting it back."

"But get it back we will, Doyle." Christ, he did not want to talk about the war. "I need a fresh drink…."

Doyle touched his arm and said, "Tomorrow, at nine, in the garden." Harry nodded and turned away from Doyle, and found himself face to face with one of the AVG pilots whose name he could not remember. The man peered at him as if trying to get his eyes in focus, or to remember who Harry was. He looked down at the glass bowl cradled in his arms as if it were something fragile and very expensive. Having reassured himself it was still there, he looked up at Harry again, and spoke, slowly and carefully.

"Eddie Rector said to bring this to you," he said. "You have to drink it down quick."

"What is it?"

"It's a 'gomenasai,' 'gomen' for short. It's a Jap drink." He saw confusion on Harry's face. "Well it's not really Jap. We made it here. It's got a little bit from each one of those bottles back there," and gestured at the bar. "One guy counted 53 bottles. Before he fell on his ass. It tastes like shit, but you gotta have a drink. Everybody does. It has cocktail onions in it."

"Why do you call it a 'gomenasai'?"

"Gomenasai means 'pardon me', in Jap. They call it that because you drink it, you say gomenasai, because then you usually puke. The name is appropriate, I think."

"Ed sent it over?"

"He would have brought it himself, but he's outside vomiting."

"Jesus," Harry said, looking down into the murky brew."

"Just dip your glass into it," the man said.

Harry did just that. He took as little as he could and tasted it. Alcohol, just a heavy alcohol taste with no other flavor. Except maybe a hint of onion. It was vile. As soon as he tasted it, a couple of the AVG pilots came over, raised their glasses and toasted the AVG. Harry drained his glass, carefully. He waited, but there was no nausea, and someone was already filling his glass with good whiskey. He raised it to the pilots and said, "To

Colonel Chennault," and everybody drained their glasses. Then the AVG pilots raised their glasses to toast Olga, Kunming, and Madame Chiang Kai-shek. Harry drained his glass each time, and each time his mood improved.

By now Harry loved the AVG and everybody else in the Silver Grill. He remembered Olga and decided he would have to look her up if he ever got to Kunming. But right now, what was more important was Lucy, and what's-his-name Collins. He walked over to their booth, and they looked up, surprised, but pleased to see him. He raised his glass and said, "To Lucy and Peter." Lucy got up then and kissed his cheek, and said how happy she was that he was her friend. Collins started up too, but had difficulty, whether from parachute injury or whiskey, Harry could not tell. And he did not care, just raised his glass and said, "Cheers," and to himself, "bloody Brit."

Silence fell over the room and someone announced that the AVG quartet would sing, *Deep in the Heart of Texas*, and "everybody better join in, all you Brits included!" A couple of the AVG singers had pistols strapped to their hips, and the four looked like Western gunslingers, but happy ones. Even Squadron Leader Newkirk joined in the singing and clapping.

At the end, somebody yelled into the microphone: "Fuck the Japs" and two shots were fired into the ceiling.

"Christ, are there any girls upstairs?"

Everybody looked up at the ceiling. "What about our guys up there with them. Somebody better take a head count."

And just then shouting started all over the room.

"Happy New Year!"

"Happy 1942!"

CHAPTER 12

The Secret Garden
Rangoon, Burma
January 1, 1942

It had been a grand party all right, they all agreed later. Everybody had enjoyed it, except maybe Squadron Leader Jack Newkirk. But even 'Newquack' had enjoyed most of it. Harry had seen him drinking and singing and laughing with the rest. It was when the shots were fired that Newkirk started looking serious, as he sometimes did, and then looking distinctly unhappy when he had to break up the fist fights – the AVG against the Brits. Not that there was anything serious, although there were ladies screaming and beer got spilled on senior RAF uniforms. Newkirk even turned a blind eye to the jeep races that ended the evening. There was nothing else that he could do; he was left un-mounted, left behind by someone who had borrowed his jeep without bothering to tell him. If not delighted by that, and Newkirk was not, he was reasonably good natured about losing his jeep, and there were numerous volunteers willing to drive him home. The breaking point came several hours later – when four of the alert pilots were not in their aircraft at the end of the runway as the dawn arrived. Newkirk had enough. This was War after all. He fined each of the derelict pilots 100 dollars. This was an enormous sum for what they saw as a small transgression. After all, the Japanese bombers never did come that morning. Newkirk would never agree with that, but later he did give the pilots back their 100 dollars.

Harry also found Newkirk treating him rather coolly for the first day or two of 1942, and did not know why. His recollections of what happened in the early hours after the arrival of the New Year were a bit uncertain. He remembered shots being fired and everybody laughing about it. It was only much later, when rumor had it that Newkirk had started the New Year badly hung over, that he understood why.

Harry's first hours of 1942 were a blur, but he did get home, and he did remember to set his alarm clock so he could make his 9 o'clock meeting with Doyle on New Year's Day. He felt both numb and nauseous as he slipped into their secret tea garden. Doyle was already there. He had arrived minutes earlier, and was pulling cups and his thermos from a bag. After exchanging best wishes for the New Year, Doyle got right to business.

"The Japs are shifting their troops around in Thailand," he said as he brushed dead leaves off the top of the table. This was the first time they had met in the tea garden in days and there was no sign that anyone else had been there. "They're probably building up their force to push across the border into Burma. The Brits have no idea where the Jap army's main thrust will come from." Harry watched the steam rise from the coffee that Doyle poured from the silver thermos. When both cups were full, Doyle screwed the thermos top back down. Then he went on:

"The Brits have no intelligence coming out of Thailand, none at all. Some of them think the Japs won't try for Rangoon directly, but come into Burma through the Shan States, way north of Rangoon. That would put them in position to grab the Burma Road and cut the supply line into China. Others think the Japs will come from the south. They're already at Victoria Point, the south end of the isthmus. From there they can push all the way north to Moulmein, and then west to Rangoon. Either way would be easier than coming directly east from Thailand, over the hills and the rivers. Coming that way they would have three major rivers to cross."

Harry tried to visualize all of this movement, following a rough map in his head. "If the Brits know which door the Japs will come through, will they be able to stop them?"

"No," Doyle said. "The Brits won't be able to hold the Japs for long, wherever they come through. That's the American Consulate's opinion. They'll fall back on Rangoon pretty quickly. The hope is that they can hold the Japs long enough to buy time for reinforcements to arrive. The word is that there are British and Indian Army units on their way from India." Doyle shrugged..

"But the fight on the ground will be over pretty quickly."

"Yes, I think so."

Harry leaned back and looked around their secret tea garden. It looked abandoned, as desolate as he felt. Last night had been so far from the war.

The singing and the cocky jokes made the world seem bright with promise again. And that was only hours ago. He could still taste the whiskey.

"On the other hand," Doyle said, "if the Brits had any intelligence, it could be a big help. If they knew exactly where the Japs will cross the border, they could be waiting for them. Their defense would be more effective. It would buy more time. In any case, Harry, the Brits have come to us for help." Doyle let that sink in, and then went on.

"The Brits don't have a clue what's happening inside Thailand. They tell me that when they had the opportunity to set up an intelligence apparatus some years ago, their respect for Thai neutrality kept them from doing it. Now they're blind, just when they need eyes in Thailand to see what the Japs are doing. They want us to be those eyes, Harry. They want us to put agents into Thailand."

"Agents!" Harry all but shouted the word. He shook his head in disbelief. "Christ, Doyle, it's a little late for that. You know how that's done – in theory, anyway – and it's not easy. There must be some other way to get a look at the Jap build-up. Aerial reconnaissance flights would be the obvious way. If the Brits can't fly them, maybe we can get the AVG to do it. But, agents...."

Doyle kept his voice flat. He did not want to argue. "The Brits have flown over the areas where they think the build-up is taking place, but they're not seeing anything. The Japs could be moving by night. Or they have broken their forces down into very small units that are just hard to spot from the air. The areas we're talking about are in the hills and jungles. It's rough country with a lot of trees. It will take an agent to find out what's going on in there."

My God," Harry said, "putting agents in place takes time. To do it properly can take years."

"I agree, Harry, but we don't have the luxury of time."

"What are we talking about? Months? What can we possibly do in a few months?"

"Weeks, Harry. Two weeks at most. Two weeks to get an agent into Thailand and find out what's going on."

"My God, you're serious."

"I am serious, Harry. The Japs must be about ready to move. We have to try."

Harry leaned way back in his chair and blew out a mouth full of air. "Let's think about this," he said. "What are we looking at? One agent and no time to train him. In the time we have, we need to find the agent, recruit him, and get him into Thailand." He sat up straight. "So, step one: we find the agent.

What are our prospects? Do the Brits have a candidate? Do you?"

"The Brits don't have a candidate. I don't have one. I haven't had time to think about it. This was put on me ten minutes before I came to meet you."

Harry was only half listening. "Let me think out loud," he said. "We need somebody to go into Thailand – and then come back again. Even if we found a Burmese to do that, I doubt that we would want him. A Burmese wouldn't survive the experience. An Indian? There are a lot of Indians on the road, walking out of here. They are all heading for India, but maybe we could get one to walk into Thailand instead. His story would be that he wants to set up a new business there to replace what he lost in Rangoon."

"Maybe," Doyle said, "but an Indian coming from Burma probably wouldn't survive either. The Thais would probably figure him for a British spy – even if the Japs didn't."

"It has to be a Thai, then."

"Maybe," Doyle said, "but where do we find a Thai? Do you know any? I don't. We won't have any time for vetting. The Thai are allies of the Japs now. We find a Thai, and he could be a spy for the Japs. We would never know."

They sat for a while, just thinking, until Doyle finally spoke. "Frankly, Harry, I think a Thai would be our best bet. He would at least get into Thailand, and he would be able to move around inside. Whatever information he brought us would have to be evaluated against the possibility that it's being fed to us by the Japs."

"Better than nothing?"

Doyle shrugged. "I don't know. I would say it is."

"Well, then let's do it. Let's find a Thai."

* * *

"Lucy, do you know any Thais?"

"I knew some in London."

"How about in Rangoon?"

She thought about it. "I don't know any Thais here. There were some businessmen, but my father dealt with them. I think they left when the bombing started."

"Shit," Harry said, and mumbled something that Lucy did not hear. She got up from her chair, walked to where he was sitting. She leaned over him and pressed a hand on each of his shoulders. "If there's something I can help you with…."

"Not if there aren't any Thais here."

"I don't know what you want to do, but there may be another way. Tell me what you need exactly."

"I need a Thai who can go into Thailand, who can look around there a bit, and then come back here."

"Look around for what?"

"Look around, find out what's happening along the border, see what the Japanese are doing."

"Ah," she said, "to be a spy."

"Well… some people would probably think that."

"Is this for the Americans, again?"

"For the American Consulate."

She looked deeply into his eyes. "Maybe," she said. "Maybe there is someone." Harry sat up, put his arm around her waist and was not even conscious of it. He waited to hear more. "It's not a Thai," she said, and Harry slumped back in his chair. "An Indian?" he asked.

"A Chinese," she said, and before Harry could react she added, "Well, not Chinese, actually, Sino-Thai. Half Chinese, half Thai."

"Brilliant!" Harry said. "That sounds good, better than a Thai. Is he here in Rangoon?"

"Yes, but it's a she, Harry."

"Oh, dear, a lady. Friend of yours?"

"I knew her in London. I never think of her as Thai, although she's more Thai than Chinese. Her father is a banker in Bangkok – a money lender, actually. He sent her here a month ago when the Japanese stormed into Thailand. After what's been going on here, I'm sure she would rather be back in Bangkok now."

"Interesting," Harry said. "So, she might be willing to go back to Thailand if we asked her. But if she would rather be in Bangkok, how would we get her to come back here to tell us what she saw?"

Lucy shrugged. "It's like the coolies working on the dock…."

"You mean we give her a lot of money."

"No, money probably would not work in her case. We can find another way to make her do what we want."

"Do you know a way?"

Lucy pursued her lips and looked at him for a long moment. "My father. She is very devoted to him. He did a lot for her father once. I think she would do anything he asks."

"Can we get your father to ask?"

She sighed. "I will talk with him."

* * *

Harry heard from Lucy early the next morning. "My father wants to meet with you. Come by the hotel as soon as you can."

Harry was at the Strand within the hour and went directly to Louie's suite. "Come sit, Harry." Louie pushed out a chair for him. "Lucy told me about the Thai girl. What exactly do you want her to do in Thailand?"

There were different ways to answer the question, but with Louie there was no point in being anything but direct. "To collect information."

Louie nodded. "This is not something you need for an article, I take it?"

"I was asked to help by the American Consulate."

"Ah, the American Consulate." Louie sat back. "So, at least it's not for the British. Collecting information in Thailand right now is something the British must be very interested in."

"I can't say the American Consulate would not share it with the British. I'm dealing only with the Americans."

Louie nodded. He reached over, poured whiskey into two glasses, and handed one to Harry. He sat back in his chair and looked thoughtful. "There are several things that concern me, Harry. What exactly will the girl be expected to do? Will she need to ask many questions? Will she speak only with the Thais, or will you also expect her to speak with the Japanese?"

"She will not have to speak with anyone on my behalf. I will give her a list – a verbal list – of things that I would like her to keep an eye out for. She will not have to ask questions of anyone. I need her only to observe. But I do need her to come back here and tell me what she saw. I will not ask her to do anything that might endanger her."

"It's the times that are dangerous, Harry, and she's just a girl. The roads are crowded with refugees. There's a good bit of thuggery. Just traveling to the border is dangerous. In a week or two, when she tries to return to Rangoon, it will be even worse. Lucy told you that the girl is Sino-Thai. It turns out that she is more Thai than Chinese, which in this case is fortunate. If she tries to enter Thailand now, she will have to hide her Chinese blood. The Thai are allies of the Japanese, and that makes the Chinese their enemy. If she is identified as Chinese, she will be suspect. We may never see her again. I'm sorry, Harry, I'm not trying to make this more difficult than it is."

"I appreciate your pointing these things out. There will always be things that I see differently than you do, or a Thai, or a Japanese."

"I know her father and I know her. I think I understand what you want to do. I think it's possible. There is risk, but it can be managed. I would not encourage this if I thought the risk to the girl was too great."

"Then you'll talk to her and introduce me?"

"I will explain what needs to be done. If she agrees, I will introduce you."

He sat quietly for a while, considering something. "Let me suggest something," he finally said. "If you give me the questions you need answered, I think I can do it all. The girl need never meet you – which may be a lot safer for her. If she never meets you she will not have to worry about having an American connection. I can also get her to the border with my trucks. If I handle it all, we can move quickly. And it will probably be safer."

As Harry listened to this, he heard over Louie's voice the echo of one of his espionage tutors, a man who had learned all he knew about spying from the British masters of the craft: "Don't ever give up control of your operation, Harry. There's always the clever agent who wants to hold the reins while he lets you think your hand is on them. So, be on the watch for the clever one, the one who wants to move you aside and be in charge. Don't give him an inch. Be tough. He won't show it, but he will respect you for it."

Harry could not imagine getting tough with Louie and not regretting it very quickly. But he had to try something, if not toughness, then a plea from the depths of his inexperience. "Louie," he began, "I appreciate what you're doing, really appreciate it. I think it's a great idea that you handle as much of this as you can, but I need to meet the girl. If I didn't and something went wrong, I would feel terribly guilty about it. I will bear the responsibility if anything happens to her, and so I think I need to meet her to satisfy myself that she can do this. I promised the Consulate that I would personally deal with this. So I can't just push it all off on you."

Louie had watched Harry's face closely as he spoke. At the end, he said simply, "Very well, Harry, if that's what you need to do. We will do it the way you want. I'll have Lucy bring the girl to you. "

* * *

"Sumalee, this is Harry."

She was smiling. He knew she was Lucy's age, but she looked younger. Her clothes looked expensive, yellow silk with a pattern of colorful orchids on her shirt and billowy trousers. She stood up when Harry came into the room, and brought her hands up together in front of her face in the Thai greeting. "*Sawadee*, Mister Harry," she said. When he was closer, she offered her right hand to Harry. Faced with her bright smile he could not suppress his own as he took it. This was not what he expected, a sweet-looking, happy teenager.

"I'm pleased to meet you, *Khun* Sumalee," he said, remembering to put the honorific before her name, Sumalee. "I understand your home is in Bangkok. I hope things here in Rangoon have not been too unpleasant ."

"Not at all. Actually, I was enjoying Rangoon until the Japanese bombers came. Rangoon is so much more cosmopolitan than Bangkok. The shops here are much nicer. It must be from having all those British here."

She seemed so much at ease that he wondered if she knew why they were meeting. "Lucy has told you why I wanted to get together?"

"Yes. You want me to make a trip to Thailand."

"And how do you feel about that?"

"I'm looking forward to it. I'll be able to spend a few days in the countryside."

"You're not concerned about traveling?"

"I know that getting to the border could be difficult, but Louie will help me with that. Once I'm at the border things will be easy."

"Oh," Harry said, a little skeptical.

"There is a place where I have crossed the border many times," she said. She looked almost shy when she added, "It's not a regular border crossing. It's the way I go when I carry money for my father."

"A smuggler's route," Harry said. He said it quietly, to himself, but Lucy heard and gave him a cold stare.

"I know the people there," Sumalee explained. "My father has known the families for many years. They help me across the border when no one needs to know."

"And when you're in Thailand…?"

"Louie said you want me to visit some towns along the border and remember things I see. He told me the names of the towns. It's where my father has friends."

"Your friends must not know what you're doing, you understand that? They must not know about me."

"Yes, I understand. My friends will think I am taking a country holiday from the bad times in Rangoon. They know my father is Chinese. Many of them are Chinese, too. They know I won't want to meet any Japanese soldiers."

"And you're willing to come back to Rangoon afterwards?"

"Yes, of course," she said, brightening up. "My friends are here. Even now, Rangoon is much more interesting than Bangkok."

"You sound as though you've thought this through. I'm glad of that." He took out his list of questions, that had probably been prepared by British Intelligence. "I have questions here, things I am interested in that you will probably see or hear about. Please don't write anything down, either now or later, and don't worry about forgetting anything. We'll go over this list several times, and we'll go over it again once you get back. You'll remember the worthwhile things. What you forget won't be worth remembering. The first question on my list concerns oxen. What is the current market price? Are people talking about oxen prices going up?"

* * *

"It was like a textbook," he said to Doyle later. "She must be the perfect agent. She's perfectly suited to go where we want her to go. She knows exactly how to do what we want. It seems instinctive with her. She's an experienced smuggler, for god's sake. She's bright and very cool."

"And very attractive, I take it," Doyle added. "Twist any man around her finger?"

"She is good-looking," Harry admitted. "Not like Lucy. She's more of a kid, happy and innocent."

"Childlike, perhaps?"

"Yes," Harry said, "she's cute, like someone's daughter."

"That's an interesting way to put it. I thought she was not much younger than you."

"She's not, but a year or two can make a big difference."

Doyle nodded and smiled. "I see. But you think she can do the job."

"Oh, she'll do it all right," Harry said quickly. A moment later he looked pensive, uneasy. He picked up his coffee cup and put it down, and then ran a hand through his hair. In that moment strain showed on his face. He looked very tired. "What if something happens," he said, "just a little bit of bad luck – not even related to what we're doing – and all this could go to hell. I think of what Louie said: 'The times are dangerous.' To me this has been mostly an intellectual exercise, trying to outwit the Japs. If I mess it up, so what. Nothing happens to me. But I think about the girl.... My God, Doyle, what if something happens to her?"

"All kinds of bad things could happen, but they probably won't. You've done all you can. You've chosen your agent well. She knows what she's getting into. She's got Louie to help her, and that eliminates most of the real risk. This is a very simple mission, Harry. You did your job well, and she'll be fine. It's unfortunate that she's so attractive. It makes it hard to think of her as your agent. But that's what you have to do."

CHAPTER 13

In his preoccupation with preparing his first agent for her mission into Thailand, Harry had been neglecting his daily AVG briefings. After breaking off with Doyle, he drove over to the airdrome and caught Newkirk just as he was going to a meeting with senior RAF officers.

"I don't have time, Ross," he said, "Nothing much is going on. Ed Rector should be over at the Silver Grill by now. Why don't you drop by there, and he'll bring you up to date. I'll be there later."

The Silver Grill sounded like a good idea. Harry felt he needed a whiskey to chase Doyle's coffee, and maybe something to eat.

"There's nothing going on," Ed told him. "There hasn't been a Jap airplane over Rangoon since Newquack arrived – and he's starting to take it personally. He thinks they're avoiding him, keeping him from making a score."

"What's going on?"

"I think after all the airplanes they lost on Christmas Day, the Japs are licking their wounds. Oh, they'll be back. It's just a matter of time."

Harry tried to get something to eat then, but the choice was limited to asparagus and cocktail onions. He sipped his whiskey and thought about that for a while, and then wondered where Sumalee was, and if she had crossed the border yet.

"Harry."

He turned, and Rector was looking him right in the eye. "You might want to be out at the airfield early tomorrow," he said.

"Early? How early, Ed? You expecting a raid?"

"I'd be there at sun-up," Rector said, then looking down into his glass, added, "Yeah, it's a raid, but going the other way."

It took Harry a moment to understand. "You mean it will be us going after them."

Rector nodded. "That's right. Newquack has decided that if the Japs are not coming here to us, he's going out to find them."

Harry's face lit up. "Damn! That will be the first time anybody's taking the war to the Japs."

"I think so," Rector said. He gestured for Harry to keep his voice low.

"How many of you are going?" Harry's voice lower now, his tone confidential.

"It's small, only four airplanes. I won't be going. It will be Tex, Bert, Jim Howard and Newkirk. Listen, Harry, this is all very top secret, but I'm sure nobody will mind if you're out there when the boys come back. So maybe not sun-up, but come by the field at 7:00, maybe 8:00 o'clock. Have breakfast with me."

* * *

Harry was at the airfield just minutes after 0700 hours and drove right to the AVG area. He parked near a P-40 that was by itself with a number of the ground crew standing around it. Ed Rector was kneeling up on the wing, talking with the pilot inside the cockpit. As he approached, Harry saw the Panda Bear painted on the airplane's side. It was waving a paint brush: Bert Christman's airplane. Rector looked down and saw him. "Harry, hang on a minute. I'll be right there," he said, and hopped off the wing a moment later. "Come on, Harry, let's go on over to the mess hall. We have time for eggs." He jerked his chin back over his shoulder at the P-40 and said, "Bert's kind of upset. He was halfway to Thailand when his engine started running funny. The other guys went on." He glanced at his watch. "They should be there about now. Lucky guys."

* * *

Newkirk's raiders were almost there, 300 miles away, approaching the airfield at Tak in Thailand. They were flying almost side by side, close enough to see Jack Newkirk jerk his thumb over his shoulder, the signal to drop back and get in trail behind him.

They saw the specks in the sky at the same time, airplanes climbing away from the field. In moments they could make out the fixed landing gear and open cockpits that identified them as the nimble little Nakajimas. The Japs had probably not even seen them yet, but Jap airplanes already in the sky meant that the P-40s would have to hit the airfield and get out fast. They saw more airplanes on the ground now, more Nakajimas, propellers turning, ready for takeoff.

Newkirk reached the near edge of the airfield. Right behind him, Jim Howard saw him bank away steeply to attack a Nate flying by itself, and then got just a glimpse of the Jap airplane tumbling out of control. That was not on the schedule, but it did not distract Jim Howard, a serious young man focused on the mission. He had come here to destroy the Jap airplanes on the ground, and that, by God, he would do – no matter how many Japs were in the air. He pointed his nose down to increase the angle of his dive. On the runway ahead, a Nate burst into flames when he touched his trigger.

Behind Howard, Tex Hill had his hands full of spitting wildcats – as he would later put it. Tex had stolen a look down at the Nakajimas taxiing along the airfield. When he looked to the front again, there was Howard right ahead, and Newkirk some distance off. But between Tex and Howard was a third airplane that should not have been there. A Nate! With all its guns firing at Howard!

No time for the gunsight. Tex slewed his airplane's nose toward the Jap and watched his tracers chop into him. The P-40 shuddered with the recoil. Tex stopped firing only to feel the thumps of something striking his airplane. Then the sky was empty. No airplanes anywhere. And just like that, from nowhere, came a Nate right at him. Head on! Instinct held his trigger down and the Nate twisted crazily. It was on fire and headed for the jungle. Tex's engine was shaking itself silly now, as if trying to tear itself apart.

Howard knew nothing of Tex's problems. His eyes were on the Nates lined up along the runway. He zoomed over them, finger on the trigger, and flames leaped into the sky from one plane after another. Something to the side caught his eye. He swiveled his head and saw… a grandstand! People jumping out of it, falling, running, trying to get away. Then he was past the line of airplanes.

He pulled back on the stick to climb and turn and start another pass, and something struck his airplane. Smoke gushed from under the cowling. The engine died.

He looked up ahead and in the distance saw the other two P-40s racing for home. For an instant he was as close to being frantic as he had ever been in his young life. His cockpit was quiet, no sound but the wind slipping by. He was alone. His airplane was dead, and he was going down on an airfield that he had just shot up.

But Howard was not one to feel sorry for himself. He got back to the business at hand. He was too low to have choices; his sole option was a wheels-up landing. He rolled his canopy back and urged his rapidly descending airplane toward the far end of the airfield. The jungle was thick there. If he could reach it, he would make a run for it.

His fingers moved as methodically as his brain. He was about to lower the flaps when the engine coughed. He eased the throttle in, gently. The engine started to run. The prop spun faster and faster.

He was over the edge of the airfield now and eased back on the stick. The airplane started to climb. He blew out the mouthful of breath he had been holding, and closed the canopy. He looked out to one side, then quickly to the other. On his right was a Nate. On his left was a Nate. The Jap airplanes were flying in formation with him. The pilots were not looking at him, but staring down at the airplanes he had set on fire. They had no idea he was there. Not yet. Very gently, more back pressure on the stick and the P-40 started to rise. When he was high above the Nates, he turned west and headed for home.

* * *

Ed Rector and Harry had finished their eggs and were sipping their second coffee when they heard the two P-40s pass overhead. They walked outside and stood by the runway to watch them land. The airplanes were down, but still a good distance off. A squinting ground crewman yelled, "It's Tex and Newkirk."

"Where the hell's Howard?" Rector asked. There was no answer to that.

The two P-40s taxied to the AVG area and shut down their engines. The sound of another airplane overhead could be heard.

"Here he is, here comes Howard!"

As Ed and Harry got close to the two P-40s that had just landed, they could hear Tex's drawl over a burst of laughter. "All these guys were sitting right there in a grandstand out by the runway. We knocked the Japs down right in front of them. We put on a great airshow, but the spectators all ran away." Tex turned to watch the arriving P-40 touch down on the runway. "I guess that's Howard. I gotta talk with that guy."

Harry followed the small crowd that walked along with Tex to where Howard parked his airplane. There was a big smile on Howard's usually serious face when he slid back the canopy.

Tex yelled up at him. "Hey, Jim, climb down from there and have a look at your airplane." Howard came down, and everyone stood back while he and Tex walked around the P-40. With a piece of chalk one of the ground crew had given him, Tex circled bullet holes in the tail and fuselage of Howard's airplane. "That's eleven. Did you see him?"

Howard looked incredulous. "See who?" he asked.

"The Nipper who put all those holes in your airplane." Howard bent over to get a closer look at the tail of his airplane. "It's the guy you don't see who gets you," Tex told him. "We were coming down on the field and I noticed there were more than three of us in the pattern. There was a guy right on your tail, Jim. I got him. I saw him explode. While I was doing that, there was this other Jap airplane I hadn't seen making a pass on me. He put some holes in me, I know that."

They walked as a group over to Tex's airplane. His crew chief was finishing putting circles around the bullet holes in that P-40. "There's 33 of them, Tex." Tex just shook his head.

Newkirk walked up just then. "Congratulations, Jack," Howard said when he saw him. "I saw you get the Nakajima that you spun off into the jungle."

"Thank you," Newkirk said, not hiding a smile. "What happened to you?"

"I went down and strafed – like I thought we were supposed to."

Tex shook his head. "Damn, Jim, you are a lucky guy. All those Jap airplanes flying around, and all that anti-aircraft fire from the ground.... It was not a good place to be."

"I figured I could do some damage," Howard said, "before they could react. Did you see those guys in the grandstand falling all over each other to get away?"

Newkirk looked puzzled. "I saw them," Tex said. "I guess it was Thai big shots. They probably got invited to see the Jap Air Force in action. Well, they got to see some action all right."

"You made just one pass, Jim?" Newkirk asked. "How much damage did you do?"

"Just one pass. Left four or five Jap airplanes burning. I wanted to go around again, but my engine stopped."

There was total silence while everybody looked at Howard until he felt compelled to explain. "It was probably ground fire." He said. "I was ready to belly in. The engine suddenly caught and started running. I don't know what it was. I came home at full throttle with no problem."

Newkirk shook his head this time, and turned to one of the crew chiefs and said, "Check out Howard's engine. I want to know what his secret is."

Ed Rector was standing next to Harry. "Isn't Howard something? He doesn't even look shook up."

There was the sound of an aircraft engine passing high overhead.

Everyone looked straight up. "Damn," someone said, "Jap recon airplane." From behind them came the roar of an airplane taking off. A P-40, rushing down the runway, lifted into the air. "Erik," somebody said. "He's chasing the Jap."

"Never catch him. The Jap's too high."

They watched Erik Shilling's P-40 climbing out from the airport. "Well," one of the pilots said, "the Old Man said we can expect a raid 24 hours after a Jap recon airplane goes over. Anybody want to bet against it? I got a hundred bucks says the Japs are coming."

There were no takers.

CHAPTER 14

The Japanese bombers did come back the next day, a little ahead of expectations, in the pre-dawn darkness. It was the first Japanese raid by moonlight, when interception was difficult. Three Sally bombers groped through the darkness outside the city, and dropped their bombs on what they thought was a small airstrip where the RAF dispersed some of its airplanes at night. The bombs caused no damage. They fell mainly in the rice paddies.

The next day the Japanese tried it again, by daylight this time. Twenty nimble little Nate fighters came first, to draw the AVG P-40s into the sky. They flitted around, skirmished with P-40s, and burned up fuel. Then they left. The AVG airplanes returned to the airfield to take on fuel. And that was when the bombers came, hoping to catch the P-40s on the ground. It did not work out the way the Japanese hoped. The AVG airplanes got back into the sky and claimed 18 bombers and two fighters.

The next day, the Japanese tried once more, lost five bombers and eight fighters, and that was it. The losses were too much for the Japanese now. They halted their daylight bombing, and for the coming weeks, would return to Rangoon only by night.

Like everyone else during those days and nights, Harry kept his eyes in the sky, but his thoughts were on the Thai-Burma border where his agent – his only agent – was hopefully collecting information that would help defeat the Japanese. Early one morning, after a night of listening to the drone of Japanese bombers overhead and the occasional "blap!" of a bomb exploding somewhere in the city, Harry picked up the telephone and called Louie's suite at the Strand. There was a minute or two of buzzing, crackling and strange voices that faded in and out and said things like, "Hello, hello, old chap. Is that you, Reggie?" Finally a voice said, "Louie, here,"

"Louie, good to hear you. It's Harry. Wanted to see if you had heard anything from our friend, the one you gave a ride upcountry."

"No word, Harry. Wasn't expecting any. Say, Harry, can you come by my room this evening? Around sunset, say. There's something I want to show you."

The sun was already down when Harry got to the Strand. He went directly to Louie's suite. "You're not to worry about Sumalee, Harry," Louie told him as soon as he walked into the sitting room. "We have arrangements to pick her up, but until then it's a 'no news is good news' situation." He handed Harry a whiskey. "But that's not why I asked you over. Please, have a seat."

Harry sat and sipped at his whiskey. He caught Louie looking at him as if he were being evaluated. After a while Louie said, "You Yanks are great hunters, aren't you? You've got bison and bear, deer and squirrels, and.... The ones that look like they're wearing a bandit mask, what are they called, Harry?"

"Raccoons, I think, but...."

"You like hunting, do you, Harry?"

"I haven't really done much. Plinked some birds with a bb gun."

"We will have to introduce you to serious sport then. You'll come hunting with us?"

"Yes, I'd like to. When?"

"Tonight," Louie said.

"What are we hunting?"

"Fireflies."

"Fireflies?" Harry repeated.

Louie got his feet. "We'll leave here in about ten minutes. Let's see, you'll need some dark clothes. I think we can find you something to wear. Come, let's see what's in my closet."

They walked to the closet in next room. Louie rummaged through it and pulled out trousers and then a coat. He held them up to the light, grunted his approval, and handed them to Harry. "These should do."

Harry fingered the soft material. "Louie, this looks like a new suit. I can't wear it to go hunting."

"You can," Louie said, "It's quite perfect. Here look at this." He was pulling something long and narrow from a second closet. It looked like a gun case. He laid it on the bed to undo the snaps. He picked something out of the case and swung it around to let Harry see, first snapping into place the fat round drum that was the magazine. It was a wicked-looking thing.

"A Thompson," Harry said, "a 'Tommy Gun'. That's a submachine gun. You're going hunting with that?"

"You'll have one too, Harry," Louie was quick to reassure him. "Lucy's chaps found them at the port. We've got at least a dozen of them."

"But you can't ...." Harry stared to say, but then shut up. What did he know about hunting? Louie glanced at him. "The suit looks good on you, Harry. A little short in the arm, but it's a good dark color. It will do fine tonight."

A young Chinese in a dark suit walked in. "Ah, Peter," Louie said. "Get us another Tommy Gun for Mr. Harry and one for yourself. And don't forget the extra magazines." As the man walked out with a "Yes, sir," Louie explained: "My batman."

Louie led Harry and Peter through the hotel's side door, where there was less chance of being seen with the weapons. Many Rangoon residents carried sidearms now, but not Tommy Guns. The Thompson was unusual, but many would have recognized it from popular Hollywood films as the favored Chicago gangster's gun.

Louie's shiny black Cadillac waited outside. "I think I had better drive," he said when the driver got out to open the rear door. "You get up front, Harry. Peter, get in back with the guns and ammunition." Louie told the driver to go home for the evening, then got behind the wheel.

They drove down Strand Road to the warehouse. They were driving on just the parking lights as a blackout precaution, but Louie turned even those off before he pulled into the warehouse compound. As they rolled into the parking lot, the Indian watchman appeared, looking at them warily. "Jumbo, it's me," Louie said, "You come inside with us. Bring your sleeping pallet into the warehouse for tonight. And don't go outside again. Peter, you make sure all the doors are locked."

Louie had flashlights for both of them, and they needed them to find their way to the office area upstairs. Some light came in through the windows that Louie opened wide. "Hopefully we're too high for the mosquitoes," he said. "Get comfortable, Harry. We'll have to wait a while. We best not talk much. Sound carries far at night."

They stood by the windows for a while and looked out. The river was glossy black with silver glints of reflected light here and there. Beyond the river, everything else was the same dull shade of black in which no individual forms could be distinguished. Harry wondered how they would see what they were hunting. What were they hunting anyway, a duck or a bird of some other kind that Louie expected to fly by their window? He wanted to ask Louie, but he knew he would get no real answer. For a while he just watched Louie, who stood by the window and seemed to be trying to peer through the blackness, sometimes hanging halfway out the window to see what was directly below. Peter joined them, and eventually they pulled chairs under the windows and sat down. And waited.

Harry was dozing when the sound of engines pulled him back to consciousness. The unsynchronized rising and falling drone of the Japanese bomber engines. They were coming over Rangoon now, at night, when interception was difficult. He could make out the shadow of Louie hanging out the window. As the engine noise got closer, Louie pulled his head back inside and said in a near whisper, "Ready, Harry? Have your gun ready. It won't be long now."

"Yes," Harry replied as quietly and started to get up. He stood in the window next to the one where Louie was hanging halfway out, but Louie was looking down, not up at the sky where the bombers were. The engine noise was getting closer and closer, and Louie said, "There it is!" just as Harry saw a light flare up below. It was unmistakable – out on the quay a lantern was being lit, then another and another. In the dancing shadows Harry could make out the figures of men.

"Out, out, damned light!" Louie shouted in his best Shakespearian voice and opened fire with his Thompson. It made a hellish clatter. "Spray the landward side, Harry," he shouted over the noise. "They'll be running for the road. Peter, get the one there, going for the river!"

Harry stuck his Thompson out the window, pointed it down and pressed the trigger. The gun banged and jerked like a thing alive; it surprised and almost frightened him. He saw sparks fly up from the road where it had been pointed. He jerked his finger off the trigger and then pressed down again hard, when he had it pointed where he thought he saw shadows move. Sparks flew again, from rocks the bullets were striking in the parking lot, giving him a sense of control and power. Then the gun would not fire at all, although he pressed the trigger again and again. Peter handed him another magazine.

It was quiet now.

"I'm sure we winged a couple," Louie said conversationally. "Peter, I think I saw yours running for the river. He might have dropped in. He may have jumped, but I think you got him. I think I saw one of yours being dragged away, Harry. We'll wait a while before we go see."

Harry was wide awake. He could see nothing out there now. It was mostly dark. A single lantern flickered weakly. He had a brief recollection of another light flaring brightly for just an instant. Then either Louie had shot it out, or the lantern had tipped over and drowned itself. It seemed that at least they must have accomplished what Louie had set out to do.

"Well, that's firefly hunting for you, Harry," Louie said. "Damned quislings," he added. "But thank God for the mistakes they made. Their lights were too weak. I doubt the bombers could see them. And they didn't light them until the bombers were right over us. It was too late then. I expect they will get better with time."

It was near daybreak when Louie decided to leave the warehouse and see what damage they had done. The air was fresh, and the sky over the river was starting to brighten. They could see things easily now. A half dozen lanterns lay scattered along the quay. They stood over one that was mashed down as if someone had fallen on it. "Blood." Louie said, pointing at a dark spot with his toe.

After getting a good look around the area, Louie said, "I think we hit one or two, and terrified the rest. They won't be lighting their lanterns on our quay tonight. Come, Harry, join me for breakfast at the Strand. I've had some eggs flown down from Kunming."

CHAPTER 15

Harry stretched out his arms and it felt good. It was cool and pleasant in the dimness of the Silver Grill, like lazy afternoons long ago when no one gave any thought to Japanese airplanes suddenly appearing in the sky. There were no other customers now. He had come in well after the lunch hour, not expecting much, but found a treat. The young lady on duty behind the bar knew him as a friend of Louie. She cooked up a can of mushroom soup, a prize that someone had found on the docks, and served it to him with saltine crackers fresh out of their waxed wrappings, still crisp in Rangoon's humidity. It was an incongruous, comforting meal that took him back to relaxed afternoons at school, when his main concern was to finish a book and there was no threat of bombs suddenly falling from the sky.

He was bent over a week-old newspaper, nibbling on a rare dessert of chocolate biscuit when the AVG pilot came in. He looked like most of them, blond and blue-eyed, tall and slim. It was Ed Rector's friend, and Tex Hill's, the third of the AVG's three musketeers, but Harry could not think of his name. Then it came suddenly: Bert Christman.

"Bert," he said, "come, grab a seat."

Christman was the artist, the AVG's cartoonist. Harry did not know him well, but he seemed likable enough. Quiet, reserved, almost shy, a gentle Panda Bear, or at least less aggressive than Rector and Hill.

"I'm going to meet Ed Rector here," Christman said, and glanced at his watch. "I'm an hour early." He turned around, looking for the waitress. He saw her at the bar, and gestured with both hands. "A big one," he said, "a cold one, please." Satisfied that she got the message, he slid into the booth across from Harry.

"Day off?" Harry asked. The AVG pilots generally did not get to the

Silver Grill until sundown or later.

"It is a day off as a matter of fact. Jack Newkirk said to take a couple of days and count it as sick leave."

"Sick leave?" Harry said, "Nothing serious, I hope, nothing catchy."

"Nothing you can catch. Something caught me. A Nate."

A Nate, the open cockpit Japanese fighter. "So a Nate caught you," Harry said, and looked at Christman with fresh interest. "What happened?"

Just then, the waitress came with a large frothing glass stein of beer. Christman picked it up, tipped it in a salute to Harry, and took a big swallow. When he set the stein down he said, "Sorry, but I really needed that. You asked about the Nate. It was the other day. I don't know if you saw any of this from here in town, but out by the airfield we had Nates all over the sky. They came out of nowhere. Must have been 30 of the little buggers. They're nimble as hell. I was leading a flight and we were letting down when they jumped us. It was like a rain shower of bullets. Bullets everywhere: hitting my wings, poking holes in the fuselage, ricocheting around inside my cockpit! I twisted and turned that airplane, but I just couldn't get away. Pappy Paxton was behind me. He really got blasted. He had to crash-land at Mingaladon. They dug bullets out of his shoulder and his arm. He's still laid up."

"What about you?"

"They never touched me, but my airplane was riddled like a sieve. I had to jump out of it."

"You parachuted? That must have been interesting."

"A piece of cake, as our British friends say. I was just happy to get out of the line of fire. But I did think a lot about Paul Greene on the way down. Paul's the one the Japs tried to shoot while he was hanging in his parachute. I was so low when I went out that they probably didn't even notice me."

Harry shook his head. "That's quite an experience, something new for an artist."

Christman took another big swallow of beer, and laughed. "Actually, it's my life catching up with my art."

"How's that?"

"You probably don't read the funnies. I used to draw *Scorchy Smith.*"

The name sounded familiar. "I remember *Scorchy Smith*. It was the comic strip about airplanes, wasn't it?" Thinking about it put a smile on Harry's face. "You were a comic strip artist?"

"Yeah, I was. Scorchy was a pilot, a mercenary – which is what I am now, if you listen to what some call the AVG."

"I recall Scorchy lost in the jungle."

"That was a long time ago, Harry. That was back in 1936, when I first took over the strip. Another guy had started it, and I finished the jungle adventure. After that one, I put Scorchy to work in China, working for a Chinese warlord. Would you believe that?"

"You're putting me on, right, Bert?"

"No sir, that's the truth."

"So then you followed Scorchy to China."

"I did. I spent so much time at airports drawing airplanes that I took flying lessons. I really enjoyed flying, so I became a naval air cadet. When the chance came to go to China with the AVG, I jumped at it."

"Hey, guys!" a shouted greeting from Ed Rector coming through the door. He was looking spiffy in tightly creased khaki trousers and a khaki jacket with many pockets. Harry raised a hand in greeting before turning back to Christman. "Bert, that's a wonderful story. I'd like to write a piece about it – when I think I can get it by the censors. I know I can't write anything personal about you guys now."

Christman hesitated. "It's one thing if you're one of the big hero pilots, like Jack Newkirk. The journalists are all over him. All I did was to get shot down."

"It's not that," Harry said. "I want to write about you and Scorchy."

"We'll talk about it, Harry"

"What's going on here, guys?" Rector arrived at their booth. He had come via the bar and carried three glasses and a fresh bottle of whiskey.

"We're talking about *Scorchy Smith*, Ed."

"Isn't that some story? Bert's not only a great pilot and a talented artist, but he's a clairvoyant. Did you know that when Bert and Tex and I were flying off the aircraft carrier Ranger, Bert drew a comic strip called the *Three Aces*. It was all based on our actual adventures."

"Now Ed's putting you on, Harry."

"Listen, guys," Rector said, "we can't be talking about art right now. Time is running out. I got the afternoon off, but I'm on alert tonight." He turned to Christman. "If you and I are going to accomplish our mission, son, we have to go as soon as I finish this drink."

As Harry watched Rector pour a half glass of whiskey for each of them, he asked, "What mission is that, Ed?"

Looking down at the whiskey he was pouring, Rector asked, "Are you a Catholic, Harry?"

"No."

"Know anything about Catholics?"

A puzzling question. Harry thought about it. "I guess it depends on what you need to know. Going religious on us, Ed?"

"No, no, Harry, it's nothing like that," Rector was quick to reassure him. "It's just that Bert and I are going over to this convent. Maybe you want to come along."

"Convent, Ed?"

"Yeah, over by the post office. I think it's called the Sacred Heart Convent. You may have noticed it; it's hard not to. There are all these sweet young things walking along the sidewalk there. It's a girls' school. And it turns out that all these charming young ladies are confined to quarters. Bert and I are going to see if we can liberate a few."

"You're going to the convent to pick up girls? That is something new and daring. The nuns will have your ass."

That's why we need to know some things. When we meet the nuns, how do we address them? As 'Miss?'"

"I think 'Sister' would probably be better."

"Okay, Sister. Then there's the one in charge. We're going to ask for her."

"That's probably the 'Mother Superior.'"

"See, that's stuff we need to know. You better come with us, Harry."

"Thanks, guys, but I need an afternoon off. I'm not up to a high-stress assault on a convent."

"You don't know what you're going to be missing."

"It's what I'm afraid of. You can tell me about it."

"Okay, Harry," and they were off, eager to get going. He watched them leave. Christman held the door and Ed stepped back to let a man in a crumpled suit enter. The man stopped just inside and tried to peer into the dim depths of the Silver Grill before his eyes were fully adjusted from the brightness outside.

"Hi," he called. "Anybody in here?"

"Over here," Harry said, and waved his arm over the back of his booth. The man squinted at him and walked over. He held out his hand. "Hi, my name's Johnnie Morris. I just got into town." Harry told him his name and they shook hands.

"Sure is quiet around here. I was expecting gunfire, cannons going off, bombs exploding, but it's just awfully quiet. What are you doing here in Rangoon, besides having a whiskey, I mean? "

"I'm a writer," Harry said. It came more or less automatically now.

"A writer, huh? Well, that's what I am too. I work for UP, the wire service, covering south China. They sent me down here to cover the fall of Rangoon." He sat down across the table from Harry and put on a pair of spectacles. "Let's see, you're Ross, you said, Harry Ross. I know that name."

"You do?" Harry said, more skeptical than surprised.

"Yeah." Morris started searching through his pockets, and pulled out a wad of what looked like badly crumpled newspaper cuttings. "My files," he said, and started separating the wad into individual pieces that he smoothed out on the table. "Let's see if I have any of your clips here. You wrote a piece on the Burma Road, as I recall, and a background piece on the American volunteers."

That surprised Harry. He had, in fact, written articles just like that. It was part of the attempt to establish his "cover". He had passed those and a few other pieces on to Doyle, who said he would send them to Washington, where one of Wild Bill's minions would try to plant them in some newspaper. It must have happened, although Doyle had never said.

"What newspaper did you find them in?"

"I don't know, I don't remember. Who do you write for?"

"I don't know," Harry said. "I'm a free lancer. I send articles off into the void, and never know who will publish something."

That must have been a good answer; Morris never raised an eyebrow. "Well, I don't seem to have any of your pieces here," he said and Harry felt very disappointed. "The ones I have are mostly from the *New York Times*." He shoved them across the table to where Harry could see. "Who is Slim, but the way?"

"Slim?"

"Yeah, 'Slim from Scarsdale'? It's a nom de guerre. The censors don't let the newspapers print the full names of Americans in combat. Here," he said, and shoved another clipping to where Harry could read it:

American pilots earlier raided the Raheng airdrome in western Thailand, where three Japanese airplanes were shot down in dogfights and four grounded planes were burned. One of the American pilots, known as 'Slim' of Scarsdale, N.Y., said the raid was 'like a football game. Two of us blocked out the Japanese while other planes strafed Japanese aircraft on the ground. It wasn't any trouble knocking those boys off,' he said.

Harry laughed. " 'Slim from Scarsdale', I guess I do know him. Nobody calls him 'Slim,' but I was at the press briefing where he said that."

"Well, who is he?"

"Squadron Leader Jack Newkirk. He grew up in Scarsdale. He's the guy leading the American Volunteers here."

"Scarsdale Jack," Morris said. "That has a nice ring to it. I'll have to remember. Tell me, what has been happening here? I've been out of touch for a few days."

"Well, let's see, the Japs have been avoiding Rangoon by day, thanks to

Scarsdale Jack and his boys. The Jap bombers come by night now, when it's hard for the AVG to find them. When they come over, the British throw a lot of anti-aircraft fire up at them. They don't seem to hit much. And the Japs can't see in the dark either, so we're pretty safe on the ground. During the day our guys go over and shoot up Thailand."

"How about the big Jap ground attack on Rangoon?"

"Everybody's waiting for it to happen."

"Do they know where the Japs are going to try to come in?"

"If anybody knows, it's the Brits, and they're not saying."

"Given their record, the Brits don't know. But the city is quiet; it looks pretty calm. I wasn't expecting that."

"That's not calm you see, it's death, rigor mortis. There's almost nobody left in the city now. Most of the population is somewhere on the road, walking to India."

That made Morris look up at him. "Good Christ! Is that right? The people are gone? They deserted their city. That means the labor force is gone, and there's nobody here but some British – and you drinking whiskey? And the Japs are coming!"

Harry nodded. "That more or less sums it up."

"Christ, that's terrible," Morris said. He looked stunned. "Now I'm going to have to rewrite my whole first paragraph." He pulled over a used glass and poured himself whiskey from the bottle Rector had left. Then he slumped back in the booth and sipped at it.

"You know what the good part is, Harry? The way the British are fighting it, this won't be a very long war."

* * *

"You didn't tell me I was a published author."

Doyle was turned around in his chair, admiring all the foliage grown wild in their secret garden, the shifting shades of green that glimmered in the setting sun. It was obvious that no one else was coming here. He finally turned back to look at him. "Sorry, Harry, a published what?"

"Author, published author. The UP guy, Morris, knew my by-line. He saw articles with my name in newspapers."

"Yeah, there may have been something like that. Clippings from some newspaper. Probably got sent out in the last diplomatic pouch. I would have brought them, but I didn't think it would matter much to you."

"Of course it matters," Harry said it a little testily. "It's my cover. I need to know what's going on."

Doyle chuckled. "Sounds more like pride of authorship to me," he said. "I'll bring the clippings next time. I'm sorry. Harry, I've been a bit preoccupied. Everybody is getting worried about what the Japs are doing. I mean really worried. Even the Brits don't believe their own reassurances. When's your girl getting back? The Thai girl?"

"My agent, you mean. It shouldn't be long. Louie has something worked out where she can signal for his trucks to pick her up as soon as she's back in Burma. If it all works, we should hear from her in a couple of days."

"Doyle nodded. "Good. I hope it's soon. I hope she can tell us something."

"Reminds me, shouldn't we have a code name for her?" Harry's tutor in the principles of espionage had stressed that one must never refer to an agent by a real name, lest it somehow be overheard. Sitting among the weeds in the garden the threat seemed remote.

Doyle raised up in his chair and looked around carefully. He whispered, "She does have a code name, Harry. Washington assigned it. Her code name is 'Mango.'"

"Mango?" Harry said. "Like the fruit?" His first agent code name, and he was not sure he liked it. "That's an odd choice, isn't it?"

"I don't know, Harry. It's the first agent code name I've ever seen. I don't think it's a bad choice: a sweet, luscious fruit, native to Thailand. It's probably some Washington wallah's idea of what to name a delectable Thai female. A mango, sweet and delicious when you bite into her."

CHAPTER 16

Days melded into one another. Rangoon was quiet, dead quiet. It seemed to Harry that the only things moving on the streets were British armored vehicles and thieves. It was wise to be armed, and Harry never went without a pistol in a little leather bag. British infantry officers, not part of the usual crowd, had started showing up at the Silver Grill and at the bar at the Strand.

Days became routines. Harry was up at the crack of every dawn, off to the airdrome for the morning briefing by Squadron Leader Newkirk. No one called him "Newquack" now. He was "Scarsdale Jack." A journalist had put the name in print and it stuck. Even the *New York Times* used it. Scarsdale Jack had added a marauding bomber and two more Nates to the two already in his bag, and the five victories made him the Panda Bear's first "Ace". He was kept busy running the air war and briefing journalists, and his appearances at the Silver Grill were rare now. Other AVG pilots continued to visit. There were not many alternatives.

Aside from the flying, a pilot's life became ordinary, almost dull. Distractions were few, to be sought out, savored, and passed around when found. The assault on the Sacred Heart Convent was a gem, as Bert Christman told Harry:

" 'Ah, Mother Superior,' Ed said to her. 'We would like to have a look around. We've heard so much about the ceilings in the chapel, and the courtyard we've been told is beautiful.' 'Ceilings?' Mother Superior said. She didn't know that the ceilings in the chapel were anything special. And Ed didn't give her time to think about the courtyard. 'But we certainly don't want to take up your time,' he told her real quick. Then Ed got this surprised look on his face, as though the idea had just struck him. 'Maybe there's a young lady, a student or someone on your staff, who's free.' 'Ah, yes,' Mother Superior said. 'One of the teachers is still here, and I know she's free now. I'll find her.' And she did, and it was a lovely young creature, Estelle by name, and Estelle took us all over the convent, to the chapel, to the library, and she showed us the dining room. We weren't halfway through the tour when Ed asked if she had a friend, and of course she did. She found her friend quickly, and we took them to the Strand that evening. Ed was going to show them off at the Silver Grill, but that seemed a little premature."

"And you'll see them again," Harry asked.

"Oh, yes. They're wonderful girls, and Ed has a real romance going. I've been seeing Estelle every chance I get."

* * *

Harry's main preoccupation was waiting for his agent, wondering when she would return. But the summons startled him when it came. It was early morning, and Harry was in the final pages of a third-rate mystery when the telephone rang and snapped him back to sunny Rangoon from a drizzly village in Yorkshire. It was Louie. "Your lady friend is here. The one who's been traveling. She would like to see you."

He made it to the Strand in record time and went directly to Louie's suite. It was code name Mango, Sumalee herself, who answered Harry's knock. She was in silk again, a frock in bright colors and flowers, on delicate shoes with high heels that showed her shapely legs to full advantage. She was stunning. And smiling, barely keeping herself from laughing out loud, so happy to see him. She was as lush and delectable as the fruit she was named for, made all the more desirable by the dangerous journey she had just completed.

"Harry," she said, took him by the hand, and led him to one of the leather chairs. "I'll bring the coffee. We're alone. Louie is at the warehouse, and he took Peter with him." If there was an invitation in that, Harry missed it totally. His interest was in what she could tell him.

She brought the coffee, and it was all very social for a few minutes. They exchanged some words, the pleasantries, and then Harry could wait no longer. He took out his notebook and unfolded a map.

"Your holiday in Thailand. How was it?"

"It was very nice, actually, Harry. Thank you."

"I'm glad to hear that," he said. "It wasn't too scary?" She shook her head. "I guess you didn't see many Japanese?"

"Oh, the Japanese were quite nice," she said. "They were very polite. They even bought us dinner." She was pleased with herself, he could see that. She was waiting for praise, but all he could think of saying was, "The Japs bought you dinner.... How...how did that come about?"

"They felt bad about our car going off the road."

"Your car went off the road...." A sinking feeling. "You don't mean Louie's vehicle? Along the border?"

"No, no, not Louie's car. It wasn't at the border. I was with my girlfriends, near Tak."

"Tak," Harry repeated. A Thai town; he knew the name. "That's a long way from the border," he said and looked at his map to find it. When he put his finger on it he said it again, "It is a good way inside Thailand. What were you doing there?"

"It was dull in Mae Sot where I was staying. Mae Sot is a border town and kind of rough. But nothing much was going on there; no one knew anything. I saw very few Japanese; everyone said the Japanese are all in Tak. So my friends and I decided to go to Tak." She was on the settee and just then crossed her legs, exceptionally fine legs, as Harry noted for a tiny fraction of a moment.

"Now wait a minute, Sumalee," he said, setting his notebook down to give her his full attention. "This is very important, and I'm not sure I'm following you. Someone told you that the Japanese were in Tak, and you went there? And your girlfriends went with you?"

"Yes," she said, and as that did not clear it up for him, so obviously unfamiliar with Thailand, she went on. "My girl friends are Chinese-Thai like me, but everyone thinks they are just Thai. They live right at the border, at Mae Sot. After a few days, nothing was happening. I said to someone, 'There are no Japanese here.' My girlfriend said, 'The Japanese are all in Tak now.' 'Well,' I said, 'if all the Japanese are in Tak, then the good shopping must be there.' My girlfriends like shopping as much as I do, and they agreed. So we drove off to Tak in my girlfriend's Buick. It's a big car, a convertible – but we had our umbrellas to shade us from the sun." She added that quickly, so Harry would understand that she was in no danger of getting a tan.

"There were five of us girls, and the driver," she went on. "Tak is really not too far from Mae Sot, but just outside the town, we came on a herd of ponies blocking the road, and the driver tried to go around them. He drove us into a ditch and the car almost tipped over. The Japanese helped pull the car out. It was their ponies, you see. The Japanese officer apologized. To make up for it he said, he would take us to dinner at a famous Chinese restaurant in Tak. He was a major."

"So the ponies belonged to the Japanese?"

"Yes, the Thai major said the Japanese bought all the ponies in Tak. Remember, when you and I first met, you asked me a question about the market in oxen. Well, the Japanese are buying all the oxen in Tak, and ponies and horses as well. Even some elephants, I understand. I said to the Thai major that the Japanese must be big eaters of meat. He said the Japanese were not eating these animals…."

"Hang on. Who is this Thai major?" Harry was starting to get a strong impression that she was enjoying his confusion.

"He was at the dinner at the Chinese restaurant – which I really don't think is very famous, although it was quite good for a place like Tak. There were four Japanese officers with us. Two were lieutenants, one was a captain, and the oldest one was a major. So there were two majors there; the Japanese major and the Thai major. The Thai major spoke some Japanese. The Japanese major spoke good English. He had lived in London once. He sat next to me because he wanted to talk with me about England, which he said he loved."

"So the Thai major was at the dinner with the Japanese officers? And he told you that the Japs didn't eat the animals they were buying. What were the Japs doing with them?"

"The major, the Thai major said that the Japanese were trying to train the oxen and the ponies to carry things, to pull things. He told us that in the Thai language so the Japanese would not understand. He thought it was very funny: the Japanese try to train them. When they harness them, the animals run away. He said the Japanese simply do not understand Thai animals."

Harry thought about the Japanese training the animals and wondered. "What about the Japs, did they say anything about the animals and what they're doing?"

"The only Japanese I spoke with was the major, and he only wanted to talk about England."

"You told him you lived in England?"

"Yes," she said, and Harry remembered his early concern about the Japanese learning of her stay in England and assessing her guilt by association. So much for that theory, he thought.

"Did any of the Japanese talk about the war?"

"The Thai officer was the only one who wanted to talk about the war." She wrinkled her nose when she said that. "He complained a lot. He was angry about the airplanes that attack Thailand. He believed they were all British, and he blamed Mr. Churchill and British imperialism. He told us that in Thai, but he repeated it all in Japanese so that the Japanese officers would understand him."

"His attempt to make a good impression with the Japanese imperialists," Harry noted. He asked some more questions, trying to get some feel for what the Japanese talked about during dinner, but it seemed most of their conversation was in Japanese. Little was said in English. Only the Japanese major had a real command of the language, and he apparently said nothing about the war or his duties in Thailand.

"Well," he said when he was finished, "You did an incredible job of dealing with the Japanese. We'll learn a lot from your meeting with them."

She turned her eyes down when she said, "I hoped you would be pleased. I know you did not expect me to speak with the Japanese, or even want me to. But when we first met the major and he spoke good English, I thought it was an opportunity to learn something."

"I am pleased. At least now I am, knowing that you got away with it. It was a dangerous situation. I would never have risked putting you in it."

"It's the way a thing ends that matters," she said, and looked up at him as though expecting him to say more. As far as he was concerned, the matter was finished, at least for now. She was right, it was how the thing ended, but the chances she took to do it were something else. It did not seem to bother her, but it bothered him.

"Look," he said, "I would like to go over the list of question that I read you when you set off on your trip. They may bring back things you noticed, but have forgotten."

He read through the list, and there were things she remembered. "The Thais don't seem too concerned about the Japanese," she told him. "The Japanese are good about paying for things. They have helped the upcountry Thai economy – even when they don't know it. When the animals they buy run away, they often go back home, and the owner can sell them again."

She continued, "The Japanese tell the Thais that they are partners in the Co-Prosperity Sphere. The Thais may not understand what that means, but it pleases them to hear the Japanese call them partners. In Mae Sot, people complain more about the Burmese than the Japanese. Which is very funny," she added, "because many of their ancestors are Burmese."

Harry did not understand that completely and said, "They complain about the refugees, you mean, those who have fled from Burma because of the bombings?"

"No, not the refugees, there are not many of them. They complain about Burmese who stay in the town now. They call themselves members of the Burmese Independence Army. They say they will help the Japanese take

Burma away from the British, and are just waiting for the Japanese to send them back into Burma. Some of them were students and act like intellectuals. The Thai say that they wear spectacles, drink tea with milk, smoke cigarettes all day, and act like British."

Sumalee's answers to many questions were negatives – negatives that puzzled Harry. She had seen no Japanese tanks, no big guns and almost no trucks. She did see some small guns on wheels, but they were pulled by animals, not trucks. (The very ones being trained, perhaps.) Japanese soldiers marched not on roads, but in the fields or in the jungle alongside the road. They never seemed to move in groups, at least not big groups, but were strung out along the route of march, and walked alone or in clusters of two or three. If they had gear, it was not trucks, but horses or oxen that carried it. And bicycles. Soldiers pushed bicycles laden with baskets full of things she could only imagine. And when they rested, the soldiers sat under trees by themselves or with a few comrades. It seemed almost sad, she thought.

There was something else she remembered. "Soldiers cutting small limbs from trees and hanging them on their bicycles, and soldiers who decorated themselves with the leaves and bushes. They walked in the jungle and it was difficult to see them."

There was something the Japanese major said. " 'Life is so different now. I must learn not to be afraid of tigers, to be an example to my soldiers. They are all afraid of tigers.'" She reflected on this and said to Harry, "I don't know why they fear tigers. There are no tigers in Tak or Mae Sot, or anywhere near the roads in between."

Without thinking about it, Harry commented, "The Japs will find their tigers – in the jungle." Later, when he sat and wrote his report he thought about tigers.

"The major said he had lived in Bangkok first, then Pitsanuloke. Now he and all his soldiers have moved to Tak," Sumalee said.

Harry just nodded. He had exhausted his questions. He tapped his notebook and said, "There's an awful lot of information here. I don't understand it all, but someone will. You did a wonderful job. Better, much better that I or anyone else could have expected. I'll have to get back now. I need to put all of this down on paper and get it to people who need it."

Her face glowed with the praise, but only momentarily. "Can't you stay and have a drink with me? I can call the kitchen and get something to eat."

"Sumalee, I would really love to, but this is too important." They were both on their feet now. "Louie's at the warehouse?"

"Yes," she said, and raised her face to him to let him kiss her cheek.

He needed to write it all down. He knew he had something good, and he wanted to get it to Doyle quickly. He could compose most of it in his mind as he drove. First he would have to see Louie. Louie would understand what all of this meant, if anyone did. By the principles of espionage, he should not be sharing this information with someone like Louie. Unless he did, he would not know what he had. Besides, Louie probably already had it all. Directly from Sumalee, he suspected.

Louie never said a word, just sat on the edge of his chair and listened. When Harry finished, he sat quietly for a while, then got up and stepped to a map of Southeast Asia on the wall.

"I think she's given you their main invasion route," he said. He looked up at the map. "My understanding is that the Japanese headquarters was here, at Pitsunaloke." He tapped a black spot east of Burma. "Now it seems the bulk of Japanese forces have moved to Tak, closer to Burma. And here is Mae Sot, on the border." He traced a red line with his finger. "Coming from Tak and on past Mae Sot is the only real road that leads through the mountains and into Burma and goes to Moulmein. If the Japanese can get past Moulmein, and over the Sittang River, the way to Rangoon is open."

Louie went back to his chair. "The British will be watching that road, waiting for the Japanese tanks, for artillery caissons and massed infantry charging into Burma. The Japs won't do that. The Japs won't be on the road; they'll be in the jungle. They will go through the same mountain passes that the road does, but not where the British will see them. They'll be in the jungle. Their Burmese friends will lead them, and the British airplanes and the AVG won't see them. And that is what I think Sumalee has given you."

CHAPTER 17

"You have a good report here," Doyle said as he finished reading Harry's first "Mango" report. "It sounds like real intelligence. Including Sir Louie's comments was brilliant. It pulls everything together. The report should make the dimmest British staff officer sit up and take notice."

"Do you think it will actually have an effect on what the Brits think?"

Doyle shrugged. "I don't know. The report gives them exactly what they asked for: an agent's view of what the Japs are doing inside Thailand and how they're doing it. There's enough here to show them where the Japs' main thrust will probably come from. That has to make an impression on them. I expect their intelligence officers will recognize the value of the information. Whether the brass will credit it is something else; it may not fit their preconceptions. We can't do much about that. The fact remains that you and Miss Mango produced exactly what the Brits said they needed, and you did it very well."

"Thanks," Harry said, "I'll pass that on to Miss Mango. Do you have any idea what the Brits are thinking at this point?"

"I can't say I do. They are probably not as convinced as they were a week ago that the main Jap thrust will be in north Burma. Your report should help with that. Otherwise, they're waiting for the Japs to make their first move on the border, and waiting for reinforcements."

"Any sign of the reinforcements?"

"Not that anyone's seen."

"So what do we do now?"

"I don't know, Harry. There's not much we can do. The only agent we have is Mango, and we can't send her back again. Maybe you can go up to the border and see what comes across." And then he added quickly, "Just kidding, Harry. Don't even think about it."

"I'd like to be able to do something."

"The time will come, Harry. The time will come."

* * *

It was just after sun-up when Harry parked the little roadster in the street along the side of the Strand Hotel. He had spent most of the night awake, tossing, thinking about what he might be able to do. He had come up with nothing, except that maybe talking with Louie would give him some ideas. He went directly up to Louie's suite and knocked on the door. If Louie was still in bed, Peter would be up and about, getting ready for the day. Nothing happened and he knocked again. He was about to turn away from the door when it opened. Standing there was Miss Mango, sleepy-eyed and tussled-looking.

"Oh, Harry!" She was as surprised as he was. She was in a short white shift, probably a night dress, and was barefoot. She seemed smaller, more delicate. She looked cute, like somebody's daughter as he had once described her. He was not expecting her here, and was not quite sure what to say.

"What a nice surprise," he said finally. "Is Louie in?"

"No," she said. "He went off with Peter. They needed to be at the warehouse early this morning. I'm here alone." She held on to the door, waiting for him. He hesitated, then, "Well, Louie's not here, but you are. Why don't you come downstairs and have breakfast with me in the dining room? They've got fresh food. It looks like it's right off the dock....."

"Why don't you come in?" she said, "I can call for coffee. We can get whatever you like."

He wanted to go into the room. There was trust in the eyes looking up at him, and something like vulnerability. "No," he said, "let's go downstairs. The baker's been busy. There's fresh bread, breakfast rolls, more food than I've seen in weeks. Somebody has been bringing butter and flour and everything else right from the docks."

"It's probably Louie," she said with a little laugh. "All right. I'll join you. I need to get dressed. Will you wait for me?"

"I'll be downstairs. I'll get us a good table. I'll grab the good things before they're all gone."

"I'll be down soon as I can."

He walked down the stairs feeling a little foolish. He had managed to confuse her and to disappoint himself. Perhaps he was just doing the professional thing, not going into the room. He could not put himself in a position that was even the least bit compromising, with Louie or Lucy, or even Doyle – should Doyle ever learn of it.

By the time he reached the lobby, he knew he was kidding himself. It was not compromise he was concerned about, it was the girl, the idea of being alone with her. There was something about the way she had looked in that doorway. He could still see her. He knew he was attracted to her, but seeing her in that little nightdress made him want to grab her. And that might not have gone over very well with her. This was something new to him. He did not know how to handle it. He needed time to work it out.

There were plenty of tables; the dining room was nearly empty. Those with important jobs, like the military officers, were already gone; the others, like the journalists, had not bothered to get out of bed yet. He sat down at a table, but did not have to wait long. She came in wearing another pretty dress, one he had not seen before. It was as if she never wore any of her dresses twice.

"I'm glad we decided to come down here," he said. "It's very pleasant." And it was. The room was cheerful, and bright with the morning sun. There was a smell of fresh coffee, cinnamon and newly baked bread. "I wasn't expecting to see you this morning."

"I have a room here now," she said, "just around the corner from Louie's suite. Louie thought it would be safer for me here at the hotel than at my bungalow in town."

He waited, but she said nothing about why she had been in Louie's suite, and he did not ask. He invited her to join him and inspect the long buffet table where breakfast was laid out, practically buried under things not seen in Rangoon for weeks. Breads and buns and cakes baked in the hotel kitchen, fresh eggs and meats, cereals and fruits. The Strand must have had a benefactor busy on the docks, and the hotel's good fortune was reflected in the mood of the staff, Anglo-Indian girls mostly, who had stayed on despite the bombings. They looked happier than they had since early December.

"I can't believe they have all this food."

"It's Louie," Sumalee said, "It has to be. He spends all his time at the docks. He has a lot of people there now, and he's been working hard. He said there are too many ships to unload and things to be moved to China. And he has to work fast before the Japanese come and take it all."

"And they probably will." he said. "What will you do then? Do you have any thoughts about going back to Thailand?"

"I don't want to go back to Thailand. I enjoyed my holiday there. Life is quite normal and the Japanese aren't much of a bother. Everyone lives well, but it's a dull place, very...," She looked for another word and found it, "provincial." she said. She smiled at Harry and looked very pleased with herself. "Louie wants me to go to Kunming. I think that would be more interesting, don't you? What about you, Harry? Will you go to Kunmimg when you leave here?"

"Yes, I think so," he said, because it was most likely.

"Oh, I'm so glad!" She clapped her hands. "We can go together. I will have a friend in Kunming." She sounded so pleased that he stopped in the act of reaching for a cinnamon bun to look at her. "I'm glad you'll be there," he said.

They carried their selections to their table, and were served coffee and tea. When they started to eat she asked, "Where do you live now, Harry?"

"I live in a little bungalow across town."

"Do you live by yourself? Do you have servants?"

"I never got around to getting servants. I have the whole bungalow to myself."

"That's very sad," she said, "to live all alone. I had servants at my bungalow. They lived at the back of the garden with their families. I never felt alone. But when the bombers started coming at night, I could not sleep."

The bombers were coming over almost every night now. Not in big formations as they had by day, but by twos or threes, moving across the sky, waiting for the signal fires that would show them where to drop their bombs. They knew there was nothing that could catch them at night, and often kept their running lights on as they passed over the city, as if to taunt the AVG and British pilots who could not fight them at night. They were dropping mostly fire bombs now, scattering them over areas of the city where wooden structures stood close together. Some nights they set off conflagrations that would burn the rest of the night and all the next day. The city always smelled of smoke now.

"I'm not too concerned about the bombers," he said. "Not because I'm brave, but because I'm not in an area where they have any reason to drop a bomb. It's just a small collection of bungalows, middle-level British officials mostly, and business people. There are a few Indian families, and some Burmese too."

"The Burmese are the dangerous ones now," she observed. "They light the fires to guide the bombers at night. They get bolder every day. They always hated the British, and now they don't fear them. If they see a British alone they attack him. Many have guns now. Louie says they steal guns from the ships. Be careful," she advised him. "If they know you live by yourself they may attack your house."

"I don't expect any problems. The Burmese in my neighborhood know I'm not British. They leave me alone. They have no quarrel with Americans."

"But you look like the British," she said, "and that's dangerous. This is a good time to be Asian." Harry laughed at that. "It's true," she insisted. "It's a little complicated, but it's true. If the Burmese thought I was Thai, it might be a problem. The Burmese don't like the Thai, because of wars they fought 400 years ago. But most Burmese think I'm Chinese, and they respect the Chinese, or fear them, so they let me alone. If the Japanese think I'm Chinese it would be a problem, but it's easy for me to tell them I'm Thai. The Japanese and Thais are friends now, and the Japanese say they are the friends of all Asians. So you see, Harry, in the end it is better to be Asian than British."

He enjoyed listening to her reason it out. She spoke with great seriousness, but her sense of humor was just under the surface and often showed through. Despite the intensity with which she spoke, he knew she was very conscious of him. The café staff was quite good at anticipating the desires of their guests, but she was better. The coffee pot was not set there for her to pour, but as soon as there was but an inch of coffee left in his cup, she sent a subtle signal to the waitress. He felt very well taken care of; he could get to like it.

"You should move into the hotel," she said, reading his mind. "We could do this every day."

"This is nice, isn't it? But I'm not sure how long all the good food will last, and I couldn't afford a room here anyway." She put on a disappointed look and he added, "Maybe we can share. I can move into your room." That provoked a delighted giggle.

"What a good idea," she said, "Louie would be so pleased. The two of you can share my rent."

"I think I better stay in my house."

"You must like it. Is it very nice?"

"Pretty ordinary, I think, but it has a pleasant little garden. The furniture came with it. It's comfortable, it's quiet. It's out of the way of the Japanese bombers."

"It sounds nice. I would like to see it some time."

"I'd love to show it to you. We can have a picnic in the garden one night, if the mosquitoes are not too bad, and watch the Jap bombers fly over."

"You would have to have me back at the hotel before the bombers come."

"I have an idea. Do you know the Silver Grill?" She knew the name, of course, everyone did, but she had never been there. "It's where the pilots go, the Americans pilots, isn't it?" she asked.

"That's the place," he admitted, "The very place. We could go there one evening for dinner. Afterwards we could drive by my bungalow and have a drink there, or go back to the Silver Grill."

She listened with obvious interest. "That sounds wonderful," she said. "Will I meet the American pilots? They're every Rangoon girl's dream."

"I'll see what I can do," he said, and felt a small twinge of disappointment.

* * *

As Harry pulled into the warehouse compound, Louie was walking around a mountain of whiskey cases in the side yard, waving his hands in the air and yelling Chinese at a group of workers. He saw Harry and called to him in English, "Minute, Harry," and then went back to haranguing the workers. When he exhausted himself he walked over to Harry, shaking his head.

"Damned whiskey," he said when he got closer. "Always a problem, but I never thought we'd have too much."

"You can't have too much whiskey."

"You can," he said. "Look at it!" He looked back over his shoulder. For a minute they both stared at the stacked cases of whiskey that loomed over them. "We need room for other things. Damned workers! I tell them that, but they keep bringing it here. Every ship in the port seems to be full of whiskey now. The market has changed. Other things are in demand. The price of whiskey is down to nothing."

"I'm surprised. I would have thought whiskey is in great demand. It looks like Rangoon is going back to the good life. I just came from the most wonderful breakfast at the Strand. My sources say that it's the result of your largesse."

"Huh?" Louie said, as if not sure what Harry was talking about. "Well, there's so much stuff piling up on the docks now. I told them to send their trucks and I would fill them with whatever they wanted. It will all go to waste in a couple of weeks." He glanced back at the whiskey. "Wish they would take more of that."

"You mean we're not back in the good times?"

"We are in the eye of the storm, Harry. We are in the calm before the maelstrom overwhelms us."

"That's quite poetic, Louie."

"Perhaps it is, but it's also true."

"But things look so much better than they did a week ago. Why is that?"

"It's man's infinite adaptability." He saw uncertainty on Harry's face and tried to explain. "The Japanese bombers came, the workers fled, and the port shut down. You and Lucy got things moving again. Then the British government saw what it needed on the ships, and set the Army to unloading. Then Chiang Kai-shek saw what China needed there. So now the British Army is all over the port, there are Chinese workers everywhere, and goods are being unloaded. And somehow everything seems normal again. The problem is that the damned Chinese workers put too much value on whiskey."

"So that's what's happening. I can see why things are better at the Strand and the Silver Grill."

"Enjoy it while you can. There's not much time."

They started walking toward the shade of the warehouse, when Louie suddenly stopped. "Ah, while you're here, there's something I want you to look at," he said. "Come over this way." He led Harry around the warehouse to where it fronted on the quay and faced the river. They walked to the far end, where a shed stood, sided in corrugated metal. Louie stopped at the door. "Chap in here I'd like you to meet," he said.

There were four people inside. Harry recognized only Peter, who nodded a greeting. He, a man in business clothes, and another dressed like one of Louie's dock workers stood around the fourth, who was sitting at a small table. The seated man was dressed in a white shirt and *longyi*, the sarong Burmese men wore.

"Harry, I'd like you to meet Captain Shinsui Ichiro of the Imperial Japanese Navy."

A joke, Harry thought, but not completely sure. With Louie one could expect anything, even a Japanese officer, perhaps an old acquaintance, who happened to drop by for a drink. "How do you do," Harry started to say, but Louie went on speaking.

"Captain Ichiro has been living in Rangoon for years. Funny how we were just talking about man's adaptability. The captain is remarkably adaptable. He's fluent in the local language. He dresses like a Burmese, walks like a Burmese and talks like a Burmese. He has a Burmese wife and two Burmese children. His closest neighbors have forgotten that he is not Burmese. What do you think, Harry, does he look Burmese to you?"

Louie picked something off the table and handed it to the man. "Here are your glasses, Captain. Put them on." When the man did, Louie turned back to Harry. "There. Now he looks like a proper Burmese intellectual, don't you think?" And in fact, he did.

Louie looked around. "Ah, Peter. Go fetch us some tea. Don't forget the milk. The Captain likes milk in his tea." Peter went out the door and Louie turned back to Harry.

"Harry, I'd like you to talk with the Captain. His English is quite good. He grew up in the States."

"You did?" Harry said, turning to the man.

"Yes. In New York City," the man looked up at Harry. He started to stand up, cautiously, watching Louie all the while. When he was upright, he extended his hand to Harry. "I'm very pleased to meet you," he said. "My friends call me Eddie." He looked back at Louie and added, "Not Captain." Harry had no problem understanding him. He was soft spoken, but his pronunciation was good, though harsher, more guttural than the Chinese or the Burmese whose English Harry had grown accustomed to.

"Where did you live in New York?" Harry asked.

"In Queens. I went to school in Brooklyn. I studied to be a pharmacist there."

"You must have lived there a long time?"

"Almost 20 years, from the time I was six."

"And then you came to Burma? When did you get here?"

"I have been here over four years. I have a wife, a business, two children."

Peter appeared with the tea. "Harry, why don't you sit," Louie said, and Harry joined the Japanese at the small table, where Peter served them. Louie stayed in the room and drank his tea standing. Peter and the other two went outside. Harry caught just a glimpse of them at the edge of the quay, drinking tea, joking and eating biscuits. He turned back to the Japanese, and they started to talk.

The man was easy to talk to, and before long they were calling each other by first names. Harry found himself liking the man, who talked with nostalgia about his old tree-lined neighborhood in Queens and his family's summer excursions to Rockaway Beach and Coney Island. He was still very young when he decided to become a pharmacist. It was a respectable thing to do and would bring him a good living. It was an opportunity to help others, and in time he could go into business for himself. He was already working at a drugstore in Jackson Heights, when relatives who had lived in Burma visited his family. An uncle regaled him with stories of adventure and opportunity in Burma, of tropical nights and beautiful women. It was almost two yeas later when he set off on a tour of Asia. Burma was on his itinerary, and when he got there, he found it was all that he had been told. Within a year, he had his own business and a beautiful wife.

"But why didn't you leave when the troubles started?" Harry asked.

"Christ, if I were Japanese, I sure would have gotten out quick when the bombing started. I would have been afraid that the Burmese would tear me apart."

"No, Harry," Ichiro said, "The Burmese are a gentle people. They would never do anything like that, not to someone they know. I had become one of them. When I married I acquired a whole family, uncles, aunts, step-brothers. My wife's mother and father are like my own. I established a pharmacy in the neighborhood where my wife's parents lived. Everyone in the community knows them, and I was quickly accepted. I helped keep everyone there healthy. I know the medicines. I'm not a doctor, but I'm good at diagnosing illness, particularly the tropical ones. I know the problems that follow poor sanitation and I think I was able to make the whole neighborhood a better place. How could I leave that? Many are dependent on me, not only my family. The people tried to protect me. I was accepted as a Burmese, and then one of Mister Louie's friends found me." He looked toward Louie and shrugged his shoulders.

Louie took this as a signal to join in. "Captain Ichiro needed to disguise himself as Burmese and he did an exceptional job of it. It took my chaps quite a while to find him."

"I did nothing wrong, Mr. Louie."

"Not in your terms perhaps."

"I tried to help the people."

"The people you helped are the chaps in the bombers who fly over us every night," Louie told him, then turned to Harry. "If your friend Eddie here were Burmese, we would call him a Quisling. But he's Japanese, so we can call him a spy."

"I am not a spy. I am a pharmacist."

Louie looked around. "It's getting stuffy in here. The hot tea didn't help. Let's get out on the quay where there's a bit of breeze. Come on, Harry." He turned to Ichiro, and called him by his English name. "Edward, you come too."

It was on the edge of the quay looking down at the river, that Harry realized how stuffy it had been in the shed. His shirt, sticky and wet, clung to him. Air moving over it felt cool. He, Louie and the Japanese stood side by side looking across to the ships anchored in mid-stream. In the sky overhead a pair of pursuit aircraft circled. They were probably British; no one seemed concerned.

"Oh, God, here they come again," Louie said and turned to look at a line of trucks pulling into the yard. "Let's go see what they're bringing. Come on," he said to Harry. He threw a few Chinese words at Peter, who stood nearby, and a quick glance at the Japanese, now standing by himself.

They were halfway to the trucks when from behind them came three quick pops. Pop! Pop! Pop! Gunshots! Harry froze in mid-stride. Beside him, Louie never flinched. Then a splash from something falling in the river.

"Aw, fuck," Harry said and turned around. Peter stood at edge of the quay looking down at the river. He was alone.

Harry turned to Louie. "You didn't have to kill him!" He shouted it.

"There's no choice, Harry. We can't keep a chap like that. The war's too young."

"No choice! Why did you kill him? You could have given him to the British."

"That would not have been a solution," Louie said. He was calm, trying to explain. "They would have treated him very harshly, then shot him in the end."

"Oh, shit. Then you could have let him go. He was not involved in the war. You could have let him go back to nursing sick Burmese."

"Well, not really, Harry. Nursing sick Burmese was not his interest. Peter, bring the thing we found."

Whatever it was that Louie wanted, Peter had it in his pocket. Louie took it, unfolded it, and held it in front of Harry's face. "Look, look at this, Harry. It's his map of Rangoon. It shows targets marked for airplanes. Look, Harry, it includes two hospitals. This one was hit. And here, the airfield. See all the marks? We talked to his Burmese neighbors. Ichiro was always interested in the airfield. Many of the airport workers lived in his neighborhood. He treated them especially well. That's how he collected all this targeting information. He was responsible for many deaths."

"You didn't have to kill him," Harry said. "He was just a man. Just a nice little man."

Louie sighed. "A spy can be a nice little man. It doesn't make him any less a villain." He took Harry by his shoulder then, not gently, and turned him so that they were face to face. "Harry," he said, "Harry, listen to me. What you saw there, what Ichiro told you, that was not what he was. He did live in America, and studied English there. He may have lived there a half dozen years or more, but not with his family. His family never left Japan. He was with the Naval Attache's office in Washington. The Chinese Embassy knew him there.

"What he told you about Brooklyn and going to Rockaway Beach, that was his legend, his cover. Maybe he wasn't a captain as I called him, maybe that was too exalted a rank, but he was a Japanese Naval intelligence officer. I swear to that. He was trained and put here to do one job. To find the targets for the bombers and to guide them in when Japan was ready to strike. He was a Japanese spy, not some misplaced Japanese-American refugee. You have to understand that, Harry."

CHAPTER 18

January 19, 1942
Rangoon

Estelle, Dorothea and Sue hit it off from the first moments of their meeting at the Silver Grill. Estelle and Dorothea already knew each other, of course, but Harry was not sure how these two Anglo-Indian girls from the Sacred Heart Convent would take to a Sino-Thai young lady who had matriculated in London.

"If I have to deal with these English ladies, who are really Indian," Sumalee said when he told her that they would join Ed Rector and Bert Christman and their ladies, "you will have to introduce me in my English name, which is Susan, but everyone calls me Sue. And don't say I'm Thai, just that I'm Chinese."

"Of course," Harry said, having some idea now of pecking orders.

"Oh," 'Sue' added, "and don't tell them I went to school in London."

"They will know," he said.

"Yes," she said, with a smile.

He need not have worried. The chemistry, or whatever causes these things, was just right. Within moments of Sue's introduction to the other two, the three huddled together in one of the Silver Grill's high-backed booths, giggling and sharing very personal secrets – or that's how it looked. Harry worried at first that it was just play-acting with Sue. After the appropriate interval, he leaned over to her and whispered, "Come, I will rescue you. Come with me and meet some friends."

She looked up at him, not with annoyance exactly, and said, "If you don't mind, Harry, I would sooner stay with my friends."

And all he could think of saying was, "Oh, all right."

Ed and Bert were at the bar, where Ed was entertaining a pair of RAF officers with tales of aerial daring-do. Bert sat a few stools off, intent on his sketch pad. Over Bert's shoulder Harry could see that the drawing had caught Ed in full flight: eyes wide, nostrils flaring, hands chasing each other like a P-40 after a Nate.

Bert was totally engrossed. When he finished, he looked up and seemed surprised to see Harry there.

"Good one," Harry said, "You got Ed just right."

"Thanks, but Ed's easy. I need something challenging."

"How about the ladies?" Harry asked.

"Ah, indeed." Without another word Bert followed Harry to the booth. The women were so preoccupied that they never noticed their arrival. "It was so small," Dorothea was saying, and showed just how small it was with an inch of space between her thumb and forefinger, and they all laughed. Bert sat at a table across from them and started to draw. Harry watched as he captured these wonderful young women in the bloom of youth on paper, their pretty faces, their beautiful clothes, their total absorption in each other. Sumalee, with long hair spilling over her shoulders, exotic eyes and lips full of promise, looked the most sensual of the three. Lush, even in black on white. The other two were pretty, but plain in comparison, more composed, more made-up.

When the women finally noticed Bert and what he was doing, they all wanted to see the sketch right away, but they waited patiently when he asked them to. He finished with a final flourish of his pen, then slid into their booth to show what he had made of them. There was silence first, while they considered it, then cheerful laughter and a studied discussion of features that might have been done better or could have been worse.

Harry felt a little left out of this, and he was. He looked to see what else was going on. Two AVG pilots standing nearby with their drinks were talking quietly. He heard the words "infiltrating" and "Thailand" and when one of the pilots acknowledged Harry with a nod and tip of his glass, he joined them.

"So they've started," he said.

"Oh, yeah, they've started."

"Did you hear about the elephants, Harry?" This from behind. Ed Rector had come up without Harry noticing.

"Elephants?" Harry said, turning to Rector. "I haven't heard anything about elephants."

"We went on this mission," Ed said. "The Brits requested it. We were to go up near the Thai border, up to Kawkareik – that's the first town in Burma. There's a British brigade up there, and they're getting frantic. They were guarding the road that comes in from Thailand, and they saw these elephants lumbering down the road toward them. There were Japs riding them. The elephants were carrying a lot of stuff. A couple even had machine guns mounted on them. The Brits figured there were about a dozen elephants, two Japs on each, and maybe five times as many Japs walking behind, and they were all coming down the road, right at them. The Brits wanted us to go up and strafe the whole shebang. I took a couple of the guys, but by the time we got there, there weren't any elephants or any Japs. Which was just as well. I would feel real bad shooting an elephant."

Several British ladies strolling around the room had stopped to listen. "Where did the elephants go?" one of them asked.

"They just walked off the road, into the jungle. That's what the Japs have been doing up there, staying off the roads. The Brits told us the Japs are commandeering all the animals on both sides of the border. They're grabbing any animal that can carry something."

"Oh, the poor animals," another lady said. "Why are the Japanese doing that?"

"They're using them as pack animals, to carry their equipment. That lets the Japs stay off the roads. They just walk all over the area. They're always in small groups and they stay in the jungle. They use the animal trails, and nobody sees them. They're like ghosts. We get calls to attack the Japs infiltrating across the border. When we get there, we don't see anybody. The Brit troops may be able to spot them from the ground, but when the Japs are walking in the jungle, you can't see them from the air."

"Well they can't walk on water," one of the pilots said. "The Brits will stop them when they try to cross the Salween River."

"They'll cross it all right."

"Yeah, what are they going to use to get across?"

"They'll use boats. They're bringing boats with them. What do you think they're carrying on the elephants?"

One of the ladies spoke up. "A friend of mine – quite well connected – says that the Japanese are buying boats from the Burmese, buying them, mind you. The Burmese will sell them anything." There was something in the way she said it that made them all see the truth of it. The group fell silent, until one of the pilots said, "Oh shit, the Japs will be here in a week."

Two others said simultaneously, "I need a drink."

Rector was looking over at the door. "Hey, look, it's Newquack, come to honor us with his presence."

Two of the pilots nearest the door dropped to their knees, stretched out their arms out before them and lay flat on the floor, kowtowing Newkirk. "Hail Scarsdale Jack," they cried in unison, then slowly raised off the floor, but stayed on their knees. "Hail, mighty leader of the Sharks of the Sky!" one of them cried, and kowtowed Newkirk a second time. "Hail, great destroyer of flimsy airplanes made in Japan!" cried the other.

A chorus came from the area of the bar, "Hail Broadway Jack! Hail defender of the Burmese skies, defender of the Silver Grill!"

Newkirk stood at the door where he had stopped, and watched the proceedings with a small smile. When it seemed over, he waved to the room. "Thanks, fellows," he said, and was greeted by more cheers. Right behind him were more AVG pilots, a few Harry had not seen since the AVG's training days at Toungoo.

"Who are these guys?" Harry asked.

"First Squadron guys, the Adams and Eves. They're going to replace the Pandas."

Harry went up to Newkirk. "Hi, Jack, how are things?"

"Well, young Ross. Haven't seen you in a while. Missed you at the press briefing this morning."

"They're keeping me busy, Jack," he said, not adding that, as the *New York Times* was getting everything on the war as well as the AVG's operations, there was no longer much "intelligence" to get from the press briefings. "What have you been up to, Jack?"

"We've been spending a lot of time on the border, both sides of it, shooting up the Nippers."

"Nippers?" Harry asked. He could not recall hearing the term before.

Newkirk laughed. "You're a scholar, Harry. It comes from the Japanese language. It's what the Japs call where they live. Japan is 'Nippon', as the Nippers say."

"Ah, so," Harry said, in his best Japanese accent. It was all very funny just then.

Newkirk went on. "We've been shooting up Jap airfields in Thailand, escorting British Blenheim bombers on their missions. The Brits are asking us to do more ground attack, to support the British infantry."

"Sounds like a job that needs doing."

"It is, but it's not a job I like. It's a dangerous job, probably the most dangerous job we can do. You can always dive away from a Nipper who comes after you in the air. But when we're flying ground attack, everybody is shooting at you. All their goddamn machine guns, and every goddamn Nipper soldier is lying on his back and shooting his rifle in the air. Jesus

Christ! There's nothing you can do. It's hard not to get hit."

Harry did not know what to say. He just nodded. "Listen, Harry," Newkirk said, "here's something you might be interested in. I sat in on a British commanders' meeting tonight. The Japs are in Burma, in big numbers. Maybe two divisions. They marched right across the mountains from Mae Sot. Now it's up to the Brits to hold them on the other side of Moulmein. The bright side is, there's supposed to be a Chinese Army marching down from Kunming."

"Good Christ," Harry said. "Two divisions! How many Japs is that?"

"The Brits say as many as 30,000."

"That's the end of our world as we know it. How about the Chinese, will they get here in time?"

"No," Newkirk said, matter of factly, "I doubt it."

Harry felt a little numb when he went back to join Ed and Bert and the girls in their booth. There had been no doubt in his mind that the Japs were coming to Burma, but now they were here and it was a shock.

"You're very quiet, Harry," Sumalee said.

"Oh," he said, "I was just thinking about some of the stories I heard here tonight."

"They're very funny, aren't they," she said, which for a moment seemed strange until he remembered that she had been listening to Ed's repertoire, and his stories could be hilariously funny. "It's getting late," he said. "Are you interested in a drink at my place, or would you like to stay here?"

"Let's go to your house," she said.

* * *

Harry parked in the small driveway that curved past the front of his bungalow. It was pitch black once he turned off what little light came from his shielded headlights.

"Watch your step, Sue. Grab my belt and walk right behind me. There are brambles right next to the path. They'll catch your dress."

Once inside he lit a lantern. The drapes were already drawn, blackout fashion. The lamp cast a soft amber glow that made the living room look inviting. It was a very ordinary room, but in the soft light it looked good.

"It looks very comfortable," Sue said.

"It's fine for the amount of time I spend here, which is not much. It will get stuffy very quickly. I can't open the drapes unless I turn off the lamp. Let's go out in the garden and have our drink there. The mosquitoes aren't bad."

A few minutes in the darkness of the garden and they could make out the forms of the chairs on the little veranda and the shrubs that bordered it. Tall trees stood around the house that, in the darkness, loomed over them like black cliffs. It made them feel like they were standing at the center of a deep valley. What they saw of the sky right overhead was bright and sparkled with a hundred stars.

"Look at the stars," she said. "It's quite beautiful. I never look at the sky anymore." He guided her to one of the teak chairs and then went to get their drinks. Scotch for both of them, water in his, coke in hers. "I like it very sweet," she told him.

They sat and sipped their drinks and listened to the night. It was alive with the buzz of insects, the whirr of wings, the secret scuffling of things in the bushes. It was hard to imagine what might be out there. It gave Harry a little shiver. It did not seem to bother Sumalee. After a while she said, "I enjoyed the Silver Grill. It was exciting."

"You didn't dance," he said.

"Ed wanted me to. Maybe next time. I like your friends. I like Dorothea and Estelle. I liked Bert very much. He's very talented. And he's not like the other pilots. He's quiet, more thoughtful. Ed is very charming. He's very good with the ladies, isn't he? But he's much wilder than Bert. He's more like the others."

"Bert said he will give me the drawing he made of you."

"I liked the drawing. Did you think it was good? It made me look a little...wild."

"The drawing was very good." He laughed. "I don't think 'wild' is the proper word. How about 'exciting'?"

She laughed then. "Exciting? You think so?"

He did not reply. He was listening to something else. Over the hum and buzz of the insects, he could hear a drone that was growing stronger. .

"The bombers," she said.

He listened a while longer. "There are two of them, or maybe three. They're not close to us." He remembered that she said that bombers going over at night bothered her, and asked, "Do you want to go inside the house?"

"No, let's stay here and watch. Maybe we'll see them go over."

Harry smiled at her in the darkness. She was not afraid. He would have been surprised if she were. She was quiet now, and they both listened. He knew that like him, she was waiting to hear the hollow booms of bombs exploding far away. In the end there was nothing, and the engine sound faded into the night.

"Well," she said, "that's it? No bombs tonight?"

"If they fall near the river we might not hear them here."

"Oh," she said, and after a pause, "Another one is coming."

He heard it then, the rising-falling drone of unsynchronized engines, more distinct now, closer. "Just one this time," he said. "He's not far away."

They watched the sky while the sound got louder and closer. "There," she said. The bomber passed over the trees, into the part of the sky they could see. Two small lights, like the stars around it, moved side by side, between them a shadow.

"He has his running lights on. He's going to pass right over us."

They both sat very still now, as if moving or even breathing would betray them to the men in the machine above the trees. It was eerie, watching the shadow of the bomber drift over them. It was not very high. At the moment it was directly overhead, Harry had a frightening thought. If a bomb was dropped just then, they would never know it. They would never sense it coming. In ten seconds their lives would just end. He caught himself counting when he got to five. He laughed aloud then and said, "Now we're safe."

"That was exciting, Harry." She stood up. He caught her movement, but could see her only as a shadow. He thought she was looking at where the bomber disappeared again over the trees. "Waiting to hear the bomb?" he asked.

"No, I don't want to hear a bomb. Not tonight. That would spoil it. This was like watching an exciting play. But no one must get hurt and spoil it."

He could sense her facing him, then moving toward him. Maybe like a cat she could see him in the dark. He felt her hand on his shoulder. She sat down next to him on the teak chaise, and pressed close. His hand brushed her cheek, and she leaned closer. He felt her face against his. They sat like that for a while, saying nothing. Then he asked, "Another drink?" He meant it to be funny. She reached over and pinched his thigh.

After a while, she took his hand and put on the front of her dress, where he could feel buttons, and skin where the buttons were undone. He stroked her with his fingertips, then felt her push his fingers under the dress where she was soft and warm. He leaned over to kiss her, hesitant. Did nice Thai girls kiss? And quickly found that he need not have been concerned. She shifted, to give his hands more freedom, and then he felt her hands on him.

"Do you want me to take off my dress?"

"Yes," he said, his voice husky, his mouth dry. He thought of the scuttling in the bushes. "Maybe we should go inside," he said.

CHAPTER 19

Friday, January 23, 1942
Rangoon

The Japanese bombers came again that Friday, in daylight, the first time since Christmas. Two dozen Nates came first, in the morning, and dove on the airdrome. There may have been bombers with them, but afterwards no one was quite sure. Three RAF Hurricane fighters had just arrived from North Africa, and they bravely went up after the Nates, as did a half dozen AVG P-40s. The Hurricanes were lucky to escape their first encounter with the Japanese. Not long after they landed, the sirens went off again. This time there were about a dozen bombers and about twice as many Nates. Three RAF Buffaloes went up, and ten AVG P-40s. When the day was over, the AVG claimed 17 victories, the British none. One British airplane and one American airplane went down. Later it was reported that both pilots were killed.

Harry did not get to see any of the action that day, which was to the north of the city. He was preoccupied elsewhere, at the native port on the riverfront where the Burmese fishermen kept their boats. A lead from Doyle took him there. A Burmese fishing boat had returned after weeks in Thai waters. The Burmese captain had sailed among Japanese warships. He had witnessed many things, but he was not willing to talk with the British about them and kept out of sight. Doyle thought perhaps an American could succeed where the British had not.

Harry would have succeeded, had the fisherman known what he was looking at, or at least had some idea about numbers. The captain knew his fish and he knew the sea. He knew nothing at all about warships or troop transports. Even so, Harry might have had a decent report on enemy naval strength, had the man been able to give him numbers. But he could not. In the captain's mind there was "one" thing or there were "many" things, but there were no words for what was in between.

In the days before this, when not involved with what he thought of as "spying," Harry was totally engrossed with Sumalee and his memories of their night together. His mind became a cinema that played back scenes repeatedly, sometimes when he least expected it, and the night became even more exotic than it was. It was not that he did not recognize the exceptionally romantic reality of it. He knew it had been an incredible night in the tropics. Soft, balmy air, enemy bombers droning overhead, a beautiful woman giving herself to him.

God, she was beautiful! His mind replayed it in all its graphic detail. When he lit the lantern in the bedroom and first saw her naked, her body was a wonder, better made than any he had ever seen in a painting. Or even in those photographs he had leered at back in school. She was not shy about any of it, and that surprised him. She was pleased when he looked at her and even more pleased when he touched her. She presented herself, turning her body in ways that made it easy for him. If anything, he felt shy when she reached for him, and then did the things he had only read about. It was the most remarkable night he had ever spent. He had great hopes of repeating it. Soon.

He had been with her twice in the days since. Once at breakfast, and once when she came with him to the Silver Grill in the late afternoon, but "only for a quick drink, Harry." When he suggested they go to his house, she said, "Wait." Wait for what he wondered? At night he fell asleep thinking of her. Mornings he awoke feeling her next to him. Once he was sure she was there. He felt both disappointment and a rush of pleasure when he realized that he was remembering a dream. And what a wonderful dream it was. Later, when he shaved, he looked at his face in the mirror for a long time. "You are besotted," he told himself, "you lucky bastard."

Driving back from the fishing port, he found himself nearing Louie's warehouse. He drove on past it; he was not ready for Louie. He drove on to the Strand instead, hoping to find Sumalee in her room. He did not, so drove on to the Silver Grill. It was still early. None of the pilots would be there; he could have a quiet drink. He would wait and see what turned up.

The girl behind the bar greeted him with a smile. "There's a note for you," she said. He took it from her, an envelope, plain, not from the Strand. "Did a young lady drop this off?" he asked, still hoping.

"No, it was a man from the airdrome."

Plain paper inside, a few words scrawled across it, difficult to decipher. He read it twice before he understood: "Harry, Bert got killed today. We bury him tomorrow p.m. at church of Edward the Martyr. If we can find him." The signature was harder to read than the rest. It said, "Ed Rector."

* * *

"It was murder!"

The pilot all but yelled the words. Harry stood with a small group of early arrivals in the quiet of the church yard, all of them uncomfortable now. The pilot looked right at Harry then, as if he had done something wrong. "Put that in your newspaper," he said. In the air in front of him he used his fingers to block out the words of the headline: "Bert Christman Murdered by Japs!"

Harry had nothing to say to that. Nor did any of the others.

Perhaps fortunately, the truck bringing the wooden box with Christman's remains arrived just then. A half dozen AVG jeeps and a pair of staff cars followed. The cortege halted near the open grave, and Rector, Hill and four other pilots got out of the jeeps and walked around to the back of the truck. They were all in khaki uniforms. They were the pallbearers.

They stood some distance off from the back of the truck, as if reluctant to get started. Harry caught a whiff of it then, the sickly-sweet smell of death, just as Tex Hill said, "Come on, guys, we got to do it. Let's go." Tex stepped up to the truck and put his hand on the box. The others joined him. Harry fell in step with the small procession that followed the box to the grave. A man waiting there was also in uniform. He told the pilots to put the box on the wood slats laid over the pit. The pilots set the box down, stepped back and saluted. Then they turned and walked to where the rest of the mourners stood. Well back from the grave.

"Lord," Harry heard one of the pilots say, "what a horrible goddamn smell." Even from where he stood, Harry could smell it. Embalming was a luxury not used now, and bodies deteriorated quickly under the Burmese sun. Everyone stood quietly and tried not to think of it, waiting for something to happen. After a while, Ed Rector walked over to him. "What's holding us up, do you know?"

Harry shook his head.

"Did you see Dorothea? She was supposed to be here."

"No, I haven't seen any of the girls," he said, and then, more quietly, "Ed, I'm really sorry about Bert. I liked him. He was a good man."

"He was. We were together for a long time. I never thought I'd go to his funeral. You don't think about that."

"One of your guys said the Japs murdered him."

"Yeah, that's what it amounts to. They shot him while he was hanging in his parachute. We found a couple of places where bullets hit him. One went through the back of his neck. That's probably what killed him." He shook his head, shivering at the memory of it. "We were flying together yesterday. I made a couple of passes on the Japs and Bert was right behind me. Then he climbed away. I never saw him again."

Ed looked to where a civilian sedan was pulling up on the grass verge nearby. "Look," he said, "there's Dorothea with Estelle," as the two got out of the car. "Poor Estelle, she must be devastated. She and Bert really got on. Your girl is there too."

Harry saw Sumalee behind the other two. Tex walked over then and said, "I'm going over to be with the girls."

"Do you know what we're waiting on?" Ed asked.

"We don't have a padre," Tex said. "He's at the other burial over there." They looked across the cemetery to where a group of British officers stood ramrod straight. A bugle started to the play "The Last Post."

"It must be the Brit pilot who got killed yesterday," Ed said.

"It's not," Tex said. "It's a Jap pilot. It's the guy we shot down near the airport. The Brits are burying him with full military honors."

"Good Christ!" Ed said, his face flushing with outrage. "I can't believe that. The Brits and their goddamn chivalry, for Christ sake! It's too bad the goddamn Japs didn't know about chivalry when they saw Bert hanging in his parachute."

"Come on, Ed," Tex said, "let's go over to the girls."

Harry turned to follow them when someone called his name. It was Morris, the journalist from the Silver Grill.

"Greetings, Ross," he said. "I'm sorry we meet on such a sad occasion. The cartoonist, was he a friend of yours?"

Harry nodded. "Yes, he was."

"I'm sorry. The man had talent."

There was nothing more to say. Across the grave they could see Ed and Tex talking with the girls, disagreeing about something. It seemed Estelle wanted to get closer to the grave. Harry could see Ed shaking his head.

"What the hell is that smell?" Morris said, looking up as if he would find it in the trees.

"What have you been up to?" Harry asked, for something else to think about. "Are you working on anything big?"

"The usual stuff," Morris said. "The air raids, mainly, the same as everybody else. The funeral will get a paragraph or two. What I would really like to do is get up to Moulmein. The Brits will go head-to-head with the Japs there before long. It will be a real mess then. I'd like to get up there while it's still possible to travel. Get the lay of the land; get some background. Then, when the curtain goes up, I'll be able to write about it from Rangoon. A few of us have been looking into it."

"Will the Brits let you go there?"

"They said they would. But they say they can't give us any transport. We'd have to get our own. You wouldn't have a jeep handy, would you?"

Harry thought about it. It sounded interesting. "Maybe I can get one."

Morris looked at him for a long moment. "Well, maybe you want to think about going up there with me."

A small group was walking across the cemetery toward them. "I think the chaplain's coming. Let's get together at the Silver Grill when this is over. Maybe we can work something out."

The service was over quickly. The chaplain was a man of experience. He said prayers, a eulogy, and words of condolence. Then he dismissed everyone before the coffin was dropped into the grave. Estelle started to shake with sobs then and tried to break away from Ed, who shook his head and held her even tighter. Finally Dorothea put an arm around her and walked her back to the car. Harry saw Sue and thought she was going with them, but she left the others and walked to a long black Cadillac parked behind their sedan. Harry recognized it as one of Louie's cars. He hurried to catch her before the car pulled out. Sue saw him and rolled down the window.

"We're going over to the Silver Grill," Harry said. "Come join us there. Better yet, drive over with me. We can have a drink and go on to my place."

She looked at him, wistfully, he thought. "I would love to, Harry, but I can't. Louie is entertaining visitors from China. Without Lucy here, he needs me. I'm so sorry. We'll do it another time."

Another time, he thought, another empty evening.

* * *

January 29, 1942

Harry checked the load on the jeep, clicking off items from a list in his head. It looked good. Everything was there, jerry cans of gasoline, boiled water, mosquito nets, canned food. Enough to be self-sufficient for a week. Morris was not looking his way just then, so he tried to slip a canvas shelter-half behind the seat. Wrapped in the canvas was a Thompson submachine gun. It made an unwieldy package, awkward to place without Morris noticing.

"What the hell do you have there?" Morris was looking at him now. Harry thought about it and unwrapped the Thompson.

"My, my, old chap," Morris said in his best British officer's voice. "The pen is mightier than the sword, you know."

"So they say, but I've never found a Parker that could outshoot a Thompson."

"Ha, ha," Morris said, in normal voice now. "It may not be sporting for a journalist to carry one of those, but I'm glad you're bringing it. And it's not just the Japanese chaps I'm thinking of."

Harry knew exactly what he meant. There were stories every day now about Burmese attacking unwary British, and some of the stories were probably true. The Thompson was a good dissuader if they needed it. What Harry had not shown Morris was the .45 automatic pistol he kept in a leather portfolio that he intended to keep very close to him. He had more faith in the .45 being near when he needed it. The Thompson was a luxury.

"Well, let's get on our way then," Morris said. "With luck, we'll be in Martaban before midnight."

The road followed the curve of the Gulf of Martaban. It was in reasonably good condition, they were told. Rain was many weeks off, and while it stayed dry, there was nothing they might meet en route that they could not drive over or go around in the jeep. By evening they should be at Martaban, the village where the road ended, where the road met the sea. They would stay there overnight. In the morning they would take the ferry to Moulmein.

In an hour they were well beyond Rangoon, out among the rice fields and the small hills, where life went on as it had for centuries, as if the British had never come. Except where the road took them through a village, which was not often, they would see people rarely, and then usually working in the fields. The only traffic they met was an occasional oxcart or a strolling water buffalo. The few Burmese they did see waved or called a greeting as they passed. But for that it was the two of them, mile after mile, alone with their thoughts, alone with the sound of the engine.

From time to time Morris got bored and needed to talk. In his short time in Rangoon, he had made good contacts among the officers at the British headquarters, and hoped to get some feel for the coming ground war from them. He was bothered when he found the British high command totally out of touch. Despite the Japanese triumphs around them in Malaya and Singapore, there were still officers who looked on the Japanese as inferior troops they would defeat easily when they finally met. "There are still senior officers who expect the Burmese to rise up against the invading Japanese," he told Harry. "It's hard to believe."

"It's not so hard to believe," Harry said. "It fits in with what I've been hearing. The Brits have their heads in a basket."

"That's not where I would say they have their heads."

"You sound like you have the inside word. Where does Moulmein fit into the Brits' thinking?"

"Moulmein is where the Jap must be stopped. It's where the Jap can be stopped. At least that's what Sir Archibald thinks, and he's the Commander-in-Chief." Morris went on:

"You'll see when we get there. Moulmein sits right on the estuary of the Salween River, where it meets the sea. It's wide there, a mile and a half across. Sir Archibald thinks that a few Brits and all that water will stop the Japs. Not all the generals agree. Some think it's an impossible place to defend. A retreat from there would be by river steamer."

Two miles outside Martaban they came to the first roadblock, four Indian troops with a scout car parked across the road. Morris produced a letter from British headquarters in Rangoon. That got them a snappy salute and a quick invitation to proceed. There were two more checkpoints before they entered Martaban.

There was not much of Martaban town that they could see. The sun had long set, and they drove in the glow of the jeep's blackout lights, little slits in the painted-over headlights. There were no street lights, and most of the shops were closed and dark. The ones still open showed only the most cautious glimmer of light. Black shapes of trees lined the sides of the street, guiding them down an uncertain path, which they followed slowly, until a voice shouted, "Halt!" A turbaned Indian soldier stepped up, shone a light in their faces. Morris held out his letter.

When the soldier returned it, Morris asked, "Are you 16 Indian Infantry Brigade?" A long pause stretched out; the soldier was not going to answer. Morris said, "I'm a friend of Major Causey. He's with 16 Indian Brigade. Is he in Martaban tonight?"

"If you will wait here please, sir." The turbaned soldier stepped back into the darkness, from where, a moment later, two others emerged to take his place. They stood quietly alongside the jeep. "Sorry, Harry," Morris said. "A long shot, but I thought it was worth a try. I wasn't expecting to get arrested as a spy." That would be an interesting turn of events, Harry thought.

It was ten minutes that seemed an hour. Two men emerged from the darkness, one in a turban, the other in an officer's hat. A flashlight was in their faces again, but briefly, then turned off. "Ah, Morris," a British voice said, "it is you. What the devil are you doing here?"

"If that's you, Causey, I might ask you the same thing. I thought you were up in the hills."

"Where are you staying tonight?"

"At a guest house. Just as you enter town, they said."

"Ah, yes, it's right ahead. Look, why don't you let my chaps take your jeep over there. You'll run into something driving about in the dark. I expect you'll want something to eat. I'll join you. There's a decent curry house not 50 yards from here. We can walk over."

"Sounds good," Morris said. "Let's go, Harry."

They would never have found their way without Causey leading them. They could smell the curry house, but not see it. It had no lights showing on the outside. The inside was a jungle of moving shadows, cast on the walls and floor by the candlelight. Causey ordered beer while they waited for their curry.

"We'd have been lost without you, Causey," Morris told him, "but I wasn't expecting to find you in Martaban."

"We've been here a few days."

"I thought 16 Brigade was up in the hills, guarding the road from Thailand."

"We were," Causey said. "Then the Japs came."

Morris and Harry looked at him, thought he was joking at first, but then realized that he was not. After a long silence, Morris said, "The Japs came, and…." He let the question hang in the air.

"We left. Rather hurriedly, I'm afraid."

"You left. What about the Japs?"

"They were right behind us, but not as quick."

"Where are they now?"

"Encircling Moulmein, I expect."

The conversation had turned unreal. The man must be joking, Harry thought. As he and Morris waited, trying to keep their thoughts from showing on their faces, Causey started to shift in his chair, uncomfortably. He turned first to Harry, then back to Morris.

"Look, chaps," he said, and leaned in close toward Morris. "We were up in the hills at Kawkareik, guarding the road from Thailand. I'm the brigade's intelligence wallah – you know that, Morris – and that makes me feel somewhat responsible for what happened. I was in the teak business for years, lived in this part of Burma much of my life. I know the land; I know the people. For a week I had been getting reports from the local hunters that the Japs were coming, right through the jungle. I reported all of that. No one in Rangoon believed it. Even my brigade was skeptical. Then, five days ago, there they were, the whole Jap 55 division in our backyard. Our Colonel decided there was nothing for it but to get out. Fight another day. We retreated right down the Kawkareik road."

Causey took a long pull of his beer. He put the glass down and shook his head. "Nothing went right. We had an accident at a river crossing. The only ferry there was sunk. We had to leave the brigade's trucks and equipment on the wrong side of the river. We came into Moulmein on the 25th. They sent us right over here. There's nothing over here, but there was nothing else to do. The brigade's morale was lost on the Kawkareik road along with our trucks and equipment."

"Jesus," Morris said. "I'm really sorry about all that. What happens now?"

Causey shrugged, looked to see if anyone was too near their table before he spoke. He kept his voice low. "The Japs have been coming at Moulmein for the past few days, but very quietly. People coming in from the villages tell us they've been in the clothing markets, buying up *longyis* and shirts. They're trying to look like Burmese and staying away from our patrols. There's been no contact so far. That makes it all very difficult for our regular Army chaps to even believe they're out there. Moulmein will be surrounded in a day or two, and then it will start."

"Good Christ," Morris said, then looked over Causey's shoulder and added, "Ah, better times. Here comes the curry."

* * *

They were up at dawn the next morning. Causey wanted them at the ferry jetty before 7 o'clock, to get an early boat to Moulmein. The Salween River was a lake where they stood, the water placid and glowing like silver in the mist that rose from it. They could see two of the ferries, long double-decked wooden steamers tied to the jetty. Alongside one was a line of Indian soldiers. Causey was nearby, talking with two officers. When he saw them he raised his hand in greeting. A few minutes later he walked over. Morris gave him a cheery hello. Causey just nodded. He looked grim. "Good morning, gentlemen."

"Is this our boat?" Morris asked.

"Ah, yes, it is," Causey said. They stood looking at the boat for a long moment. Finally Causey said, "I don't think it's wise that you go over to

Moulmein this morning. The town is under attack."

"The town's being attacked now?" Morris asked.

"As we speak. They came at first light, broke through the perimeter."

"Does it look bad?"

"Well...." Causey hesitated. "Let's say it's not likely to be a good day in Moulmein today."

* * *

"...and was that an understatement!"

Harry paused to get his breath while Doyle poured coffee from the thermos. Their secret garden had become a jungle since they last met. "I'm listening," Doyle said. "Go on."

"Causey went over to Moulmein on the first ferry. We never did see him again. Morris and I hung around the waterfront most of the day. Everybody in town was there. Every once in a while a boat came in from Moulmein, with wounded usually, and we got news of the action. It was pretty grim. After the first attacks, the Brits moved their headquarters up on a ridge that overlooks the town. By noon there was a lull, but in the late afternoon the Japs attacked again. The fight went on for the rest of the night. By morning, the Brits were pushed up against the water. All they could do was get out. It was Dunkirk all over again. Every boat for miles along the river was lined up on the waterfront. Some of the troops built rafts or started to swim across. The boats left in a storm of bursting artillery shells and machine gun fire. The Japs were already on the jetty when the last ferry left."

"And do you know the strangest thing of all?" Harry's question was purely rhetorical. He had to tell Doyle this one. "In the middle of the battle the Brits changed commanders. There was no reason except that the new man just happened to arrive. During the afternoon lull, the brigade's new brigadier went over on a boat. He had just arrived in Martaban from his previous command, but British Army headquarters in Rangoon decided that as he was there he was now in charge. They replaced the brigadier who had been handling things in Moulmein for months with a guy who just got there and knew nothing about what was going on. Later, Morris asked one of his Brit friends why they did that. They told him that the brigadier was a 'charming' man who would 'do no harm'."

Doyle shook his head. "The Battle of Moulmein, all over in 24 hours. It's a total disaster for the Brits. They've been talking about it here. Moulmein was one of Burma's most important towns, the heart of the teak and rice trade. The Brits have been there since the 1820s. Losing it the way they did is a great shock, to the Brits, to the Burmese, to everybody who hears about it."

They sat quietly for a while, mulling over this disaster. Doyle started putting away the tea things. "Listen, Harry," he said. "I want you to write down everything you told me, everything you remember about the battle at Moulmein. I'll send it on to Donovan. Spying on the Brits isn't our job, but I think Washington could use some perspective on this. I expect the British account of the battle won't be quite like yours."

CHAPTER 20

Lucy's back!" She said it right in his ear, shouted it practically. It brought him out of his chair. "Lucy's back!" he repeated in self defense, just a reaction. He felt silly now, standing there, facing her. She was grinning at him, looking absolutely beautiful.

"Sue," he said to her, "I've been looking for you." And he had been. He had been slumped in a chair in the lobby of the Strand for the last hour, watching, hoping to catch her passing through. He had not seen her in days. And now here she was, and he had not seen her coming. She had sneaked up behind him, jolted him out his reverie, a reverie about her.

"Listen," he said, "Let's go to dinner tonight, or go for a drink, or at least come over to my place."

"But, Harry, Lucy's back."

"That's wonderful," he said. "I'm looking forward to seeing her. But how about tonight?"

She put on a sad face now. "Harry, I think Lucy would be very unhappy if she saw us together." She looked around the lobby then.

"She doesn't have to see us together. Nobody does. And what if Lucy does see us together? There's nothing between us. I don't think she would really care."

"She would care, Harry. Very much. I think we should wait a few days. You should see her, talk with her. I had better go now."

"Sue...."

* * *

"Lucy, it's great to see you back. Rangoon hasn't been the same without you."

He held her hand and looked at her. It was like seeing her for the first time. She was a beautiful woman, much more beautiful than he remembered. More beautiful than Sue even, but very different. Sue was a child compared to her, still a girl. And that was Sue's attraction. She exuded femininity and youth like a powerful perfume. He suddenly felt guilty, thinking about Sue while looking at Lucy.

"Lucy." He took her by both hands. "Let's go in the bar, have a drink. You have to tell me about all the exciting things you've been doing."

"It wasn't all so exciting, Harry," she told him after they got their drinks. "It was work. A lot of it was tedious. I spent my days trying to convince people that my father and his business would survive after Rangoon was gone. Then I had to find ways to make sure that it happens. I even spent time with your Colonel Chennault, talking about airplanes."

"You met Chennault! Did you spend all your time in Kunming?"

"There and Chungking."

"You met the Generalissimo?"

"I did, and the Madame. It was Madame Chiang who introduced me to Colonel Chennault."

"And you talked with Chennault about airplanes?"

"Yes. When Rangoon is closed to us, everything going to China will have to come through India, and from there over the Himalayas by airplane. I talked with the Colonel about the best way to do this and about CNAC's capabilities."

"See-Nack." He pronounced it as one word, as she did. "And what is CNAC?"

"China National Aviation Corporation. It's General Chiang's airline. They're flying the Himalayas now. Colonel Chennault says the American Air Corps will also operate regular flights from India. There's a lot to do to assure that my father is able to continue his business under the new circumstances."

"Why did your father send you? Why didn't he go himself? I know you're very capable, but he's the man in charge."

"Harry, do you really need to ask that?" There was a long silence while she looked at him with something like disappointment. "I'm a woman. My father knows that in these circumstances I would get more attention from the Chinese generals and even from your Colonel Chennault than he ever would. And there's Madame Chiang. My father thought the two of us would get along well. And we did. My father is a very intelligent businessman. That's why I went in his place."

"The ways of the Orient," Harry said.

"Also," she continued, "I had to get my father's house in Kunming ready. It's in the hills beyond the city with a beautiful view of the lake. You'll love Kunming, Harry. My father will probably want you to stay in his house."

"I look forward to Kunming, although if I get there it will only be after the Japanese take Burma, and that's not a happy thought."

"My father said he hasn't seen much of you lately."

"He's been busy. I've been on the road."

"You must go to see him."

* * *

"Well," Louie said, as Harry came to the end of his account of the Battle for Moulmein. "I didn't expect the British to hold Moulmein long, but I did not expect them to fold so quickly. I assume you've written up a report on this – for your newspaper. I wonder if you could pass me a copy of that. It would be interesting to some of our military chaps."

"Of course," Harry said, "I'll get you a copy." It was the last thing Harry wanted to do, to give Louie copies of anything he had written, newspaper articles – or a letter home for that matter. If Louie had plans to use him as an agent, his responsiveness to such a request would confirm to Louie that he was on fertile ground. On the other hand, it was difficult to say no to the man when all he asked for was a draft of an article being sent to a newspaper.

"Rangoon's end is coming, Harry. Have you decided to come up to Kunming with us?"

"I'm not sure, Louie. I think so, probably. My only other choice is India. I think China is the better one for me."

"Whenever you're ready for Kunming, let me know. I have an airplane that comes here almost every day now. When you're ready, we'll just pull off a case or two of whiskey and make room for you."

"Thank you. I'll remember that."

"I have a house in Kunming, outside the city. You're welcome to stay there as long as you want."

"Thanks again. How much time do you think we have left in Rangoon?"

"It's impossible to say. Too much depends on the British. They may be able to hold the Japanese for a while, a few weeks, perhaps. But when the Japs break through this next time, things will crumble very quickly. I'm already evacuating. I started as soon as I heard Moulmein fell. I'm not sure we can get everything we need out of our warehouse and off the docks in the time we have left."

* * *

After taking Moulmein, the Japanese 55th Division moved up along the east bank of the Salween River, destroying pockets of the British 17th Indian Division where they found them. The British moved across the river, deployed along the west bank and prepared to defend the river crossings.

The soldiers of the British 17th Indian Division were Indians or Gurkhas, good troops who fought bravely when they met the Japanese. But they were raw troops for the most part, and had been trained to do battle on the vast plains of India. In Burma they fought for their lives in banana plantations and among the rubber trees. By day, Japanese planes came from airfields in Thailand to bomb them, and all they could do was lie on their backs in slit trenches and fire their rifles at the sky. By night, the Japanese soldiers came. They were expert now at moving in the jungle, and came silently under the cover of darkness. Close to the British troops, or already among them, they charged in screaming with their bayonets fixed on the ends of their rifles, and the clashes often ended in hand-to-hand fighting. When they overran a position, they butchered the British wounded. In time, the British soldiers stopped taking Japanese prisoners.

British officers who had regarded the Japanese as a third-rate soldier saw him quite differently now. The British became masters of strategic retreat. They decided to withdraw from their positions along the Salween and moved farther west to the Bilim River. They passed the orders to withdraw over their radios in the clear. The Japanese heard and reacted quickly. Lightly equipped and accustomed to operating off the roads, the Japanese troops reached the Bilim almost before the British did. Now they threatened the British withdrawal route across the Sittang, the last of the great rivers before Rangoon. It was the last obstacle the Japanese Army would have to cross.

The air war was proceeding apace. In late January, the AVG in Rangoon was reinforced by the arrival of its First Pursuit Squadron, the Adam and Eves. There were 12 fresh pilots now, and 12 fresh P-40s. The Second Squadron Panda Bears were tired and their airplanes worn. They were scheduled to return to Kunming in early February, but in the meantime Jack Newkirk remained the boss of the combined squadrons. The AVG airplanes were now dispersed at night to small air fields outside the city – named after popular brands of whiskey – where they were less likely to become a target of Japanese bombs. Swarms of Nates came by day to draw the P-40s into air where they could be destroyed by the overwhelming Jap numbers. Jap bombers came by night trying to hit Migaladon and find the dispersal fields. The Japanese were not having their way with the AVG easily. By the end of January, the AVG had destroyed its 130th Japanese airplane.

Between actions, everybody listened to the radio, which now reported day-by-day accounts of the battle for Singapore. On 13 February the Japanese were reported to have crossed the strait and were on the island itself; on 15 February Singapore fell. The British in Rangoon got ready to evacuate.

* * *

Harry was spending a rare mid-afternoon at the Silver Grill catching up on his reading of dated American news magazines, when someone slid into the booth across from him.

"Well, Harry Ross. How you doing, Harry?"

"Morris, what are you up to? You sound like you need something."

"It's just that I have an idea."

"Oh, oh."

"Can you get us a jeep?"

"Oh, shit.... Where do you want to go this time?"

"I think it's time to visit the British positions along the Sittang River."

"I don't think so. I don't want to leave Rangoon right now."

"Boy, you must have something good going on here. I can't think of a single reason not to leave Rangoon for a few days. There's been fierce fighting along the Bilim. The Japs will be pushing across the Sittang before long. Anyway, if you change your mind, let me know."

Harry felt bad about turning him down. Morris had a nose for action. If he felt that the Sittang was the place to be, that was where things would happen. Harry felt particularly bad because his decision revolved around a woman. It was all about Sue. Sue was what he thought about, what he lived for. But he could not get near her. It was frustrating, infuriating. He needed to get this resolved, one way or another. Great events were happening and his own life was centered in his groin.

* * *

"Sue," he said. "Dinner? Drinks? At least come over to my place. An hour. I can get you back here in an hour." He had caught her passing through the lobby of the Strand.

"It's awkward, Harry. I live here. Louie is right around the corner. Lucy has a room here now too. If I leave with you, the staff will see me. They'll tell Louie."

"Sue, the staff doesn't have to see you. And what if they do? What if they do tell Louie? What the hell does that matter? It's you and me, we're not doing anything wrong."

That seemed to make her think. She frowned and looked pensive, and that stoked the warm feeling in his stomach. "Harry," she said, touching his arm, "I have an idea. You know where my room is. Here's the key. Come up there tonight. At 10 o'clock." She pressed the hotel key fob into his hand. It felt like a big wooden phallus.

Ten o'clock. It had never been so hard to wait. His mind was a cinema again, playing scenes of what would happen. Flesh, firm, rounded flesh. Eyes, hands, mouths, everything in play. Jesus! He looked at his watch. Ten minutes. He could start now. Walk slowly through the lobby, looking in shops as he went, moving gradually, quietly, toward the stairs.

Outside her door he stopped and listened. Quiet. He slipped the key into the slot. It went in easily. Jesus, he thought. The movement of the key was like a metaphor. The thought made him smile. He pushed the door open. It was like the sitting room in Louie's suite, but smaller. "Sue," he said, quietly. There was a light from the next room. He went slowly, quietly, pushed on the door.

Oh my God! The bed was a tangle of bodies. He recognized Sue, her thigh, her leg. Then he saw her face. Mouth open, eyes squeezed shut, she was completely entangled with someone else, a male body, hard, muscular, pounding, pounding, pounding down on her. He started to step back.

"Ah, Harry." A voice from the bed, Louie's voice. "Won't be a minute."

"Oh, fuck," Harry said, and went back into the hallway. He did not even try to be quiet.

* * *

"I've thought about it, Morris. I want to go up to the front lines. I'll get us a jeep." As he said this he thought I must sound like a chump trying to join the Foreign Legion. But Morris never noticed, or pretended not to.

"Hey, that's great, Harry," he said. "Let's get going before this war ends."

* * *

The Sittang River
February 21, 1942

They could see the river now. It was a long way to the other side. "It's over 500 yards wide here," Morris told him. The road had taken them to a ferry crossing not far from the bridge. It looked like a military camp, although a disorganized one. There were tents scattered about, soldiers who looked like they were resting. A truck or two could be seen moving around the perimeter of the area. The rest were parked.

"I hope there's somebody I know. I'll ask for Major Causey. I don't know if he made it out of Moulmein."

They started walking toward the bridge and came to two sets of railroad tracks that went over it. There were soldiers walking ahead of them, and they fell in step with a Sikh. "I'm looking for Major Causey," Morris told him. "He's with 16 Brigade."

"I'm sorry, sir, but 16 Brigade is still on the other side of the river."

"Ah," Morris said, "can we walk across the bridge?"

"I wouldn't advise it, sir. The Japanese have the hill on the other side. They have a machine gun firing on the bridgehead."

They turned from the bridge and walked along the bank instead, trying to get a good look at the long steel girder bridge. There was not much activity on it they could see, a few soldiers here and there, some walking across, others standing and looking down at the water. "What the hell's going on?" Morris said. "Nothing's moving. You would think something would be moving across the bridge. Let's get out there and have a look."

The defensive positions guarding their end of the approach to the bridge did not seem like much, slit trenches and a machine gun pit, soldiers brewing tea. No one paid them any attention. The bridge was long, 1,650 feet from one end to the other. Because it rose gradually from where they stood, they could not see to the far end. After walking a hundred feet or so, they could see work parties ahead, struggling with something.

"There's your problem," Morris said. When Harry raised an eyebrow at him he added, "We're walking on it."

"What do you mean?" Harry asked.

"This is a railroad bridge. It's not usable for truck traffic. Do you see what those guys up ahead are doing? They're laying sleepers alongside the rails, making a deck for the trucks to drive on, a wooden road." Harry realized then that they had been walking by railroad ties stacked along each side of the bridge. "At least it looks like they're getting near the end of their job."

They reached the first of the work parties and Morris went up to a young British officer. "How long will this take?"

"Not long, sir. We expect to have the lorries moving across before dark." He looked them over. "I'd be careful," he said. "You can't get much beyond here without being in range of Jap snipers. They also drop an occasional mortar on us. Might I ask the nature of your business, sir?"

"American observers," Morris said, "Lend-Lease and all that."

The officer smiled. "Lieutenant Gordon." He held out his hand.

There was something about Morris and his ways that the British took to. Harry did not know what it was, nor did he particularly care, but tonight it got them a place to pitch their tent, a warm meal and some friendly chat.

The British officers here were of another sort. Officers of the British Indian Army, they commanded Indian troops and spent their careers in India, far from British Army Headquarters. They had a grip on the local realities. They spoke highly of their troops, complained little and said nothing about a high command they did not understand. The only complaint Harry heard was that their battalions had been "milked" of experienced officers, who had been sent off to replace British losses in the Middle East campaigns. Lieutenant Gordon promised them a tour of the bridge and the east bank in the morning. As Gordon had predicted, the first trucks started moving across the bridge at nightfall. The British withdrawal across the Sittang was now underway.

Harry awoke with the dawn. Everyone else had been up a while, including Morris who stood nearby with a tin cup of tea. It was quiet now. He could hear cocks crowing, and in the distance the clatter of a machine gun. It took Harry a while to realize that the truck engines he had fallen asleep listening to were quiet now. He and Morris walked to the mess tent, where they found biscuits and things floating in gravy that Morris thought were lentils. They decided to leave their own tent up. From what Gordon had told them, it was not likely they would get far beyond the bridge on the east bank, if they got across the bridge at all. They started toward the bridge and met Gordon on the way.

"We have a bit of a problem," Gordon said, when Harry asked why no trucks were moving. "A lorry came off the sleepers and got wedged crosswise on the bridge. It's jammed in the girders and they can't tip it into the river. The sappers will have to practically disassemble it. It may take hours."

Morris put on a dark, disappointed look. "But, come along," Gordon said. "We can walk around it. We'll have to be careful as we get near the far end."

Harry and Morris walked across the bridge on either side of Gordon, who might have been taking a stroll across London Bridge. He chatted on about temples he had seen and ancient buddhas he had examined as his brigade retreated from Moulmein. Gordon's war sounded like a temple tour.

"As we get nearer the end of the bridge, you'll get a better look at the two hills just beyond. The nearest has a pagoda on it. We've named it Pagoda Hill, of course. The other has a huge gilt Buddha. You'll see the Buddha glinting in the sun. That's become Buddha Hill to us. The Japs got up on the two hills yesterday. They command the approaches to the bridge from there. It's damned awkward. Some of our chaps will try to clear them later this morning. It should be a good show. I hope you get to see some of it."

An Indian trooper ran toward them. "Careful, sir. Careful, sir. Machine gun." He pointed to the end of the bridge.

Gordon stepped to the edge of the bridge and looked out over the river to the hills. "Look, chaps," he said, "you can see Pagoda Hill and Buddha Hill right over there. The machine gun that has us ranged in is on Pagoda hill. We can watch the attack from here. If it's successful, we may be able to stroll along the east bank afterwards."

"Why not?" Morris said, and sat down to wait, dangling his feet over the side of the bridge.

It was not long before flashes on the hill and puffs of smoke signaled the beginning of the British attack. They could hear the sound of big guns firing from somewhere well beyond the far end of the bridge. "Our mountain guns, 19-pound howitzers," Gordon said. The shelling went on for 20 minutes, until there were clouds of smoke drifting across both hills. Silence came suddenly, but lasted only seconds before machine guns started to chatter. Above the gunfire they heard the shouts of men. "Our Gurkhas," Gordon said. "They're going in with bayonets and *kukris*."

They could hear it, but see little of what was happening. Occasionally, if they concentrated on a clearing in the jungle that covered the hills, they might see men rush across it, and sometimes fall. It went on for a long time before there was silence again, this time punctuated only by an occasional rife shot or short burst from a machine gun.

"Our chaps seem to be cleaning up," Gordon said. "I think we can go on now."

They walked to the end of the bridge to where a small party manned the positions guarding it. Beyond they saw a line of trucks that stretched into the distance. They had been standing here for hours, delayed by the truck wedged on the bridge. Several trucks were burning, men standing some distance off, watching. Others showed damage from the machine guns and mortars on Pagoda Hill.

Gordon stopped where two officers were trying to get the trucks moving again. To Harry and Morris he said, "Walk along the river if you like, but go south, away from Pagoda Hill. There are still Japs up there."

They walked along the river, while Gordon stood watching. "Not much to see here, Harry," Morris said. Coming from the south were small groups of soldiers walking toward the bridge. "The Gurkha attack on the hills will make a good story. I'd like to talk to some of the soldiers who were there."

They turned away from the river and walked back to Gordon, who stood with an officer whose uniform looked not as fresh as his. He had a Tommy gun slung over his shoulder. He looked weary.

"…and then the Japs stood up to surrender," he was saying as Morris and Harry walked up. "They waited for the Colonel and his Gurkhas to walk toward them, then threw themselves down. There were machine guns hidden behind them. They killed the Colonel and most of the Gurkhas."

"That's the kind of detail I like," Morris said to Harry quietly, as they walked back to the bridge. Gordon had told them to go back – it sounded like an order – while he stayed behind to talk with soldiers who kept arriving at the bridgehead. He caught up while they stood looking at what little remained of the wedged truck that had caused the first of the morning's problems. It had been literally taken apart. Most of it had been thrown in the river.

Gordon did not look happy. "The road is jammed with trucks for miles back. We have to get them moving. The Japs are very close now. They've infiltrated from the south and they're attacking."

"What happens now?" Morris asked.

Gordon looked up at the girders, and then from one end of the bridge to the other. "The sappers have wired the demolition charges. They may have to drop the bridge in the river. We can't let the Japs have it. If they get across tonight, they'll be in Rangoon tomorrow."

A machine gun started firing. It sounded near. "We'd better get over to the west bank," Gordon said. There was a lot movement on the bridge now. It seemed confused. Soldiers ran past them, going both ways. Gordon moved to make room. "We're putting more people on the bridgehead," he said, "beefing it up."

A machine gun started firing again, even closer now, and rifles joined in. There was no question it was Japanese firing on the bridge. They could hear the plink! plink! plink! of bullets striking the steel girders. Instinctively they ducked and started moving faster.

They were more than halfway across when Harry heard Morris say, "Christ, look at that." He was standing at the edge of the bridge, holding on to a girder, looking back at the far bank. Harry looked to where he pointed.

South of the bridge he could see a group of soldiers lying on the bank with the river at their backs, firing up at the jungle beyond. "No, no," Morris said, "over there." He was pointing at the bank alongside the bridge, where several Burmese families were wading out into the river.

"I thought they were trying to make the bridge, but it looks like they're going to swim for it." Several were in deep water now and started swimming, just as the machine gun opened up. Harry thought he could see the splashes where bullets hit the water near them. And then there was nothing. No Burmese walking, no Burmese swimming. Just what looked like bundles of clothing drifting in the current.

"Let's get on with it, chaps," Gordon said. "Tea will ready when we get there."

* * *

February 23, 1942
Sittang River Bridge

The Brigadier of 48 Brigade, Noel Hugh-Jones, was the officer responsible for making the decision to drop the bridge in the Sittang River if it became necessary. He was very aware of what would happen if the Japanese got the bridge intact, and he was growing more and more concerned as the Japanese attacks on the east bank grew in ferocity. .

Harry and Morris abandoned their tent for the night and found shelter on a hill that stood a distance from the bridge but overlooked it. Gordon told them to go there, and then went off to check in with his unit. Once night came, the gunfire became even more intense. From where Morris and Harry lay on their stomachs, peering into the darkness, there was nothing they could see, but flashes of rifle fire and machine gun tracers that reached across the river toward them or arced at the bridge.

After hours of this, they dozed, only to be shaken awake by an enormous explosion that was followed by another, and then yet another. Morris rolled over, hard against Harry. "Jesus Christ!" he yelled. Debris rained out of the sky. When the last fragments of steel and concrete stopped falling, there was silence, absolute silence, as if the world had been paralyzed by the shock. Across the river Harry saw the sky brightening with the coming dawn. After a while he could make out the bridge. Two spans were in the river. From somewhere beyond came the sound of voices, many voices, all Japanese, all talking at once.

After a long while, they watched Gordon climb slowly up the hill. He looked shaken. His face was ashen, his hands trembled. He sat down next to them, but seemed not to want to meet their eyes. He looked furtive, like a man with a terrible secret.

Morris tried to bring something normal back to the day. "Well," he said, "at least the Japs won't get us so easily now."

Gordon turned to look at Morris. He smiled and looked out over the river then, and the damaged bridge. He picked up what might have been a fragment of girder and threw it toward the bridge. After a while he looked at Morris again. "You are quite right, Mr. Morris,' he said. "The Japs would have a devil of a time getting us now. But I doubt they care. They've got the whole British Army over there."

Morris nodded and kept looking out over the river. It was only after a long silence that he dared to ask, "What do you mean?"

"The British Army, most of it, it's over there, on the other side of the river. You know, Mr. Morris, we have one brigade over on this side of the Sittang. But our other two brigades are over there, on the east bank. That's where the Japs are. The Japs will tear them to pieces."

"You're saying they blew the bridge with most of the British Army on the wrong side."

"That's what they did, Mr. Morris, that's what they did. They blew up the bridge too early. They cut the lifeline to our troops. Two-thirds of our army is over there, trapped on the Japanese side of the river. They won't have a chance in hell against the Japs."

CHAPTER 21

Not two-thirds of the whole British Army, Harry," Doyle said. "Only the two-thirds that was supposed to defend southern Burma." He laid the report on the table and looked up at Harry. "Ah, well, it's all the same. It's the end of things as we know them. Rangoon is finished. It's just days now. You better take Sir Louie up on his offer to fly you up to Kunming. Get yourself out of here as soon as you can."

"What about you?"

"The Consulate is making arrangements. We'll all be out of here in the next day or two. I may have to go to India first, that's where everyone else seems to be going. I may even take a bit of leave there. Then I'll see you up in Kunming."

Harry started to say something, but Doyle had not finished. He held up his hand. "Don't worry about it. I'll find you. I'll be in touch with you there."

Harry nodded. The meeting was over, their time in Rangoon ended. They sat quietly and looked around the ragged, overgrown garden that had become their regular meeting place. It didn't look much like a garden now. It was a patch of jungle again, except for an indistinct path where they had tramped their way in and out, and the bare spot around the table where Doyle periodically plucked the more menacing of the encroaching weeds. It was suddenly very sad.

"Wonder if we'll ever see this again?" Harry asked.

"Doubt it," Doyle said. "Doubt it matters. Doubt we'll remember it a week from now. We certainly won't the next time we're in Rangoon – in a dozen years, maybe. Another week and this will be a Japanese tea garden, and no one will remember the spies who once lurked here."

"Think it will be that long?"

"Before we can come back, you mean?" Doyle shrugged. "I don't know. Maybe not a dozen years, but it will be a while, a few years anyway. Well, Harry…." Doyle started to his feet..

"One other thing…," Harry said, feeling rushed now. "Do you really think I should go up to Kunming with Louie's airplane? I could probably hitch a ride with the AVG."

"Louie's the way to go, Harry. Get on him now; there's not much time. It's best for us to have Louie help you get set up in Kunming. There's no one could do it better. You'll meet a lot of people through him." Doyle looked closely at Harry's face. "You don't have a problem flying up to Kunming with Louie, do you?"

"No, of course not," Harry said, "I just thought …. Well, anyway, I'll try to see him today." It was time to change the subject. "Listen, Doyle," he said, getting to his feet and offering his hand, "it's been fun, fighting the Japs, fighting the Brits."

"We'll do it all again, Harry, in Kunming."

They shook hands. It was not much of a goodbye, nor did it seem like it had to be. Harry let Doyle exit the garden first, against the improbable chance that some passer-by might see them together. There were no passers-by now; had not been for weeks. It did not really matter; Harry wanted to sit among the weeds and think. There was no way he could have explained his problem with Louie. Christ, he had not even seen Louie in weeks. Well, maybe not that long, but not since the gratuitous shooting of the Jap spy at the warehouse. Except when he walked in on Louie, in bed, Louie entwined with Sumalee! Christ, he still could not believe he had done that! It was the most embarrassing thing he had done in his life! It must have been as embarrassing for Sumalee, and probably for Louie too. What could Louie possibly think of him now? The way he had strolled into Sumalee's bedroom – in the middle of the night! As if he knew Sue very well indeed. Or worse, that he was taking advantage of his "professional" relationship with Sue. Christ, what a mess. And now he had to get up to Kunming – on Louie's airplane, for Christ's sake. How could he possibly ask Louie that now?

In the end, it was all worry for nothing. Not 20 minutes later, driving by the Strand, he saw Lucy. She was parking her car and waved him over. "My father said to tell you that we'll be finished here in two days," she said. "He thinks it best that you fly to Kunming with us then. You can come later, of course, but things may be more difficult.

"Oh," she said, and pulled an envelope from her bag, "I almost forgot." She handed it to him. An invitation of some sort.

He was so relieved by what Lucy had said that he completely forgot the envelope. It was not until much later that evening that he opened it. It was indeed an invitation, a handsome engraved card with the crest of the Royal Air Force that invited him to the dedication of the new officers' Club at Mingaladon Airdrome. Not a complete surprise; the Brits had been working on a new club for weeks, since the original one was gutted during a Japanese bombing raid.

It was who might have sent the card that puzzled him. The few British RAF officers he knew were gone. His American pilot friends, Rector, Newkirk and the rest were back in Kunming. There was no one else he could think of. Maybe it was his growing reputation as a journalist. Little chance of that, but he would go. If the Brits were optimistic enough to open a new club as the Japs were closing in on them, he would help them dedicate it. If he could still get to Mingaladon then. The dedication was two days from now – a long time off.

The city was unraveling quickly now. Just driving anywhere was dangerous. Cars bunched up in convoys to discourage Japanese agents, Burmese nationalists, or whoever was taking potshots at them. A drive across the city was a journey on the outskirts of hell. Some part of Rangoon was always burning. Smoke was everywhere. It rose in dense black columns from the burning docks and warehouses, and drifted across the city in long dark clouds, like harbingers of an early monsoon. Streets were clogged with debris from bombing raids and from the destruction that came with the looting of long-shuttered shops and abandoned homes. Gangs roamed the city, the inmates of prisons, the insane, the lepers. All set free when their keepers fled Rangoon. It was said that the zoo animals had also been freed, and all the reptiles. And that seemed to frighten some people more than had the fall of Moulmein.

Harry was too preoccupied witnessing the sweep of history to be concerned about his own mundane drives across town, or the release of zoo animals, or the neighbors he rarely saw – until the day he no longer had neighbors. One morning he peered out over his garden wall and saw no movement in his neighborhood, no sign of life. Even the birds seemed to have fled. That was the day he took a room at the Strand. The desk clerk recognized him as a friend of "Mister Louie." "Would Sir require a suite in Mister Louie's wing?" he asked. "The floor below might be better," Harry said. The separation would make them less inclined to party, and "just a regular room would be fine". "Ah, of course," said the clerk, not really understanding. He gave Harry the key to a very ordinary room.

The Japanese Air Force had come back to Rangoon by then. More than a hundred Japanese airplanes appeared in the sky over the city on 26 February. There was little to oppose them. Nine AVG P-40s and six British aircraft went up and acquitted themselves well. Japanese airplanes fell from the sky, like ducks with broken wings, or straight into the ground like arrows. It was hard to get an exact count. No one was eager to go into the jungle to see where the Japanese airplanes fell, or to wander the rice paddies looking for them. When the Japanese returned the next day, only six AVG aircraft were fit to fly, and no British airplanes took off. Harry spent much of both days under a tree next to a shelter by the Strand. He held a book he pretended to read, but spent the time thinking, mostly about his life to come in Kunming. There were no departure instructions from Louie yet.

That was the evening he drove to the airdrome, one in a convoy of cars that had formed at the Strand. At Mingaladon, the cars dispersed to park near the new officers' club, and Harry pulled alongside a glossy black Buick. It looked brand new. The driver was just getting out, a young man with a vaguely familiar look.

"Nice car," Harry said. "Looks brand new."

"It is. I just picked it up at the Buick Agency." There was pride of ownership in his voice. They both stood back from the car to admire it. "I always liked the Buick," the man said. "Always wanted one just like that. Got lucky, I guess. The keys were in it, and no one was there."

Harry turned to look at him. "You, ah . . . just took it?"

The man shrugged. "I figured it was me today or the Japs tomorrow." His eyes met Harry's then. "You're Ross," he said, "aren't you? Harry Ross. Eddie Rector said to make sure you got the invitation." He held out his hand. I'm Paul Frillman."

"So you're AVG. I'm surprised we haven't met."

"I've seen you at the Silver Grill a couple of times, and at the cemetery recently. I did the service for Bert Christman."

"Did the service…?"

"I'm the AVG chaplain."

"Oh, the Padre," Harry said. "I've heard about you." Rector had spoken of the Padre. A good guy, he said, not your standard Holy Roller, not just a preacher, but a guy who does things that need to be done, a guy you could count on – and not above having a couple of cool ones with the guys. "Pleased to meet you," Harry said, and he meant it.

"I had to come tonight," Frillman said as they walked to the club together. "To show the AVG flag. I doubt there will be many of us here tonight."

The party was well underway. In its previous incarnation, the RAF Officers' Club was always a quiet place, almost dreary, but tonight there was no question that everyone was having a wonderful time. You could tell by the crowd of happy faces, ruddy and glistening with sweat, by the volume of noise: clinking glasses, shouting and laughter, a hundred voices speaking all at once. Strange accents: New Zealanders, South Africans, but no American voices could be heard.

"Replacements, a lot of them," Frillman commented as he looked around the room. "The New Zealanders over there are bomber pilots that got here a couple of days ago. They're already competing with the Australians and the South Africans for the most rowdy prize. The Brits don't have a chance in that contest."

"Where's the AVG?" Harry asked.

"Well," Frillman said as he looked around, "the Pandas have been replaced. They're back in Kunming. The First Squadron is here now, but the few airplanes they still have are dispersed to auxiliary fields outside the city. They're trying to hide them from the Japs. Most of the pilots are living out in the boondocks near their airplanes. A few of the guys are still in town, and they'll probably show up here tonight. Mostly, the AVG is just tired, the pilots and everybody else."

They pushed through the crowd to the new long bar, then stood back to admire it, a highly polished dark beauty with a shiny brass rail. An RAF officer proudly told them, "We had a dozen little Burmese buggers polish the teak for two weeks. Then we had two RAF engineers brighten up the brass. Had to use the RAF for the brass. Can't trust the local buggers to do the fine work."

A big portion of the crowd at the bar suddenly shifted to the piano and left them some room. They sipped their drinks and Frillman turned to one of the British officers still at the bar. "Well, hello, Denny," he said, "Seems a bit silly, this dedication. The Jap Air Force will be drinking here in a couple of days."

Denny smiled a toothy smile. "You Americans are always getting the wind up," he said. "You mustn't worry. The Japs won't be getting anywhere near here for a long time yet. We'll still be here in June to celebrate your… what do you call it, Independence Day?"

"Freedom from British Empire Day," Frillman corrected. "And it's in July, not June."

"Ah, well, July then. The RAF will be here." He raised his drink. "Cheers!"

Voices around them were growing louder, trying to be heard over the boisterous singing from the group at the piano. A handful of AVG pilots finally appeared, and Frillman introduced them. They looked tired. A familiar face or two among them, but no one Harry really knew. One was Squadron Leader Bob Neale, who had replaced Jack Newkirk as the AVG Commander in Rangoon. They got their drinks and looked for seats, and seemed not much interested in talk, except for Neale who sought out the senior British officers.

Harry was not in a talking mood either. Looking for the W.C., he came across a small group of journalists huddled in a remote corner, discussing travel plans. Off to the side, sitting by himself and staring into his drink was his recent travel companion, Morris.

"Morris! You're still here. I thought you had fled Rangoon."

"Oh, hi, Harry. Tomorrow, maybe tomorrow. A couple British ships are evacuating civilians to India. That's not where I want to go, but I don't have much choice. I don't have priority to go by air."

"What about the truck convoys driving up to Kunming over the Burma Road?"

"I don't know," Morris shrugged. "I hear the Japs have already cut the road. I would rather drive if I could."

"Good luck," Harry told him. The whiskey made him sleepy. He was ready to go home to the Strand. He went off to tell the Padre he was leaving. When he found him, Frillman said there was no need to drive back to the city tonight. There were a lot of empty bunks at the airdrome. He would be sleeping here, as would many of the others.

* * *

A great roar jolted Harry out of a sound sleep. An airplane went by his window. He bolted out of his bunk before remembering he was still at Mingaladon. Another airplane roared by. They were taking off. His watch said it was 4:00 a.m. He stumbled to the window and watched a long line of trucks driving by. British trucks with RAF markings. This was not an hour for the Brits to be doing anything. Over the engine noise came the sound of voices, loud, agitated.

"What the hell's going on?"

No answer for a while, then a shout. "Fucking RAF is pulling out!"

"Can't be!"

"Fucking is! That's them there. Leaving!"

"No one said they were going."

"They're gone! Look! The Brits are all gone."

"They wouldn't pull out without telling us. Even Brits wouldn't do that."

But the Brits did. Harry got out on the tarmac, out where the AVG had gathered. One of the crew chiefs walked up to Squadron Leader Neale. "They're gone, all right. The RAF is gone. 'Dispersing' they said, to airfields up north. They took everything, all their air-warning equipment. What they called the 'radar'."

A crewman nearby said, "That 'radar', it never amounted to shit. We never got more than a couple of minutes' warning from it." After a pause he said, "But now we'll get nothing."

Bob Neale shook his head. "All right, bitching about it isn't going to help us." He turned to Frillman. "Get everybody together. We need to start moving."

Almost all the AVG were already there, so it took Frillman only minutes to round up the strays. Altogether there were maybe two dozen. They stood and looked at Bob Neale. Neale finally nodded at them and started talking. "By now you all know that the Brits have left," he said. "It puts us in a bad position. Without the British 'radar', we're sitting ducks. The Japs will be on us before we know it. We have to get out of here – as soon as we can. The pilots who still have working airplanes will fly out. Everybody else will go by road. And that means we need to move quickly. The Japs are 20 miles away. They could cut the road anytime. So let's go! Let's get the trucks loaded. Frillman here will take the first bunch that's ready. He'll take the first convoy."

Frillman looked at Neale in surprise. "I'm the chaplain," he said. "I'm not taking any convoy anywhere."

"Sorry, Padre," Neale said, "It's the Old Man's idea." He pulled a small sheet of paper from a pocket and pushed it at Frillman. "A radio message from Chennault. We got it this morning." He looked down at it and read it aloud. "The Old Man says quote: 'Convoys start this morning. Frillman takes the first one'." He held the message out to Frillman.

Frillman glanced at it. He shrugged. "The Lord's Word," he said, "I guess we go." He caught Harry's eye and winked. "Now I know why the Lord put that Buick out in front of me. That convoy will be led in style."

"What about the road out of town?" a crewmen at the back of the crowd shouted at Neale. "We heard it's been cut."

"Our information says it's still open. When you guys get rolling, our P-40s will be sweeping the road ahead of you. The pilots will keep an eye on you until you're past the Jap areas. But we've got to move. Let's do it!"

There was a great deal of bustle, men running every which way. Harry backed up against the hangar to avoid being run over. Everybody's leaving, he thought. And I'm standing here. Today was the day Louie was supposed to leave. Or was it yesterday? Harry started for his car. He needed to get back to the Strand and find Louie or Lucy or somebody.

"Harry!" Lucy was running toward him. "We've been looking for you. Peter is still at the Strand in case you came there. Louie said you would be here. We're leaving as soon as our airplane arrives. Are there things at the hotel that you need?"

"There's nothing there I need. I'm ready. "

* * *

"Here, Harry, take this," Louie said, handing him a glass of whiskey. "You see the river over there? Can you see our warehouse?" Rangoon was falling behind them as the DC-3 climbed. The city was burning. Anything of value to the Japs was being destroyed by British demolition teams. The docks were blanketed by thick black smoke, but he could still make out Louie's warehouse easily. "Your warehouse is not burning," he said.

"Can't afford to burn it," Louie said. "I'll need it. We'll be back."

That made Harry want to laugh, but he took a big swallow of whiskey instead. The whiskey would make it easier, put everything in perspective. He sat back and tried to relax. He watched Louie move through the cabin being generous with his bottle of whiskey. All the seats were full, taken by Louie's minions or hangers-on, and Louie poured generous measures of whiskey for all. It brought an air of holiday cheer to their departure. He turned to look at Lucy across the aisle. She was looking out the window. She seemed sad, lost in her own thoughts. He watched her for a while, when a thought suddenly struck him. He leaned over to her.

"Where's Sumalee?"

"In Kunming," Lucy said. With a sly smile, added, "Waiting for you."

CHAPTER 22

Harry! Welcome to China!" Louie's words pulled him out of a comforting sleep. "That's the Salween River down there," Louie said, pointing out the window. "We're crossing it now. Harry looked down at gnarled hills and finally made it out, a black ribbon twisting through the hills, almost buried in them.

"We're in China. Burma's behind us."

Burma was behind them now, in more ways then one. For an hour Burma had been an undulating dark green sea of jungle passing beneath them. From the airplane, the land looked flat for a long time before it gradually turned into hills, but still stayed green. In time the hills got higher and seemed to lose their color, to dry out and turn drab brown. Harry looked out the window and tried to follow the twists of the Salween while Louie talked.

"You can't really make it out from up here, but it's a tough place. The gorge the river flows through is hundreds of feet deep. It can't be crossed easily. Over there, to the left, is the bridge. You can just make it out. It's the only bridge for a hundred miles. It carries the Burma Road across the river and into China."

A uniformed Chinese crewman interrupted, handed Louie a slip of paper, a message form with a vertical line of Chinese characters. "Hmmm," Louie said as he read it. He turned to Harry. "Change in plans," he said. "I won't be going out to the villa tonight. The Generalissimo has invited me to dinner. He wants an update on Rangoon. You might want to stay in Kunming this evening. We have a flat in town. It's Lucy's really. She's planning to stay there a few days. It's quite nice, convenient to the fancy shops." He turned to Lucy then. "I thought Harry might like staying with you tonight. I'll be staying in town for dinner. "

She looked pleased. "Oh, Harry, stay at the apartment. There's lots of room."

Louie turned back to Harry. "Lucy will make it nice for you. The girls will be able to show you around town, get you oriented. When you get bored with that, you can move out to the villa. It's a bit out of town, but you'll have a car to use." They might have been going on a holiday. Did Louie say "the girls" would be able to show him around town? That meant Lucy and….

They touched down at dusk. As they taxied in, Harry got glimpses of AVG P-40s scattered about the field. Several near the end of the runway, probably standing alert, others in sheds, cowlings off, men working under shielded lights. Chinese soldiers, many of them, standing around, and coolies, all in what looked like blue pajamas.

The airplane rolled to a stop. From the window, Harry watched a half-dozen cars pull alongside, shiny black sedans, like Frillman's, but not Buicks, at least not the first one. Harry recognized it from photographs, had seen one or two in New York, a Cadillac V-16 Fleetwood limousine, with a spare wheel mounted on each front fender and an open chauffeur's compartment. Kind of flashy, even for Louie, he thought. Maybe the Generalissimo sent it. The other cars were garden-variety Cadillac sedans.

The stairs were rolled up and Louie was the first out. "Come on, Harry," he said. Cool air had been seeping into the cabin, and the air was cold where Harry paused at the top of the stairs. Rangoon was sweltering, but at its 6,000 feet, Kunming was experiencing late winter. He looked at the mountains not so far away, and thought he saw snow. Louie saw him shiver. "There are clothes in the apartment," he said. "Lucy will outfit you."

Louie took his arm, and then Lucy's, and walked them to the second car in line. "Harry, I hope you don't mind the diversion to the flat," he said, holding the door. "I think you'll enjoy it." When Harry and Lucy were both in, Louie closed the door, but stood by while the others from the C-47 sorted themselves out among the waiting vehicles. When everyone was settled, Louie tapped on the door, gave Harry a small salute, and walked to the first car in line. Peter waited there, holding the door.

The six cars pulled out together, a small convoy to make it easier to get through the checkpoints. There were salutes, and many rifles were raised in their honor by Chinese soldiers lining the road. It was almost dark now, and like Rangoon, the only lights were the dim slits on painted-over headlights. Louie's car turned off, and when Harry looked back, he saw the others had gone their own way as well. They were alone.

"There won't be much to see tonight," Lucy said, "I'll take you around town tomorrow." Bumping through the darkness, Harry lost all sense of time, but it did not seem to take very long to get to the apartment. They stopped at a building, just another shadow in the darkness. Closer, it seemed sizable, four stories tall. Its edges were rounded; a modern form set into the side of a small hill.

"From photos I've seen of Kunming, I was expecting shop houses," he said to Lucy.

"Oh, there are a lot of those," she said, "but this is Louie. He built this place about a year ago. He brought an architect from London, but in the end designed it himself. He didn't want a villa in town. The idea of living anonymously in a flat appealed to him. So he did this. It's quite nice. You'll see."

The building was set back from the street; the entrance recessed in a curved wall. The two main doors might have been glass, but were covered now with canvas and only the edges of silvered frames showed. Inside was total blackness once the doors closed behind them. But only for a moment, then light engulfed them.

They stood in a spacious lobby. Heavy blackout curtains kept the smallest glimmer of light from falling outside. Everything was new and very modern-looking. The walls were long graceful curves of highly polished light-hued wood that contrasted with black lacquer tables and chairs that stood on shiny metal legs. Directly across, a pair of silver panthers arched across black lacquered doors, the entry to the lift. Three Chinese ladies stood there, in slim black dresses like uniforms. They bowed then, and in a single voice said, "Good evening, Miss Lucy." They must practice that, Harry thought.

"Good evening, ladies." Lucy returned the bow. "Thank you for waiting." The three ladies giggled in unison.

The lift had ebony walls and silver-framed mirrors. The control panel was silver, with amber buttons that glowed softly when you touched them. When they reached their floor – the top floor, Lucy said – an older Chinese man waited by an open door across from the lift. He was dressed like an English butler.

"Butler Chen." Lucy said. He inclined his head to Harry.

In Harry's mind, living spaces in China's cities were cramped. It was not so here. The flat was huge, what he could see of it: the main room and the hallways that extended out from it. The entire far wall was a graceful double curve shielded by draped blackout curtains. "Is that all window?" he asked. "The view must be magnificent."

"You can see a bit of Kunming from here, the nicer part of it," Lucy said, and to Butler Chen she added something in Chinese. He switched off the light and pulled aside a small section of blackout curtain so Harry could look out. As his eyes adjusted he could make out dark shadows against a lighter background, the tops of trees silhouetted against the sky. Below, all was black, flat black except where a few places were shiny black, reflecting light from the few stars that poked through the clouds.

"What am I looking at?" he asked, "The shiny areas there."

"It's the lake, where you can see it through the trees. Green Lake, Jade Green Lake."

He thought of a map. "Not the huge lake on the edge of Kunming?"

"No, not that one. That's lake Kunming. What you see is a small lake, right in the city. Green Lake. It's very pretty. It's surrounded by a park. You'll see it tomorrow." When they moved from the window and the lights came back on, she said, "Come, I'll show you your room."

That was when Sue walked in. She looked like a vision, tall, imperial, beautiful. She wore a white robe, not Chinese, but something a guest might find in the dressing room of a grand hotel in Europe.

"Harry!" she said, and looked as surprised as he was. "I knew you were coming to Kunming, but I wasn't expecting to see you tonight!" She came to him and pressed herself against him. He gave her what he intended to be just a friendly hug. He realized he was very happy to see her.

Lucy left them then, and for a while he and Sue sat close together on a lounge. Harry told her of his last days in Rangoon. She told him about her first days in Kunming: How primitive the city was! There were no decent shops now, not since the war started. Before that, while the French in Indochina still came here on holiday, things were not quite so bad. There were good dress shops then, with wonderful things that came all the way from Paris, or at least the fashions did even if some of the sewing was done right here. And pre-war there were certainly good French restaurants, and shops where you could buy the delicacies of Paris in a can – the tin can, a wonderful invention of the French mind. But now the French lived in Hanoi under Japanese rule, and never came here. Forbidden to ride their own railroad to Kunming! Imagine that! What a pity. Kunming had become a backwater. Compared to Rangoon, Kunming was provincial, dirty and disorderly. It was no longer a nice place to live. She shuddered and looked around the big beautiful room. "Thank God Louie thought ahead." She sighed.

Lucy reappeared to announce that Butler Chen would serve a light dinner. "I've asked Chen to do French," she said, looking at Sue. "Louie would want Harry to start his life here with the cuisine of old Kunming."

"French food is the cuisine of old Kunming?" Harry asked.

"Louie thinks it is," Lucy said. She showed him where he could wash up. When he returned, the table was set.

"Fish soup," Lucy said, "with fresh fish from our lake."

"Bouillabaisse," Sue corrected.

Next, a lobster salad in mayonnaise. "Louie's favorite," Lucy said. "Lobster St. Jacques."

"Lobster St. Jacques?" Harry repeated it as a question.

"That's what Louie calls it. He first had it at Cap St. Jacques, the Vietnamese resort, near Saigon."

"Ah," Harry said, as if he knew, but he had no idea where Cap St. Jacques was. He would have to ask Louie some time, or Sue. But not tonight.

The final course was "Not Peking duck, but duck a l'orange." For dessert there was a choice: "Crepes Kunming," which Lucy described as "swimming in a peculiar-tasting local rice liquor. It makes your insides burn," or "a simple chocolate mousse." Ah, the mousse, but before Harry could choose, Lucy told him, "I've ordered the Crepes Kunming for you. I'm sure that's what Louie would want."

Harry finished the meal relaxed, totally relaxed. It had been a great meal, even the crepes proved edible, and it had been a long day – and there was a bottle of cognac on the table from which Sue refilled his glass whenever he sipped from it.

"That was the best meal I've had in months," he said. "It makes it hard to believe there's a war on."

"The war has moved on," Lucy said. "The Japanese bombers don't come here any more, thanks to your AVG friends. You will have to go see them, maybe tomorrow."

Sue yawned elaborately. "Such a long day," she said. "All this cold weather.... I think I'm ready for bed."

Lucy looked at Harry, saw his eyelids droop. "I think we all are. Come, Harry, I'll show you your room."

She took him down a hallway. "This is your room," she said, opening a door. When Harry looked down the hall, she added, "That's Louie's room. The library is over there, then Louie's office. Beyond is my room, and past that is Sue's." She looked at Butler Chen waiting in the hallway. "If you need anything, ask Butler Chen."

Butler Chen laid out a pair of Louie's pajamas, and hovered until Harry dismissed him. It was only then that Harry felt comfortable enough to take a good look around. It was not just a room, but a small suite. There was a bathroom, quite sizable, with a small dressing room attached. Best of all, there was a small alcove across from his bed that could be used as sitting room or a small dining area. It had windows on three sides that probably looked out on the park. He would wait until morning to find out. This is really nice, he thought, and silently blessed Doyle for pushing him to have Louie bring him here. It had been a long day; he was tired now. A quick bath and then bed.

He had just put his head on the pillow, it seemed, when he heard a sharp 'click, click', like a door being opened. He must have been asleep; for a moment he thought he was back at Mingaladon. It was too quiet for that. But someone was in the room with him.

"Harry, are you awake?" she whispered.

"Sue?" He could see nothing. The blackout curtains kept out even starlight. It was totally dark.

"I hope I'm not disturbing you, Harry." Her voice came from across the room, where the small alcove was. A rustling of fabric, a small thin opening appeared where she drew back the edge of the blackout curtain. Light from a few insignificant stars filtered in and the darkness was no longer as intense as it had been.

She came alongside the bed. He could make out her form, and reached for it. She was wearing something very soft, a nightdress, he guessed. He felt her put a knee on the bed, and then bring her other leg across. She was kneeling over him now, straddling him. He reached up and felt only warm skin. With his finger he traced the contour of her belly. Her nightdress was gone. She lowered her hips to his and moved them slowly across him.

"Sue, Lucy will hear us."

"She won't," she spoke as quietly as he had. "And if she does, she won't care."

"What about Louie?"

"She won't tell him."

"That's not what I meant." He put both hands on her waist to hold her still. "Listen Sue, we need to talk. About Louie."

She leaned forward and put her mouth on his, her lips warm and moist. She drew back and started moving her hips again. "Don't worry about Louie," she said. "Don't think about him. Not tonight. Think about me. Think about me. Think only about me."

And for the next hours it was all that Harry could do. He was totally focused on the sensations that her smooth, firm body brought him as she moved it against his. In the darkness he could not see what her hands were doing, or how her body moved, but he saw her in his mind and that increased the intensity of what he felt. He lost all sense of time and place.

There was nothing but his sense of touch, nothing but pure sensation. It was near morning when he fell into a dreamless sleep.

The smell of coffee awoke him, and the gentle scent of warm croissants laid out on the small table in the alcove. The curtains were drawn from the window. He sat up. There was no sign of Sue, just Butler Chen walking back toward the door. "It's eight o'clock, Mr. Harry," he said in good English. "Miss Lucy wished to know when you were awake."

"Please tell her I'm awake now."

He put on the robe laid out for him. He wore nothing underneath. The pajamas he had worn to bed had disappeared with Sue's arrival. He had just tasted the coffee when there was a gentle knock on the door. "Yes?" he said, thinking Chen had returned, but it was Lucy who walked in.

"Good morning," she said. "Did you have a good night?"

"Very good," he said, and looked away from her. His neck burned with guilt. "I feel like a guest in one of the grand hotels," he said. "I like the view." He looked toward the window where he could see a panorama of Green Lake and the park around it. When Lucy looked there, his eyes quickly swept the room, hoping not to see Sue's nightdress draped over a chair. But nothing incriminating had been left behind; even the bed looked orderly. He relaxed. "The coffee is wonderful," he said, raising the cup. "Did Louie have it sent from Paris?"

"It's the cook who gets it. He worked for a French restaurant here, when the French still came here on holiday. I think Sue plans to take you out and show you some things. You'll need clothes. I've picked out some of Louie's. Butler Chen will bring them. You can ask him for anything else you need."

That made him feel even more grateful. And added to the weight of his guilt. "I don't know how to thank you – and Louie. God, I live in his house, I wear his clothes. I'm starting to feel like his son."

Lucy frowned. "You mustn't say that, Harry. Louie would be very disappointed." She saw that he did not understand. "He's fond of you," she said, "but not like a son. He looks on you as a friend. You must treat him that way. Treat him as an equal."

"Treat Louie as an equal! How do I do that?"

"Treat him as a friend, not as a …," she looked for a word, "benefactor."

He reached for her, started to pull her to him. He felt no resistance. He let her go. Jesus, he thought, she was like his sister, but that would not be a wise thing to say to her. If Sue wasn't so easy…. God, what a terrible thing to think. How could he think that?

"Lucy," he said, not sure how to continue, and moments passed. Finally, he said, "I think I understand. Louie is my friend. I'll do more to show it."

It was mid-morning when Sue walked him the short distance to Green Lake. The park was full of people. "Young people come here at night," she told him, "but in the morning the park is like the garden of an old people's home, where the inmates can exercise, practice dance steps, meet friends."

There were people doing all of that, and more. Classical singers whined to the screech of strange stringed instruments. Vendors sold tea, hot buns, and rice gruel from pushcarts. Harry could have spent the morning watching, but Sue wanted him to see the shops, the vestiges of the former French presence.

A rickshaw took them to a tree-lined street where the shops looked worn but modern, if not quite French. Chinese shop girls wore frocks and hair cut short in the European fashion. The shops were few; the street short, bordered on one end by old Chinese shop houses, on the other by an open air market. Business at both ends was brisk, loud and raucous. Harry wanted to investigate, but Lucy was expecting them for lunch.

"Ah," Lucy said, "I'm glad you're back, Harry. Louie telephoned. There's a dinner tonight you must attend, a chance to meet people. Oh, and there's someone here to meet you."

She walked down the hall to Louie's office. A stocky man seated in a leather chair stubbed out a cigarette as Lucy opened the door, then waved at smoke that hung like a curtain in front of his face. He was coarse-featured, his hair trimmed to short bristles. Probably Louie's age, but he looked much older. If asked to guess the man's occupation, Harry would have said, "gangster." He would not have been far off.

He was Louie's special assistant, Lucy said. He would drive Harry to dinner. His name sounded like "Charlie."

"Good to meet you, Charlie," Harry said.

"Cha Lee," the man corrected him, pronouncing it properly, with drawn-out vowels. "Friends call me Shanghai Cha Lee." He added, "You too call me Shanghai Cha Lee."

"Shanghai Cha Lee. Do I have it right?" Harry held out his hand. Cha Lee took it and smiled. He seemed satisfied.

"Mister Shanghai Cha Lee will see you get to the dinner," Lucy said. "But we'll have to find you something to wear."

As they poked through Louie's wardrobe, Harry asked, "What exactly does Cha Lee do?"

"Whatever Louie wants. He's like an aide-de-camp."

"Like Peter in Rangoon?"

"More than that. Louie and Cha Lee started out together in Shanghai many years ago. He'll take good care of you."

And Cha Lee did. He drove them in a Ford sedan, a recent model that was worn and scruffy-looking. Harry thought they were headed toward Lake Kunming on the edge of the city, but before they got to where they could actually see the lake, Cha Lee turned into a large compound, a military installation of some kind. Soldiers manning the gate recognized Cha Lee and raised the barrier quickly. Cha Lee parked next to a large gymnasium-like building.

Inside, a hundred round tables were set up, ten rows of ten. Twelve chairs at each table were occupied by men already eating the food. Cha Lee made for one side of the room and went down the rows to where two chairs were vacant. He gestured for Harry to sit, and from a bag he had carried in, took two bottles of premium scotch whiskey and two of five-star cognac. "Chinese whiskey no good," he explained as he filled a water glass with whiskey for Harry, then gestured to the others at the table to help themselves. Their table was suddenly a very friendly place.

Louie walked up just then. "Harry, I'm glad you made it. I've got to sit with the chaps up front. Cha Lee will take care of you. I'll introduce you around later." Harry watched him walk back to the head table. Everyone there was in uniform, colonels, generals, field marshals, whatever. Only Louie and one other man looked like civilians.

There was almost no conversation among the guests; everyone just ate and drank until the speeches started. Harry tried to follow what was going on, but even with Cha Lee's help he could not. There were occasional burst of clapping, a bit of laughter, and even a few cheers. Each of the half-dozen speeches ended with a toast. Harry stood with the rest of them, raised his glass, touched it to his lips. He had replaced the whiskey with water, knowing many toasts were coming.

The tables were cleared then and set with bowls of fruit, and the guests at the head table rose and started moving through the room amidst shouts of "*gambai, gambai*," as glasses were upended.

The other man at the head table, who like Louie was not in uniform, stepped up to Harry's table. Cha Lee got to his feet immediately, bowed deeply, and cocked his head to listen when the man spoke. Just then a small man, also in civilian clothes, came up behind Harry.

"I'm Eddie Liu, the General's translator," he said to Harry in reasonably good English. "The General would like to welcome you to China. He would like you to *gambai* with him."

Cha Lee picked up Harry's glass, poured the water in it into a fruit bowl, and filled it to the rim with cognac. The General already had his glass in hand. He clicked it with Harry's and said, "*Gambai.*"

"*Gambai! Gambai!* " others at the table shouted.

Harry took a swallow of cognac, a big one, but when he went to set his glass down, he could not. Cha Lee had a finger on the glass's bottom and kept it pressed to Harry's mouth – smiling and nodding at Harry all the while. "*Gambai, gambai,*" he said. "Drink down, drink down."

Harry had no choice. He swallowed and swallowed and drank all the cognac that did not run down his chin.

"Very good! Very good!" Eddie Lou shouted.

The General laughed. The guests at the table and others nearby clapped.

Two other generals, or field marshals, or whatever they were, came by and Harry had to repeat the performance. Now that he knew what would happen, he took charge of his glass. He made sure there was no more than a finger or two of cognac in it.

Eventually Louie came by. He saw the cognac-stunned look on Harry's face and said, "Come on, let's go outside for a bit." They went and stood outside the door. Inside they could hear the toasts continuing.

Louie looked him over and laughed. "Cognac can be a shock to the system if you're not expecting it. But at least you met Tai Li."

"I met everyone," Harry said, woozy and only half-listening. "Which was Tai Li?"

"Stocky chap in civilian clothes. The first one you *gambaied* with."

"Ah, yes. He was with Eddie the interpreter. He's the one who started it all. So who is Tai Li?"

"The Director of the Bureau of Investigation and Statistics, a man you must know."

Harry swayed as he thought about it. "Ha," he said, "he sounds like a huge bureaucrat."

Louie smiled. "He's the Chief of the Secret Police, actually, and of Chiang's Intelligence Service. He has agents everywhere. Claims tens of thousands of them, all around the world. Wherever there are Chinese. And he probably does. There's no one quite like him."

Harry considered this. "Really?" It seemed amusing. Tai Li the Spymaster. He thought about it; he had heard the name. Doyle had invoked it at least once. Ah, yes, one of his "espionage" instructors had spoken of "Tai Li". He remembered now. "A scoundrel," the instructor had called him. "A warlord, an unsavory thug, an opium lord, a thief!" It was all coming back to him now. He almost laughed aloud when he remembered the best epithet of all: "A man reputed to have killed his own mother."

"My God," Harry said. Maybe it was not so funny. "So that was Tai Li? I have heard of him. The man is ..." It took him another moment to find the right word. "... a legend."

"He is a legend," Louie agreed. "The man who can't be killed. At least that's what they say, those who have tried." Louie chuckled when he said that.

"Are there many of those?" Harry asked, quite seriously.

"Oh, quite a few," Louie said. "But...," Louie paused to wave a finger in Harry's face. "Tai Li is the man you must know if you want anything done in China."

"Right," Harry said. He held up one of his fingers and waved it at Louie. "Tai Li is the number one. The man I must know. You see, Louie, I'm learning."

"You are learning, and that's important, because now that he's met you, Tai Li will remember you."

"I'll certainly remember meeting him; he's a legend. But why would he remember me?"

"Because he does; Tai Li remembers everyone – at least everyone who could be of use to him. It's part of his charm."

Louie was still smiling, but Harry was not. To be remembered by Tai Li – it sounded like a threat.

CHAPTER 23

She found him in the bird and flower market. It was easy enough to do. He was the only American there not wearing a uniform or something that resembled a uniform. The uniformed Americans were poking through the stalls, looking at the birds in the cages, at cheap ceramics, at carvings of wood and stone, at ancient things that were not really as old as they looked, although you would never know it. One American was playing a bamboo flute, but not very well.

"Harry." His name came above the wavering wail of the flute. He turned – and found himself looking right into her face. He was surprised she remembered his name. He recalled hers – after a long anxious moment – once he remembered who she was. She looked older than he remembered, and not as exotic as that first time they met. Months had passed since then, and he had a familiarity with Asia now that made him more comfortable with exotic beauty.

"Olga," he said when he remembered. "Olga Greenlaw. You've moved from Toungoo."

"We had to, it was way back in December." She gave his face a long searching look. "But you can't have been here very long. Jack Newkirk has spoken of you. We have a Kunming chapter of the "Greenlaw Hotel" now, and Jack comes by regularly. And Eddie Rector has talked about you, and some of the others. They told me how you were a party boy in Rangoon, and gave them that wonderful New Year's party."

"You're well informed," he said.

"The boys come and talk to me. You'll have to come by. Do you have a car? I'll show you where it is." She searched in her bag and found some paper.

"Have you been at the hostel," she asked, "where the boys are staying?"

She drew a small map. "There," she said, tapping the map with her pencil. "That's where we are. And the hostel is right here. It's a big place, conspicuous, you'll find it easily. You have no excuse now, not to see your friends."

* * *

He told Olga that he would come by to see her soon, but it was really the AVG hostel he wanted to visit. He drove a gray Ford sedan that Louie had loaned him and found the place as easily as Olga said he would. It was an imposing building, the largest in the area. It had been the administration building of an agricultural college and had a red-tiled Chinese roof with upturned eaves. A half-dozen long stone steps led to a landing where four tall columns flanked the wide entrance.

He parked and started up the steps just as Chennault came out of the building. The Old Man was in a rush, heading for a staff car just pulling up, but he stopped and held out his hand. "Ross, good to see you," he said. "We'll talk when I can get some time." As he turned away, he said over his shoulder, "See Jack Newkirk."

"Yes, sir," Harry said. "I will." Chennault was already in the car.

Inside, the building was bright with fresh paint, like a newly renovated college dorm. Two men in sweat shirts and khakis stood talking at the bottom of the stairs. He asked where he might find Ed Rector. He had telephoned him to say he was coming.

"Upstairs," one said, "the pilots' bar, at the end of the hall."

He went up the stairs and turned down the hallway. Where doors were open he could see rooms that were spacious and bright. The bar was easy to find; he just followed the laughter. There were a half-dozen pilots inside and someone had just told a joke. Rector sat at the well-stocked bar, the others at a card table.

"Harry," Rector said, getting off the stool. "Glad you could get over here."

They started to talk, trying to bring each other up to date, when Harry heard his name spoken. Jack Newkirk stood in the doorway. "I thought I saw you walk by," Newkirk said. "When you have a minute, I'm down the hall."

"I'll come now, Jack," Harry said, and to Rector, "Back in a couple of minutes." He and Newkirk walked down the hall to a small room that was half bedroom, half office.

"I heard you had made it to Kunming," Newkirk said. "I saw you on the steps with the Old Man. He wanted me to take something up with you."

Newkirk paused then, invited Harry to sit, and took the chair across from him. He looked uncomfortable, as though not sure how to proceed.

"Look," he said suddenly, jumping right into the murky water, speaking quickly. "I don't know how this fits in with what you're doing, but …we need intelligence. We need to know what the Jap Air Force is doing in Thailand. We know where their bases are, but we don't know where they keep their airplanes on a given day. Now that most of the AVG has been pulled back to China, our P-40s don't have the range to fly over the Jap bases in Thailand, so we can't confirm where their airplanes are. In recent days they've been clobbering what we have left in Burma. We think they're doing that from north Thailand, from Chiang Mai, but we're not absolutely sure. Frankly, Harry – between you and me – if we know for sure where we can catch the Jap airplanes on the ground, we can hit them, hit them really hard!"

Harry listened, carefully, even as it became obvious that what Newkirk wanted was well beyond his capabilities – even if Doyle were here, and even if Doyle could go directly to Donovan. He did not see how it could be done, but he could not tell Newkirk that. Instead he said, "I'm not sure we have the means right now, Jack, but tell me exactly what you need."

"Well, Chiang Mai is probably our best bet." Newkirk sat back, looking more relaxed now. "We need to know what airplane types the Japs have there now. We need to know how many. Do they still line them up along the runway like they used to? We need to know what time the Jap pilots stand-to in the morning. We assume they man their planes at daybreak, but do they all sit on the ground in their cockpits and watch the sun come up? Or do they fly a dawn patrol? We have to assume there're a lot of anti-aircraft guns at Chiang Mai. But what kind and where are they? There's another airfield south of Chiang Mai, along the railroad, a place called Lampang. We need the same questions answered for that."

"That's a tall order, Jack. What's your timing? How soon do you need all this?"

"I could use it right now. But – if you can get anything at all on where the Japs are hanging out – any time will do."

"I'll do what I can, Jack." What else could he say?

Newkirk gave him a telephone number, a line straight to him that Harry could use any time of day or night. Harry thought of Doyle again. Doyle would enjoy the sense of action, even if he could not help.

Well, there was Louie, always Louie.

* * *

"... and that's what Jack Newkirk said he needed, Louie. Chennault is looking for a way to hit the Japs, to hit them hard."

They talked as they rode in one of Louie's Cadillacs along a road that led toward the mountains. Louie was driving. He had insisted that just the two of them go for a drive when Harry said he had something to discuss. It must have been the way he said it. Louie had raised his eyes and said, "Delicate?" Then, without waiting for an answer: "Come, Harry, I'll show you the mountains. It's a quiet drive; you'll enjoy it."

"Interesting," Louie said now. He slapped his hand down on the Cadillac's steering wheel and leaned forward, looking at something far down the road. "I hope Chennault can bring it off."

"I do too," Harry said, "but everything is contingent on his getting this information. Is there any way we can help him get what he needs?"

Louie did not answer right away. He looked through the windscreen, intent on the road ahead. After a while he said, "There's only one man who can get that kind of information, and that's Tai Li."

"That's what I thought," Harry said. "And Tai Li is a friend of yours."

"Colleague," Louie corrected.

"Colleague, then, but you can ask ."

"No, Harry, I can't. I'm sorry, but this is one I can't help you with."

"But this is the big one, Louie! This could really hurt the Japs. We can help make it happen. Look, can't you go to Tai Li, tell him that Chennault needs this to kill Japs? The Japs are the enemy. We're all fighting the same war."

Louie took his eyes from the road, looked at him very directly for a moment. Then he turned back to stare out the windscreen. "No," he said finally, "we're not all fighting the same war, Harry. That's something you need to learn. The Americans are fighting the Japs; the Chinese are fighting the Japs – and each other. The Chinese Communists loom large in Chiang Kai-shek's mind, larger than the Japs most of the time. The Japs are not always the main enemy."

"But the AVG is part of the Chinese Air Force. Christ, the AVG is the Chinese Air Force! Claire Chennault works for Chiang Kai-shek; Tai Li works for Chiang Kai-shek. Doesn't that at least put them on the same side?"

"Harry, let me tell you a bit of recent history. Not so long ago Tai Li offered to work with Chennault. He said they would both collect intelligence on Japanese targets and then share whatever each got. Anyone with just an inkling of their respective capabilities knows that Chennault can do only an occasional reconnaissance flight over a Japanese base, while Tai Li has spies everywhere, probably even in the Japanese Air Force Headquarters. Despite that, Chennault turned Tai Li down."

"Turned him down! Why would he do that?"

Louie shrugged. "Chennault knows China – as one day you will. He understands the Chinese and their politics. He knows what Tai Li is. He knows how Tai Li got to where he is and how he stays there. Chennault is a realist, a practical man. He knows that in a relationship with Tai Li he would lose more than he could ever gain. Maybe Chennault was influenced by the British. The British have no use for Tai Li at all, no taste for his 'secret police'. I've heard senior British officers call Tai Li 'the Chief of the Chinese Gestapo'."

Louie paused to let this sink in. Then he added, "So you see, I cannot go to Tai Li for information to pass to Chennault. And I can't tell him it's for somebody else. He would see no reason I would want such information – except for Chennault."

Something to think about, but before Harry could begin to get his thoughts together, Louie added one more thing. "What I've just said, Harry, you must not repeat, certainly not here in China. Tai Li has his spies everywhere. And that's not just hyperbole. The walls in Kunming have ears, believe me. It's why we went for a drive."

Harry nodded. "Thanks," he said, "I'll remember that." He stared out the window at the brown hills that were getting closer, and ran his mind over what he had just learned. He was not ready to give it up yet.

"What about Chennault himself?" he asked. "Can't the Old Man get that kind of information through his own channels? He has Chiang Kai-shek's ear. Chiang wants to destroy the Japanese, and the AVG is his most effective weapon. Why can't Chennault go to Chiang and ask him to order Tai Li to get the intelligence he needs?"

Louie shrugged. "Chennault is too wise for that. He would have nothing to gain, he knows that."

"I don't see how there's nothing to gain."

"Well, suppose Chennault did go to Chiang, and Chiang agreed to give Tai Li an order. Tai Li would salute smartly and say, 'Yes, sir.' And then – quite properly – he would turn the order over to his organization and let it work its own way through the bureaucracy. Nothing would ever be heard of it again. Whatever happens, Tai Li can cover himself. It's how he survives. I'm sure you believe that Chennault is close to the Generalissimo, and so he is. But no one is closer to the Generalissimo than Tai Li. Tai Li is Chiang's guardian. He's kept Chiang alive and in power for many years. Chiang's trust in Tai Li is total."

"Christ, Tai Li sounds like the devil!" Harry said. "I think I'm beginning to understand." He sighed, "But we still have to find a way to get

Chennault what he needs."

That made Louie smile. "You are a persistent bugger, aren't you? Well, you can ask Tai Li yourself."

"Sure, I can tell him it's for the front page of the *New York Times.*"

"No, but you can tell him it's for Chennault."

"Wait, Louie, wait!" He held up his hands, calling a time-out. "If you're being serious, I'm not following you. You can't tell Tai Li you want information for Chennault, but I can? How does that come about?"

Louie took his foot off the accelerator and let the car drift to the side of the road. When it rolled to a stop, he turned to look directly at Harry and started to explain.

"It comes about because you can get away with it. You can tell Tai Li that you want information that will help the AVG destroy Japs. If you ask him, it's not a matter of what's being asked, but who's asking."

"I don't understand."

"If you ask, then it's you Tai Li will be looking at – and thinking of how he can use you. Tai Li is always looking for instruments he can use to pursue his own goals. Right now he needs to look at the Americans. He knows he needs an American or two, to tap into all the money America is bringing to China. But the situation is new for him; it's difficult for him to know who might be useful. So he will look you over. He will see your connections to American newspapers, to Colonel Chennault, to American diplomats and military officers. All of that will interest him. It will make him want to do things for you. So all you need to do is ask him for the information Chennault needs – you will get it! That is not the way he would see the request if I asked."

"The last thing I want to do is to piss off a guy like Tai Li. I'm just getting started in China. You're suggesting that I manipulate the master. That's rather presumptuous, isn't it?"

Louie laughed. "It is presumptuous. We won't even talk about consequences. There's no question that you will have to be careful. But I'm sure you can get away with it."

"If he gives me something, he will expect something in return."

"Yes, but you won't give him anything. There's so much going on, so much confusion here. He knows that finding the lever to manipulate the Americans will not be easy. He won't expect to succeed with every American he approaches. You'll be one of his failures."

Harry kept his eyes out the window and said nothing.

"Take your time, think about it, Harry. In the end it comes down to how badly you want this information. All I can do is arrange your meeting with

Tai Li. And may I point out, that's not insignificant. It will make me your associate. So you must be successful. If you disappoint Tai Li, it will blow back on me as well. Both of us will be in trouble."

Harry shook his head. "Tai Li is the devil. Even Chennault won't deal with him. And now I must?"

"It's not Chennault's job to deal with the devil. Dealing with the devil is what you've been put here to do, Harry. That's your job."

Harry laughed. What a great line, he thought. It's one to tell Doyle, and his old espionage instructors, if he ever saw any of them again. Dealing with the devil: so that's what espionage was.

"All right, Louie," he said, "let's go do it."

* * *

On the appointed day, they drove to a house not far from Louie's flat at Green Lake. It was a big house with a wide veranda that overlooked a spacious garden with a small pond at its center. A pretty young lady waited for them on the veranda. In good English she said it was "too bad" that it was so cool and that they could not sit outside, and led them to a sitting room. A servant came behind her and brought them drinks. Not five minutes later Eddie Liu, Tai Li's interpreter, walked in.

"Very nice day," he said in greeting. His wide smile shrank a bit; he looked almost sad. "Ah, the General," he said, "General Tai Li regrets…." He let them hang there a bit, to imagine the worst. "… that he will be late, but only a few minutes. He is very busy. As you can well imagine."

Harry could well imagine. Louie and Eddie spoke in Chinese, while Harry wondered if they were related. They shared the same surname, but they certainly did not look as if they came from the same family. The servant came back into the room then, with a fresh bottle of cognac. He filled a glass from it, which he placed on a small table next to the empty leather chair across from Harry. Just as he stepped back, General Tai Li entered. He walked directly to Harry, inclined his head, and spoke in Chinese. Eddie Liu translated.

"The general welcomes you to his home, Mr. Harry. In the future he hopes to see you here often."

Tai Li nodded at Louie and said a few words that were not translated. Then he stepped to the chair where the cognac had been set. He looked at them and nodded.

"Please," Eddie Liu said, "please sit."

Tai Li took a big swallow of cognac, mumbled something to Liu.

"You have business you wish to discuss...."

Louie had briefed Harry on how the meeting would go. A few minor pleasantries, then directly to business. Tai Li had no interest in discussion; a waste of time. So Harry laid out his case, quickly, concisely, saying just what Jack Newkirk had told him. For Tai Li's benefit he added the certainty that once he had the information, Chennault would go on the offensive. He would attack the Japanese, destroy their airplanes and kill as many of them as he could.

Eddie Liu stood by Tai Li's chair and translated as Harry spoke. By the time Harry reached the end of his brief, there was a smile on Tai Li's face. When Eddie Liu finished his translation, Tai Li raised his glass of cognac and said one word. Eddie Liu went to a drinks cart at the side of the room and took two glasses from it. He handed one to Harry, the other to Louie. Tai Li rose, and personally filled their glasses with cognac.

"The General would like to make a toast," Eddie Liu announced. Glasses were raised. The General spoke.

"To the success of Colonel Chennault!" Eddie Liu translated.

"To the success of Colonel Chennaut," Harry and Louie repeated.

"*Gambai!*" Tai Li said, in a voice louder than before.

"Bottoms up," Eddie Liu said. Harry learned his first word of Chinese.

They drained their glasses and set them down. Tai Li shook hands with Harry, bowed to Louie and walked from the room.

"The General thanks you for coming," Eddie Liu said. The meeting was over.

* * *

"That's it?' Harry said as they walked down the path to their car. "How did we do?"

"You did well," Louie said. "You didn't waste the General's time. He didn't waste yours. You will get your information."

"You think so?"

"We've already toasted Chennault's victory. It may take a week or it may take two, but you will get what you asked for."

* * *

To say that Harry was pleased would be to understate how he felt by orders of magnitude. For an hour he walked on air. When reality returned, he knew that Tai Li might just treat his request in one of the ways that Louie had suggested: turn it over to his minions and let it disappear in the bureaucracy where nothing would ever be heard of it again. But if he got what he asked for – and Louie certainly seemed sure that he would – it would be the biggest thing Harry had ever done in his life.

Harry wished Doyle were here, or that he could tell Rector about it. Or go to Jack Newkirk and hint that something was on the way. It would be wonderful if he could do that, but he knew he could not. Telling Newkirk anything at all just now was simply not wise. The process he had put in motion was complicated; the information might never arrive. Tai Li had to query his agent in Thailand through whatever means he had; the agent had to get the answer back to Tai Li – after he surreptitiously counted airplanes or did whatever he needed to do. It would be dangerous for the agent. Touch and go. He could be grabbed by the Japanese while counting airplanes – or betrayed by his own radio when he transmitted what he saw. There were too many possibilities, most of them bad. It was best not to say anything at all.

* * *

He used the days of waiting to get to know Kunming. Louie took him to restaurants and introduced him to people he should know; Lucy showed him other things, the markets and the villages and even the cemeteries where the people went to hide from the Japanese bombers. The nights were for Sue. She came to him almost every night; it was almost a routine: Droopy-eyed and yawning after dinner; she was always the first to bed. Later, the "click-click" of his bedroom door opening brought him to action stations. He knew the feel of her now, the smell of her, the taste of her, he had explored every square millimeter of her geography. Familiarity did not diminish his interest or his excitement; it only intensified it.

In the mornings Lucy still came to have coffee with him in his little alcove. If she knew what went on in the night, she gave no sign. The three of them were great friends now, almost like family. Life in the apartment went on more smoothly than he could have imagined. Louie had yet to make an appearance there. Harry had no idea where he was living, and never asked. Lucy claimed not to know; Sue said nothing about it at all. He was probably living at the home of one of his mistresses, Lucy said once.

The war went on, but far from Kunming. The Japanese bombers had never returned to the city after their devastating defeat by the AVG in December. Harry read the newspapers when they came, always late, and he listened to BBC. But the news was censored and he could get more from a quick chat with Ed Rector than he ever could from a month of newspapers.

The war in Asia was not going well; the Allies were not winning. Rangoon had fallen, and the Japanese were pushing north, driving the British Army ahead of them. The Japanese were headed for India. But there was concern that they would try to push across the Salween River and follow the Burma Road all the way to Kunming.

The AVG still had some of its P-40s in north Burma, at an RAF airfield, a place called Magwe. From there they continued to strike at Japanese targets. Everyone knew it was just a matter of time before the Japanese came to obliterate Magwe and the AVG there.

Harry was at the flat, staring at a map of north Burma when Louie telephoned. "Come to my office," Louie said, "you know the one," and Harry did. It was the office of one of Louie's smaller companies, an out-of-the-way place where he and Harry met occasionally before going on to lunch or dinner. Louie hid away there when he wanted to be alone.

"I have a packet for you," he said when they met. "From General Tai Li. He asked that you forgive him for not giving it to you directly, but he had to leave Kunming for a few days. He thought you would want it as soon as possible."

Harry's heart pounded as he opened the packet. He looked at the bundle of paper. "It's all Chinese," he said, and felt disappointed.

"Let me see it," Louie said. He took the packet from Harry and paged through it. "It's just the top pages," he said. "That's the original report in Chinese. Under it is the English translation." He passed the English to Harry and kept the Chinese version. They both started to read.

"It's all here," Louie said, "even maps. Chennault will be pleased."

Harry knew Louie was right. They had done it!

"Ah …." Louie interrupted his thoughts. "There is one thing. Tai Li's has a request."

Harry looked up. "Oh my God," he said, "the Devil wants his due."

"Indeed he does. Tai Li said to me: 'If Chennault is victorious, I want to see his victory on the front page of the *New York Times*."

Harry remembered to breathe again. "That's it?" He laughed. "If it happens, it will be on the front page of the *Times*. I guarantee it."

He had the packet in Newkirk's hands within the hour. Newkirk paged through the material, then started reading it, intently. He suddenly looked up at Harry, said, "Stay right here," and left the room, taking the documents with him.

He was back in minutes, excited. "I gave it to the Old Man. He's going over it now. He thinks what I do: It's exactly what we need."

Harry was on his feet then, happy, excited – exhilarated even. He could have hugged Newkirk. They shook hands instead.

"I'm glad it's what you need," Harry said, trying to look casual, as if reports like this came into his hands every day.

"We owe you one, Harry," Newkirk said, "We owe you one, Chennault and the whole AVG."

"Let's see how it works out," Harry said.

The very next day, March 22, the Japanese came to Magwe, the RAF airfield in north Burma where the AVG still based some of its P-40s. The Japanese came with over 250 airplanes. The bombers came first. They passed over the field in three waves and pounded it with their bombs. Then the fighters came down and worked everything over with their machine guns. By the time it was over every AVG P-40 had been destroyed or damaged – and two AVG ground crew had been killed. Harry learned about it that evening in a telephone call from Newkirk.

"The Old Man is really pissed off," Newkirk told him. "Come by the field tomorrow. Be there early. We're going to do it."

CHAPTER 24

March 22, 1942
Kunming, China

"Who are these people?" Harry asked, looking out the window of the operations shack. The tarmac looked almost crowded with people clustered around the shark-nosed airplanes parked along the side of the apron. They were Americans, civilians mostly, but there was a good smattering of uniforms among them, starched and pressed uniforms that the AVG did not own. He could see the smiles and hear laughter, as if the day was a holiday. The only serious faces were on the handful of AVG ground crew readying the airplanes for flight.

Newkirk came to the window to look. He shrugged. "It's Kunming's growing American community. Today is a big thing for them, after what happened at Magwe. The word's gotten around that the AVG will hit back." He shook his head. "It's an open secret. Everybody's here to see us off. It's a county fair."

"Come over here, Harry," Newkirk said as he turned away from the window. "Take a look at the map. I want to show you what we're going to do. The Old Man said that you can feel free to write whatever news stories you want – just don't release anything until all our airplanes are back."

The map on the wall showed China's Yunnan province and below it, the northern parts of Burma and Thailand. "We're going to hit the Japs at Chiang Mai with ten P-40s. It's a long way from here. The Japs know our P-40s don't have the range to get there from here. So they won't be expecting us. That's the beauty of the plan. We're going to give them a big surprise."

Newkirk put his finger on the city of Kunming near the center of the map. "We take off here this morning, and fly south to Loi Wing." Newkirk's finger moved down the map. "Loi Wing is right here, on the China-Burma border. It's our maintenance base, all the AVG's heavy repair work is done there. There's a good airstrip, and even a nicer American Club. We'll refuel our airplanes there and then fly on to Nam Sang." Newkirk pointed to a blue dot on the map, near the eastern edge of Burma and its border with Thailand.

"Nam Sang is a small British auxiliary airstrip. It's in the middle of nowhere. We'll get there at dusk when there's almost no chance of some stray Jap airplane passing by and seeing us. We'll top off our fuel tanks, get some sleep, and then take off before dawn." Newkirk's finger moved east across the map and stopped at Chiang Mai. "Here's our target. The airfield at Chiang Mai is less than an hour from Nam Sang. We'll attack just as the sun is coming up. According to the information you gave us, the Jap pilots will be walking to their airplanes just about then. We should catch them on the ground."

"You're going to hit Chiang Mai with ten airplanes?"

"Six, actually. Bob Neale will lead those six. I'll take a flight of four south of Chiang Mai, to a town called Lampang." Newkirk's finger now followed the green line that was the railroad going to the southeast from Chiang Mai. "From Chiang Mai it's about 40 miles to Lampang. Your report said the Japs have some heavy bombers based there. The Old Man picked it as our secondary target. My four airplanes will hit the Japs we find there. On the way back we'll join the fracas at Chiang Mai. Then we come home retracing the route we took through Burma. We should be back in Kunming day after tomorrow."

"Sounds good."

"It is good. It's the Old Man's plan. When I briefed the pilots this morning, Ed Rector said, 'The Old Man can think like the Japs. They won't be expecting us.'"

"Ed's going too? Anybody else I know?"

"Well, there's Ed, Charlie Bond, Greg Boyington, 'Black Mack' McGarry – I don't know if you know him. The pilots are volunteers; everybody wanted to go. The ones we picked are the best we have."

Newkirk took a step back to see the map better. "It will be a good operation." He turned to look at Harry. "You helped, Harry." Newkirk was smiling as he said it. A real smile, the first Harry had seen on Newkirk's tired face in a long time.

"I hope I helped, Jack, but you're the guys who have to do the work." He stuck his hand out to Newkirk. "Jack, I know you have things to do. I'll see you when you get back. Good luck and good hunting!"

Out on the apron he decided to find Ed Rector, and looked for P-40 number 36. When he spotted the airplane, he saw Rector was kneeling under the wing with his crew chief, sorting through things spread on the ground. He stood up when he saw Harry.

"Hey, Harry, come on over here. I'm just going through my survival kit, maps and candy bars. You know where we're going, I guess?"

"Yeah," Harry said.

"I figured you might." Rector looked toward the south. "It's a long way from here, and nothing but jungle." He shivered then. "Well, I've got my survival chocolate bars."

Harry gave him his hand. "Good luck, Ed. The beer's on me when you get back."

"That sounds good. I'll see you, Harry." He was back to sorting maps and candy bars before Harry had gone two paces.

Harry continued down along the apron toward the runway where the P-40s would take off. He passed Chennault deep in conversation with Bob Neale. The Old Man looked up as he passed. "Mornin', Ross," he said, and turned back to Neale before Harry could say anything.

When the P-40s took off, Harry saw the Old Man looking after them, long after they were out of sight, then walk by himself to the operations shack. Harry went back to wait at the Green Lake apartment.

The next day passed quickly, almost unnoticed. The day after that Harry waited from early morning for the telephone to ring, but no call came. That evening he let Lucy and Sue talk him into dinner at a Chinese restaurant. He was not really concerned. Newkirk and the others must have been delayed, probably by rain in Burma. It was mid-morning of the day after that, March 25, when the call finally came. It was Ed Rector.

"Hey, Harry," he said, "if you have time, come on over to the billets, buy me that beer."

Harry drove the gray Ford to the hostel in what must have been record time.

"The Old Man asked me to brief you," Ed said. They were in the pilots' bar. Ed had pulled a couple of cold beers from the cooler, and sat across from Harry at one of the card tables. "There's no one around right now," Ed said. "It's a good time to talk."

"I've been waiting to hear. Did everything go all right?"

Ed scrunched up his face. "It was a damn good mission. We hit the Japs hard. But it cost us." Harry felt something inside him sink. "Let me tell you from the beginning," Ed said. "You were here when we took off. When was that, two days ago? It's like two weeks."

"We flew to Loi Wing. The plan was to refuel there, and then go on to Nam Sang. But we got into Loi Wing late and had a problem with the refueling, so we stayed overnight." Ed smiled, for the first time since he started talking. "You should see that officers' club. It's like a high-class country club in the States. Huge windows with an incredible view of the mountains...." He stopped talking suddenly. "Well, anyway .... The next morning was all fog and rain. It cleared up in the afternoon and we flew on to Nam Sang.

"Nam Sang was really different. It's a small British field, primitive compared to Loi Wing. We got there at dusk and refueled our airplanes in the dark. The Brits stored the fuel in tins; it's been there for years. We had to pour it through chamois skin to filter the gunk out. But they gave us a meal and we got some sleep. We got up at 4:00 a.m. There was no moon. It was pitch black. The Brits used lanterns and truck headlights to mark the runway. Once we got in the air, all we could see was the glow of our own exhaust stacks. I was in Neale's flight, and the six of us circled over Nam Sang while we waited for Jack Newkirk's flight to join us. Jack and his guys never showed up. I figured it was just poor visibility. After about 20 minutes, we headed for Chiang Mai.

"Visibility on the way was poor, haze, and a lot of smoke. The rice farmers burn off their fields this time of year. We couldn't see anything on the ground. When we got close to Chiang Mai, Charlie Bond took the lead. Charlie had flown over that area before, on a recon flight. He recognized the mountain that's off to one side of the airport, waggled his wings and led us down in a dive. I could just make out the city under my port wing. I knew the airport was at the southwest corner, but I couldn't see anything there.

"I was number five in line. Black Mac McGarry was behind me. The two of us were going to fly top cover while the four others strafed the airfield. When we got down to 5,000 feet, I finally saw the Jap airplanes lined up on the field, a lot of them. Our guys made their first pass and I could see Jap airplanes start burning.

"The Jap anti-aircraft artillery and machine guns opened up then. You could see the tracers chasing after our strafing airplanes. Anti-aircraft shells were bursting around me and Black Mac, and coming awfully close. It wasn't long before Charlie Bond and Bill Bartling climbed up to where we were. By then there were a lot of Jap airplanes burning and the raid was over. Charlie Bond started leading us back. Neale and Boyington climbed up way on the other side of the field and flew back separately.

"It wasn't long before I realized that Black Mac was falling behind. I circled around and tried to get alongside, but he was flying so slow that I flew right by him. He was really losing altitude by then; smoke was coming from his engine. There was a ridge ahead that he wasn't high enough to clear. Suddenly, he just turned the airplane on its back and dropped out. He was about 1,000 feet above he trees when his chute opened. I saw his P-40 crash into the side of a hill and burst into flames. Mac landed in a clearing about 200 meters away. I saw him get to his feet and wave. I flew over him and threw him a bar of candy. Charlie Bond dropped him a map. That was it. We tore up the Japs at Chiang Mai all right, but we lost Black Mac."

"Is there any way to get him out?"

"I don't see how. It's rough country. Nobody would ever find him there. Even if he could walk to the Salween River and cross into Burma, he's still nowhere. That whole area is Jap country now."

They sat quietly for a while, finally remembered to drink some beer. "Want another one, Harry?"

"No thanks, Ed. I feel bad about Black Mac," he said, and remembered there was more. "What about Newkirk's bunch?"

"That was the other problem. Newkirk didn't make it back, Harry."

A hammer blow to his chest. He could not believe what he just heard. "What do you mean, Newkirk didn't make it back?"

"Jack Newkirk went down. He crashed."

Harry's mouth went dry. It took him a long moment before he could ask: "What happened?"

Ed looked away, shook his head. "We're not sure. He was supposed to take his flight to Lampang." He stopped talking and looked at Harry as if trying to decide something. "I know you're going to put some of this in the newspapers," he said, "but not what I'm going to tell you now. Okay?"

"Okay, I won't put in anything you don't want."

"Okay. I told you we flew circles around the airfield at Nam Sang while we waited for Jack, but we never saw him. Jack's four airplanes took off after we did. He was supposed to join us, and then all ten of us would fly to Chiang Mai together. It turns out that while we flew circles and waited for him, he flew straight on to Chiang Mai. He never tried to rendezvous. That means he got to Chiang Mai before us. He wasn't supposed to fly anywhere near the airport, and he didn't. That would have cost us our surprise. Instead he shot up the railroad station."

"I don't understand," Harry said.

"Neither do I. But when he shot up the station, the Japs knew we were in the air. That's maybe why there was so much anti-aircraft fire at the airfield. They'd been alerted. Jack's guys were surprised when he dove on the station. They didn't even fire their guns. They just followed Jack and the railroad to Lampang. We don't know how far south they got, but they never saw any Jap airplanes. Jack turned the flight around and headed back to Chiang Mai. On the way they all shot up some barracks, and then Jack dove down on a tank that was driving along a road. The tank either hit him with its gun, or Jack just flew into the ground. That happens sometimes. They call it target fixation. All we know is that one of the guys with him, 'Buster' Keeton, looked down and saw a fireball roll along the ground. It was only later that he realized that the fireball must have been Jack Newkirk."

"Jesus," Harry said, shook his head. And after a while, "So that's it. Scarsdale Jack is gone."

"He's gone, Harry."

Someone had come into the room, but they barely noticed, until he came and stood by the table, looking down at them. "Newquack," he said. "You guys talking about Newquack?" Harry looked up. It was the dark, stocky pilot that Harry recognized as Greg Boyington.

"Harry, you know Greg?" Rector said. "He went to Chiang Mai with us."

Without waiting for Harry to say anything, Boyington said, "Poor Jack. He got the word."

Harry stared at him. "Got the word?"

"Yeah, 'the word'. That's the feeling people get that they're not going to live through something. Jack got the word at Loi Wing.... You know, back when we were flying together in the Navy, Newkirk was an affable gent, he was 'Smiling Jack' himself. But that night at Loi Wing, boy, he didn't want to talk at all – about anything."

Rector took a thoughtful pull at his beer. "Tell Harry what happened at Nam Sang, Greg."

"I was getting to that. It's an RAF emergency field, a real lonesome place. Jack and I were in this bamboo hut that the Brits use as a washroom. A RAF sergeant came in and told us not to drink the water – or even brush our teeth with it. And there was Jack, dipping his toothbrush right in it. 'Hey, Jack,' I said, 'didn't you hear what the man said?' Jack just looked up and smiled. 'You know,' he said, 'after tomorrow, I don't think it will make any difference at all.'" Boyington turned to look at Rector.

"You know, Ed, I feel bad about Jack... but he didn't do us any favors when he shot up the Chiang Mai railroad station."

Ed just nodded. Boyington went on then. "It sure is funny. Black Mac and I spent most of the evening at Loi Wing looking out the window and drinking scotch. He'll make it back. I wouldn't be surprised to see him come walking in here one day."

He walked over to the small bar and went behind it. They watched him select a bottle of scotch and pour himself a large measure. He turned to them and held up the glass.

"To poor Jack," he said. "To Scarsdale Jack."

* * *

Lucy looked up from a book as he came into the Green Lake apartment. "Louie called," she said. "He wants to see you. At the 'little' office. He said you know where it is. He said it's urgent."

"Ah, Harry," Louie said when he got there. He looked relieved. "I'm glad you came so quickly. It's a bit awkward. Tai Li has sent you a gift."

"A gift?"

"Yes, he's quite happy with page one." When he saw no comprehension on Harry's face, he added, "You haven't heard, I suppose." He picked a sheet of paper from his desk and started to read:

"Page One, New York Times, 25 March 1942. Headline: 'U.S. Fliers in Burma Smash 40 Planes; Seven Fires Set at One of Two Enemy Airfields Raided in Thailand'. Quote: 'Pilots of the American Volunteer Group smashed forty planes at the Thai airport of Chiang Mai today in a dawn raid that caught the Japanese by surprise. Lampun, to the south was also raided, but the results were not revealed....'"

Louie stopped there and looked at Harry. "At the end of the piece it says...," and he started to read again, "'The enthusiasm of the returning American pilots was dampened, however, by the death of their squadron leader, Jack Newkirk.'" .

When Louie looked up, Harry just nodded.

"I'm sorry," Louie said.

"I'm glad we made the front page of the *New York Times*, but it wasn't me, Louie."

"That really doesn't matter. Tai Li doesn't know that."

It struck him then. "You can't have seen the *Times* already. It won't be here for days."

Louie held out the sheet of paper to him, all Chinese characters. "The Chinese Embassy in Washington sent a cable. Tai Li passed this to me. He's quite happy. He believes you did everything you said you would."

"Great. Then I'm off the hook."

"Well, perhaps. There is the matter of the gift." Louie walked over to the small lacquered cabinet where he kept the whiskey. "Harry, we should have a drink." He poured generous measures into two glasses. "Harry, I was thinking.... Chap like you, man-about-town, should have a place for himself, somewhere he can go and not be troubled. I mean, please do use the Green Lake flat as your permanent residence. I certainly want you to, and Lucy loves having you there...but you really need something like my little office here, a bit nicer, perhaps, where you can entertain, privately. I know of a wonderful little flat...."

It was all too much for him. The success of the raid, now the coverage in the *New York Times*, but most of all, the loss of Jack Newkirk. Harry was in no mood to talk about something as mundane as a flat. He needed a private place, he knew that, but this wasn't the time. "Yes, I would like that. We can take a look at it, maybe sometime next week."

"Actually, I think you need something now. A place to put your gift."

This was completely unlike Louie. He was not one to insist. He must be feeling pressure of some kind, from Tai Li probably. He could feel Louie's eyes on him now, watching, waiting for him to say something. What was all this about having his own flat, he wondered. Did Louie want him out of Green Lake? Had he found out about Sue? Probably not, but if he had, Louie was too much of a gentleman to throw someone out just for bedding his mistress. It had to be something more serious. It had to be Tai Li. The gift. It was the gift from Tai Li that brought him here. Oh, goodness....

"Louie," he said, "why am I getting a feeling that it's not a bottle of cognac that Tai Li has sent me."

"No, it's not cognac, Harry," Louie rolled his eyes and got to his feet. "Come on," he said. "She's in the room down the hall. Nice girl, Shanghai girl. You'll like her, you'll see."

He did not know what to expect, but he did like her. She was a nice girl, a few years younger than he was. She wore a tight red dress, one of those Chinese things, very tight, with a high collar and a slit down the side that showed off a good body and nice legs. Her hair was cut short and modern-looking, like the girls on the French street. She had a pretty face, but wore too much makeup. It made her look older, too serious. Her eyes were dark, brilliant. They flashed with life and held his when he looked at her. Her look was questioning, but confident, almost challenging. He took it all in, looking at her longer than was polite, but he really liked what he saw. "Well, she is nice," he said to Louie. "I appreciate the thought, but I can't...."

Louie stepped close to him, spoke quietly. "Look Harry, we can't just send her back. We'll take her over to the small flat and you can keep her there. Tai Li would be offended if you send her back now. It wouldn't be good for her either. Send her back in a couple of months; it will be fine."

"A couple of months! Louie...."

"Let's step out in the hallway for a minute." He nodded at the girl as he held the door for Harry. A few steps down the hall he said, "Between us, Harry, I doubt she speaks English very well, but I'm sure her comprehension is quite good. You must be careful what you say around her. Know what I mean?"

When Louie said, "Between us," Harry knew exactly what that meant now. "Yes, I understand. She's a Trojan horse. But I can't just keep her, Louie."

"If you want to play the game and stay on the good side of Tai Li, you'll keep her, just for a while. It's a great honor he's doing you. In the usual course of such things, you'd be bored with her in a few months anyway. Then you can send her back and Tai Li won't lose face. Nor will she, nor you. Everyone will be happy."

"What if I just tell Tai Li that it wasn't me who got the headline in the *New York Times*."

"Harry, this is not to joke about. It's just for a few months. I have the flat where you can keep her. It's not just you. I have money in this game too, you know."

"It just doesn't seem right, Louie."

"It's not a matter of what's right. You're in China now, not London, not New York. The Chinese bosses have their ladies stashed all over town. You're in their game now. If you want to stay in it, you'll play by their rules."

Harry nodded. "All right, let's go look at the flat."

Later, when he reflected on it, Harry realized his life was getting complicated. Here he was, for all purposes, alone in darkest China. His closest friend was a Chinese with a murky past and mysterious connections – on whom he had become totally dependent. He was bedding the man's ward and sometimes lover, and lusting after his daughter. Now another Chinese, one of the most powerful of all, had honored him with the gift of a Shanghai girl, a gift he could not turn down. She was attractive enough, and he quite liked her. But if he bedded her, she would turn into a Trojan horse and report his most intimate grunts back to the man who gave her to him, the man who was the devil himself. The Shanghai girl's job was to steal his secrets – the secrets he stole from others, which had become the purpose of his life. And although no one around him seemed to notice it much these days, there was a war going on. He wondered what Doyle would say about all this.

CHAPTER 25

My God," Doyle said, "You're doing an incredible job, Harry." Doyle had turned up in Kunming, finally. Chennault himself had helped him find Harry. He sent Doyle to Ed Rector, and Rector summoned Harry to the airport. He and Doyle met in the dark corner of a hangar, just long enough to arrange a proper meeting, which they were having now, in a tea shop of Harry's choosing. Doyle spoke before Harry could even begin to explain what he had been doing.

"You've really scored big here, Harry," he said, giving him a long look, examining him. "Donovan heard from Chennault how you were responsible for the Chiang Mai raid."

"I was hardly responsible for the raid," Harry said. "All I did was give Chennault some information."

"Ah, but that's your job, Harry. And you did that well. And how did you do that, by the way? We all wondered."

And so Harry carefully explained about Tai Li, how he met him through Louie, and how Louie helped get the information. There was nothing boastful in the way he spoke about it, but a bit of cockiness crept into his voice as he went on. He was a veteran now, who had taken risks, while others dealt with the bureaucrats in Calcutta.

"And now you're living with Sir Louie."

"His daughter actually. I mean, I'm not living with her. I'm living in her flat...."

"Great!" Doyle said.

"I have this other flat...," he started. "And there's the problem of this gift from Tai Li...."

"We're not supposed to accept gifts from our contacts, I think. Better keep that to yourself. As far as the flat goes, bring accounting for whatever funds you need to our next meeting. You really are doing a great job, Harry."

Doyle was getting to his feet. It was not a good time to try to explain Tai Li's gift, Harry thought. It was all too complicated. Even if he understood the complications, what could Doyle do? Quote some government regulation against accepting gifts? Ah, well, they could talk about it some other time.

But it was good to be back in contact. Doyle was somebody he could talk to, his lifeline, his link to Uncle Wild Bill and the world left behind. A dull world, actually, when he thought about it, compared to the one he lived in now. That thought brought him back to all the complications of his life.

But it really was good that Doyle was here. Doyle was the one person he could share all of this with – once they had the time. It did disappoint him though, that Doyle had said not a word about Jack Newkirk. Neither had Louie, for that matter. But you could not blame them. There was so much going on and they probably never thought of it. But Jack Newkirk was gone. He felt it, but it was almost as if nobody else knew, or cared. It was as if Newkirk had never been.

Harry went back to the small flat that evening, poked around in a cabinet and found a bottle of cognac. The Shanghai girl stood off to the side and watched him. She had not spoken a word so far; he was not sure she even spoke English. Poor kid, she was probably totally intimidated by him, had probably spent her whole day waiting for him. He took another glass, filled it with cognac, and offered it to her. She took it from him, smiled, and looked pleased. He clicked his glass against hers and said, "*Gambai!*" That she understood. She tipped her glass back and did her best, gulped down half a glass of the cognac. Then quickly put the glass down and raced for the bathroom. She looked a bit green, Harry thought. He could hear her gagging. He stepped to the window, looked out, and tried not to hear.

When she came out after a long while, she looked washed-out, tried not to look at him. He went and sat down on the small loveseat and patted the space next to him. She hesitated, but finally came and sat by him. Then she reached for her cognac glass, looked him right in the eye as she drank from it. Two swallows, small ones. He was touched by the gesture, what he took as her desire to please him. It made her very appealing.

He leaned toward her, put his mouth close to her ear, and whispered: "The AVG is getting a dozen new fighters, E-model P-40s. Tai Li would love to know that." He gave her a secret that was no secret, but maybe Tai Li would hear it from her first, and be pleased. He would help her play the game.

He sat back. She would not look at him at first. He knew she understood, and waited while she thought it through, tried to decide. Finally, she sat back, turned to him. There was a smile on her face, a small one, a bit uncertain, but real. "Thank you," she said.

Sex with her that night was the best Harry had in China up to that time. It felt more illicit than anything he had ever done with Sue.

* * *

Over the next few days, he and Doyle had a series of meetings, mostly while they walked though Green Lake Park in the early morning when only the old people were there. There was a lot to discuss. They needed ways to communicate. They had codes to agree on, meeting places to choose; they had operational plans to discuss, even their own futures to consider.

"Your Uncle Wild Bill has your career well planned," said Doyle, who had spent much time in Calcutta meeting with Uncle Wild Bill's representatives. They had finally reached what Harry had been waiting for, the tasking from on high that would define his life in the coming months, for the rest of the war even. He was so eager to hear what Doyle had to say that he stopped dead in his tracks. Without really noticing, Doyle simply took him by the elbow and moved him along.

"We have reports that an anti-Japanese underground has formed in Thailand, but we have no real proof of it. The thinking in Delhi was that because of your successful penetration of Thailand with the Mango Operation...."

Doyle stopped walking then to look directly at Harry. "In fact, Harry, you have a distinction. You are the only American spy to ever run an intelligence operation into Thailand." He slapped Harry on the back. They started walking again and Doyle went on.

"Thailand is your prime target now, but not your immediate one. Thailand is long range. Your more immediate concern is the Chinese and what they are doing." When he saw surprise on Harry's face he said, "Yes, our Chinese. It's our allies you'll be spying on. We need to know their secrets. We need their secrets so we can move the Chinese in ways that will help achieve our goals – not just theirs."

They moved off the footpath to stand by the edge of the lake and look out over the still surface of the water. "Blame it on your own success," Doyle said. "Once Wild Bill learned about your relationship with Tai Li, he saw your purpose in life."

"Oh, Lord." Harry shook his head. "That's what Louie said."

"Said what?"

"That I had been put here to deal with the devil."

"Tai Li is the devil, eh? That's a reasonable assessment. But dealing with the devil is only part of it. Wild Bill also wants you to keep in touch with Chennault. Not as a spy, but as an objective observer. He wants periodic assessments of Chennault and AVG capabilities to factor into estimates of where the war is headed. The AVG is the only American group that seems able to beat the Japs."

Doyle picked up a stone and tried to skip it across the lake. It struck the water once and disappeared. He shrugged and went on. "Our military presence in Kunming will grow, vastly. That will create all kinds of complications for us. There will be fiefdoms and rivalries and turf wars. It will be American versus American versus Chinese. There will be other Americans in touch with Tai Li. You job will be to maintain a relationship with Tai Li outside the official framework. Whatever he thinks, he must never know with any certainty that you're an intelligence officer."

"That may not be easy. Tai Li won't keep me around because he likes me. He looks to those who can be useful to him."

"He must think you are. Does he accept you as a journalist?"

"He sees me useful as a journalist. I think he's more interested in my contacts with Chennault and the AVG. You have to understand – I don't really have a relationship with Tai Li. I've met him twice, I think."

"A little tenuous, perhaps, but a relationship nonetheless. Even if you didn't have one, it wouldn't matter much, because Wild Bill thinks you do. So if you did not have a relationship with Tai Li, we'd have to create it."

"This is getting too complicated for me, Doyle. I'll just try to stay in touch with him."

"Good. Do your best."

"And what about you? Will you be here as an official of the American embassy?"

"Actually not. Nothing is settled, but it looks like I'll be here as part of the Army, as a civilian political advisor attached to the office of the Commander-in-Chief. You've heard, I suppose, that a general named Stilwell has been named C-in-C, but he's walking around in the jungle now, fleeing the Japanese hordes with the British." He shook his head at the thought. "So, you have a lot to do, Harry. You must maintain your relationships with Sir Louie and his daughter, with Mango, and most importantly, with Tai Li. Also, you need to think about how we get back into Thailand. It won't be as easy from here as it was in Burma. It's a long way from here, and there's a lot of mountain and hostile folk in between."

"I'll think on it," Harry said. "I'll think on it."

* * *

As the days wore on, and turned into April, Kunming started to earn its name as "the City of Eternal Spring." Harry had found a Chinese house with a beautiful garden, where tea was served at any hour. It was near the center of the city, but set apart from its neighbors, almost secluded from them. The location was convenient, the setting more elegant than their tea garden in Rangoon, and it was pleasant to sit there, washed by the cool sunshine of Kunming. A great meeting place, Harry thought, and told Doyle about it as soon as he could.

"This is a nice spot," Doyle agreed when he first saw it. "It makes me think of Rangoon, of how hot and unpleasant that place could be."

"It wasn't that bad," Harry said.

"It was, you just don't remember." They sat and sipped their tea. When they said 'tea' garden here, they meant 'tea'. Harry would have to remember to bring coffee; he was sure he could get the staff to make it.

"Harry, there's something going on," Doyle suddenly said. "Something big."

"What?"

"I don't know. They won't tell me. I'm on the staff now, you know, General Stilwell's staff, but I'm the ultimate outsider. I hear the Army people whisper when I walk by, 'Gasp, it's Donovan's man.' They're all friendly as hell, offer me cigarettes, take me to lunch, but they won't tell me anything."

"Doyle, are you putting me on, or just feeling sorry for yourself?"

"Maybe," Doyle said, which answered nothing. He sighed, theatrically. "Ah, the real story, Harry: The real story is that there is something going on, something big, and they won't tell me. But it's not something that everyone knows. It's very hush-hush. I doubt there are three people in Stilwell's headquarters that know about it, and they talk in whispers. I'm not sure that even General Stilwell knows."

"Then what are you crying about?"

"I don't like to be left out of things. It happened to me once or twice when I was a child. In Rangoon the British shared much more with us than our people here do. It's part of the fiefdom syndrome I warned you about, Harry. You haven't worked with the staffs. The thing that concerns me is that when things are held so tight, it may not be the right people who get to know. Staffs are not doers. The people who make things happen are people like you and me, Harry."

"I get your point, and I don't disagree, but what do you want me to do?"

"Nothing, Harry, nothing. I just want you to know. Now, on to the important things...."

Harry would not remember the rest of what they talked about, when he thought back on this conversation later – after it happened.

CHAPTER 26

Girls! Girls! Girls! A dozen, at least! Chasing him through a beautiful garden. They weren't wearing much, little silk things at most. Some wore nothing at all. They giggled and he laughed. He stumbled and went down in the soft grass. They were on him then, held his arms and legs, everybody laughing now, but he could not get away. Then the girls all went quiet, looked at each other. Now we have him, now what shall we do? Poke him! Touch him! Grope him! They reached for him, poked him, all giggling again. One touched him where he least expected it! "Don't!" he said. "Don't do that!"

That woke him. The sheer incongruity of it. He suddenly realized Sue was there, naked, kneeling on the bed, one hand stroking his stomach. Was it that or the dream? He was thoroughly aroused and her other hand held him, her fingers curled tight.

"You're so big now," she said, looking down at him, "like a buffalo." That made him even more aware of himself, sent a little tremor pulsing through his lower regions. He dared not move. He closed his eyes and tried to think of something else. "Just like a buffalo," she said, her voice soft and sweet.

"But an old buffalo," she added and sounded accusing now. Her grip tightened; it pulled a little gasp from him. "Old buffaloes are always a problem, did you know that, Harry?"

What a time to talk about buffaloes; it made him open his eyes.

"Old buffaloes," she said, her eyes peering deep into his now. "Old buffaloes don't stay in their own field. They don't want to plow the same field every day. They want something new."

Oh, shit, he thought and started feeling less like a big buffalo. He could even feel himself diminish. But she held on, gave him a quick tug.

"Sue!" he said, "That hurts."

"You think that hurts? Do you know what they do to old buffaloes when they stray? They cut it off. Right here. At the root!" A fingernail circled him, sharp on tight skin. "After that, the buffalo stays in his own field."

"Sue, what are you talking about?" he asked, and tried to sit up. He knew damn well what she was talking about: She knew about the Shanghai girl! She had sensed it, somehow. Christ! He had been so careful.

"Ah," she said. She was looking down at him again. "Not big like a buffalo now," and loosened her grip. She bumped her bottom to the edge of the bed, stood up and sounded sad when she said, "And now it's morning. Lucy will be awake soon." With that she turned and walked out of the room, still naked, carrying her little nightdress in her hand.

He stared at the door. Should he be relieved or upset? He knew where the buffalo talk was headed, and he did not care for that. But she had him feeling like a buffalo, a big one. Then, just like that, she walked out on him. He still felt like plowing something. He lay back on the bed, trying to cool down and think.

She could not really "know" anything. There was no way. She was guessing, or maybe it was some kind of a female sixth sense. He had come back to Green Lake late on a number of occasions recently; there were even a couple of nights when he did not come back at all. But he had a reason each time, or at least a cover story. There was so much going on in Kunming just now, and when he did not have a real reason, he told her he was with the AVG guys and stayed at the AVG hostel when he was out overnight. Ed Rector or one of the other guys would always cover for him if it came to that. God, he did not want to spoil what he had here with Sue – and with Lucy.

By the time Lucy knocked on his door, he was so relaxed that he almost told her to come in before he realized he did not have his pajamas on.

"Just a minute, Lucy," he shouted toward the door as he pulled on the bottoms. It was ironic, the one night he and Sue had done nothing, he was not wearing anything when Lucy came.

Minutes later they were sitting in the alcove, sipping the coffee that Lucy brought. This was the best part of the day. Everything was fresh. The smell of the coffee was wonderful, and he was never disappointed when he tasted it. He and Lucy sat in companionable silence, sipped at their coffee and watched the world brighten as the sun came up.

"Will you be out again tonight?" Lucy asked.

He thought for a moment. "Yes," he said finally. "Tonight's the governor's dinner for the AVG. Do you know if Louie will be there?" He had not seen Louie in days.

"He will be, if he's in town," she said. "What's troubling you, Harry? You don't look very happy this morning. Not looking forward to the dinner?"

"It's not that so much, it's just that I'll be coming back here late again. I haven't seen that much of you and Sue in the last couple of weeks."

"These are busy times. You needn't be concerned about us. One of Sue's friends has come by several times while you were out. I think he's taking both of us to dinner tonight."

"Oh?" said Harry, and wondered....

* * *

He got to the little flat where he kept the Shanghai girl. She ran to the door when she heard him, took his hand, and led him to the small dining table. He sat down and watched as she brought soup and rice and two simple vegetable dishes she had made for lunch. Now that they were friends, the clothing she wore in the flat was simple, usually a light blouse and cotton trousers, and the heavy makeup was gone. It made her look younger, but harder somehow, tougher than Sue or Lucy, as though her life had been difficult – which it undoubtedly was. She smiled often now and rarely took her eyes from him. That was flattering, but at the same time he was totally comfortable with her. He was sure she trusted him, and he knew that he could trust her. Whatever else they were, they had become friends.

He had a mission that day. He needed to find out more about her. He knew now that her English was quite usable. Her comprehension was excellent, and her ability to speak improved each time they met. It was time to ask questions.

"Now," he said, when lunch was over and they sat on the couch to which she had led him, "tell me about yourself. Where did you live when you were a little girl?"

"Shanghai," she said, "I always lived in Shanghai. Shanghai was my life, my home. I thought I would always live there."

"And your father and mother worked there?"

She nodded.

"Where did your father work?"

"On Nanking Road. Do you know Nanking Road? It's a famous place. There are many shops, goods from Europe, from everywhere. My father worked in a shop."

"Was it his shop?"

"Oh, no. Only rich men owned shops. We were not rich."

"But you were not poor. You went to school."

"Yes, we were not poor. We had many things, a radio, a Victrola. I went to school every day. I had no brothers, no sisters. My mother wanted everything for me. She sewed dresses for the English ladies and made more money than my father. She spent her money so I could learn English. And so that I could learn to draw."

"Like an artist?" He sketched with his hand in the air.

"Yes," she said. She got up and ran into her little bedroom. She came back with a large sketch pad, sat down right next to him and started turning the pages. He could see they were filled with sketches, but she moved so quickly that he could not make them out.

"Here," she said, stopping finally at a fashion sketch, a lady in a long dress, very elegant looking. "My mother wanted me to draw like this, dresses that the English could see. Then she could sew them."

"Ah," he said, "you were like a fashion designer. Was that your ambition? Is that what you want to be?" he asked.

"Want to be…?" She looked at him, puzzled.

How to explain…. "When you were a child, what kind of work did you want to do when you were as old as your mother? What was your ambition? Your dream? To be an artist? A designer?"

"Ah, my dream, yes, I understand." She looked down and thought for a long moment before answering. "My dream was to meet someone."

"Meet someone … to marry, or…?"

"No, not marry. To help me."

"Someone not to marry, but to help you. Help you how? To get a job? To learn more about fashion?"

"No, no," she said. "Help make my life easy. Get money, get a nice house." She turned her face away from him, to think or because she was embarrassed, he could not tell. He tried to help with what she wanted to say. "Well, let's see, you didn't want a husband, did you want a boss…?"

"Yes," she said, looking at him again. "Yes, a boss."

"A boss? You wanted a job!"

"No, no, not a job." She shook her head to emphasize that, got to her feet, took his hand. "Come," she said, "I will show you." She led him into her bedroom, the smaller of the two in the flat. The bigger was reserved for when he came. It had a big bed and a view of the garden. It was where they made love. He had been in her bedroom just once, when Louie first showed him the place.

Her room was neat, bright, and colorful. A cot with a stuffed tiger sitting on it, a chest of drawers, but his eyes leapt to the walls – lined with colorful posters, a dozen at least, each one advertising soap, or cigarettes, or whiskey. And silk stockings apparently. He had seen others like them in restaurants in Kunming and in the fancy shops that Sue took him to, but he had never really looked at them; they were just advertising after all.

"Do you like them?" she asked, her eyes bright with a collector's pride.

"Quite attractive," he said, although he was not certain that he would want them on his wall.

She watched him looking at the posters. "Pretty girls," she said.

Ah, pretty girls, of course. He was not thinking. The object of each poster was a pretty girl, or two sometimes. Each wore a shy smile and a nice dress. Their poses differed, but, standing or sitting, they were always modest. Any one of the girls could have been the nice Chinese girl next door. The product being advertised seemed like an afterthought. A bottle of whiskey, a bar of soap, or a pack of cigarettes that was placed almost inconspicuously along the side or in the bottom margin.

"They are pretty girls," he said, and he meant it. "They're not photos. They're painted, aren't they? Is that what you would like to do, paint the girls?"

"No," she said, looking disappointed that he did not understand. "I want to be the girl. The girl everyone looks at."

"You want to be a model?" He thought about that, shrugged. "Well, if that's what you want …." He turned to look at her. She was pretty enough, as pretty as the girls in the posters, but she did not have their innocent look. That could be painted in he supposed. "A boss, you said. What kind of boss could help you be a model?"

She blurted it out: "A gangster!"

He laughed. "A gangster? Where did you learn that word? Do you know what a gangster is?"

"Yes," she said, "I know. A boss, a big boss. The boss everyone listens to." She stepped up to one of the posters, looked at the girl in a green high-collared dress, who was seated demurely in front of her dresser, lost in thought apparently, not even looking at the oversized bottle of scotch whiskey at her feet.

"This girl was the sister of my school friend. Her family was poor. She met a gangster. Now she has a nice flat. She goes to nightclubs and to the most expensive restaurants. She drives everywhere in a Buick. All the poster girls are girlfriends of big boss gangsters." She sounded disappointed that he did not know that.

"So you want to be a gangster's girl, a gun moll. I guess I see your point."

She did not know what a gun moll was, but tried to explain what happened to her dream. "When I finished school, I thought I would meet a gangster, a nice one, but the Japanese came. Everyone fled from Shanghai, even the gangsters."

She looked so sad then, that he felt he had to say something. "You didn't do so badly. You found the biggest gangster of all." He knew she would not take it quite the way it sounded, but she frowned.

"General Tai Li does not like posters," she said.

* * *

He thought of her all the way to dinner. The governor of Yunnan Province was hosting the AVG tonight. Getting to his mansion at the top of a hill that overlooked the city meant driving over narrow, twisty roads crowded with people, carts and animals. Driving required his full attention, but his thoughts were with the girl.

He had felt sorry for her at first, but now he was starting to accept her situation as the natural way of things. This was China, after all, and life in Shanghai even before the war was a different world. What did he know of it? Shanghai had been a shining symbol of modern China, a Sino-European metropolis that was also one of the most depraved cities on earth. Rich people lived wonderfully well and the poor starved. What real options did an ordinary girl there have, except to do her best to survive? At that his Shanghai girl had proven adept.

Her past was not his concern, but her future might be. By local rules she belonged to him. He could probably do with her as he pleased and get away with it. Not that he had any bad intentions, but his mind had seized on the thought of what a good spy she could be – not for Tai Li, but for him.

She was quite bright, not as bright as Lucy or Sue perhaps, and certainly not nearly as sophisticated as those two. But she was clever, and shrewd, and calculating. She could fit into Chinese society in a way that neither Lucy nor Sue ever could. She was born to survive.

How to take advantage of this natural talent? He was already using her, in a very small way, against Tai Li. Through her he could feed things that he wanted Tai Li to believe. But Tai Li had other sources, and in time he would see the discrepancies in what she reported. Her credibility would wane, and with that, her usefulness to Tai Li – and to Harry as well. Before it came to that, he would need to find another way to use her, to find a target he could direct her at, somewhere outside Tai Li's circle. He needed to talk to Doyle.

The governor's mansion was big and impressive, as befitted a descendant of the warlords who had previously ruled the province. Like them, the governor had his own army, and much of it was on display at the palace that evening. Whistles blew and arms waved Harry into a parking place, and a small squad escorted him across the courtyard to the path that led through the garden. They left him there, with a touch of ceremony, to find his own way down the worn stepping stones strewn with pine needles. Paper lanterns that dangled from tree limbs lit his way. Where the path ended, marble steps lined by two rows of soldiers led to an open door. At the top he was greeted by a colonel.

The colonel led him into a drawing room that was something out of old Europe. The governor's love for France was well known, as befitted a man who ruled the part of China closest to French Indo-China. The colonel introduced Harry to a short man with a shaved head and spectacles that magnified his crossed eyes. The governor took Harry's hand, bowed, and said something that sounded very French. He did not look much like a warlord.

Another Chinese colonel led Harry to the "play room", really the bar, that was already crowded with the AVG. It was a big room, with heavy drapes and French furniture, and the AVG had taken it over. What were probably priceless antiques got little respect from the pilots. The Panda Bears had pulled delicate chairs together into a protective circle that they sat inside of, and drank and laughed and looked out on everyone else. Others leaned on fine tables or sat on them. Another group sat on the marble floor or sprawled full length on expensive rugs. Through the cigarette smoke and the din lurched a troop of white-coated waiters, balancing trays of drinks that were depleted before they got carried very far.

There were others in the room besides the AVG. A group of senior Chinese officers stood to the side and watched. A gaggle of American Army officers stood nearby, in a corner, wearing stern faces. Suddenly, all faces, American and Chinese, turned toward the entrance. Olga Greenlaw had walked in.

She was gorgeous in a green silk dress that glowed like emerald in soft light. The dress fit her perfectly; it could have been French-made or Chinese. Like Olga, it looked exotic. The Chinese officers got to her first; she seemed to know many of them. One kissed her hand. The AVG waved at her and shouted greetings. Her face glowed as she waved to the loudest and nodded greetings to the others. She saw Harry and waved a hello at him. At least he thought it was meant for him, and he waved back. He noticed a Chinese looking at him then. It was Tai Li, who nodded. Harry nodded back.

Ed Rector stopped on his way to the dining room and invited Harry to join some of the Pandas at their table. The dining room was really the terrace, but it was all glassed in, roof and all, so that the guests would not notice the chill if the night turned cold. The floor was covered with pine needles; the pine smell heavy in the air. The most senior Chinese were already seated at tables in the front. The AVG squadron leaders and vice squadron leaders were in the next row, sharing tables with Chinese colonels. Neither Chennault nor Harvey Greenlaw was able to make it, and Olga was one of the few women there. She took her seat at one of the front tables and was quickly the center of attention.

The Pandas' table where Harry sat was close to the back wall, near the door that offered easy access to the bar if service got slow. But that never happened. The staff was efficient, drinks flowed and the food came quickly. It was Chinese with a Western touch, and there were forks as well as chopsticks. Dinner proceeded smoothly, until dessert. "Precious eight pudding," Rector read the name from the menu.

"What the hell is that?" somebody asked, and the Pandas looked worried. One of them went up and asked Olga. "It's stuff made out of eight different kinds of fruits and nuts," he reported to them when he returned. "And each one's a different color." When the explanation ended there, some one asked, "What then?"

"I don't know. You eat it, I guess."

Harry looked up, just as Doyle walked by, and almost failed to recognize him because of the uniform that he wore – of a U.S. Army lieutenant. He had noted a table of American officers near his own, but had his back to them and never looked there. That must have been where Doyle had come from. He watched Doyle walk down the hallway, headed for the men's room, probably. No one was looking, so he got up and followed.

It was the men's room all right, a bright and elaborate display of chrome and marble, and facilities enough to handle a terrace-full of hard-drinking generals. Doyle stood alone by a row of marble sinks, his back to Harry. As he came up behind, Harry hummed a tune, the words known to everyone now.

You're in the Army now.
You're not behind a plow.
You'll never get rich
By digging a ditch,
"I'm in the Army now!" Doyle sang out the final line.

"So this is your new cover?" Harry said, looking at the second lieutenant bars on Doyle's shoulders. "You could at least have made yourself a captain."

"It was second lieutenant or private first class," Doyle said. "I modestly chose the lesser rank." He looked at the row of polished wood doors across from them, and gestured with his chin at the exit. They stepped outside, into the hallway, walked a few steps to a small alcove where they could stand inconspicuously, and see anyone approaching.

"I think I told you, Donovan wanted me attached to Stilwell's staff," Doyle explained. "Stilwell didn't want any civilians around." He shrugged. "I either became a soldier or found other work."

"So Uncle Wild Bill made you a soldier."

"The Army made me a soldier, Uncle Bill just let them. I'm a soldier for the duration, I guess, but I'm still working for Uncle Bill. It gets confusing. It means I have a lot of bosses. Hey, before we get diverted, let me ask you something serious: Who is that fascinating woman sitting up by the governor's table, the one all the generals are falling over? She's not Chinese, but very exotic-looking. She waved at you in the bar."

"You mean Olga, Olga Greenlaw. She's the wife of the AVG executive officer.

"So that's Olga," Doyle said and, as he thought about her, added, "Wow! Isn't she a great-looking woman. How about introducing me?"

"That wouldn't be good tradecraft; besides, isn't she a bit old for you? She must be over 30."

"If that's what old is, I'll take it. I watched her with those Chinese generals. She just wraps them around her fingers. She looks like one smart lady."

"She is a smart lady. The Old Man made her the AVG's historian. She keeps the Group's war diary and does a little newspaper for the group."

"You'll have to tell me more about her at our next meeting." Doyle stepped into the hallway, looked both ways to assure no one was coming. "Harry, you may have the answer to this. Do you know about any airplanes being brought in here?"

"There are airplanes coming here all the time now. The AVG has received some new E-model P-40s. The Chinese got some P-43s."

"Those are all fighters, aren't they? What about bombers?"

"There's always talk about bombers. Chennault's plan was to have a second AVG that would have been made up of bombers, but as far as I know, that idea was overtaken by the start of the war. I'm sure the Army will bring in bombers from India before long."

"All those airplanes are coming in from India?"

"Where else? Everything comes from India or via India. The AVG guys went to Africa to get the E-models, then flew them here by way of India."

Doyle shook his head. "It's not that. There's something else going on." He looked at Harry a long moment, hesitating. "Do you know of any airplanes coming from the other way?"

Harry thought about that. "The other way is from the east. It's all Japanese in that direction."

"Yeah, I know, but where would American bombers come from if they were coming to China from the east?"

"That doesn't make any sense, Doyle. They would have to be coming from Japan."

Doyle shrugged. "There's something going on that involves American bombers coming from the east. The staff guys at Stilwell's headquarters who know, aren't talking, but one of my Chinese friends got wind of some thing. He says it's very hush-hush, but it involves receiving American bombers coming from the east."

"That doesn't make any sense," Harry said.

"Well, then see if you can find out what's going on."

CHAPTER 27

Find out what's going on. Well that should be easy enough. Now that he had experienced a certain success in dealing with "intelligence problems" - unexpected as that success might have been – Harry believed that his instincts were good, and that he could trust them. And his instincts told him that if he wanted to find out anything about mysterious bombers coming from the east, it made no sense to poke around with the underlings, but to go right to the top, to the Old Man himself. Chennault was directly involved with everything that concerned airplanes, American or Chinese. He would certainly know what was going on. And he owed Harry, for the information that made the Chiang Mai raid possible. Harry drove to the airport early the next morning, figuring he could catch the Old Man at his office there.

"Nope," the Old Man said. He leaned way back in his chair, stared at the ceiling and looked thoughtful. "I've been asking for bombers for months, Harry, but nobody's told me they're on the way. And if they ever did come, they would come from India, not Japan. You sure your man didn't get his directions mixed?"

Harry shrugged. "I'm not sure of anything, sir, but let me ask you this: If something like this was going on, if somebody was delivering airplanes to China and you didn't know about it, but some low-ranking Chinese officer did, what would that mean?"

The Old Man did not hesitate. "Politics," he said.

The surprise must have shown on Harry's face, so the Old Man explained. "There's an awful lot going on. Stilwell's bunch is trying to establish itself with the Chinese. The Army Air Corps is trying to find its place. Why, hell, even our Navy is trying to get a foothold here.

Everybody's holding their cards close to their chest. And it seems like everybody's main concern is the pecking order. I'll tell you, Harry, it's getting to be as bad as Washington here." The Old Man stood up. A clerk was waiting at the door with an armload of papers. "Look, Harry, if I do hear anything about bombers coming from the east – or from the west for that matter – I'll get in touch with you. I would appreciate if you do the same for me. Give my best to your Uncle Wild Bill."

As Harry walked back along the apron, a small truck went by, carrying some of the pilots out to their airplanes. "Harry!" someone shouted and then waved. "Stop! Stop!" the same voice cried. Brakes screeched and the truck jolted to a stop. Ed Rector hopped off. He stood and waited for Harry to reach him. "Come on, Harry," he said, "walk along with me out to my airplane."

"Where you guys going?" Although they had sat next to each other at dinner the night before, Harry knew there were questions not to ask unless they were alone.

"We're going south, down to Loi Wing. We'll be there for a few days, to fly morale missions."

"Morale missions? I'm not sure I know what that is. Last night somebody said that AVG morale had hit rock bottom, and that morale missions were to blame."

"Yeah, well, that's right. Our morale has gone to shit because we're flying missions to boost the morale of the Chinese troops. Do you follow that? No? Well, here's how it works. The Brits in Burma are in full retreat. A Chinese division was sent down to help them, and then the Chinese get smashed by the Japs. Now the Chinese are on the run too. Everybody's demoralized, but General Stilwell has the answer: Order the AVG to fly strafing attacks against the Japs, have us get down low where the Chinese troops can see the whites of our eyes. That will raise Chinese spirits, Stilwell says, boost their morale. That's what a 'morale mission' is supposed to be, Harry. But what morale missions are really doing is getting our airplanes shot up and destroying AVG morale. And they're not doing much to cheer up the poor Chinese trooper who is getting his ass chewed off by the Japanese."

"I don't follow that, Ed. Chennault is in charge of the AVG, and the AVG is part of the Chinese Air Force. How does Stilwell get to give orders to the Old Man?"

"You're behind the times, Harry. The Old Man doesn't like the morale missions any more than we do, but he has no choice. He's got to take orders now. He's back in the U.S. Army Air Corps, you knew that, didn't you?"

Harry nodded. He had heard someone say that Chennault had been recalled to the U.S. Army Air Corps, but had not really thought about what that meant.

Rector was still fuming. "The morale missions are nothing but a waste of fuel, and they're bloody dangerous. It makes us easy targets, and the Chinese troops get strafed as often as the Japanese. Visibility down there is very bad. The Burmese forests are burning; there's haze over everything. When we see a troop column on a road, we often can't tell if they're Japanese or Chinese. We have no communications with the Chinese troops, which is a terrible thing when you can't tell friend from foe. The AVG was created to defend China from the Japanese Air Force, not fly low-level missions against troops. Chennault knows all that, and he agrees that the morale missions are crazy. But General Stilwell is in charge of the whole theater – and U.S. Army Colonel Claire Chennault is just one of his officers now." Rector turned to look Harry straight in the face.

"I bet you just saw the Old Man, didn't you? Did he tell you he's going to be a Brigadier General? That's part of the deal he got to go back to the Army."

"If the Old Man has been pulled back into the U.S. Army, what happens to the AVG?"

"The word is that the AVG will be disbanded on the fourth of July, which seems fitting, doesn't it? We'll be replaced by an Army Air Corps fighter group."

"Does Chiang Kai-shek have anything to say about all this?"

"I don't know, but we all still have contracts with the Generalissimo, even the Old Man. I guess the contracts will stay in force until 4 July."

"What happens to all you guys after the fourth?"

"Nobody knows. They tried to induct us into the Army Air Corps, but that turned into a total disaster. They sent this guy Bissell, Colonel Clayton Bissell, to talk to us. He's an arrogant son-of-a-bitch; treated us like children. Told us to sign up right then, and that if we tried to go home first, our draft board will greet us when our ship docked. He really rubbed everybody the wrong way. You can't do that with the AVG. Our guys are pretty independent, and all of us have commitments to get our U.S. commission back once our AVG contracts end."

They were near the P-40s now, and could see the pilots in their cockpits or climbing in. "I better go; the guys are almost ready to take off. Look, I'll be back in a couple of days. We'll talk then. Hey, look over there, the CNAC C-47 has just arrived." Harry turned toward the runway to see the twin-engine transport land, wheels throwing up plumes of dust as they touched.

"Tell you what, Harry, if you want to see something funny, go over to the ramp and watch the passengers unload."

"What do you mean?"

"Just go watch. You'll see."

It was on his way, so Harry stopped to watch. The C-47 had taxied to park near the operations shack. A half-dozen Chinese employees of the airline were gathered near the aircraft door to help with baggage or do whatever else was required while the plane was on the ground. As the passengers started to deplane, most of them American army officers, the Chinese bowed politely to each one as he passed, and shouted out a greeting. It took Harry a moment to realize what it was they were shouting:

"Piss on Bissell! Piss on Bissell! Piss on Bissell!"

An AVG crewman was standing nearby, watching. He looked at Harry and started to laugh. "Our guys taught them that. They think it's a polite greeting."

* * *

"So you don't think there's anything in our mysterious bombers from the east?"

"No, I don't," Harry said. "The Old Man would know if anybody did. And he has no reason not to tell me."

"He might," Doyle said, "if the secret's big enough. You might not have 'the need to know.'"

Harry shrugged. "The 'need to know', huh? You may be right, but The Old Man sure seemed sincere."

"I've often seen you looking very sincere while you were telling a bold-face lie. It's a useful talent to have."

Doyle was in uniform, but he wore it casually. He had no necktie, and his garrison cap was stuffed in his belt. Harry had also taken to wearing khaki-colored clothing, particularly when he was meeting Doyle. It made him less conspicuous now that there were more and more khaki-wearing Americans in Kunming. It was good camouflage.

Harry had been paying little attention to where they were going as they walked through the park around Green Lake. They reached one of the old pavilions, where in the mornings there was usually a small crowd having stand-up breakfasts from portable food stalls that sold noodles and little steamed buns. Past that was a trash pile and, as usual, there were several dirty old bums picking through it. One had just exhausted the culinary possibilities and stumbled out on to the path and almost ran into them. Harry could not help looking at the man. He wore a tattered vest and ragged shorts, and his legs and arms were filthy, stained and caked with muck. He dropped something and, without breaking stride, Doyle bent down and scooped it up. It was a greasy-looking thing, probably something used to wrap food. Doyle balled it up in his hand, and Harry shuddered. He pretended not to notice.

They turned a bend in the path, where they were hidden by shrubbery from anyone behind, when Doyle said, "Aren't you going to compliment me on my agent? And our pass?"

"Your pass?" Harry said.

Doyle sighed. "There are times I despair for you, Harry." He flipped the ball of greasy paper in the air and caught it. "Brush pass," he said, "with the Green Lake quick-drop variant." Harry looked completely puzzled now.

"That was my agent, Harry, and we just made a pass."

"That filthy beggar?" Harry turned around as if to see if the man was still there.

"For God's sake, Harry, don't go staring at him now. People will think we're spies. Yes, he's my prime agent, that chap. He's under 'filthy beggar' cover. It's quite effective."

Harry couldn't decide if Doyle was pulling his leg or not. The whole idea was so preposterous that it had to be true. "Doyle I can't believe this. What can you possibly get from a beggar?"

"Well, a complete report of your movements, as one example." Doyle looked around to assure there was no one in sight. He uncrumpled the greasy wrapper and extracted from it a small but clean sheet of paper. It was covered in Chinese characters. "Something for our translators," he said. He stuck the slip into his pocket and threw the greasy wrapper into the bushes. From a trouser pocket he pulled another wad of paper, a couple of sheets folded over and covered in typewritten English. He handed them to Harry, and Harry started to read. It took maybe 15 seconds.

"Goddamn it, Doyle," he said. "You have been watching me."

"Not I, old man, it was the filthy chap. It's just practice for him." What Harry had read was the comings and goings of one "gentleman" and two "madams" at the "Green Lake House". It gave times that the three, individually or together, departed and returned. It did not take Harry much time to realize it was a record of his, Lucy's and Sue's movements over the last ten days or so. It was a surveillance report. Harry had seen them in training, but never paid much attention to them.

"He's been hanging around your end of Green Lake for almost two weeks," Doyle said, "going through trash piles and just hanging around. You never noticed him, did you?"

Harry was not about to admit to anything. He just stood and looked off toward the lake.

"It's just an agent training exercise, Harry. There are a couple of teaching points. I assume you never noticed this chap, but who would? Don't feel bad. Who notices a beggar in a town full of them? This is just the kind of fellow Tai Li would use, or the Japanese if they could. I'm also thinking about your young lady from Shanghai. I know you would like to aim her back into Tai Li's boudoir, but have you considered her use in a more humble role against the Japanese?"

"What, poking through Jap trash piles?"

"No, not that, no trash piles for the young Miss Shanghai, but you might think of making her into someone inconspicuous who could survive in a Japanese-occupied city and collect information on simple things like Japanese truck movements or train cargoes, information we can pass on to Chennault's people. It's humble stuff, but very necessary to win the war."

"What about your beggar? You going to keep him watching me?"

"Actually, we're going to put him into Chungking. It's all very hush-hush, right now, but his target will be a European gentleman we think may be a spy for Germany, and also collecting information for the Japanese. That's why I put our filthy friend on you. You're a Westerner and you're a spy. It's good practice for him."

"Damn," Harry said.

"Now, now, Harry. You have to face up to it. In our profession you need to get used to being followed around without taking notice. An innocent man never notices his watchers, does he?"

They lapsed into silence then, walked along, Harry deep in thought. "You know, Doyle," he said finally, "This is all bullshit, but I liked your presentation. You made your point. It gives me things to think about. Where did you get this guy anyway?"

"I caught him poking through the trash in our compound. I was sure Tai Li had sent him. But he was so genuinely upset to be found in a trash pile – and it turns out he's a Christian. He learned a good bit of English in a missionary school. He hates the Japs, hates the war. When the Japs came, his school closed. And that was the end of his career prospects."

"He's Christian. That means he can't be Tai Li's man?"

"He can be, I suppose. Could be Tai Li's brother for all we know. Even if Tai Li sent him, it won't matter. We'll use him against targets that won't upset Tai Li. The information he will collect will be as interesting to Tai Li as it is to us. We certainly won't use him to penetrate Tai Li's organization. That way lies perdition."

"You keep saying 'we'. Who is 'we'?"

"Ah, that's my next agenda item. You and I are no longer alone here. Donovan has sent us some helpers, and more are enroute. Our new comrades are experts, one on Chinese culture, and one on the Japanese. They were professors at some school in New England. They both seem very knowledgeable and have ideas on not only what we should be doing, but how we should do it. They're the ones who suggested more use of filthy beggars and other invisibles. They also know a lot about what's been happening in Washington."

"So what's been happening in Washington?"

"Donovan is creating a new organization. He's recruiting like mad. As is his wife, I'm told. You know more about this than I do, Harry. They're both well-placed socially, and they're recruiting all their friends. The wife, all her old school chums...."

"Ruth," Harry said. "Donovan's wife's name is Ruth. She's a Vassar girl."

"Auntie Ruth? I understand she's a wealthy woman. I heard a little bit about all that when I was in India, and more from our two professor friends. They say that Donovan is recruiting his law partners and his old school mates. He's in the early stage of creating a strategic intelligence organization. At least that's what the professors call it. They say it will be big. It will reach around the world. It will be very secret. It will carry out espionage and sabotage – and a lot of things you and I have probably never even thought of."

"Sounds exciting."

"Well, it is. And you and I, Harry, we will have been there from the beginning."

They looked at each other, thoughtfully, but only for a moment. "Okay," Doyle interjected. "That finishes all the mundane stuff. Now, Harry, tell me all about the marvelous, the mysterious, the beautiful Olga Greenlaw."

CHAPTER 28

A few nights later, when Harry got back to the flat, Lucy told him, "You just missed your telephone calls. She looked at a note she made for herself. "Let's see, first there was Ed Rector. He said he was back from the south and not flying tomorrow, and how about a drink. Then Louie's tailor called and said your new shirts are ready. The last was an American, Captain Anderson, I think he said. It was something about an interview he was trying to schedule for you, but he wasn't successful yet."

Harry's ears twitched when he heard the Anderson name. That was Doyle calling an emergency meeting. That was unusual, and could not be anything good. By their standing arrangements, it would automatically be a car pickup at 7 o'clock the next morning. Doyle would be walking along the road from the Army compound where he lived, and would be hitch-hiking as Harry drove up.

"Oh, and I've heard from Louie," Lucy said. "He's been traveling, with the Generalissimo apparently, and now he's back in Chungking. He said to say 'hello.' He wasn't sure when he will get back here."

It was after dinner and Sue was not in sight. He assumed she was already in her room. She had not been sneaking into his bedroom since the night of the "buffalo", and otherwise seemed to be avoiding him. "Is Sue already in bed?" he asked.

"Actually, she's out with her new friend, Chinese chap, a colonel, I think."

"Oh," Harry said.

"Yes, I think he's one of Chiang Kai-shek's intelligence officers."

"Well, good for Sue," he said. Life was getting even more complicated.

The next morning he rose early to get the first order of business out of the way, a quick car meeting with Doyle. He saw Doyle when he was still a good distance off. There were few motorcars on the road, but people everywhere, and a procession of animal carts. Doyle must have been the only Westerner for miles. He turned when he heard the car engine, and stuck out his thumb. Harry pulled over. "Going my way, soldier?" he said as he pushed open the passenger door.

Not even a small smile for that. Doyle looked serious, even grim. "Start driving, Harry. I want to read you something," he said and unfolded a sheet of paper. "This came in our channel last night. Our bomber mystery is solved." He started to read:

The U.S. Army Air Corps reported that on April 18, 1942, 16 B-25 Mitchell bombers bombed Tokyo and four other Japanese cities. After leaving Japan, the bombers flew on to airfields in China that had been prepared for them. As of this time – middle of the night in Washington, yesterday," Doyle interjected, "none of the crews have been in contact with their headquarters. Because of bad weather over China, the aircraft may have diverted to other airfields in friendly territory. It is also possible that some of these aircraft and their crews have landed or crashed in Japanese-controlled areas of China. We request that you query all sources for information about these aircraft and their crews. The reaction of Colonel Chennault and any knowledge he might have of the preparations made in China for the crews would be most interesting. Signed, 'Donovan'.

"Good Christ!" Harry said. "This is absolutely incredible. We bombed Japan! Where the hell did those airplanes come from? Are these the bombers we've been looking for?"

"They're our mysterious bombers, I'm sure of that. They came from 'Shangri-La'. That's what the Army said in their cable to Stilwell's staff, and that's all they plan to release to the press. So 'Shangri-la' it is for now. What you need to do now, Harry, is to get to Chennault as soon as you can. Find out what he thinks about the raid, but the most important thing is what he knows about the missing bombers and their crews. If they've come down anywhere in China, there had to be Chinese who saw it. Chiang Kai-shek's people must know by now.

"And try to find out what the hell was supposed to happen. The cable talks about 'airfields in China that were prepared for the planes'. Chenault had to be involved with that. If the bombers never got there, why didn't they? I'm sure you won't be the only one trying to talk with Chennault this morning. Every American in China has probably received the same kind of cable we have. Try to get there first, Harry. Tell the Old Man he owes you for Chiang Mai."

Harry dropped Doyle and drove right out to the airfield. Chennault usually went out to the field in the early morning to watch his airplanes take off on their dawn patrols. The airfield was quiet when he arrived, and Harry was afraid he got there too late. But he found the Old Man in his office at the field, sitting at the small desk, staring out the window, deep in thought. He looked tired, the lines in his face deeper than Harry remembered.

"Ah, Mister Ross," he said, "I thought you would be out here this morning. Stilwell's people had up me up in the middle of the night. I expect you want to talk about Doolittle's Raid?"

"Doolittle, sir?"

"Jimmy Doolittle, he led the raid on Tokyo. An American boy like you should know who Jimmy Doolittle is."

"I do, sir. Jimmy Doolittle was one of my heroes when I was a kid. He was the race pilot who set all the speed records. But I didn't know he led the raid."

"He did. It's not generally known yet, but it will be."

"What do you think of the raid, sir? Did they cause much damage?"

"Sixteen B-25s could not do much real damage to Japan. What they did was destroy the confidence the Japanese had that they were safely out of America's reach. It was a brilliant operation, one for the history books."

"We have a report that there were airfields in China prepared to receive the airplanes."

"That something I've just learned myself. I had no foreknowledge of the raid. No one asked my help to prepare airfields or to do anything else for Doolittle's airplanes. What I know about the raid is what I've learned in recent hours, mainly from Stilwell's staff."

The Old Man stopped there, turned to look at Harry directly. "What I'm going to tell you is not for publication. I assume you will prepare a report for Donovan. This is for Donovan, no one else."

Harry nodded.

"Stilwell is still charging around Burma with the British. On his staff here, he has an Air Officer, an Army Air Corps Colonel named Clayton Bissell. I've had some dealings with Bissell, but I found out just this morning, that his main purpose in coming here was to make preparations for the Doolittle raid, to organize airfields where the raiders could land after they bombed Japan. He was so secretive about his mission that he never told me about it. And that was a shame. We have an air-warning net that covers most of eastern China. Bissell organized a couple of airfields all right, but when Doolittle's B-25s arrived in China, they came in the dark, and when the weather was bad. They couldn't find the airfields. Had Bissell told us they were coming, we could have plugged an AVG radio station into the east China air-warning net and talked most of the bombers right in to a friendly airfield. Because we were never told they were coming, there was no way to communicate with those airplanes. They were on their own over unfamiliar terrain."

"So what happened to the bombers and the crews?"

"We don't know yet. We know they're down. They crashed – or the crews bailed out in the dark. Those were the only things they could do. The Chinese are doing their best to find them."

"Christ," Harry said, "I don't understand, why would Bissell not tell you?"

"I don't know that, Harry. It might have been bureaucracy or politics. Or plain stupidity maybe. Whatever it was, it cost us 16 good airplanes and possibly a lot of good men. There is one other thing you should know. Whatever caused the problem here, Washington shares in the blame. The planners in Washington made an outrageous mistake. They overlooked the effect of the International Date Line, the fact that China was a day ahead of Washington. Because of that the bombers got here a day earlier than Washington told even Bissell. We know some of the bombers over-flew one of the airfields that Bissell prepared. Because the planes arrived a day earlier than anyone thought, the Chinese turned out all the airport lights. They thought it was a Japanese air raid."

"So what happens now?"

"We wait and we pray. The Chinese are doing what they can. It's a goddamn shame. We were to get those airplanes. We could have used them." The Old Man shook his head. He looked more frustrated than tired.

Back in his car, Harry looked at his watch. He could make a meeting with Doyle and report on what he had learned from Chennault, pick up his new shirts, and still make lunch with Ed Rector.

CHAPTER 29

Harry walked along Kunming's French Street. Or that was how he thought of the street where all the good shops were, the ones Sue had introduced him to. And it was where Louie's shirt maker was located. There were also a few restaurants that Sue had taken him to, including a "bistro" that served an almost edible water buffalo "beefsteak" and French fries. With his new shirts in a box under his arm, he got to the bistro early. It was popular now with all the new American arrivals, and he wanted to be sure of a table overlooking the street for his lunch with Ed Rector. In his rush he collided with a man coming through the door. "Excuse me," he said as he pulled himself back and collected himself.

"Watch where you're going, Ross. You're not in Burma now." The voice was so familiar that Harry turned around to look at the man. "Morris!" he said. "My God, where did you drag in from?"

"Burma."

"Burma? You were there all this time? I thought you left weeks ago. When did you get to Kunming?"

"Twenty minutes ago, enough time for one drink. Come on, you can buy me another." At that Morris turned and went back through the door. "Did you know they have Armangac here?" he called back over his shoulder. With Harry right behind, he bounded up the stairs and reclaimed the table he had just vacated. The Chinese waiter was still cleaning it up. Morris slapped him on the back. "Garcon!" he said, "Armangac! Two big ones, *s'il vous plait*." To Harry, "My alcohol level is dangerously low."

"I don't remember you as a big drinker," Harry said.

"It's turning into a long, dry war. A man has to adapt."

"I'm meeting Ed Rector here. You remember him?"

"I sure do. He can buy me a drink too."

When they were seated, Morris said, "I heard what happened to Scarsdale Jack. I'm really sorry about that. He was always a good story."

Harry nodded. He did not want to talk about it now. "I thought you went to India."

"I started to. The night we inaugurated the new RAF officers' club at Mingaladon. Then I found an AVG convoy forming up, and I joined them." He ran a hand through his now bushy hair. "It was a long drive. I went only as far as Lashio. I ran into Shi Ti-weh and his bunch there. They convinced me that all the news of the world would come from there as soon as the Japs caught up with us. They were almost right about that, but the food wasn't great and there was never enough to drink."

"Shih Ti-weh? Who is that?"

"Stilwell, General Joseph W. Stilwell. It's what the Chinese call him. Even up here you must have heard that China is now the "Allied China Theater", that Chiang Kai-shek is its Supreme Commander and Stilwell is Chiang's Chief of Staff. That puts Stilwell in command of the Chinese forces that were sent into Burma to save the British bacon. Have you met him yet? "

"Stilwell? No. I haven't seen him around here. I don't think he's spent much time in China."

"Maybe not since the war started, but he was here before that, back in the thirties. He was a military attaché then. He speaks Chinese. He's not a very personable man, but he wears his uniform nicely. When the AVG convoy reached him up in Lashio, the boys had been on the road for days. They were looking for a place to rest up, and something to eat. He treated them like bums. 'A disgrace to the U.S. Army', he called them to their faces." Morris chuckled at the memory. "Because they're not in the U.S. Army it didn't really bother them too much."

"I hear the Chinese troops are putting up a good fight in Burma."

"Well, they were. They fought like tigers at Toungoo."

"Did you get to see any of that?"

"No, I was up north of there, with Stilwell. He was setting a trap for the Japs in the Sittang Valley. The idea was that, after mixing it up with the Japs at Toungoo for a few days, the Chinese would start falling back. They would lure the Japs north, where Stilwell was waiting with the main force of Chinese troops. And then a British regiment got itself into trouble over in the Irrawaddy Valley. They got trapped by the Japs, and yelled for Stilwell to save them. Stilwell took his tanks – the only ones he had – and an infantry division – and charged off to save the British. He did that all right, but he weakened the Chinese line, and the Japs punched right through.

That was the beginning of a disaster. Right now, even as we speak, the Brits, the Chinese and Stilwell himself are all in a race to stay ahead of the Japanese and get out of Burma."

Harry shook his head. "Jesus," he said. "But the Japs can't push much farther north, can they? They're already over-extended."

"Yeah, well, that's what the British say. That's what the British have been saying since Moulmein fell. And they will be saying it when the Japanese are marching down the streets of New Delhi." Morris shook his head then. "I don't know what will happen when the Japs get to India, but as far as Burma goes, Burma is lost."

"How did you get out?"

"An occasional airplane goes in to bring stuff to Stilwell. On the way back it brings out wounded and an occasional civilian like me."

"Where's Stilwell now?"

"Hopefully, still ahead of the Japs. He's in north Burma somewhere, heading for the Chinese border. Chennault will send him an airplane when he calls for it. He's been too proud to leave so far."

"Christ, he could almost qualify for the British Army."

"I don't think the Brits want him. Actually, Stilwell is not really as bad as all that, although abandoning the Chinese line to save a British regiment is going to cost everybody dearly. The Chinese could have really hurt the Japs there – maybe stopped them – if he hadn't done that. It could have been a real Chinese victory. It must really piss off the Generalissimo."

"So what happens now?"

Morris shrugged. Just then Harry saw Ed Rector's head pop up the stairway and look around. Harry waved and Ed walked over. Harry was not sure Rector and Morris would remember each other, so he started an introduction.

"You know Ed Rector? You guys met at the Silver Grill."

Morris stood to shake hands. "Yeah we know each other. How you doing, Ed." He turned back to Harry. "Actually, Ed and I met even more recently."

"You did? Where was that?"

"Burma," Rector answered, and winked at Morris. He took a beer the Chinese waiter offered and held it up. "Cheers," he said, and they all drank.

"I'm waiting, Ed," Harry said. "Don't be mysterious."

Rector all but finished his beer before going on. "I was flying some recon missions for General Stilwell, trying to keep track of the Jap advance. Usually I would just fly back to our field, make my report, and they send it on to Stilwell by radio. One day I flew over an area where I knew he was bivouacked in a little town. It was very picturesque. I landed on a polo field and found a couple of American officers. They said he was resting at the British club, right on the edge of the field. I walked over, met a couple of his staff and gave them chapter and verse on where the Japs were. About that time I saw Morris here, sitting at the bar, all alone, having a beer. He looked lonely, so I went over and had one with him. It was a nice beer. Morris got them to put ice in it. "

"That made it drinkable," Morris said.

Rector nodded and went on. "I appreciated that beer. It was hot work down there in Burma. We were both hungry too. There wasn't a whole lot, but the cook made a mean crumpet that we soaked in brandy and ate with honey."

"Have you flown down that way recently?" Morris asked. "Do you know where the Japs are now, Ed?"

"Hot on the heels of the Chinese, at least the ones I saw. Everybody's heading for the Salween River."

"Will the Japs be able to cross the Salween?" Harry asked.

"If they do, we're all in big trouble. There's just a single bridge. The Chinese should be able to hold them. If the Japs get across it, they're in China and there would be nothing between them and Kunming."

"And I thought it was already as bad as it gets," Harry said.

"It will get worse," Morris said, "I promise you. But right now I've got to find myself a haircut."

"The barbershop's on the other side of the street," Rector said, "about three doors down. It's called 'Marcel of Hanoi.'"

After Morris left, Harry asked, "Do you have any more good news for me.?"

"Well, let me think. Did you hear about the pilots' revolt?"

"You're kidding. What happened?"

"Last time I saw you I think I told you how low AVG morale was, because of the morale missions and other things. And the guys were complaining about our airplanes being in bad shape and not getting replacements for them. Or not getting any new pilots either, to replace the ones we've lost. The last straw came when we were down at Loi Wing. The Old Man ordered a flight to escort some British Blenheim bombers to Chiang Mai. Can you imagine? Chiang Mai is where we lost Jack Newkirk and Black Mac. It's a Jap beehive. The Blenheims are slow airplanes, and the guys thought they were being sacrificed on a hopeless mission. Somebody drew up a petition refusing to fly and offering resignations. Twenty-eight pilots signed. I was not one of them"

"What happened then?"

"It was getting pretty bad, and then Tex Hill made a speech. He said things had changed since we signed our contracts. America was at war now. It was not just what we wanted, anymore. All that ended at Pearl Harbor. It was our country we were fighting for now. Then, Tex volunteered to lead the mission. Five of us volunteered to join him."

"So you flew back to Chiang Mai?"

"Nope. We took off, but the Blenheims never rendezvoused with us. Bad weather, they said."

"Wonderful. Now what? Do the resignations stand?"

"The Old Man had some talks with the pilots. It's obvious he agrees with their views, but he has to execute the orders he gets from the Generalissimo and Stilwell. He has no choice. He told the pilots they had a choice: his orders or a 'dishonorable discharge.' Nobody wants that. I think the Old Man will just sit on the resignations. He needs the pilots. And the pilots aren't pressing the issue. Everyone would just like to forget the whole business. I think it's already over."

"So it's back to the war."

Ed picked up a freshly poured beer and nodded. "It's back to the war for everybody."

* * *

It was like a family reunion that Harry found when he arrived at the Green Lake flat. Butler Chen let him in, an unusual smile on his face. He saw Lucy first, and she looked happy. And then he saw Sue – and Louie, sitting side by side on the lounge in the living room. It was the first time he had seen Louie in the flat. It was first time Louie had visited there since they had come from Rangoon. Louie stood up and pulled out a chair for Harry, next to Sue.

"Harry, old boy, come join us," he said.

Feeling of guilt twisted in Harry's bowels, and dread that the confrontation he saw in nightmares was about to happen. But just for an instant, and then he knew it would not. "This is quite a grand occasion," he said as he sat down. He stole a glance at Sue. She looked particularly well-behaved, hands folded on her lap, a small smile of innocence on her face. "You must be through with your travels," he said to Louie.

"Yes, "Louie said, "I spent time with the Generalissimo. I just got in from Chungking. I wanted a chance to see everyone here, and thought I better do it while I have time. The girls and I have had quite a chat already. I understand everyone is happy; everyone is busy. I was about to retire to the library for a brandy. Come along, Harry, we can chat there."

They left the girls behind and went to Louie's den. Louie brought out the glasses and the brandy, and poured a generous measure for each of them. He handed one to Harry, but then, instead of sitting down himself, started roaming the room, looking at pictures on the wall, at the books on the shelves.

"You look a bit…unsettled," Harry said.

"I suppose I am."

"Anything I can help with?"

"No, thank you, Harry. It's the war." He sipped at his brandy, thoughtfully. "There's so much to think about right now, so many changes coming. I need to find new ways to do things. Change is always disconcerting."

Harry said nothing, just waited. He knew there would be more to come; Louie was in that kind of a mood. Another reflective sip of brandy and Louie went on.

"The loss of Rangoon and the Burma Road has caused me real problems. The things China wants are coming in a dribble." Another reflective sip. "Mind you, I said 'wants', not 'needs'. What China 'needs' will arrive in a torrent, once the Americans have their supply line organized."

" 'Needs', 'wants'?" I'm not sure I understand your distinction."

"What China 'needs' are the machines to fight the war. The Americans will provide all that. What China 'wants' are the luxuries the Chinese upper classes now find they cannot live without. And it's the 'wants' that become my problem."

As he became engrossed in explaining, Louie finally sat down. "It was simple enough before," he said, "while we had Rangoon and the Burma Road. I found the goods that were wanted, negotiated the price and delivery to Rangoon, and sent everything up the Burma Road. Now Rangoon is closed to us, and the Road is gone. How do we get what we want now?"

The question was rhetorical, Louie continued. "Well, we buy goods from America, have them delivered to India, and fly them here. Simple enough, isn't it? If you have airplanes. Your President Roosevelt has already promised Chiang and Stilwell 100 cargo planes. The Generalissimo has ordered another ten for CNAC, his own airline, the China National Aviation Corporation. That's just the beginning."

"So," Harry said, "things sound pretty good."

"Well, they're not, not for me. I'm not ready. I need to find ways to deal with this."

"I don't think I understand."

"Well, let me put it another way. You know, Harry, in my days on the Burma Road, and before that, I did a lot of unusual deals, but I was always a legitimate businessman." He reflected on that and added, "Well, I may have done a bit of smuggling, but only when I had to. No more than your average man, I'm sure." Another sip of brandy.

"My father and his father were traders before me. They did their business with Europe and America, and I simply followed in their footsteps – as a good son does. And then the Japanese made everything difficult. I had to become creative. It was the way to survive. When the Burma Road opened, everything was made easy. Since it's closed, it's been hell. Another drink, Harry?"

Louie poured two fresh cognacs into their crystal snifters, then went on. "So, now I must start over. I must become even more creative – and less legitimate. And that troubles me. The way into China now will be by airplane. Most will be flown by American military pilots. The lowly cargo handlers will be Chinese, of course. Certainly those who work for CNAC will be. Having Chinese in the system will simplify the problem to some extent. So, while the things China needs for the war will come almost automatically, the things that China 'wants' are not things that American aid will provide. These are things the Americans will not want to deal with: gold and opium and whiskey and fine watches. But the demand is great, far greater than the demand for books on democracy."

"I think I see what you're getting at," Harry said. "Your job is to fill the gaps where American aid does not provide."

"Ah, exactly. I will necessarily deal with high-quality cargo, gold, say, or whiskey. Some of these things can simply be shipped under false manifests, with the people handling it well paid to look another way. But there are other high-quality items – watches or medicine – that I need new ways to deal with. A small bag of very expensive watches is worth a small fortune. The cargo airplanes have two pilots and a radio man. One can be paid to carry the bag. Watches and medicines can go like that, and opium perhaps. That's the easy part. Tobacco, like whiskey, must be moved in large quantities, which is more difficult. It's a tough business, Harry."

Harry sat, thinking. "I see your problem, but I find it hard to believe that the Chinese elite expect to get the things they always got. As if there was no war on."

"Ah, now you've hit the nub of the problem. There is a war on, but it's not ours. It's not a Chinese war anymore. Once Pearl Harbor happened, and the Americans came into the war, the destruction of the Japanese war machine was assured. That's how the Generalissimo sees it. And his officers. And our business leaders. Of course they want what they've always had. Why not? With the Americans here to fight the Japanese, the Chinese can turn to more important things. They can go back to fighting Communists and drinking good scotch whiskey."

"You're kidding."

"I'm not. The Doolittle raid simply reinforced this thinking. Doolittle showed that the Americans can strike in the heart of the Japanese homeland – without any need of Chinese assistance. The Chinese see the writing on the wall now. The Japanese will be finished off by the Americans. It will require only time. It's a very happy position for the Generalissimo – and all the rest of us Chinese."

"Everybody knows about the Doolittle raid now?"

"Everyone in Chungking is talking about it. They found some of the crews, you know."

Harry wanted to ask about that, but Louie was still very preoccupied with his own concerns. "There's another troubling aspect to all of this," he said, and went on before Harry could phrase his question. "And that's dealing with the Japanese-controlled areas of China. I suppose you know there's a good bit of trade that goes on between free China and the China under Japanese control. It may benefit the Japanese as much as it benefits us. It's a different kind of business. It's dealing with the devil – like you do, Harry. Next week, I'll be meeting some chaps from Nanking and Shanghai. We will establish routes to bring our goods through Japanese lines."

"I'm amazed," Harry said. "Isn't that very difficult?"

"There are always people who must be bought off, of course, Chinese and Japanese."

An idea was percolating its way up through Harry's mind. "You mentioned Shanghai," he said. "Will you actually be dealing with traders from Shanghai?"

"I don't expect to go into Shanghai. We will probably meet on neutral ground, somewhere outside the Japanese areas, but yes, I'll be dealing with the traders from Shanghai."

"Do you think it would be possible to get someone, a Chinese, a job in Shanghai with one of the big traders?"

"I think so. I don't see where it would be a problem at all."

"How about gangsters? Can any of these traders be considered gangsters?"

"Oh, yes, I believe every one of them is a proper gangster. You just tell me what kind of gangster you need."

"One who sponsors advertising posters."

That raised Louie's eyebrows. He bent his head and looked deep into the depths of his brandy glass, considering. Finally he looked up and shrugged. "If it's posters you want, Harry, it's posters you shall have."

By the time they finished their talk, Harry got Louie to agree to find a Shanghai gangster to hire his Shanghai girl. He put it in terms of needing a way to solve his problem of keeping the girl, while mindful of her desire to get back to Shanghai. He thought Louie probably knew exactly what he wanted, and Harry could live with that. It had been a good session with Louie all around. He had a new operation. And Louie's comments on the new economic realities and high-level Chinese views of their role in the war could be turned into a very interesting intelligence report. He congratulated himself. It was not a bad day's work.

CHAPTER 30

"A brilliant report, Harry," Doyle said after he read it. "Very enlightening; Washington will be pleased." He folded the report in half and stuck it under his shirt. "Now, you mentioned this girl from Shanghai. Tell me about her."

And so Harry explained how he had been working with this girl from Shanghai as a potential agent, and how he had worked out an operational plan to insert her into the center of Japanese-controlled Shanghai. Once there, she would report on Japanese activities and also on Chinese economic plans and activities. He acknowledged that he met the girl through Tai Li, but avoided getting into the gifting aspect of the relationship. That was impossible to explain at this point.

"Brilliant!" Doyle said again. "An excellent plan. Sir Louie will find her a job, identify a 'patron' who will take her in. And once she's there, she reports back to you. How will she communicate with you?"

"Initially, I will use Louie's good offices. She will send reports back through the business channels he establishes with his counterparts in Shanghai. He will explain the girl as a family link, a young niece who wants to stay in touch with daddy."

"And you are daddy. That's sweet. Will you train her in secret writing?"

"Not initially, just a simple open code. If it looks like the operation is working, we can use Louie to bring her out. I can train her in secret writing then, or in radio transmission if that looks feasible. I think it's best to wait and see how she does once she's back in Shanghai. This is our first one Doyle, and we don't know what kind of access she will have to any information we want, or even how well she will be able to function in Shanghai."

All of this was true, and Harry was most concerned by it. But he was even more concerned by the fact that he had not yet broached the idea with the Shanghai girl. She had no idea that she was on her way to Shanghai. He would see her right after this meeting. God, he hoped he could sell her on the idea.

Doyle was still talking. "... and you're absolutely right about that, Harry. I'm very impressed with how well you've thought this operation through. I'm sure Uncle Wild Bill will be very pleased. This may be our first agent behind Japanese lines in China. A splendid feat, Harry."

Harry smiled a modest smile.

"But enough of this spy business," Doyle said. "Did I tell you that I met the enchanting Olga Greenlaw? She's quite a woman, Harry. Given all your connections with the AVG, I'm surprised you never tried to put a move on her."

"I hope that's not what you're thinking, Doyle. She is Mrs. Olga Greenlaw, after all."

"But Olga seems such a free spirit. I have heard things about her. And the pilots. She's quite a favorite, it seems."

"She is a favorite of the pilots, a friend to some, a mother to others. To a few, perhaps a wishful thought."

"What a delicate way you put it, Harry. You must be fond of her yourself."

"She is a nice woman, but there's more than that. She's part of a special group that I doubt would take kindly to an outsider sniffing around, particularly a U.S. Army lieutenant – on General Stilwell's staff, no less. "

"Well, it's something to think about."

And so they thought about it. It was a pleasant afternoon to do that. They sat in the garden of their courtyard house, in comfortable silence, and sipped at their tea from time to time. The staff recognized them now, and knew not to disturb them once they had what they ordered. So they just sat and thought, Doyle about the enchanting Olga; Harry about the Shanghai girl.

"Just so you're aware of it," Doyle said after a while, "one of my new jobs is to deliver dispatches and such from Stilwell's office to Chennault. That means you'll see me from time to time at the AVG hostel or at the airport. That's how I got to meet Olga."

"Just be careful, Doyle," Harry said.

* * *

"So, how was your day?" Harry asked. The Shanghai girl was puzzled. He had never greeted her that way before. When he handed her a great loaf of the crusty French bread she liked, and the frosted pastries she loved, a twinge of concern became mixed with her delight. Harry had never brought her anything like this before. "Is something wrong?" she asked.

"No, no, I just wanted to see you. I have time. I can spend the evening here. I brought some champagne too. I got it all at the old French hotel."

"Oh, Ha-Lee," she said, calling him by his name, for the first time that he could remember, and giving it a Chinese pronunciation in her excitement.

"Yeah," he said, "We can have a drink, talk a little."

As he iced up the champagne, he went over his plan again. He had not decided if it would be sex first or sex later, but recognized that the timing was most important. His training had not included the use of sex with agents or informants. It was frowned upon as an espionage tool was the impression he had. Which was most unfortunate, he thought. Sex could be very useful. In this case, if he had sex with the Shanghai girl before he broached her return home as an agent, plied her with champagne and treated her with consideration and affection, she would likely be more amenable to his operational approach. On the other hand, if he waited until afterwards, and she really liked what he proposed, she would put heart and soul into her lovemaking. It could mean sex beyond his wildest imagination. In the end, he did not have to make the choice.

"Now," he said, champagne glasses in hand, toasts to their futures made, "I've been looking forward to this. I think about you often during the day, about your ambitions, your love for your home in Shanghai." She seemed to be following what he said, so he went on.

"I enjoy having you here in Kunming, especially as summer nears. We must spend more time out of doors, you and I." She nodded at that, which was encouraging.

"I know you miss Shanghai. I'm sure it's beautiful there in the spring."

"Spring?" she said. "I don't understand."

"It's a season," he said, "before summer. It's spring now in Shanghai, as it is here."

"Ah, Shanghai," she said, "yes." She set her glass down. She had not drunk very much champagne at all. She seemed uneasy, avoided meeting his eyes. Finally she turned to look at him.

"I must say something. You must not be angry. I want to go to my home. In Shanghai. I cannot stay here with you. I like you very much. But I have a letter from my mother. She said I must come to Shanghai now. I am afraid that my father may be ill." She looked away from him then. "I am worried that you are angry now."

"I am not angry," he said. "But how did you get a letter?"

"My uncle. He brought it."

"What about the Japanese in Shanghai? Are you not afraid of them?"

"Shanghai is a big city. There are many places. The Japanese are not everywhere."

He sat quietly for a moment. This was not what he expected. It made his job easy. "If you want to go to Shanghai, I can help you," he said. "But then, when you are in Shanghai, you must do things for me." She listened carefully, seemed to weigh every word. At the end she nodded.

"I know a man," he said.

"A Chinese man?" she asked.

"Yes, a Chinese man. This Chinese man will help you go to Shanghai. The Japanese will not stop you. In Shanghai, the man will introduce you to a gangster – a big boss gangster." He saw surprise on her face when he said 'gangster' and then questions. But he went on. "The gangster will give you work. He will give you money, and he will see that you have a place to live. You can see your mother, I'm sure. And…," he paused there to let her anticipate what might come, "…this gangster likes posters."

She cocked her head to one side, looked at him. She seemed not to understand, and he did not know the Chinese word. "Pictures," he said. "Like the pretty girls on your bedroom wall." She smiled then, knew what he meant. "Thank you," she said.

It was so much easier than he expected. He was not sure she understood everything. She was willing to meet his 'friend', willing to put herself in the hands of an unnamed Shanghai gangster, so long as he was a "big boss gangster," and work for him, whatever that might entail. She knew what all of that meant.

It was more difficult to explain what he wanted her to do. He would have to work on that part of it, define what kind of information she would collect for him. She did agree to write letters to him from Shanghai, and – before she left Kunming – to learn an "open code", the "special" words that would mean things that they really did not. That part of it left her uncertain, even confused. As did the idea that she would write letters to him in Chinese, which he could not read. She knew that professional letter writers could be found on certain street corners, but they all wrote in Chinese too. In the end, they agreed to put off these questions to another day.

Harry was certainly right about one thing. Putting off the sex until afterwards was the thing to do. It turned into a night he would long remember, and she probably would too.

Afterwards, as they lay in bed, she smoking and he thinking, Harry voiced a thought that had been niggling at him, "Will Tai Li be angry if you leave Kunming?"

"No," she said. "The general will be happy."

"Oh," Harry said, "why do you think he will be happy?"

"He said to my uncle that I should go."

"Go to Shanghai?"

"Yes."

"When did he say that to your uncle?"

"When he gave the letter to my uncle. He said to my uncle he would help. Just like you." She sounded pleased and added, "I am lucky. Many friends want to help me."

"Ah, shit," Harry said to himself as the light was turned on. To her he said, "So it was Tai Li who brought the letter from your mother?"

"He brought it from Shanghai. My uncle lives in Kunming. He could not go to Shanghai."

Harry saw his splendid feat of an operation slipping away. "Damn!" he said, "Damn! Damn! Damn!"

"Damn!" the Shanghai girl said her new English word. "Damn!" she said again, this time trying to put as much feeling into it as Harry did.

* * *

"It's no big deal, Harry," Doyle said. "We haven't lost anything. We just have to be careful and remember that we're sharing the operation with Tai Li."

"I don't know that we can go ahead with this. If we do, Tai Li will know exactly what I am. He will also know that Louie has been helping me."

Doyle held up his hand to stop Harry from saying something he might later think foolish. "Now listen, Harry. Tai Li will know just what we want him to know. He will know you are a journalist trying to get an insight into Japanese-controlled China. He will know that Louie is a friend who helps you out when you ask him. And that's all."

He waited to see if Harry was listening, then went on. "Here is what you are going to do: Tai Li is in Kunming right now. You make an appointment to see him. Tai Li knows that you and the girl are friends, right? So it's no secret that you know that she wants to go home to Shanghai. So you tell him you want to help. Tell him that you want to try a journalistic experiment and establish the girl as a source in Shanghai. She will send information to you. Tell Tai Li you might need his help with this, but you have ideas on how to do it. And if he can't help, you might ask Louie to help. All of this is for your research on what is happening in Jap-controlled China. I can't imagine Tai Li would not jump on this and want to help you. "

"If Tai Li helps us, what do we get from our new agent in Shanghai? Tai Li propaganda? It won't be intelligence." Actually, Harry liked the idea and wished he had thought of it before Doyle had. He did not want to tell Doyle that, at least not yet. "I'll have to clear all this with Louie first," was all he said.

"Good. I don't want you to do this if it will cause a big problem with Tai Li – or with Louie. I think Tai Li will be quite taken with the idea of helping you. He wants to put a good face on China and a bad face on the Japanese. What better way to do this than by helping an American journalist?"

"You're probably right, Doyle," Harry finally said. "We will go with your idea; it's a good one. But I will have to run everything by Louie first. I will certainly need his help. I think I know how to approach him so he doesn't have any problem with it."

"Good, I'm glad you approve. Now, I have to send a summary of our new operation back to Washington. There is something I'm not clear on. As I understand it, your Shanghai girlfriend already agreed to be our agent before she got the letter from her mother, right?"

Harry looked up at the ceiling. "Boy, this spy stuff can sure get complicated," he began.

* * *

Complicated, maybe, but so much easier than he had anticipated, as Harry realized afterwards. Louie shrugged his shoulders when he said that he wanted to meet with Tai Li and told him why. "Yes, why not get Tai Li involved?" Louie said. "He's the one who gave you the girl. Dealing with Shanghai is easy for him. I'll try to explain the need for a "proper" gangster," and rolled his eyes when he said that.

Tai Li set an early meeting. Harry was well prepared, did not waste anyone's time, and immediately got Tai Li's agreement to do what he could. The meeting was quick, so quick that Harry was left feeling that he and the Shanghai girl were very small potatoes in a Tai Li world full of agents. But Tai Li's participation meant the operation had a good chance of success, and the odds of the Shanghai girl surviving the war increased considerably.

Now he had to get her trained, had to identify what he wanted her to collect. He could teach her the simple measures she could take to protect herself, the commonsense things that almost everyone overlooked. But it was their communications system that would be the most important thing, and the most difficult. It had to be done right. He had to get the intelligence she collected in a way that would let her survive. In the end it was Louie who had the answer, the commonsense way the Chinese did it.

"Look, Harry," Louie said, "you don't want the poor girl writing you letters talking about "sacks of rice" to mean Japanese battleships and "bunches of onions" to mean cruisers. Counting the ships is going to be bad enough for her."

"So what do we do? Use bird species?"

"Oh my God, Harry, haven't you heard of the telegraphic code?"

The way Louie said it, Harry knew that a great gap in his education was about to be filled. "I guess I haven't, Louie."

"Well, I suppose we can't really expect a chap who is not a China specialist to know about it," Louie said, which made Harry feel just a little better.

"Here's how it works: The Chinese language has tens of thousands of characters. You can't send any of them via telegraph. Then a clever Chinese gentleman came up with the idea of giving each of 15,000 ideographs a four-digit number. Each four-digit number represents a word. So all one does now to send a telegram is to send these four-digit groups of numbers, which are easily transmitted. You can send anything, your Declaration of Independence, if you want. Everybody in China uses this system, everybody who uses the Chinese language. You can buy the code-books in any bookshop in China."

"But then anybody in China can read our code."

Louie sighed loudly. "Harry, think about it. I use the code. Every businessman, every smuggler, every criminal in China uses the code. And none of us want our letters read. To make what you send a secret, you simply add or subtract a certain number of digits from each group – which you prearrange with your correspondent. For example, you can add 23 to each number if you send the letter on Monday, or subtract 17 if you send it Tuesday. It makes it impossible for anyone else to read."

"Ah," Harry said, "I see." And he did; it dawned all at once. "Of course. It's so simple. It's totally incredible. Good! Now we won't need to use bags of rice, or bundles of onions. It's something Tai Li would think up."

"I'm sure Tai Li uses it, but it's not something he thought up. When it comes to business, every Chinese is clever."

"I'll have to remember that," Harry said.

CHAPTER 31

You've taken on protective coloration, Ross," the Old Man said as he regarded Harry in one of his khaki outfits. "I thought you were one of my boys."

The Old Man had just stuck his head out of the officers' bar at the AVG hostel and asked for someone to bring a map. The door to the bar was closed when Harry got there. That was unusual enough, but two pilots, neither of whom he knew well, stood in front of the door like guards. One shook his head when Harry asked if he could go in. "Meeting," the other said. "VIPs." Harry started to turn away when the Old Man saw him.

The Old Man continued to look at him, finally said, "You come inside with me, Harry. The ones in there will think you're one of ours too. This is not for your newspaper, but you will find it interesting. Take a seat at the back. Be inconspicuous."

Harry followed the Old Man into the room. A dozen or more men were seated where the card tables had been bunched together. Others sat along the back wall, and Harry quietly joined them. He looked around and saw only two AVG, Harvey Greenlaw and one of the Squadron leaders. The others were U.S. Army officers, all facing the bar and the man standing in front of it, who was speaking. He wore a crisp new khaki uniform, but with no rank insignia.

"... and there was flak," the man said. "Our airplanes were strung out for a hundred miles. My airplane was the first to fly across Tokyo. We did not get much of the flak. That was directed at the aircraft that came later. Then it was intense, but not accurate. We did see fighters in the distance, but they never came close. They weren't expecting us. If they actually saw us, they probably could not conceive that we were the enemy."

"I understand you had removed most of your guns to lighten your airplanes," one of the Army officers said.

"We removed the belly turret to make room for a fuel tank. We replaced the rear .50-caliber guns with broomsticks painted black."

The thought of flying over Japan protected by broomsticks generated some laughter, but it ceased when the next question was asked. A petulant voice that commanded silence:

"We assume that by now the Japanese have found your crashed airplane. Did you manage to destroy your Norden bombsight before you bailed out?" It was more accusation than question. Harry turned to see who was speaking. "And the bombsights in your other airplanes," the voice continued, "the others that fell into enemy hands, were they destroyed?" It was an old man, a sour face above the uniform of a full colonel in the U.S. Army. The room was still.

"We did not use the Norden bombsight, sir. It's Top Secret, as you know. We knew we would lose at least some of our airplanes to the Japs. Also, we bombed from low altitude. It was not practical to use the Norden at the heights we bombed. Our bombsight was a twenty cent affair, made by one of our pilots from two pieces of waste aluminum. It was like using an open sight on a rifle. Not secret, but most effective. "

The old colonel sounded angry now. "And how many airplanes did you lose, Colonel Doolittle?"

"I don't know, sir. We haven't accounted for all our crews yet." He paused, kept his eyes on his interrogator. "I believe we may have lost all our airplanes, sir."

"And how many was that, Colonel?"

"I'm not at liberty to say."

"Well, the newspapers in the States said there were 16 bombers in your flight. You lost them all?"

Doolittle did not respond. When his interrogator started to speak again, Chennault stood up. For the first time Harry noted the lone star of a brigadier general on each shoulder.

"Gentlemen," Chennault said, "it's time we let General Doolittle go. An airplane is waiting to take him to India, and from there back to the States." He shook hands with Doolittle then. Harry watched as the old colonel who played interrogator leaned over to one of his staff, said something, looked puzzled.

Harry stayed at the back of the room while the others shuffled out, talking quietly among themselves. A few paused to shake hands with Doolittle and wish him well, but not everyone. Harvey Greenlaw led Doolittle out.

All the while Chennault was engaged by the old colonel. "A mission is not a success if losses exceed ten percent," Harry heard the colonel say. "It's the accepted rule."

Chennault heard the man out, then said something, quietly. Harry could see surprise on the colonel's face. It ended the conversation. The colonel nodded to Chennault, turned and walked out, followed by his entourage, two lieutenants and a captain.

Harry stepped over to Chennault. The Old Man had a little smile on his face. "Were it anybody but Jimmy Doolittle," he said, "I would feel sorry for the Colonel. Apparently, he didn't hear me introduce Doolittle as a Brigadier General. His promotion was announced in Chungking, just before he flew up here. I feel a little bad about it. Doolittle was not wearing his stars because I'm wearing them on my shoulders. There were no stars to be had in Kunming, and he said he could easily replace the ones he was wearing when he got to India." The Old Man shook his head. "It's stuck in the old colonel's mind that Jimmy Doolittle is still a lieutenant colonel, and that he can still treat him that way."

"Congratulations, sir, on getting your star. I'm also very pleased to hear that Doolittle got his. Maybe there is a God."

"Thank you, Harry. I'm very pleased that Doolittle's brilliant Tokyo mission got the recognition it deserved. He felt so bad about losing his airplanes. I told him it doesn't matter. They were to become my airplanes once he got them here, so I had a big stake in what happened. And as far as I was concerned, those airplanes could not have been expended in a better way. He will be a hero when he gets back to the States."

"What about the crews, sir? Have they found any more?"

"We've accounted for six or seven. We know the Japanese captured the crew of one airplane, and maybe more. The Japs have started a massive search in east China, but most of the boys have kept ahead of them – thanks to some brave Chinese farmers. The Chinese are risking their lives and their families to help."

They walked out into the hallway together. The two pilots still stood there, now guarding an empty room. Just behind them stood an intense, anxious-looking young man in rumpled civilian clothes. "General Chennault," he began.

"Ah, John," the Old Man said, "I know you're eager to get back. Don't worry, the airplane won't leave without you." They exchanged a few words, then the Old Man turned to Harry. "Have you met John Birch, Harry? John led some of Doolittle's men out of east China."

Harry shook hands with Birch. "It's too bad the two of you won't have time to talk. John has to get to the airfield. There's a flight going to Chungking, and John's going with it. He's eager to get back to his flock."

Harry stepped away while the Old Man and Birch said their goodbyes. Birch turned and walked quickly down the hall, gave a little wave to Harry.

"Come, Harry, walk with me," the Old Man said as he started down the hall. "I'm glad you met John Birch. You may see more of him. He's a good man, a Georgia Baptist. He's a missionary in Hangchow. I've been looking for men just like him."

"Need another padre, General?"

"Actually, I asked John to lay aside the Bible and take up the sword. I want him to be part of our intelligence network. As our Air Force here grows, we will need targeting information, specific information that I can use to direct air attacks. We're not getting much from Stilwell's people. And frankly, I doubt that we ever will. Stilwell doesn't understand the airplane and its uses.

"We need to establish our own field intelligence network to get the information we need. I have been looking for old China hands. Americans who have lived in China, who speak the language and know the customs, men who can survive on Chinese food. There are not many of those. Most of the ones I know are missionaries, and John Birch is one. Another is our own AVG chaplain, Paul Frillman. I'm not sure Paul intends to stay in China once the AVG breaks up. If he leaves it will be a real shame."

He stopped walking then. "I'm telling you this, Harry, because I may need your help. The people I'm looking for will know how to live among the Chinese and how to pass through Japanese lines. That will be almost instinctive for them. What they won't know is what intelligence is. Maybe you can help teach them that. If you spend some time with our pilots, learn what they need, come up with ideas of how to get it. I know you can't do what you did for us at Chiang Mai over and over, but that's the kind of thing we need. We will be a long way from it until I can recruit John Birch and a few more like him."

* * *

"The Japs are on a rampage," Louie said. "They're tearing east China apart, looking for Doolittle's crews. They haven't found many, and that really irritates them. They think the Chinese farmers are helping your Air Force escape, which, of course, they are. So now the Japs have turned on the Chinese farmer. They're killing Chinese now, a lot of Chinese. They're burning villages. They're killing all the farm animals. It's very dangerous in east

China now. Tai Li has warned me not to go there. He 'ordered' me not to go there. He said we can't send your girl to Shanghai until all this is over."

"Shit," Harry said. "Everything slows down. Damn it! I was hoping to have her on her way in a couple of days."

"Look on the good side, Harry. You'll have her companionship for a bit longer."

"Yeah, well...," Harry ran his hand through his hair. God, it had been a long day. "Japs on the rampage," he said. "It's starting to feel like a war again. What other terrible things can happen?"

"Well," Louie said and stared into space as if considering the question. "If the Japanese in Burma crossed the Salween River and advanced on Kunming, would that qualify?"

Harry thought about it. "It might. That could be very bad."

"I thought you spent time with Chennault today. Didn't he have anything to say about the Japs closing on the Salween?"

"He didn't, no. He would have, if things there were serious."

"They're serious, Harry."

* * *

May 2, 1942
Kunming, China

Harry got to the airport well before sunup to wait for the Old Man. He was not alone; there were many others milling around in the pre-dawn darkness. Most were U.S. Army officers whose numbers in Kunming were growing by the day. There were also journalists, some Harry recognized as old-timers who rarely bothered to rise that time of day. Off to one side, he saw three of Kunming's ubiquitous Chinese Army officers, standing by themselves. From snatches of conversation that drifted his way, it was evident that everyone was waiting for Chennault. That confirmed something was going on. Harry spotted his old comrade Morris chatting with a couple of Army officers, and walked over to him.

"Hey, Morris," he said, "this must be the earliest you've been awake in years. What's going on?"

"I just want to get the details of what happened yesterday."

"What happened where?"

Morris looked at him a long moment, not sure if Harry was putting him on. "At Loi Wing," he said, "the AVG's big base. They evacuated it yesterday. Chennault was there with them. He got back here late yesterday. Most of the

AVG is in Kunming now. Look over there. Ever see so many P-40s?"

Harry peered into the darkness and saw nothing. Only where light spilled from one of the hangars, could he make out the shapes of several of the long-nosed P-40s. There might have been more than usual, but he could not really tell.

"Oh, that evacuation," Harry said, and walked on, leaving Morris wondering if there was something Harry knew that he did not. In fact, Harry had heard nothing of the evacuation, or even that Chennault had been away and just returned. If whatever happened was big enough to take the Old Man out of Kunming and then make everyone want to talk with him when he got back, it had to be pretty big stuff.

The journalists were getting impatient, but they were not kept waiting long. Chennault's car pulled up in front of the operations shack, and everybody clustered around it. Harry hung back, stayed on the perimeter, wondering how he would get close to the Old Man without calling attention to himself. The Old Man solved the problem for him.

"Gentlemen," Chennault, said as he pulled himself out of the car, "one of my officers will brief the press and the U.S. Army in the hangar, the one over there where the lights are." When no one moved, he added, "You will hear all about our withdrawal from Loi Wing." He looked at his watch. "The briefer is starting right now."

Shouts came from members of the press: "We need to talk with you, General," with all emphasis on "you."

"Later," the Old Man said. "Go hear the briefing now. We can talk afterwards."

They started moving, the Army officers briskly, as a group. The press straggled after, reluctantly, individually. Eventually only three Chinese Army officers and Harry stood with the Old Man by his car.

Chennault turned to the senior of the three Chinese officers. "Wang," he said, "I'll see you in my office, in a minute. Have the boys get you a cup of tea." The three Chinese saluted. "Thank you, General," the senior one said. As the three walked away, Chennault turned to Harry.

"Well, young Ross, I saw you lurking in the background, trying to stay hidden. Come walk with me. I'm sure you have an important mission."

They walked into the ops building. Chennault looked around and found a small, vacant office. "Come on in here," he said to Harry.

"Sir, I don't want to take up your time, but I was concerned about the situation at the Salween River. I need to bring Colonel Donovan up to date."

"Nobody really knows what's happening at the Salween. You can tell Donovan that the situation is confused. Everyone is racing toward the river.

The Chinese Army and the refugees think they will be safe if they can cross it, but the Japanese Army is close behind. You know we evacuated Loi Wing yesterday. We expect the Jap Army to be there today. That means the Japs will be inside China, but still west of the Salween River."

The Old Man went on. "Losing Loi Wing was a serious blow. We had to leave 22 of our airplanes there. They were being repaired. We had to burn them all. Most of our personnel and our remaining airplanes are here at Kunming now."

"Is the whole Chinese Army in Burma on the run? And what happened to the British Army?"

The Old Man's face looked sour. "Everyone is in retreat. The British are walking to India, what's left of them. The Chinese who can't reach the Salween are fleeing into the mountains. The Chinese fought well. Some are still fighting. But they're disorganized now. There's no leadership."

"What about Stilwell, sir?"

"Stilwell." The Old Man repeated the name, went silent. He looked across the airfield, peered into the darkness. "I cannot read that man," he said finally. "I do not understand him. He radioed me, asked where his airplane was. He said he wanted to fly out of Loi Wing. That was two days ago. I told him everything was arranged. An airplane was standing by. It would pick him up whenever he wanted, and our Third Squadron would escort his airplane. I didn't hear anything back from him. Then yesterday, as we were pulling out of Loi Wing, he radioed me. 'I'm staying here,' he said."

"He's staying in Burma?"

The Old Man frowned. "He can't stay in Burma very long. We did finally send an airplane to get him. He refused to board. He put some of his staff aboard and sent the airplane to India. He told them to set up a headquarters for him there. I guess that's where he's going." Chennault's black eyes peered at Harry. There was a disgusted look on the Old Man's face.

"I don't understand," Harry said. "He can't stay in Burma, he won't fly out...."

"He will walk. He preferred to walk, he said. He will walk through the jungle to India."

"That's incredible," Harry said. He almost laughed, but when he thought about it, he was struck by something else. "The man is 60 years old. That makes it even more incredible – admirable almost, that he wants to walk out of Burma with everybody else."

"Admirable?" A smile came to the Old Man's face, a very small one. "Is it admirable, Harry? You disappoint me, son. I thought you were learning something about the military. What Stilwell is doing might be admirable if he were a company commander looking out for his troops. But Stilwell is no company commander. Stilwell is the senior American officer in Asia and the Chief of Staff of the Chinese Army. He is in command of the Chinese Army in Burma. Now he's abandoning them. If he had gotten on that airplane, he could have been in India in hours. Or flown to Chungking. From either place he could direct the reorganization of the Chinese Army. He can't do that in the jungle."

"So what will happen now?"

"I can't speak for the U.S. Army, but the AVG needs to get organized. We must do what we can without Stilwell. I'm sending our boys out this morning to see where the Japs are, try to figure out where they are headed. The Chinese defenses have evaporated. There are no obstacles now between the Japs and Kunming."

"There's still the Salween River, sir."

"Yes, there's the river. And there's the AVG."

As Harry left the ops building, some of the American Army officers were walking toward him, coming from the hangar where they had been briefed. He was preoccupied with what the Old Man said, and just glanced their way. They were young men, eager-looking, ready to get on with the war. One was a walking wounded, a lieutenant with a huge bandage that covered his nose and much of the center of his face. As Harry drove away from the airfield, the memory niggled at him. Something about the man reminded him of Doyle.

* * *

Harry sat in the garden of the courtyard house, waiting for Doyle, and then watched wide-eyed as the same bandaged man approached and mumbled a greeting.

"Hello, Harry. Sorry I'm late." The words were slurred, hard to understand, but it was Doyle's voice all right.

"Jesus, Doyle, what happened to you?"

"Door," he said. "I walked into a door."

Harry looked at him closely, examined his face where it was not hidden by the bandage. His nose was still there, larger than it had been, and with streaks of black, purple and yellow around it and most of one eye. The upper lip was bigger too, and puffy. It looked as if it had split open and then stuck back together. There was probably no serious damage, but someone had tried to rearrange Doyle's face.

"You should get a Purple Heart for that," Harry said. "What really happened, Doyle? Come on, you can tell me. You tangled with some of those Army guys, didn't you? The Stilwell guys you work with?"

Doyle did not answer, but carefully picked up his tea cup, held it well away from him as he tried to drink and not dribble down the front of his shirt. It went well at first, but then tea squirted from his mouth as if he had a hole in his lip. He mumbled a "Damn," and readjusted. Eventually he got about half the tea down. The rest pooled on the table.

"I needed that," he said. He put down the cup and raised his hand to touch his mouth. "My toof," he said, "broken. Hard to eat. Hard to talk. I whistle." He said, "Simple Simon" and sounded like a whistling tea kettle. It made Harry laugh.

"I didn't laugh at you, Harry, when you got hit in the face and said it was a tree. It was not the Army I tangled with. It was a Marine."

"A Marine? I haven't seen any marines in Kunming."

"Yes, you have. There's at least one. A stocky guy. One of your Air Corps guys."

"You mean the AVG? Yeah, the AVG has some former Marines. You foolishly picked a fight with a Marine? Why did you do that?"

"I didn't pick a fight. I didn't do anything. I got attacked. In the toilet."

"I'm not going to ask what you were doing in the toilet."

"I wasn't doing anything, nothing to provoke an attack. It was at the AVG hostel, the toilet by the pilots' bar. I was at the sink, just standing there. This big guy, the Marine, charged out of a stall. Popped me in the nose."

"You were standing at the sink doing what? Talking maybe?"

"Well, I was telling this other guy how good Olga was looking."

"If it was Olga you were talking about, it must have been Greg who popped you, Greg Boyington. He was a Marine, and he is a good friend of Olga. Don't take it personally. He's popped a lot of people."

"Somebody told me he had been drunk for a week. He just floundered around after he hit me. Crashed out the door and into the pilots' bar. Tried to get in a fight there. Three guys held him down."

"Yeah, that's Greg. He's a great pilot, but on the ground he's a terror to all. Look on the bright side. When Olga finds out about this, she'll want to nurse you back to health. She does that with all of Greg's victims."

"That makes me feel better already. Look, much as I would like to talk more about Olga, I think we better talk about the war."

So they did. They compared what they had heard that morning, what Harry got directly from Chennault with what Doyle heard in the briefing, and then in the separate talk his group had with the Old Man.

"You're getting more from Chennault than we are," Doyle said.

"Stilwell's staff is getting nothing from him. It's like the Old Man said, Stilwell is walking around in Burma somewhere. He does have a radio, but he's talking about dumping it. It's too heavy to carry far. In the meantime, what he's sending to his staff shows that he's not exactly sure where he is, and that he doesn't have a clue where the Japs are. 'Ten miles behind us', he says. He's determined to walk to India. He has to cross 150 miles of jungles and mountains to do that. The U.S. Army is not getting any kind of intelligence through its channels now, nothing I can send to Donovan. You're going to have to stay with Chennault, Harry. That has to be the priority now. You may as well move in with him."

"The guys will put me up at the hostel if it's necessary."

"It's necessary, Harry."

CHAPTER 32

May 5, 1942
Wu Chia Ba Airfield
Kunming, China

Harry was back at the field early again, as he had been for the last two days. Despite what Doyle wanted, he had little luck seeing Chennault. The Old Man came and said, "Later, Harry," and then left before Harry could get near him.

Chennault was busy, like everyone else directly engaged with the war. With most of the AVG together in Kunming now, there was a lot to be done. There were a lot of P-40s parked around the airfield, including some of the new E-model "Kittyhawks" that were flown in via Africa. Their arrival meant that the veteran B-model Tomahawks could get much-needed maintenance and repair. To the casual observer, the two aircraft types looked alike, but there were some real differences. Both aircraft had six machine guns, but all six of the Kittyhawk's were .50 caliber guns, compared to the Tomahawk's two. Four of the Tomahawk's were smaller .30 caliber guns. More importantly, the E-models had racks to carry bombs. Chennault now had a capability he had wanted for a long time.

With nothing to do while he hung around the airfield, Harry poked around the hangars, talked with the pilots and joked with the ground crew. He climbed up into the cockpit of one of the new E-models and wondered what it was like to fly a machine like this, to soar over the mountains, to flit among the clouds, to meet a Jap pilot who wanted to kill you. He was lost in his fantasy when Ed Rector hopped up on the wing.

"Hey," he said, "You can fly this thing some other time. The Old Man sent me out to find you. He said he's sorry he hasn't seen you yet, but he's busy trying to keep the Generalissimo happy. He said if you don't mind, I can brief you in his stead."

"Let me get out of here," Harry said as he started to extract himself from the cockpit. "Let's go walk along the runway."

As they walked, Ed filled Harry in on what was happening. "Yesterday, we got hit at Paoshan. That's our airfield in South Yunnan, across the Salween from Burma. We had eight P-40s there. Fifty Jap bombers came over. Paoshan is an old walled city and it's just crammed with refugees from Burma. The Japs dropped their bombs right on them, killed thousands. Our warning net down there has collapsed, so our pilots were on the ground when the Japs came. They hit the airfield too, tore up our airplanes. One of our guys got killed by bomb fragments. The only pilot who got in the air was Charlie Bond. You remember Charlie? You met him at Toungoo."

Rector stopped in his tracks and grabbed Harry's arm to hold him in place. "You didn't hear what happened to Charlie, did you?" With no pause for an answer, he went on. Ed loved a good story.

"Charlie got up to the bombers and knocked one down. He used up all his ammunition and turned back to the field. He did a slow victory roll over the runway. While he was doing that, he didn't notice the three Jap fighters lining up on his tail. Next thing he knew – bang! His airplane was on fire. The fuel tank behind his seat exploded. He was sitting in the flames.

"But Charlie is a quick old boy. He jerked the nose up, rolled the airplane over, and dropped out. The Japs were circling him. He knew they wanted to shoot him in his parachute, just like they did Christman. He was so low that he hit the ground right after his chute opened. He landed in a Chinese graveyard and scuttled around like a frenzied crab, watching the Japs, trying to hide from them behind the burial mounds. He was so busy that he didn't see that his flying suit was smoldering – until it suddenly burst into flames!

"Charlie was lucky again. There just happened to be a stream there, and he leaped right in, lay on his back." The picture of that made Ed laugh aloud. "I shouldn't laugh," he said. "He got burned pretty bad. Doc Richards painted his hands and face with some kind of disinfectant. It turned him purple. He was a sight. When they flew him back here yesterday, somebody gave him a bottle of whiskey on the airplane. He wasn't feeling any pain when he got here."

"What about the rest of the AVG at Paoshan, did they leave too?"

"No they're still there. There's not much they'll be able to do without airplanes. Let me tell you what's happening today. Tex Hill and eight of our guys took off this morning for Yunnanyi. That's a small airfield halfway between here and Paoshan. The Old Man told them to go there, refuel and wait."

Ed stopped talking then, seemed to be thinking. "The Old Man knows something. He's been here since dawn." Rector looked at his wristwatch. "Let's take a walk over to the radio shack. The Old Man was supposed to be over there about noon. He said to bring you over. We might get some action."

They walked to the radio shack, really just a room in the operations building. Chennault's car was parked nearby. Several of the off-duty pilots were sitting by the door, enjoying the sun. "What's happening, boys?" Rector asked. "Is the Old Man here?"

"Yeah, he's inside," one of the pilots said, "sitting by the radio. Tex and the guys he sent to Yunnanyi are patrolling over Paoshan now. The Old Man told them the Jap bombers would be there at 12:30." The pilot shrugged his shoulders. "Who knows," he said.

"The Old Man knows," Rector said. "If he said the Japs will there at 12:30, they will be there at 12:30. I guarantee it. The Old Man can think like the Japs. Come on Harry, let's go inside."

The Old Man was sitting right in front of one of the big radio receivers, staring at its large circular dial. He turned when they came in, glanced at his wristwatch and said, "Ross, come sit over here," indicating a chair next to him. "You will find this interesting."

Harry sat down in the chair; Rector took another nearby. "I'm waiting for the Japs to hit Paoshan again," the Old Man said. "I have our radio man at Paoshan on the horn here. He just went outside to see if anything's happening yet. The Japs should be there about now."

They sat quietly and stared at the radio. It crackled with static every now and then, but otherwise was silent. The Old Man looked at his watch again. "They're late," he said."

There was a loud crackle, then: "General Chennault. Are you there? We can hear the Jap engines. They're coming now." A crackle of static, then: "Jesus Christ! Sorry, sir! They're strafing the field, a line of Jap fighters."

There was no sound at all for a while. Finally: "Here come the bombers. I can see them."

"Where are the bombers?" the Old Man asked.

"They're high, still over the city. They seem headed this way. Wait! I can see smoke up there now. I think... I can't make it out. Let me go outside. I can see better there."

"Go ahead," Chennault said. "Go out where you can see them."

There was a long silence. Then crackle, crackle, and "It was Japs going down. I could see smoke coming from three of them. Wow! I can see them from the window now. They're dropping like flies."

"Who's dropping?" the Old Man asked.

"I'm not sure, sir. Let me get back outside real quick."

They sat in silence, the Old Man shifting uncomfortably in his chair, looking at his watch, looking at the window. He was sitting too low to see out. "Damn!" he mumbled once under his breath.

Suddenly from the radio: "It was Jap fighters I saw burning, sir. The first flight of bombers passed over us. There's another flight of bombers coming now. Three vics of nine. The P-40s are chasing after them."

The Old Man turned to Harry. "Three big vics, nine each. Twenty-seven bombers, and that's the second wave. The total must have been over 50."

A minute later, the radio crackled again. "They're dropping their bombs. The Japs are dropping their bombs now. They're dumping them over the rice fields. They are turning away. The Japs are turning away."

"Where are the P-40s?" the Old Man asked.

"Chasing them, sir. The P-40s are chasing them. They're almost out of sight."

"Let me know when the flight reports in. If we have any losses. How many Japs went down."

While they waited, Chennault turned to Harry. "There's an intelligence lesson in this for you, son,"

"How's that, General?"

"I thought they would hit Paoshan again today, but I could not be sure. Then this morning the Chinese intercepted some Japanese radio traffic. Jap bombers were taking off at Rangoon; another bunch at Chiang Mai. I know the cruising speed of those airplanes. The times they took off would put them right over Paoshan at 12:30. I told the boys I sent down there to get in the air and patrol over Paoshan. I told them the Japs would be there at 12:30. They missed it by just a little bit."

"You did great, sir," Harry said. Chennault looked pleased; generals probably did not get praised much.

The radio crackled again. "Kunming, Kunming, this is Paoshan. Do you read me?"

"Paoshan, this is Kunming, Go ahead."

"Our boys are down. Everybody's fine. We had no losses. We got eight bandits, repeat eight bandits."

"Very good, Paoshan. Well done. Tell that to the boys." He turned to Harry. "You know," he said, "my conversation with Paoshan didn't hide much from the Japs, and that's fine. The Japs know their own losses, and now they will know that we didn't lose anything. Let them think on that!"

"Yes, sir," Harry said.

* * *

Harry and Ed Rector were just finishing a late lunch of "eggies" and spam at the small mess hall on the field, when one of the AVG clerks walked up. He addressed them both. "The Old Man said not to hurry, but if both of you are going over to the hostel, to stop by his office there."

"Thanks, Paul," Ed said, then asked the clerk, "What's happening? You look a bit ruffled."

"The Old Man just met with some Chinese officers. Then he called the squadron leaders and everybody started running around. Something is up, something very big."

"You may as well stay at the hostel tonight, Harry," Rector said. "We may have some busy days."

They found the Old Man in his office. "Sit down, boys," he said and pushed aside a stack of paper he had been working through. To Rector he said, "You'll be flying again tomorrow, Ed, Navy style." He pulled a sheet of paper from his typewriter. "This is part of a message I'm sending to Chungking, to the Generalissimo," he said and handed it to Harry.

It was dated 1530 hours, 5 May, and said: "Japs on the west bank of the Salween River. Situation is desperate. Japs are meeting no opposition anywhere. They can drive trucks and tanks to Kunming unless road and bridges are destroyed and determined opposition is mounted."

When Harry finished reading, the Old Man said, "I've just heard some good news. The Chinese have blown the suspension bridge over the Salween. That will hold the Japs at the river's edge for a day or two, until they get their engineers up to throw a pontoon bridge across. That's something the Japs are very good at. It won't take them long. I'm asking the Generalissimo for authority to attack the Japs on the west bank of the Salween while they are still bunched up there."

Then the Old Man turned to Rector. "That will be your chance to be a dive bomber pilot again. It will all be up to the Panda Bears. Tex will lead you tomorrow. Now, if you could just excuse us for a moment, Ed."

"Yes, sir," Rector said, and started out. At the door he paused. "I look forward to tomorrow, sir."

The Old Man nodded at him, then turned to Harry. "I want you to report all of this back to Donovan. I doubt that Washington will get anything substantive on this situation from anybody else for days. There's a real danger here. If the Japanese Army manages to get across the Salween, there is nothing to stop them from coming all the way here to Kunming. There's no Chinese opposition left. What Chinese troops are on the roads between here and the Salween are fleeing. They're mixed in with the civilian refugees and have abandoned their weapons. If the Japs get to Kunming it's the end of the war for China. Kunming is the terminus of China's only remaining supply route over the Himalayas. If the Japs take Kunming, China is cut off from any possibility of Allied aid."

"I understand, sir."

"Get all that to Donovan. I don't care who else gets to know about it. The situation is worse than I've ever seen in China. I'll have airplanes in the air tomorrow, and we'll try to do something about it. You tell your uncle Wild Bill that, too."

Harry needed to contact Doyle right away to cable his report to Washington. But first he walked down to the pilot's, bar to find Rector.

"The word's out," Rector said, "Everybody knows the Japs are coming. All anybody here wants to talk about now is the evacuation of Kunming. But look over there, it's the only spot of sanity in the room."

In the corner, the Panda Bear squadron leader, Tex Hill, was playing checkers with Olga Greenlaw. "They all know Tex is going to lead the Pandas to the Salween tomorrow," Ed said, and just as he spoke, the Old Man walked in. Some still greeted him as "Colonel", out of habit. He went over and sat at the game table with Tex and Olga. Harry heard her say, "You want me to play both of you? I know I can beat you, General, and I know I can beat Tex, but I don't know if I can beat both of you playing at the same time."

"You will have to play both of us to find out, Olga," the Old Man said to her.

Harry watched the first two games. They were quick, and Olga won both. "I have to run out for a while," he said to Rector. "Make sure I have a room when I get back here."

"You will have a room, don't worry. But look at that. Everybody's watching to see if Olga can beat the Old Man again. Nobody's even thinking about the Japs now. They could be on the moon."

* * *

Doyle heard him out without saying a word. When Harry finished, Doyle shook his head. "Losing China is not going to sit well with the brass in Washington," he said. "It's a good report, Harry. The Army guys here know the situation is bad, but they don't know how bad. They're being briefed by their Chinese counterparts, but they don't believe them. Your piece will bring a dose of reality to what they're reporting."

"So one hopes," Harry said. "By the way, Olga was playing the Old Man at checkers tonight. She was winning, and victory made her look particularly beautiful."

"My nose hurts," Doyle said.

* * *

"See, on the wing racks here, Harry, those little bombs, they're 'weed cutters', 35-pound fragmentation bombs that we'll drop on the troops. This big fellow here," Rector said as he patted the big bomb that hung from the belly of the airplane, "This big fellow is a 570-pound high explosive bomb. The Russians sent them here a long time ago. They're all over the place, but we could never use them until we got our E-models. We tried to drop them from our old airplanes, but we could never fashion a proper bomb rack to do it. "

Harry followed Rector as he walked around the airplane, checking what had already been checked and re-checked by his crew chief. "You know how it will work, right Harry? Four of us will fly the Kittyhawks with the frags and one big bombs each. We'll go down and hit the Japs in the gorge. Four pilots in B-models will fly top cover. Tex Hill will lead us. It's a simple mission."

Somewhere on the field an engine started, and Ed looked toward the sound. "Time to saddle up," he said. As he climbed into the cockpit, Harry gave him a thumbs up and stepped back, away from the prop blast that came as the engine started. He walked over to where many of the other AVG stood, waiting to watch the takeoff.

Everyone on the field stopped what he was doing to watch the eight P-40s take off. It had rained overnight, and the planes threw up spray as they started their runs. The E-model Kittyhawks were easy to make out. They ate up more runway, and they climbed slowly, and then it was easy to see the big Russian bombs hanging from their bellies.

It would be hours before the mission was completed. Harry walked toward his car, thinking about driving into town for lunch, when Doyle pulled up alongside him in a jeep. He was alone.

"I came by to deliver some stuff to Chennault's staff," he said. "The Army received a radio message from Stilwell, his last one. He said he's signing off and walking into the jungle. He's on his way to India. He has about a hundred people with him, including a medical team. They're dumping the radio; it's too heavy."

Harry shrugged. "We don't need Stilwell. Chennault is doing okay by himself. The guys are on their way to the Salween now, to stop the Japs. I'll have a full report for you tonight. Ed Rector will brief me as soon as he gets back."

* * *

"Have you ever seen the Salween gorge, Harry?" Ed said. "It's huge. Over the eons, the river has worn its way down through solid rock. It's a mile down to the bottom of the gorge where the river is now. At the top, from one edge to the other, the gorge is miles across. The way down on the west side is steep. The Burma Road drops over the edge there and winds down through a series of switchbacks. It's one serpentine curve after another, 35 of them, before it reaches the little suspension bridge at the bottom. Most of the bridge is gone now, but it looked tiny from the top of the gorge. Across the bridge, it's the same thing, curve after curve leading up to the top. There it meets the edge of the Paoshan plateau.

"It's an incredible sight from the top of the gorge, or flying over it. It's beautiful. When the sun is right, the hills around it are ablaze with color, and the river is just a thin vein of glittering silver embedded along the bottom of those corrugated hills for miles and miles, as far as the eye can see.

"We could see activity down around the bridge, on the west side. When we got lower, we could see the Japs had brought their engineers up, and they were already putting in their pontoon bridge. They had a couple of pontoons already in place.

"When we were over the gorge and in position, Tex gave the signal. We slid into a single line and followed him down. There were a lot of Japs below us and we figured we would get a lot of ground fire, but that was not what we were thinking about. On our first dive, we aimed at the top of the gorge, on the western side, right where the Burma Road starts its way down. Tex had briefed us. The idea was to drop those big Russian bombs right into the edge of the gorge where they would blast away huge chunks of rock and start landslides that would tumble down the gorge, smash across the road, block the road and cut off the Japs.

"And that's exactly what we did with those big Russian bombs. When we finished, the edge of the gorge, where the road had started down, was gone It was blasted away. Most of it had slid on down, and took big sections of the road along with it. The Japs who weren't killed, were trapped now on those serpentine curves. They were out in the open. They couldn't go back; they couldn't go ahead. They had no place to hide.

"At the bottom of the gorge, we saw the Jap engineers scurrying around by their bridge. They had very little cover. As we flew toward them, we hit them first with our .50 caliber machine guns, then we dropped our fragmentation bombs as we passed over. I saw secondary explosions from gas tanks and ammunition stores. There were flames everywhere, rolling along the ground, shooting up into the sky. It was like the fires of hell. Then we skimmed along sections of road, shooting, just shooting. Troops, trucks, tanks, there were targets everywhere. The Japs had nowhere to hide. When we ran out of ammunition, our four guys flying top cover came down. They tried to kill everything we couldn't.

"So the raid was a success, Harry. As great a success as the AVG has ever had, I would think. I know the Old Man is pleased. The road on the western side where the Japs were all bunched up is blocked now. It's unusable in a lot of places. Many Japs are trapped along the road inside the gorge. They were there when we went back in the afternoon. They will be there tomorrow and the day after that, until we have killed them all.

"Well, I hope that gives you some idea of what happened along the Salween, Harry. I hope it's of use. I'm getting a little tired now. It was a long day, and I think I'll turn in. Morning will be here soon, and I know the Old Man will send us back to the Salween again. It's a long flight, tiring work. But it's easy work. You know, Harry, we get down low when we're shooting Jap troops. You can see them, almost see the expressions on their faces. I don't think they're even shooting back at us. It's like they're not bothering to. It's like they know they don't have a chance. Well, good night, Harry. You sleep well. "

* * *

"So the AVG stopped the Japs at the Salween and saved the world as we know it.

I'll get your report back to Washington tonight. I'm sure it will ease some minds. Do you think our crisis is over?" Doyle asked.

"It looks that way. The Old Man isn't done with them yet. If the weather holds, and the AVG can stay after them for a few more days, there will be a lot fewer Japs to try to cross the Salween again. Maybe they'll look for something easier, like chasing Stilwell."

"You stay with the AVG guys for now, but as this winds down, you'll have to give some thought to your operations. How's that girl you're sending to Shanghai?"

"I don't know. I haven't even thought about her. It hasn't been that long, but it seems like months."

CHAPTER 33

May 11, 1942
Kunming, China

"Louie left this for you," Lucy told him when he came back to the flat for the first time in many days. "He said it came from Shanghai."

"Thanks, Lucy," he said, and took the envelope. Inside, he found a half sheet of paper covered with rows of numbers. "Did Louie say what this was?"

"Only that he would send you a translation. You can give him a call. He's at his little office."

Louie picked up on the first ring, spoke a greeting in Chinese.

"Hey, Louie, greetings. Harry here. That envelope you sent…. Is it from who I think?"

"It is. We sent her right after I said we wouldn't. The Big Boss said that with all the confusion in the east, it would be a good time for travelers going the wrong way. He was right."

Harry understood Big Boss was General Tai Li. "All the numbers…. I wasn't sure."

"Ah, the numbers. I just wanted you to see the original, to see how it's done. I had to transpose that into proper Chinese, and then translate the lot into English for you. It's finished. If you're at the flat, I'll send a boy over with it. I understand you've been hanging around with Chennault's boys. They've done some good work. It seems we won't need to leave Kunming just now. Look forward to talking with you about it."

Just as Harry was about to hang up, Louie added, "By the way, I received another packet from the Big Boss for you. I'll send that as well."

While he waited for Louie's boy to bring the translation, he went looking for Lucy. She was in Louie's study, sitting at his desk, doing paper work. "Hard at work?" he asked.

"Dutifully helping Father," she said. She put down her pen, looked up at him. "He's starting to get busy now. You might have noticed all the activity at the airport. The American Air Corps is increasing its cargo flights over the Himalayas. There's a lot coming in from India now. And there will be a lot more as time goes on."

"And Louie is handling special shipments for the Generalissimo, I presume?"

She smiled. "A lot of the cargo is for the Generalissimo. It's for the war. The American share of what's being brought in will increase as more and more Americans come here. There seem to be Americans everywhere now. There are just not enough airplanes now for everything that's needed."

"So you'll be working here in Kunming ?"

"Well, Kunming and Chungking. Kunming is the terminus of the air route, but Chungking is where our customer is, the Generalissimo and his government. The work in Chungking will be political, dealing with the Generalissimo, the Madame, and all the generals. Louie will want to handle that, but I expect he will want me there too on occasion. Working in Chungking could be interesting, but there are too many official dinners. I would prefer to work just in Kunming, by myself, but I'm not sure Louie thinks I can handle it."

"You handled the whole Port of Rangoon, you should be able to handle this little backwater."

She shugged. "Kunming may look like a backwater, but it's become the main stream. It will have more than its share of undercurrents, eddies and whirlpools." She laughed then. "Sorry Harry, I'm not a poet. I don't have the words. But doing business in Kunming will become complex and even treacherous. I know my father spoke with you about how business here will be very different from the way it was in Burma. It will certainly be less straightforward."

It surprised Harry that Louie told her that they had talked. Lucy was exceptionally competent; Louie probably needed her in the middle of his business dealings, but he had always been so protective of her. Until now, Louie shielded her from the more unsavory aspects of his business. It bothered Harry that it might change now.

She stood up, stepped over to him. She took his hand in both of hers. "I missed you," she said. "I missed you in the mornings, missed not starting my day with our chats."

He squeezed her hand, got up and pulled her against him. A hug, but a careful one, a chaste one. "I missed you too, Lucy, I really did." He wanted to do more, but that would not be wise, he knew. "We can start our breakfasts again tomorrow," he said.

Butler Chang interrupted with a little cough. He handed Harry a large envelope. "From Master Louie," he said. Inside were two smaller ones.

A note from Louie on one envelope said, "Bear with me, my first attempt. It will be easier as it goes on." Inside was a sheet of paper filled with Louie's handwriting, clear and easy to read, a translation of the first letter from his Shanghai girl. He laughed aloud when he read the salutation.

Dear Kunming Big Boss,

I arrived in Shanghai only yesterday, and I wanted to thank you. I am with my mother for now, and already have a job. My new big boss is a real gangster, as you promised. He has many pretty girl pictures on his walls. He said my work will be to entertain Japanese officers. They always have money. Some are nice. When I meet them, I will try to find out for you where their airplanes will bomb, and how many there are, and other things you want to know. I thank you again. Your Calendar Girl in Shanghai.

He was touched by the note. Despite everything that must be happening to her, she was thinking of him. They shared a bond, there was no question of that. But it was professional now, not personal. He looked at the second envelope. There was nothing written on it and it was sealed. Inside were three pages, the top one a rough sketch of some kind, possibly a map. Looking at it closely, Harry decided it was probably an airfield. Notations on it were in French, which Harry did not read. He turned to the other two pages. They were also in French, in a handwriting that was difficult to decipher. When he made out the word "Hanoi," he decided it was probably a report about an airfield in French Indo-China. He would pass the whole packet to Chennault in the morning. Then he had a thought.

"Lucy, is Sue in her room? She reads French, doesn't she?"

"I'm sorry. I should have told you. She's not here. She's in Chungking, doing some work."

"Working with Louie?"

"No, her Chinese gentleman friend found her something. I think it's involved with the government."

"Do you know what she's doing?"

"Translating, or something like that. She said she would need to use her Thai language."

* * *

"... and he studied the language. He speaks Chinese and reads it. He's the U.S. Army's China expert, Harry. I first met him in Peking, in 1939 I think it was. He was the American military attaché then. He knows China and the Chinese. He's traveled everywhere, all over the country. Stilwell is as expert on China as any American you will ever find."

"Morris, you old devil, you've been holding out on me. You knew Stilwell all along, all the way back to the old days in Peking. He's an old friend and you never told me. So that's why you stayed with him in Burma."

"I wouldn't say 'friend', Harry; 'acquaintance' would be better. And I stayed with him in Burma because that's my job. It was a chance to talk with the most important American military man in Asia."

"Did you actually get to talk with him much?"

"Yes, we talked a lot. At night, in upcountry Burma, even with a war on, there's not a hell of a lot to do. At the end of the day, after the Chinese commanders made their reports, Stilwell and I sat around, listened to the crickets, and talked. About war, about life."

Morris poured the last of his beer into his glass, drank most of it in one thirsty swallow, then went on. "I don't know what you've heard about him, but Stilwell is an impressive man, an outstanding soldier. He was a real star in the U.S. Army. Did you know that he was chosen for high command in the European theater? You wouldn't know that, I suppose; it's still all hush-hush. Anyway, his future looked very bright. Then someone in Washington promised Chiang Kai-shek that one of America's top generals would be sent to China to help him. And which general knew more about China than anyone? 'Shih thi weh', old Joe Stilwell himself. Stilwell wasn't looking for that. In fact he did not want to come back to China. The real war for the men who wear stars is in Europe. That's where glory is won. For the generals, China is the end of the line."

"I didn't know any of that," Harry said. "I've heard very little about Stilwell, and most of that is from Chennault – who does not regard Stilwell very highly."

"That's understandable. For years, China was Chennault's turf. Now Stilwell is the new boy, but also his superior officer. They're vastly different personalities. Chennault is 'the Old Man'. There are some who don't like him, but from what I've seen, the AVG doesn't just respect him, they love him. And Stilwell is 'Vinegar Joe'. Did you know everyone calls him that? And he's Vinegar Joe Stilwell for good reason.

Talking made Morris more thirsty. "Garcon," he called, and held his beer bottle in the air. After he got a fresh one, he went on. "There's more to it than that, Harry. I think the problem between them is less personality than their views of war. Both are thinkers, military thinkers. Chennault believes the war in Asia can be won with airpower. Period. Stilwell does not believe it's that simple. He thinks that if Chennault begins an extensive bombing campaign, especially one that touches the Jap homeland, the Jap army will be unleashed to destroy all the Chinese air bases before the Chinese are capable of defending them. The Americans would lose their foothold here. The first job, as Stilwell sees it, is to build the Chinese Army. Then it must be equipped, and properly trained. Only then can he think about fighting the Japs."

"I'm sure you're right about that. I remember the Old Man saying that Stilwell has no understanding of the use of aircraft. Stilwell sees the airplane useful only for reconnaissance or as flying artillery to support the ground troops."

"Well, it's a little more complicated than that."

Harry was drinking beer too, more than he was used to, and feeling a bit cocky. "If Stilwell is so damn smart, how do you explain his lack of judgment in Burma, his walk into the jungle?"

Morris shrugged. "I don't know, Harry. We'll have to see what he has to say for himself once he re-emerges from the jungle – if he ever does."

"One thing I've learned," Harry said quite solemnly, "China is very complicated. Nothing works simply – if it works at all."

"You make a good point," Morris said. That surprised Harry. All he had done was to say a line that he liked the sound of. It was nothing he put thought into. He listened carefully now to what Morris had to say.

"I think what you're saying is that everything of significance in China is overlaid with politics. The war that Stilwell has to fight is very political. It's Chinese politics layered over American politics, but Stilwell doesn't want to deal with that. He really doesn't know how. American generals are above politics; the Chinese generals wallow in it. And here's Stilwell, an American general, for God's sake, who is the chief of staff of the Chinese army. It has all the makings of a comic opera.

"Did you know that Stilwell has the authority to execute Chinese officers up to the rank of major? Isn't that impressive? But in Burma he found out just how much authority he really has. There he was worrying about the Japs while the senior Chinese were worrying about how much merchandise they could get back to China before the Burma front collapsed. When Chinese mercantile interests started to get in the way of the war, he tried to do something about it – and quickly learned there was nothing he could do. The Generalissimo vetoed anything that might affect his political allies. Stilwell is very good at doing a soldier's job, but in China a soldier's job is just politics in another form. And nothing in Stilwell's career, or his life, has prepared him for that. That's Stilwell's flaw." Morris suddenly laughed aloud. "Do you know who Teddy White is?" he asked. Harry shrugged; the name was vaguely familiar. Morris went on:

"Teddy's out here somewhere. He's a correspondent for *Time* magazine. He ran into Stilwell in New Delhi and got the most incredibly succinct description of what's wrong in China. Stilwell told him – and I've never forgotten these words – 'The trouble in China is simple,' Stilwell said. 'We are allied to an ignorant, illiterate, superstitious, peasant son of a bitch.' And that's how Stilwell described the problem with the 'Peanut' as he calls the Generalissimo."

"Jesus," Harry said. "I'm glad we're all friends in this war together."

* * *

"Ross," the Old Man said, and stopped halfway down the steps in front of the hostel. He was obviously in a hurry; his car was waiting for him. He said something to the army officer walking with him, and the man continued down the steps.

He took Harry's arm, led him a few steps aside. "It was good information," he said, "very timely. Your man must have been right down on that airfield. It was a repeat of Chiang Mai. Well done!"

"Thank you, General," Harry said, then watched as Chennault went on and got into his car. He had no idea what the Old Man was talking about. Well, he was on his way to see Ed Rector. Maybe Ed would know.

* * *

"Ed," he said, "What have you guys been up to?"

"Oh, this, that, the usual thing. Tex is in Delhi, so I've been scheduling flights. Mostly patrols down along the Salween, keeping an eye on the Japs. I'm looking forward to Tex coming back. This damn office work keeps me from flying much."

"I saw the Old Man outside. He said something I didn't understand. Something was like Chiang Mai?"

"Oh, he must have meant the Hanoi raid. We did that yesterday. We caught the Japs on their airfield at Hanoi in French Indo-China and tore them up, just like we did at Chiang Mai. And we lost a guy to anti-aircraft fire, just like we lost Black Mac at Chiang Mai."

"I'm sorry to hear that. But the raid was successful?"

"It was. We sent six Pandas down. Jim Howard came back because of an engine problem. The other five hit the field. Everything went perfectly, and then John Donovan got hit. He plowed right into the runway, just a ball of flame. Here's a sheet on the raid, sort of a press release. It has the details."

Harry skimmed it. Fifteen Japanese planes destroyed, another 30 damaged. So that's why the Old Man thanked him. It was the information on the airfield at Hanoi that Tai Li had sent him. He had brought it to the Old Man the next morning, left it with his clerk, and then totally forgot it. Mark off another intelligence coup for Harry Ross! One he was completely oblivious of. He had not recognized the gift horse when it trotted up to him. Another one to tell Doyle about when he saw him that afternoon at their tea garden.

Harry was ready with his Hanoi story, but Doyle beat him to the punch. "Have a look at this. It's a cable we got this morning," he said, handing Harry a sheet of paper as he sat down. "The AVG made the *New York Times* again. I thought you'd find it interesting."

It was the story of the Hanoi raid, more or less as presented in the "press release" that Rector gave him. Harry smiled, passed the cable back to Doyle.

"That was actually us, Doyle, America's intelligence service at work." He went on to tell Doyle about the packet of information on the airfield at Hanoi that he got from Tai Li.

"It was in French, so I just passed it on to the Old Man the next day. It turns out that he had already decided to hit Hanoi several days earlier. Ed Rector told me that. The Old Man had some information from an over-flight by one of his pilots, but he didn't have all the information he wanted. He knew there would be a lot of flak, but he didn't have locations of the gun positions. Tai Li's report must have had that. Rector said that the Old Man got something the day before the raid that made him happy as a clam. That was the same day I took Tai Li's envelope over to the Old Man. Rector said that new information was what decided the Old Man to go."

"So you gave him all this valuable information and never knew it."

"I didn't bother studying it. I thought it was just some routine report on an airfield. And by coincidence, it was the airfield at Hanoi that the Old Man was planning to hit."

Doyle laughed. "Tai Li sent you information on a target Chennault was planning to hit – and you call that a coincidence."

And that made Harry feel a little dumb. Doyle was right. It was an obvious connection, and he had not seen it. The information from Tai Li could have been a coincidence, but probably was not. It was not the way the world of intelligence worked, not when you had a grandmaster like Tai Li shuffling around in the shadows.

"How the hell would Tai Li know what the Old Man was planning?" Harry asked. "Do you think Tai Li is tapped into the AVG?"

Doyle shrugged. "Of course he is. He'd be remiss if he weren't."

"Where, where's he tapped in?"

"I don't know. If there's enough money involved it could be anybody. How about your friend Ed Rector? Hey, I'm kidding, Harry, I don't think it would be any of the Americans. Ah, but there's Olga! She's a Russian, isn't she? Still kidding, Harry, I know she's from Brooklyn. When you think about it, there are a lot of Chinese involved with the AVG, some in a good position to know what's going on. Chennault has a Chinese interpreter, think about that one. He has drivers and cooks and God knows what else. But, what the hell, we're all in the same war."

Harry was thinking now. "But why wouldn't Tai Li pass information like that to Chennault directly, or send it through Chinese Air Force channels? Why would he do it through me? Why would he do it at all?"

"It could be pride that keeps him from giving it directly to the Old Man. It was you who told me that Chennault had turned down Tai Li's offer to work together. He probably thinks that if he passes information through you, Chennault will not know the real source. He thinks you're the one who got the Chiang Mai story in the *New York Times*. Maybe that's what he was expecting this time. And he'll be pleased to see that you made the Times again. You've become his cut-out, Harry, a tool that he can use. And again, you owe him. He will look for payback one day."

"But why? Why did he pass the info at all? Because he had it and knew that Chennault would use it?"

"Probably something like that. He had the information, saw an opportunity, and the AVG was the most effective instrument. It was probably just a simple strike against the Japanese. But you're looking for deeper meaning, aren't you, Harry? Well, how about this: A friend of Tai Li is doing business in Hanoi, and the Japs don't pay their bills. The strike is Tai Li's subtle message, 'Don't mess with Tai Li and friends'. What do you think of that?"

"Come on, you don't believe that, Doyle."

"I don't think that's what happened. But we have to accept that as possible. Hey, this is China, Harry, the mysterious East. Anything can happen."

CHAPTER 34

Harry thought he would probably find Morris at the bistro, and so that was where he went first. He walked there in a drizzle, water pooling on the street in glossy black puddles, except where light spilling from doorways of the fancy shops made them glittering yellow. Some of the shops were closed, the ones that sold the real imported goods that were now hard to find. The loss of the Burma Road was starting to be felt.

Coming out of a wet, dark night, the bistro felt cozy. Morris was at his usual table upstairs, near the window overlooking the street, a bowl of hot sauce propping up a book in front of him. He saw Harry crest the stairs, craned his neck for a waiter and shouted, "Garcon, another beer," then turned to Harry, now standing alongside the table, dripping on it. "Harry Ross," he said, "you have been participating in the monsoon. You are wet."

"I am wet," Harry said, and dripped some more. He reached for the book, turned the cover so he could read the title. "A mystery by Miss Agatha. Isn't that cozy? Isn't the war in China exciting enough for you?"

"It's not about excitement, Harry, it's about contrast. I sit here in the drizzle and chill of a target for Japanese bombs. So I turn to Miss Agatha to immerse myself in the life of a picturesque 1930s English village, where spinster ladies serve cyanide tea with arsenic cookies. It's all so civilized compared to China."

Harry tried not to smile, but he did. "It's a different kind of Brit from the ones we knew in Burma, eh, except … I never really got to know the older spinster ladies, but I always suspected that you did, Morris. It's what lights your candle, I suppose. Speaking of Burma, I hear Stilwell has come out of the jungle. What do you hear?"

"The same. I hear he's been out a few days. You're lagging behind the news again, Harry. Actually, I do have an advantage: an old Brit friend passed through Kunming this afternoon, on his way to Chungking. He was in India when Stilwell emerged. Do you know what Stilwell said when he came out of the jungle and saw the gathered press?" Morris looked up at the ceiling and recited, pulling the words deep from his memory:

"'We got a hell of a beating. We got run out of Burma. It is humiliating as hell. I think we ought to find out what caused it, go back, and retake it.'"

"Wow," Harry said, "tough talk!"

"Tough talk, indeed – from a tough man. It's really quite impressive what Stilwell did. It will make him an American folk hero."

"Yeah, right," Harry said. It sounded as dismissive as it was, and seemed to cause Morris some distress.

"Hey, Harry," he said, "think about it. A three-star general gives up his airplane to others, and walks 140 miles of jungle, that's full of heat and thick with vines and all the bugs and leeches that make their home there. The walk takes two weeks. There's no New Delhi veranda and Coca-Cola on ice for this general. It was all bad water and diarrhea, nasty mosquitoes, bites and itching – and he's got the Japanese Army right on his ass."

"And then ... he emerges from the jungle, and he hasn't lost a man – or woman for that matter. He had over a hundred people with him, including a civilian medical team, 'Doctor Cigarette' Seagrave and 20 of his Burmese nurses, young ladies and spinsters both. And Vinegar Joe Stilwell – resplendent in World War I campaign hat and canvas puttees, for Christ sake – leads them through the muck and mire, behind him the nurses singing, 'Onward Christian Soldiers.' No one got left behind. The sick ones got dragged out on mattresses."

"When they started their trek, Stilwell told them all that he would get them out. He said, 'You will hate me, but if you follow my orders you will get out.' He told them, 'If you can't follow orders, speak up. We'll give you two weeks' rations, and you can do it on your own.' And nobody spoke up, Harry." Morris shook his head at the thought. "Christ! I wouldn't. It tells you something about the man, doesn't it?"

"It tells me he should have taken the airplane."

"Jesus, Harry, have you no respect? The walk will make Stilwell famous. It will make him an American folk hero."

Harry shrugged, and it became even more important for Morris to make his point. "You have to look at the whole picture, Harry. Consider the Brits. Look what happened to them. General Slim led the remnant of the British Army out, Englishmen, Gurkhas, Indians, and lost hundreds. The Japs caught them crossing the Chindwin River. They had to fight their way across. They left 2,000 vehicles there and 1200 dead. It was no walk in the park, Harry, for the Brits or for Stilwell."

Harry did not try to dispute that. "So what comes now? What happens to Stilwell?"

"He's on his way back to China. He's supposed to fly to Chungking and report to the Generalissimo. He's got jaundice and worms in his guts that they're trying to clear up first."

"I'd love to be there when he reports to the Generalissimo. I suspect he's not a folk hero to the Chinese."

"Yeah, maybe not. But there's too much important stuff going on for those two to get in a pissing contest. Stilwell needs to reorganize the Chinese Army. He needs to organize all the plane loads of Americans coming here every day. He needs to meld the whole Chinese business together with the American."

"It will be tough. The AVG will soon be gone, replaced by a whole new air force. There will be bombers coming here, armadas of them, and transport airplanes to fly, oil and gasoline over the Himalayas for the bombers. The U.S. Navy is here now, did you know that? They want to set up weather stations all over the country, even in Tibet. There's talk of American intelligence organizations, propaganda efforts, commando teams. Jesus, it's going to be very complicated. Do you know if the final decision has been made about what will replace the AVG?"

Harry shrugged. "The AVG will be disbanded, that's all I know. They're still talking about what comes next. Chennault will have his own show. Word is that it will be a 'task force'. The big question is where the pilots and other personnel will come from. They're still trying to recruit AVG pilots and ground crew, but General Bissel has pissed off most of them. There won't be many volunteers from the AVG."

"Hey, Morris," Harry asked then, "have you spent time in Chungking? Some of the Pandas are there now, and I've been invited."

"If you have an invitation to Chungking, take it. It's big and sprawling and the shopping's good."

"The shopping is better than Kunming? You're kidding? "

"Not kidding. The shopping's good. It's not that it's better, it's just different."

"Different how?"

"It's not foreign imports like you find here in Kunming. Mostly it's Japanese goods, stuff made in the Chinese factories in Shanghai that are run by the Japanese. You can buy almost anything in Chungking. I can get you a new Buick at a great price."

"You're kidding?"

"I'm not kidding. The trade between the Japs in Shanghai and the Chinese in Chungking is big business. The Yangtze River ties everything together. It makes it easy to transport goods by boat, including your Buick. There are taxes that have to be paid here and there along the way, but it's big business. War or no war, commerce rules."

"Yeah, every Chinese general is a businessman. I know all that, but I'm still astounded every time I think about it."

* * *

"The grapevine has it," Doyle said, "that Donovan's office, the 'Coordinator of Information,' will get a new name. It will be called the 'Office of Strategic Services.'"

"That has sort of a nice ring to it," Harry said.

"We will be known by just our initials, like everybody else."

"OSS? That doesn't sound like anything."

"Well, it doesn't have quite ring of SOE, but it sounds okay."

"What's SOE.?"

"The British spies, 'Special' something…'Special Operations Executive,' that's what it is."

"Executive sounds better than office. But you're right, we'll just be part of the alphabet soup. Who will remembers what AVG stands for."

"American Very Good! Oh, sorry, that's what the Chinese say it means. With OSS, it's already started in Washington. 'Oh, so secret,' some say it means, because it is. Or 'Oh, so social,' because Donovan is recruiting from New York high society."

They thought about it. Whatever the name, it would not make much difference to the two of them. "Hey," Harry said, "that reminds me, the Old Man wants me to go to Chungking."

"What's the Old Man want you to go there for?"

"He wants me to meet with this missionary, John Birch. He wants me to talk with Birch about the principles of intelligence and what makes good intelligence reporting. He wants Birch to work for him."

"I don't know if you should be doing that, Harry. It's going to be really important that we keep you free of any taint of an intelligence affiliation. If you go talking with some missionary, next thing you know he'll be preaching sermons about you. If you talk with some guy about intelligence, he won't believe you're an innocent journalist. It's better somebody like me does it. We will have some people here in a few weeks, OSS people…,"

Doyle raised his eyebrows as he said that, "... whose job it is to train agents."

Harry shook his head. "You wear a uniform now, probably the other OSS guys will too. The Old Man doesn't want that. He doesn't want to scare John Birch off. His idea is that I talk with Birch, not as a spy, but as a journalist. I tell him how a journalist goes about getting information, and then puts it together in a report that has value to others. What a journalist does is not so different from a spy. The Old Man figures that all the sneaking around that makes a spy different from a journalist is something that John Birch is already pretty good at. Birch has been out in the rice fields and sneaking through Jap lines for months. The Old Man figures there's not much we could teach John Birch about that."

Doyle thought on that a while. "He's probably right," he finally said. "I'm impressed by the way the Old Man thinks. He sees things as they are, and knows how to take them to the next level. I think it's worth your while to talk with Birch, Harry, not so much for what you can teach him, but for what we might learn from him. Like Chennault, we're going to need people like John Birch."

"You authorize me to go to Chungking?"

"I authorize you, my son." Doyle made the motions of blessing him. "Go in peace." He added, "Do you plan contact with Tai Li?"

"I'm not planning that. Should I?"

"I think you should. You get along well with him. If he has time, maybe he'll show you Happy Valley."

"Happy Valley!" Harry laughed. "What's Happy Valley? A rice field paradise with naked ladies picking rice? And Tai Li is the rice picking overseer?"

"Something like that. I don't think you'll laugh if you get to see it. Happy Valley is Tai Li's big intelligence base. It's an actual valley, several valleys apparently, outside Chungking. Nobody has seen it, so we don't know for sure. We're told it's where he trains his security thugs and his spies. It's where he keeps the people who think up bad things to do to the Japs. We know a little bit, because Tai Li has been sniffing around the official American community, looking for money, and training, and equipment. That all reminds me, there are problems I need to tell you about."

"I'm listening," Harry said.

"I mentioned the SOE, the British Special Operations Executive. They are very unpopular in China right now, particularly with Tai Li. SOE has been here for years, trying to run operations against the Japanese. They've never had much success. Tai Li doesn't like them, and since the Brits lost Hong Kong and Burma he looks down on them. He thinks SOE is really here to subvert China."

"That doesn't sound good for the SOE," Harry said, "but how does that affect us?"

"Well…we think Tai Li looks on OSS as a tool of the SOE. The fact is, Donovan has had a lot of dealings with the SOE. A lot of what OSS plans to do in the war, and how it plans to do it, is based on SOE doctrine. The fact is, OSS has learned from the SOE, but it's not an SOE tool. OSS runs its own show, Harry, now and in the future. But somebody outside, watching Donovan organize OSS won't believe that. No matter how often we might tell him, Tai Li's black feelings about SOE may spill over on OSS. That's the thing we're afraid of. That's why it's important to keep you from being tainted with the OSS brush."

"Wow," Harry said, "I didn't know that spying could get so complicated."

"It gets worse. There's a U.S. Navy group here now. They're trying to get into the intelligence business. It's under a guy named Miles. There's talk about him working jointly with OSS. If that happens, I will probably get involved. I might find myself dealing directly with Tai Li. That's all the more reason for you to stay hunkered down. So you stay in the background, Harry. You're our ace in the hole."

"So, I hunker down, but you still want me to try to see Tai Li in Chungking."

"Absolutely. Just don't give him reason to think that you're anything but a journalist."

"Journalist it is, sir. Best thing is I tell Louie that I'm going to Chungking as a journalist, to cover a conference that Chennault and the other Air Corps guys are having with Vingar Joe Stilwell about the future of war in the air. I'll just ask him if there's a chance to see Tai Li while I'm there – to talk about the future of the war for a series of articles I'm planning."

"Good. That will whet Tai Li's appetite. It's all you'll have to do. If he wants to see you, he'll find you."

CHAPTER 35

May 24, 1942
Chungking, China

That's the Yangtze down there, that big, muddy river," said the passenger seated in front of him, who had obviously been this way before. As he said it, the airplane banked sharply to follow the river as it turned between the cliffs. "It's not far now to where it meets the Kailing River. Where the two rivers run together is Chungking."

Harry watched quietly. The upper half of his window was crazed, almost opaque, but there was enough clear glass to watch the scene passing below. They were low enough now to make out the families on the decks of the sampans that crowded the riverbanks. Farther out in the stream were heavily loaded rice barges and small steamers. The river became even more crowded as they went farther, and the signs of human activity on the riverbanks increased. Individual farmhouses became clusters, and clusters became villages, and the villages clung to the riverbanks that grew steeper and began to look more like cliffs. Beyond them were rice paddies that stretched inland as far as Harry could see.

Harry and a half-dozen AVG had taken off that morning on one of the transport airplanes that served Chennault. They flew high over a countryside that was brown and rugged, mountain after mountain, the occasional village just a cluster of dots along the thin line of a stream. The pilot finally brought them lower, to follow the river.

"There, you can see where the Kailing River meets the Yangtze," the passenger in front said. "Christ, look how yellow both of them are. Full of mud, but the Yangtze is muddier. Look, you can see the line where the two rivers meet. The water doesn't want to mix."

Here the cliffs that hung over the Yangtze were high and covered with the city. Buildings, bunched together, crowded the tops of the cliffs and spilled down the sides. There were open areas here and there, where bombs had turned everything into rubble, or into naked scars where bomb-damaged structures had been leveled and not replaced. And there were holes, openings cut into the cliffs, rows of them in some places, looking like the mouths of caves.

"Air raid shelters," the passenger in front said just then. "Look at them all. They've been digging into the cliffs to get away from the bombs. They live in those holes now. The Japs have been hitting Chungking hard, really hard. They've been bombing the city since 1939. I got a newspaper from home that said that Chungking is the most bombed city in the world."

A moment later he said, "Look, there's the airport. Out in the middle of the river." He turned to look at Harry. "Don't worry, it's not the one we're landing at, " then laughed and peered out the window again. "They can't use it all year round. When the river's high, the runway floods and sometimes totally disappears."

Harry saw it then, a narrow strip paved with stone. It was on a sandbar, the river almost level with it, streaming around it. A narrow bridge over the swirling water connected the sandbar to the foot of the cliff where the city began. It was hard to believe an airplane could land on that, but he knew the CNAC DC-3s did it regularly, at least when the river was not high enough to run right over the top.

They banked steeply then, turned away from the river to fly across the city. They were so low that he could not see it all. It was hard to take in. The city was big, much bigger than he thought it would be. He knew that an ancient wall ran along the top of the cliffs, and now he saw parts of it. It enclosed the old city, a maze of alleys that twisted down the hills to the river. They passed over one tall structure that might have been a tower for one of the old wall's nine gates. He thought he had seen a photo of that once, but he was not sure.

Gray was the city's color, dark gray, almost black in some places, the dull black of age. The buildings looked small from here, mostly just shacks crowded together. Everything down there looked ancient. Then they passed over a business district, or one of the new government quarters that had spread outside the old city wall. He caught a glimpse of structures that looked thoroughly modern.

Free of the city, they flew west, over miles of rice paddy. Now and then an individual compound appeared, a rich farmer's house perhaps, or a rice trader's, but mostly it was little villages, alone in the rice fields. Somewhere ahead was an airfield, named Peishiyi, from where the AVG would operate. Harry saw the flaps start to slide back on the wing as the pilot prepared for landing.

An AVG pilot whose name he could not remember stood at the edge of the apron with others, watching the DC-3's passengers disembark. He called to Harry when he saw him, "Hey, Ross! Harry Ross!" Harry raised his hand, and the pilot shouted at him, "There's a Chinese guy waiting for you out by the cars."

"Thanks," Harry shouted back, threw a salute, and wondered who was waiting. Louie probably, who else, or somebody Louie sent if he was too busy to come all the way here from the city. The exit from the small terminal was crowded with rickshaws and cars, and enterprising drivers shouting incomprehensible inducements, waving hands in the air. None of the faces looked familiar, none seemed a likely surrogate for Louie. He started looking for a shiny sedan, but saw not a one. He pushed ahead, at the same time trying to protect his small bag from the many hands trying to relieve him of it.

"Harry, over here." It was Louie. "You walked right by me," he said.

"I didn't see you," Harry said, but really meant that he did not recognize him. He had never seen Louie not wearing a suit, or at least part of one, maybe with his coat slung over a shoulder or hung over the back of a chair. But here was Louie in the gray, high-collared, buttoned-up-to-the-neck uniform that all the government functionaries wore. He looked different, more Chinese. "Car's over here," he said.

The car was a surprise too, a battered Chevrolet, painted gray once, or maybe black. "In better condition than it looks," Louie said when he saw the surprise on Harry's face. "It doesn't do to look prosperous here. Damned place is crawling with refugees from Shanghai and Nanking, gangsters, every one. The Shanghai ones are the worst. The ones from Nanking take your car to sell it. The ones from Shanghai kill you for something fancy to drive."

Pulling out of the parking area, Louie said, "Watch who follows."

Harry put an arm over the seat back and peered through the rear window. "Chevrolet, brown one."

Louie nodded. "Same chap. He's seen you arrive. His curiosity should be satisfied now. He'll drop off soon."

"Tai Li's man?"

"Yes. There are many of them here with not enough to do. It's good practice for them, I suppose. We'll see Tai Li tonight. He's hosting a dinner in Chungking. Said to bring you along. Hope you don't mind."

"Not at all. I look forward to it. Is it a long way to town?"

"Thirty miles or so. The roads are rough; it takes longer than it should."

For a while they drove in silence, Harry looking out the window. The road went up and down as they wound through the hills, steep ones, steeper than they had looked from the air, and passed through villages. There, they had to slow for traffic, mostly bicycles and people walking, everywhere. And for the cars and the trucks, and the carts pulled by animals and the carts pulled by men, and for rickshaws and sedan chairs. There was more of everything in the mix as they got closer to the city.

When the spectacle grew monotonous, Harry turned his attention back to Louie. "How's business?" he asked.

"Quite good. Too good, some days. I'm dealing in everything now, bobby pins to Buicks." He smiled. "I prefer the Buicks."

"I've heard you can buy a new Buick here. Are they really Japanese-built?"

"They're all built in Shanghai, and the Japanese are the proprietors there now. Yes, for three million dollars Chinese – that's about 15,000 American dollars – you can have a new Buick, the latest 1942 model, delivered in Chungking."

"Let's see," Harry said, thinking aloud, "How many 50-dollar articles must I write to buy one? By the way, what's the occasion for the dinner tonight?"

"Visitors to Chungking – American military and some embassy chaps. Tai Li doesn't usually do this for foreigners. I suppose he's trying to adapt to the inevitability of the pervasive American presence. There's a lot the Americans can do for him – as he sees it."

As they got into town, Louie said, "I'll take you by your hostel. Nice place, you have your own floor, separate entrance. Sorry I can't put you up at my place, but it's mostly office and crowded. I have staff there, and visitors at all hours."

Inside the city, they crawled through old winding streets, and finally stopped at the entrance to a house, a narrow doorway cut into an ancient wall. Inside, it was all bowing ladies and a labyrinth of connected rooms, none on the same level. In one door and out the other, one step up, two steps down, careful you don't trip.

"I'll never find my way out."

"Not to worry," Louie said, "I'll show you the easy way" and he did. A stairway from Harry's rooms on the second floor led down to a door that opened on an alley.

"How do I find the alley?"

"The house is number 32, the 32nd house on the street of the Wang family. You walk behind the house to this alley. There, you see the fruit vendor? That's your landmark."

"Right, and if I come in late, the fruit vendor won't be there vending."

"No, he'll be sleeping on top of the cart. He lives there."

They drove on to the restaurant, closer to the river, and made their way up to a private room on the second floor, brushing by a brace of young toughs with shaved heads, who gave them no room, just hard looks. And near the door three more of the same, and just as friendly.

"Thug school graduates," Louie said as they squeezed by. "The big chief is already here."

Four large round tables were set in a line inside the long room, a well-stocked bar at the far end. Everyone was already seated, and girls, a dozen at least, scurried back and forth, bringing food, placing it on the tables. Tai Li was at the table farthest from the door. On one side of him was an older man, an American in civilian clothes, on the other a younger man in a U.S. military uniform of some sort. Eddie Liu sat by the civilian, leaning past him, his eyes fixed on Tai Li.

Tai Li saw them, stood up and walked over, Eddie Liu right behind. He bowed to Louie, extended his hand to Harry and said some words. Louie translated for Harry. "General Tai Li welcomes you. He's pleased you could come."

Which was almost all they heard from Tai Li that evening. The two Americans monopolized him, discussing important business, undoubtedly. Tai Li listened, ate little, took small sips of his drink, spoke only occasionally. Louie said both Americans were Chinese speakers. The older gentleman was the American ambassador, the other an American naval officer who had come to China to do important things. There were many opportunities for Tai Li to meet the ambassador, so it had to be the naval officer who was the VIP tonight.

"It would be interesting to know what's going on, what Tai Li has in mind," Harry said.

"Well, in a day or two," Louie said. He would know then, and he would tell Harry.

"Are there no secrets?" Harry laughed.

"It's all secret, Harry, it has to be. It's government business. But a secret is a tantalizing thing, isn't it? The pleasure of having a secret comes from sharing it. On a very selective basis, of course."

"Of course," Harry said. "Of course."

At the end of the meal, before the serious drinking began, Eddie Liu walked over, shook hands again with Harry. "General Tai Li regrets he could not spend time with you this evening," he said. "He invites you to visit him again." He turned and said some Chinese words to Louie. Louie nodded, responded in Chinese. When Eddie left, Louie said, "Well, you get to see Happy Valley. I told Eddie I'd drive you over there tomorrow."

"Happy Valley?" Harry said as though it was the first time he heard the name.

"Happy Valley, it's a lovely place. Tai Li has a training site there. It's kind of his headquarters." Louie looked at Harry then, laughed. He added, "Tai Li's lair."

Leaving the restaurant, they had to wait at the bottom of the stairs for traffic by the door to clear. Another party had arrived and was blocking the exit, three men and three women, all Chinese. Harry threw a casual glance their way, then turned back to look again, and this time looked hard. One of the women was Sue. She saw him, nodded. Harry nodded back, but she had already turned away.

He looked at Louie, who winked. Outside Louie said, "It's her Chinese officer friend, one of Tai Li's chaps. Would you like to see her? I'll give her your address."

"Yes, please do."

CHAPTER 36

It's not so far," Louie said. "A dozen miles or so."

"It's all hilly," Harry said. "Everywhere I go in China is full of hills. Some of these hills look like mountains."

The road was bumpy, but the countryside was beautiful. Directly ahead, but still some distance off, were real mountains, steep ones, but here were soft rolling hills that dipped down into gorgeous valleys, where flowers and grass swayed in the breeze. Tree-lined streams ran through the valleys, and along the streams were pretty little farmhouses. It was peaceful, almost idyllic.

They were close to the first of the real mountains when Louie turned down a lane that ran into one of the valleys. When they reached an open area he parked the car. "We're here," he said. Just then a half-dozen Chinese men appeared, all in peasant blue. They walked toward the car, but stopped a distance away. Their spokesman bowed politely and said something in Chinese.

"Our porters," Louie said. He walked around the back of the car, popped open the trunk and stood aside. Two porters stepped up, each took a crate of what looked like wine bottles, and started back up a tree-lined path.

"Come on," Louie said, and they walked after the porters. It was a pleasant walk amid sounds of birds and running water. They came to a guard post, where the guards stared at them briefly, then stepped back. The trail started going up, and when it started getting steep, they found steps cut into the stone. At the top they could look down into another beautiful little valley. There were small houses built into the side of the slope, and an imposing structure half hidden by trees that looked like a Mediterranean villa. As they started down, they heard laughter.

"Women?" Harry asked.

Louie shrugged. "Could be. You can ask Tai Li."

At the bottom of the hill were two very substantial-looking houses. The roofs were Chinese, but otherwise they looked European. "The Bank of China built these," Louie said, "a couple of years ago, when the Japanese started bombing Chungking. The idea was that the senior staff could stay here during the bombing season."

A few temporary-looking structures stood nearby. The paths connecting them were planted with flowers. They were admiring these when Tai Li came walking down one of the paths, his interpreter Eddie Liu close behind. After bows and the exchange of greetings, Eddie Liu said, "The general is happy to see both of you here. Mr. Harry, General Tai Li said that you may write a story about what China and America will do together, but only in general terms. We must not inform the Japanese enemy of our plans. The name and the location of Happy Valley are secrets."

"I understand," Harry said. He also knew that any military secrets he might inadvertently write about would never get by the U.S. Army censors.

"There is so little here now," Tai Li said while Eddie Liu translated. He moved his arm in a sweeping gesture that took in the whole valley. "We will have to build here, schools and residences for the students and teachers, buildings for offices. We will have a political training institute. We will have a place to train guerrillas." As the General said that, he gestured to the south. "Those we can train in the other valley. And we need to train those who look for intelligence in the enemy's communications."

Tai Li stopped walking then, turned to look right into Harry's face. He spoke with emotion that came across in Eddie Liu's translation. "But my biggest dream is to have a school where our Chinese investigators will be trained by the famous American Federal Bureau of Investigation. I hope the FBI can teach the Chinese to understand counter-espionage and to practice the secret techniques. The FBI can help the Chinese to be first in Asia in security operations. Our concern is not only the Japanese invaders, but the Chinese Communists. To defeat them we need the cooperation of the Americans, and the help of the U.S. Army, the U.S. Navy, and the American FBI."

When they finished their walk through the valley, Tai Li concluded his comments by saying, "It is good that the Americans are now here." Just before they broke up, Tai Li handed Louie an envelope and said a few words that Eddie Liu did not translate for Harry. When Harry caught Louie's eye as Tai Li and Eddie Liu walked away, Louie smiled and said, "Later."

Harry and Louie were shown to a bungalow where they could rest, and then it was off to dinner in one of the Bank of China buildings that had a large formal dining room. Two big round tables were set. There were 20 people in all, and except for Harry and Louie, all were Tai Li's staff.

It started with toasts, most directed at Harry as the honored guest, and he had to drink with everyone. Even before dinner started he was drowsy. He wondered if that was the way it was intended. The conversation around him was all Chinese.

At one point Louie called his name. "General Tai Li wants you to hear some of his comments. He is speaking about the British." Harry turned to Eddie Liu, who offered a brief summary of what the general had already said:

"General Tai Li said the British have long been a problem for China. Their intelligence service has tried to establish its own agent networks in China. Their purpose is to keep China divided. Their secret police collaborated with the Japanese in Hong Kong and Shanghai. British arrogance is offensive."

When Eddie Liu finished his summary, Tai Li started speaking again. "China offered troops to the British, to help defend Hong Kong, and to fight the Japanese in Malaya and Burma. The British refused our troops. Their refusal of help is an insult. It grows out of their colonial arrogance.

"Madame Chiang Kai-shek has written an article in the American *New York Times* where she explains this British arrogance. She noted that China could not prepare for the Japanese attack on Shanghai in the fall of 1937, yet our Chinese soldiers defended the city for three months. In Singapore, the British prepared the most modern defenses for 12 years. When the Japanese attacked, the British lost Singapore in two weeks. Eighty thousand British troops were surrendered there. It was the greatest military defeat in modern history. That was only the beginning. The British lost Hong Kong and Burma. The British empire has collapsed. The British forces are poorly led. They have no will to fight. Yet the British scorn our soldiers, but still come to us, to work together they say, but really with the intention of exploiting China and its people."

Tai Li said something, gestured to Eddie Liu. They had a brief discussion, and then Eddie turned to Harry. "Do you know the expression, 'Old China Hand'?"

"I do," Harry said.

"General Tai Li wants to make some comments about this expression, but he does not want you to be offended. You are new to China, so he does not include you."

"I'm sure I appreciate that," Harry said, "But the general can say what he wants. I will not take offense."

Tai Li went on speaking then, with Eddie Liu translating for Harry. "We are seeing now among the British the return of the 'Old China Hands', some going into high places. These so-called 'Old China Hands' are the British, the Europeans, and even some Americans who have spent many of their years in China and have acquired great experience of China and its people. They believe they are experts on China, and indeed they are. They are expert at exploiting the Chinese people. They are expert at using Chinese labor to create products, cheaply, for their home markets. They are expert at dumping in China the inferior products they can sell nowhere else. And they are expert at explaining how all their exploitation of China is really for the good of the Chinese people. Those are the 'Old China Hands'. We must know who they are. We must be cautious in our dealing with them."

On the drive back to Chungking, once they were well clear of Happy Valley, Harry finally spoke up. "Wow," he said, "Tai Li really doesn't like the British, does he?"

Louie shrugged. "No, he doesn't like the British. In his own mind he has a lot of reasons for that. British defeat throughout Asia has cost them Chinese respect, not only Tai Li's. But with Tai Li there's always more than meets the eye. Tai Li resents the British, hates them perhaps. Early last year he was arrested by the British police when he visited Hong Kong. The Japanese tipped them off that he was coming. He was stuck in a Hong Kong jail overnight. They arrested him as a Nazi sympathizer, as the boss of a spy organization modeled on the German Gestapo. I think that's what their reports said. It took the Generalissimo's personal intervention to get him released. It was an affront that Tai Li will never forgive."

They drove along silently for a time, while Harry absorbed this. "It was foolish of the British to do that," Louie said. "It may have felt good to get back at Tai Li, but they have made themselves a powerful enemy in China. Probably for as long as he lives."

"By the way, the envelope Tai Li gave me, it's a letter from your girl in Shanghai. Tai Li said his people were frustrated trying to read it. It shows you how secure such a simple system can be when they don't know the key. I will put it in Chinese for you."

* * *

Louie dropped him in front of his "hostel." The little lane alongside the house was too narrow for the Chevy. "Remember, Louie said, "when you reach your alley, turn left at the fruit vendor." Harry was almost out of earshot and barely heard the rest. "And have a good night, Harry."

It had been hot out at Happy Valley, but here it was cool. A breeze from the river rustled leaves on the limbs that hung over the lane. All the foliage made the lane dark, but when he reached his alley, there was light enough to make his way. He turned left at the fruit vendor. The man was still awake, quietly rummaging through a box by the light of a candle. The rest of the alley seemed deserted, except near his door where he noted a suspicious shadow. It looked like someone standing there. For a moment his heart stopped. He stood still, watched and wondered if it might be best to go back the way he came. He could always get to his rooms by way of the main entrance.

As time ticked by and his eyes became more accustomed to the light, he was sure someone was there. A woman he decided, a woman leaning against the wall, one leg braced, the other bent at the knee. The knee was bare; he could see shiny skin reflecting what little light there was. That meant she was wearing a short skirt, and a short skirt meant she was a young woman. He thought first of his Shanghai girl, and then of Sue. The woman at the door had long hair, he could see that now. It had to be Sue then. He started to walk toward her, as a thought passed through his mind: how foolish he would feel if instead of a woman he found a wiry, long-haired assassin – wearing shorts.

She heard him, straightened and turned in his direction. In poor light and shadows it turned into a scene from Harry's youth, a vision seared into his memory: a beautiful woman in a trench coat, walking out of the mist, long black hair, almond eyes, Asian, mysterious – the "Dragon Lady" herself. That single panel of a *Terry and the Pirates* comic strip became Asia for him. The Dragon Lady inspired the dreams of his youth, inflamed them, made him long for an Asia that he knew would be full of women like her. He could never admit it; it was where Asia began for him.

When he was close enough to touch her he saw that it was Sue. He did not know what to say. He searched her face, but shadow hid most of it, and he could not make out her expression. It made him cautious. She said his name then, and the way she said it gave him confidence, made him a little bold. He took her hand, and in silence, led her to the door and up the stairs.

In the small sitting room, he turned on a lamp and looked at her face. "How did you find me?" he asked, and answered the question before she could. "It was Louie, wasn't it? Of course, who else would know of the entrance off the alley?"

She nodded, turned to look around the room, slipped off her coat and draped it over a chair. Her dress was the red the Chinese loved, short and tight and molded to her form. She walked around the room looking at things on the tables, on the walls. He could not take his eyes from her. He let them move over her, drift down her body. He felt his excitement grow.

"What is this room?" she asked, holding open the door, looking in.

"The bedroom," he said as she walked in.

He knew she was taking her clothes off. He stepped into the room, saw the red dress on the floor. He looked up to see her slide the little silk things over her hips. Before he could move, she did, and ran right into him. They tumbled on to the bed, grappled. She pulled at his clothes. He felt cool skin, firm flesh – and sharp little teeth on his thigh. "Christ, Sue!" She bit down harder. It turned into a struggle then, almost violent; the end quick. She cried out in Chinese. He gasped – a soldier taking a mortal wound – shuddered, lay still.

She pulled away, rolled off the bed, got to her feet. "Do you have anything to eat?" she asked.

"Uh...." he said, on his back, dazed, trying to think. "The ladies should have left some soup. Look in the other room, the small one with a big table." He knew he should get up and help her. It was too difficult. He lay on the bed, waited for his strength to return. She came back into the bedroom, carrying a tray.

"The soup looks good," she said. "And there are dumplings. They're still warm. Have some." She held the tray for him. He shook his head.

She sat cross-legged on the bed, ate with gusto. She wore nothing. He watched her eat, watched her face and her hands so his eyes would not stray. She would not mind, he knew that, but he would be embarrassed if she saw his eyes moving over her. He had no need to do that. He knew he would be ready for her before she finished eating.

"You're working here now, in Chungking, aren't you?" he asked.

She answered with a nod, spooned some more soup.

"Are you working for the government, for General Tai Li?"

"I'm working for the Intelligence Service, so it must be Tai Li."

"What do you do?"

"I should not talk about it," she said. She finished eating and carefully set the tray on the floor. She got on her knees and leaned in, close to his face. "I work for the language bureau. I listen to radio broadcasts from Thailand. I do other things. The Chinese are very interested in Thailand."

"They know your background, the people you work for?"

She nodded. "They want to know everything. They wanted to know about you."

"Did you tell them about our business, about your trip across the border to Mae Sot and Tak?"

"I told them I went there, but not that we worked together. I told them nothing about us – except that we made love sometimes."

He wanted to ask about others she made love with, but knew it was best not to, at least not now.

"I missed you," she said, "I thought about you. When I saw you yesterday I knew we had to meet."

God, he had missed her too. He had certainly missed the feel of her, skin that was softer than any other he had ever touched. "I missed you too," he said then. "When I saw you yesterday, I never thought we would meet again – like this, I mean."

"It is our fate," she said simply, and he knew she believed that.

* * *

"It's just like preaching, Harry, to my Chinese flock," John Birch said. "What you've said makes me see that. If I want to preach to them, to put it into Chinese, I first have to know what it is I want to say, what I want them to understand. It's only when I see a thing clearly that I can talk about it easily. Then I have to think about how I will say it, so that it will be clear to them. It's only when I have finished thinking it all through that I can preach to them. And that's what I'll do when I make my reports to the Old Man."

They were walking on the riverbank, high above the Yangtze, among the weeping willow trees in an ancient garden as the mist drifted in from the river. The old whitewashed buildings were a school now, and had some connection with the missionaries who took John Birch in as a guest.

"The rest of it, Harry, is all common sense. You asked before how I manage to move behind the lines, how I survive there. Well, there's nothing secret about it. It's common sense. You have to think about what you need to do, then you do it the way it makes sense to do it. First of all, over in east China you would never see me dressed like this. If you saw me there, I would look just like another Chinese farmer to you. I wear their clothes. I put a farmer's straw hat on my head. Unless you were up close and could see my eyes, see that my hair is not jet black, you would never know I was not Chinese.

"And moving around behind the lines, or anywhere there are Japanese, it's all just common sense. You must know where they are so you don't just bungle into them, and that's easy enough. Any Chinese farmer will tell you where the Japs are. Why? Well, first, I think it's because he wants to show you that he knows, that he's not a fool. Second, because he likes you more than he likes the Jap. And that's not because you're an American, or even a Christian, or because somehow you're a better man than the Jap. No, it's because he knows that when he meets you, you will treat him well, if not exactly as an equal, at least fairly. He knows that you will treat him fairly every time you meet him, that you will respect him as a man.

"It's for the same reason that the Chinese farmer will not betray you to the Japs. Oh, there are some who will take the 30 pieces of silver and tell the Jap where you are. Christ had Judas Iscariot, and any outsider here can have his own Chinese Judas, who will betray him to get some advantage, a handful of coins or a sack of rice. That will happen where the people are poor. It's hard to blame the Chinese farmer for trying to survive, trying to keep his family alive. He has nothing against you personally.

"But even when the Jap comes for you, some Chinese farmer will tell you when he is on the way, while he is still three or four villages away. And then it's common sense again. The Jap must come for you with a force, he must march into the fields to find you, or ride in the back of his truck over broken roads. It takes time, and he has to be careful. The Jap doesn't suddenly want to find himself in a remote rice field facing Chinese irregulars that from the distance looked like farmers. That's what is in the rice fields, Harry. It's what the Jap fears, the Chinese irregulars. Nationalist or Communist, the Chinese irregular soldier is no bother for you or me. For the Jap he's deadly.

"Ah, the Communists. If you have met Communists, Harry, you know they're not like our Nationalist Chinese friends. There are a lot of Christians among the Nationalists, and the Nationalists are led by good Christians, the Generalissimo himself, and the Madame. But the Communists, they are godless. They are more interested in fighting the Chinese Nationalist Army than they are the Japanese. You must be careful of the Communists while you are in China, Harry. They are godless, they are not our friends. One day we will have to fight them."

Birch led Harry to a bench under one of the big old willows where they sat for a while. "It's pleasant here, isn't it, Harry? The war is so far away. I think you know that I told Chennault that I would consider doing this intelligence work for him. What I really want to do is to be a chaplain. I'm an ordained minister, so they can't draft me, but I'm ready to volunteer. I want to serve God and my country both.

"The Old Man said I could do more for my country – and for China – by being his intelligence officer. He thinks that my experience here, because I speak the Chinese language and 'can eat Chinese food' as he puts it, that's what I'm best suited for."

Birch said, "The Old Man," then shook his head and laughed aloud. "The Old Man, he's a card. I really wasn't ready to be his intelligence officer, and then yesterday, I saw him here in Chungking – he's here, did you know that? I said to him, 'General, if I accept your commission as an intelligence officer, can I still preach on Sunday?' 'John,' he said, 'If you're my intelligence officer you can still preach on Sunday. You can preach on Monday too, so long as you get your intelligence work done.'"

They both laughed then. "So, John, will you join the Old Man?"

"Well, it looks like I may have to. I haven't heard anything from the chaplain corps. And the Old Man is somebody I can work for easily. He's a man of principle. He likes the Chinese people and respects them, as I do. He's not like some of the Americans who have come to China recently. They have no understanding of China, and no love for the Chinese people. To them, the Chinese have their hand out, to take whatever they can from us. They believe the Chinese will always cheat us, in whatever way they can. But that's not so. The Chinese are a proud people. They're living in difficult times. They will make their own way, without us if they have to. I have really gotten to like the AVG. I stayed at their hostel and got to know them. There are some bad ones in the group, but most of them are good people. I could work with the AVG, but they will be gone soon."

"You would do very well, working with Chennault. He certainly thinks highly of you."

"As I do of him. The Old Man said he would expedite all the paper work. He said if I did later get an appointment as a chaplain, he would support that, and I could transfer to the chaplain corps. So, Harry, I guess I may try that, work as an intelligence officer for General Claire Lee Chennault. Then I can see for myself if he is right, that it's the best way to serve both God and my country. In the meantime I can preach."

* * *

"So, you met Stilwell? I'm dying to hear what he was like. Tell me."

Doyle was eager to tell Harry. "Actually, I was one of four at the meeting," he said. "I was just the note taker. What was Stilwell like? Goddamn interesting. You know, he's still wearing the same old campaign hat that he wore in Burma. That's really a big thing to him, getting his ass kicked out of Burma. He's going to spend the rest of his goddamn life trying to get over that, but he won't. Old Vinegar Joe Stilwell, he's a crusty old bastard, very blunt, very direct."

"What was this big meeting all about? If you can tell me, that is."

"I can tell you all right. In fact, you have to know about it. It fits in with some of what you saw out at Happy Valley, what Tai Li told you. It could also have a big effect on how you and I will spend the rest of the war. There were four of us in the meeting with old Joe. Two were OSS. It was me as the resident spy, and a guy Colonel Donovan sent out here named Al Lusey. Al is an old China hand. Donovan sent him here to set up some propaganda radio stations. The other two guys were U.S. Navy, Commander Mary Miles, and his note taker, Tom something."

"*Mary* Miles? We have a Navy lady here now?"

"No, no, Mary's no lady, believe me. Mary's a tough enough fellow. He spent a lot of time out here with the Yangtze patrol, speaks Chinese. He got his name Mary back at the Naval Academy. It seems the upperclassmen get their amusement by giving freshmen funny names. Anyway, Mary Miles is out here to work on a friendship project with the Chinese, whatever a friendship project might be. He's only been here a little while, but somehow he already got tied in with Tai Li. And Tai Li seems to have really taken to him. Lusey picked up on that real quick. Whatever else Tai Li is, he's the mover here, the man you have to know if you're going to get anything done, especially the kind of things we want to do. Lusey saw this and decided to hang on to Miles' coat tail."

"Christ," Harry mumbled to himself. To Doyle he said, "That's not a good thing."

"Yeah, well, it gets worse. Miles briefed Stilwell on his friendship project, and then went on to talk about all the cooperation he's getting from Tai Li. Stilwell does not trust Tai Li at all, so right off, that gave Stilwell something to ponder. And then Lusey briefed him on OSS. Then he went on to tell Stilwell about Donovan's thinking on what OSS will do in China. He talked about guerrilla warfare, working behind the lines, sabotage, that kind of thing."

"Well, it became obvious very quickly that Stilwell doesn't like the idea of having OSS out here, or Mary Miles, or any other organization that is not directly under his command, which neither OSS nor Miles would be. Stilwell obviously has no great regard for intelligence – and he doesn't like the idea of guerrilla warfare, or things like sabotage. He said those things are 'illegal actions'. Can you believe that? He said his kind of war is 'face to face'. Dear God, next we will have to say 'sorry' and 'please' to the Japanese as we kill them."

"Strange things to say from somebody who has witnessed Japanese brutality. Where is all this going? Will Stilwell be an obstacle?"

"Stilwell has no choice. He has to accept OSS and Mary Miles, and that they won't be under his command. Their ultimate authority comes out of the War Department or the White House. So Stilwell's feelings should not come to concern you and me. What's important for us is that Miles may be anointed as the OSS chief out here – strictly because of his relationship with Tai Li. Miles doesn't know what he's getting into."

"I don't think OSS does either."

* * *

"You were at Happy Valley," Sue said. They had just made love and she was sitting on the bed, still naked, eating a fishy smelling Chinese snack.

"Yes, I was. That was several days ago. You didn't see me there, did you?"

"My friend told me. Our office is on the other side of the hill. I could not see you from there."

She got up from the bed then, walked to the bathroom. When she came back she waved wet hands at him. "I washed them. I know you don't like the fish smell." She leaned over and kissed him. Her breath was fresh; no fish smell. She smelled as she always did, a flower with a subtle scent.

"Will you work with Tai Li?" she asked.

"No," he said. "I was there to talk with him, about the war. I was there as a journalist."

"Does he know you are a spy?"

"I'm not a spy, Sue."

She smiled, reached across him to a bowl of fruit on the bedside table. A breast brushed his face. "The pears are from Kunming," she said. "They are delicious." She held one out to him. He shook his head.

"I'm not a spy, Sue," he said again. "You must not say that. People will get the wrong idea. It could be dangerous, for me, for you too."

"I never tell anyone you are a spy," she said. "Lucy thought maybe you were. I told her 'no'."

"I was thinking more of your Chinese friends, the ones who work with Tai Li."

"I would never tell them," she said. "They know I spend too much time with you. They would think I was a spy too."

"We don't want that either," he said.

She tossed what little was left of the pear across the room. It landed in a potted plant. "You worry too much, Harry," she said. She wiggled closer, put a hand on his chest and pushed him flat on the bed. Then she threw a leg over him, sat up, across his hips, facing him, her knees pinning his arms. "I am glad you do not work with Tai Li," she said.

"You work for Tai Li. You don't have a problem with that?"

"It's different for me. It's something I want to do. Something I have to do. Here I look like a Chinese, even to you. But I am really a Thai."

"I know you are a Thai." He laughed then and said, "But I remember in Rangoon when you wanted to be Chinese. You did not want anyone to know you were Thai."

"That was better for me then, better that some people thought I was a Chinese. But I was always Thai."

"Sure, you're Thai. You're working for the Chinese, and they know you're a Thai. You use your Thai language skills for them, don't you?"

"Yes," she said, "I listen to Thai radio, which is really the Japanese. I listen to other radio too." Her hips straddled his, started rocking back and forth. It was very distracting. He tried to concentrate on what they were talking about.

"What kind of radio?" he asked.

"It's private. I think you would call it secret. There are people in Thailand who have friends here in Chungking and they use a radio to talk with them."

"They're talking with other Thai people?"

She reached around behind her and grabbed him, started gently squeezing. "Sue, for God's sakes!"

"If it does not feel good," She said, "tell me to stop."

"I asked who the Thai people on the radio speak with here in China."

"It's a secret, but I will tell you." Her hand started stroking him. "Does that feel good?" Harry groaned. She went on. "The Thai people on the radio speak with me." She looked back over her shoulder. "Oh, look how big you are now."

He tried to sit up then, but she pressed her full weight down on his chest; her knees kept his arms pinned. "Sue, you have to tell me. This could be very important. Look, let's talk about this now. When we finish, we can make love all night."

She looked down where her hand was working. "The Chinese say that spies are very strong. But look, you are getting small again." She rolled off him and sat up, demurely, or as demure as she could be without any clothes. "Maybe it is better to talk now."

He sat up, pulled some covers up around him. "Yes, let's talk. Who are the Thais on the radio? Why do they speak with you?"

"Some of them live in Bangkok, but mostly they live in the north. The important ones are in Bangkok. "

"Why are they speaking with you?"

"They think I am the secretary of the anti-Japanese Thai resistance based in China. They ask for guns and other help. They ask me what they should do."

"You are actually talking with these people?"

"No, no," she said, dismissively. "The Japanese would find them very quickly if they talked on the radio. They put everything in code, and then they transmit it in Morse code. But everything they write is in Thai. The Chinese receive the message and decode it. I read all the Thai. Later I put the answer into Thai and send it back to them."

"Who decides what the answer will be?"

"One of Tai Li's officers, the one in charge of operations in Thailand. But he and the others are Chinese, so they depend on me. I tell them if the answer is right, and then I send the answer in Thai."

Harry thought about that. "So the Thai resistance in Bangkok thinks that the answer is coming not from the Chinese, but from a Thai."

"They think there is a whole Thai anti-Japanese organization here. Sometimes when I sign the message, I am the Secretary General, sometimes the President, sometimes the Finance Officer. When I use those titles, I also use different names, but the name is always an alias. Everyone understands that we cannot use real names, for security. But I am all the people in the organization."

"You're the organization and they come to you for instructions. What kind of instructions do you give them?"

"Good instructions. I tell them that for now they must wait until everything is ready. We do not want the Japanese to find them. They must quietly recruit more friends into their cells. One day the Americans will send guns. In the meantime, they must send information to me. I ask them where the Japanese are, and how many there are. I ask for the names of the Japanese officers and where they live. I tell them one day we will rise up and kill all the Japanese."

"That's incredible," Harry said. "You're a one-man – excuse me – a one-woman deception organization. What you're telling me is what we believed, but couldn't confirm, that there is an anti-Japanese resistance organization in Thailand."

"There was a resistance movement there since the Japanese invaded. They want to contact the Americans and the British, but Tai Li does not want that."

"He wants to control the Thai resistance himself."

"Tai Li thinks that what happens in Thailand is not a concern of the British or the Americans. Thailand is a neighbor of China and many Chinese live there. When the war is over, Thailand must follow China." She pulled back the sheet that covered him. "Are we finished with the talk?" she asked. "Are you ready to use this?" She took hold of him again.

"Wait, Sue. Not yet," he protested, but weakly. She was squeezing, gently, starting to stroke him. "Look, just a couple more things. In your messages to the Thai, can you ask questions that the Chinese would not know about? Can you hide from your Chinese bosses some parts of the messages you send to the Thai?"

"I think so," she said. "I write the answer in Thai language, then I give it to the Chinese cryptographer to put in code. None of the Chinese can read Thai. So they don't know what I write, except what I tell them."

"Good," Harry said. "It's something to think about. Do you know the names of the Thais you are in contact with, their real names? Do you know how many of them there are? "

"Oh, I don't know any of that, Harry. No one here knows. All of that information is secret. Don't you know the principle of cells?"

"Cells? Sure, that's a Communist idea, isn't it? "

"Yes, it is Communist," she said, "and it's a very good idea, it's what makes spying safe. If they catch your friends, they don't catch you."

"Sue, I'm amazed at what you are doing. I'm astounded at all you know."

"Well," she said, "I did go to school. I studied Political Science in London. My father wanted me to study commerce."

"And you speak Thai and Chinese and English."

"And I speak French," she said.

"I thought so. Did you learn to speak French in London?"

"There, and in Paris."

"Paris must have been exciting."

"At that time it was very exciting," she said. "There were many Asians in Paris then, mostly Vietnamese. There were some Chinese too, but not many Thai."

"Paris is where many of the Asians became Communists, especially the Vietnamese."

"That was many years before I was there. It was a Vietnamese who helped the Thai create the Communist Party of Thailand. When I was in Paris, the Vietnamese were still helping the Thai Communists. The Vietnamese Communists were very good people, but the people in Thailand do not like them."

"Did you know any of the Communists?"

"Yes," she said, "I knew many. They were always the smartest ones. They knew how the world really works, and how to make it better. They knew how to survive."

"You sound like you admired them."

"I did admire them. They were the best people I knew in Paris. I still admire them."

Harry laughed. "I hope Tai Li doesn't find out about that."

"You must not tell him."

"If you don't do what I want," he teased, "I can tell Tai Li that Sue is a Communist."

"He won't care," she said. "The Nationalist are in a united front with the Chinese Communists; they fight together against the Japanese. There's an office of the Chinese Communist Party here in Chungking."

"I've heard that," Harry said, "but what do you think Tai Li would do if he found that a Communist agent had infiltrated his organization."

"I know what he would do. He would shoot me."

"I'm not talking about you, Sue, I'm talking about Communists."

"I am a Communist. I am a member of the Communist Party of Thailand. I have been a party member since I studied in Paris." She raised herself up and bowed to him, a deep mocking bow. "Now, you hold my life in your hand."

"Jesus Christ, Sue." It was all he could think of saying just then.

CHAPTER 37

June 15, 1942
Chungking

Harry found the safe house after days of careful walking through Chungking alleys. If Tai Li's people were following him, he had to be sure not to take them where he did not want them. He played tourist, made it look like a simple exploration of the neighborhoods, all the time watching what was happening on the street around him, the process made easier by the odd little alleys he chose. He kept a camera conspicuous, pointed it back from where he had come, scanned one side, then the other, aimed right at the possible counterspies. He lingered at interesting places, temples and shrines, colorful courtyards, areas of bomb damage. He wandered through these places erratically, so a watcher would never know which way he would face next. One or twice, he convinced himself that he had spotted a surveillant. In the end he concluded no one was watching, not in any systematic fashion anyway. He was just not important enough.

Compounding the difficulties of his search was that he could not ask anyone for a recommendation, not anyone he knew, however slightly. Once he located his ideal safe house, he did not want anyone to be able to associate the place with him. It had to be really secure. It was where he and Doyle would meet. They both enjoyed meeting in the open air of tea gardens, but Doyle said their operations were becoming too complex. In the future they would require time and absolute privacy, to exchange papers and other things. Their immediate need, Doyle said, was a sterile new site for an "operational review." Harry had to ask what that was. "A review of all your operations," Doyle said. "We'll look at where we are to see where we're going." "Oh," Harry said. It was jargon, he decided, OSS jargon, brought from Washington to China by all the visitors coming here now.

Harry found an ideal little hotel. He assured himself that it was accessible and secure by walking past it a half dozen times. Set at a junction in a warren of small alleys, it could be reached from almost anywhere in a dozen different roundabout ways. And no one could follow too closely without being noticed.

The hotel was a little gem in other ways. It had a courtyard entrance. It was not a single building, but several, interconnected by garden paths. Individual rooms were quiet and isolated from their neighbors. The main building had a small dining room, a separate bar, and a sitting room that was also a library. It was not inexpensive. It served a clientele of knowledgeable traveling businessmen, Chinese mostly, but also foreigners. Harry came to check in on a quiet day and had his choice of rooms. A young chambermaid was assigned to show him the rooms available. He chose an inconspicuous one in a corner, isolated from its nearest neighbors, but accessible from a veranda or by a small back hallway. It had a sizable bedroom, a bath, a pleasant sitting room. The veranda was shielded from view by plants and a small side wall.

Following standard operational procedure, Harry and Doyle came separately. Harry had coffee ready when Doyle arrived. They sat across from each other at a card table in the sitting room. Doyle spread typewritten papers, luxuriously, on the table in front of him. He smiled. "This is more like it," he said. Harry put down a single sheet, pushed it toward him.

"Ah, so this is the most recent letter from your girl in Shanghai," Doyle said as he reached for it.

"It's Louie's version of her letter. He broke it out of the telecodes and translated the Chinese into English."

Doyle started to read aloud. "'Dear Kunming Big Boss' – that's you, I take it?"

Harry nodded and Doyle went on: "'First, I must thank you for your unexpected gift. And I did as you told me. I have two beautiful new dresses now. Thank you very much.'" Doyle looked up at him. "So, you're sending gifts? Did you pick out the dresses yourself?"

"No, I didn't pick out the dresses. That's not my thing. I sent her money. Two American 100 dollar bills. I told her it was a gift that she should use to buy dresses. But it's not really a gift; it's an operational payment. Remember what they told us in training? An agent might think he's spying for love or for ideology, but it's money that gets the hard jobs done. An agent used to regular payments knows what he's working for. I should have asked you about it before I did it, but it seemed like the right thing to do."

"A lot of money for dresses, Harry." Doyle raised his eyebrows when he said that, then let them drop. "But you did the right thing. Let's assume it will be worth it," he said, then started to read again:

" 'I have two new boyfriends. Both are colonels.'" He looked up at Harry. "Japanese colonels?"

"Yes, of course. Both are Japanese."

Doyle read on. "Both like to talk to me and tell me things. One was a teacher once. He pretends to be a teacher now. It's our game. He teaches me lessons and I must remember what he tells me. I have to wear a school girl dress, and if I forget my lesson, he hits my behind with a wooden stick. My mother kept my old school uniforms and they still fit. The dresses are small for me now, but the colonel likes them like that.'"

Doyle looked over the top of the letter. "Pervert?"

"Aging Japanese gentleman. Louie says they have this thing about schoolgirls. She's playing up to that. Doing it well, I'm sure."

Doyle shrugged. "She goes on: 'The other colonel likes me to dress nice. I picked your dresses for him. They are Western style, short, and quite daring. This colonel takes me to nightclubs. He is a very good man, and would never beat me with a stick. He speaks Chinese very well, and is trying to learn English. He takes me when he goes to dinner or has drinks with his Japanese Army friends. They treat me very nicely, as if I were a Japanese girl. I am learning the Japanese language now.

"'I am learning many things from both colonels. Some are things I think you would like to know. Maybe I can see you one day and tell you.

"'My Chinese gangster boss is also very good to me. He has other girlfriends, but I bring him the best business. My gangster boss has other businesses too; one is to deliver rice, chickens and other food to the Japanese Army airfield. He sees many things there, and I think he would tell me if I asked.

"'I hope you are well, and that I will see you one day soon. I know you can not come to Shanghai, but one day I can visit you.'"

Doyle put the letter down, looked at Harry, an incredulous smile on his face. "This is too good to be true, Harry. We've got a wonderful operation here, a classic. It's the one they tell you about in training – the one that never really happens. This is going just the way it should. Our novice spy gets access to two senior Japanese officers and they tell her things – or that's what she says. Her boss has access to an enemy airfield, and he will share his observations." Doyle shook his head. "We need to find out what kind of information she's getting from all these guys. How will she get that to us?"

"I think the telecode system we're using now will work fine. Louie showed her a simple way to double-encrypt it. That's what she did this time. Tai Li complained that he could not read her letter. His guys apparently weren't able to decrypt it. That's a good sign, I think."

"What about Tai Li, will Louie give him a copy of this?"

"Louie will give him a totally different message, one where she says she misses me, and makes some commonplace observations about life in Shanghai, the kind of stuff that a journalist like me might find interesting. Louie says Tai Li will expect a copy of everything she sends. He understands that what we give Tai Li has to be innocuous."

"For now we'll trust his judgment. Can you get me a copy of everything Louie passes Tai Li?"

"I've already asked."

Doyle stared up at the ceiling for a while, thinking. "The problem will come when Tai Li decides he wants to do his own decoding and asks Louie for the key. Meanwhile, we will have to work up questions for our Shanghai girl that will help us gauge how much she can get from these guys. We need to know where both of the colonels work and what they talk about. We need to ask questions that will draw out her gangster boss, find out what he sees at the airfield and not make him wonder why she's asking. If this operation starts to take off, communications will be the big problem."

"We always have the option of bringing her to Chungking. From what I've seen, travel between Shanghai and Chungking is no big deal, not if you have the right kind of help. If we can get her up here, we can train her in secret writing, or maybe some other technique."

"We have to think radio," Doyle said. "The British are having success with it. They team a radio operator with an agent. The operator knows all there is know about using a radio behind enemy lines and surviving. The agent goes about his spying and lets the radio man handle security and the link with headquarters. It's a bit tricky, but done right, it's very secure."

"Let's see where this goes. Maybe we want to try that."

"Okay, now the Tai Li operation. The comments you got from him at Happy Valley made a couple of nice reports." He handed Harry copies of two formal reports stamped "secret." While Harry looked them over, he went on.

"What they say about Tai Li's plans and the kind of support he expects to get from the Americans, explains the maneuvering we've been seeing elsewhere. His comments on the British – his great dislike of them – helps explain other things, like why the SOE unit was asked to leave China. We included Louie's aside about Tai Li being arrested in Hong Kong. That helps put things in perspective."

"You're doing a great job with Tai Li. Everybody's pleased with what you're taking out of your relationship. As OSS in China grows, there will be more Americans in direct contact with him. To Tai Li, many will be the "China hands" he doesn't like. He doesn't put you in that category. At least not yet. Just keep doing what you're doing and, hopefully, he will continue to be as forthcoming as he is now."

Doyle picked up a notepad on which he had written some cryptic notes. "Now, Sir Louie: I think he's what the British would call a 'splendid principal agent.' He has wonderful contacts, he's willing to help you with them, and he seems to be completely frank and honest with you. Stay on his good side. Use him as you have been. Bounce questions off him. He's bright and insightful. Even if he doesn't know the facts, his opinions are well worth recording. We'll use him to get you deeper into Chinese society."

He looked at the notepad again. "Your prime case is your luscious Thai friend, Miss Mango. She's incredible: brave, smart and imaginative. She's doing a lot of things on her own that benefit us. She has answers before we have the questions. But you're going to have to guide her more, mostly to make sure she doesn't get herself in trouble. Point that out when she starts moving too quickly. She seems to have contempt for the Chinese who work with her, and perhaps for everyone else who is not as smart or as quick as she is. When there's a guy like Tai Li around, a guy who sits back quietly and watches, he just might notice her doing something that she shouldn't be doing.

"Mango is really several operations. The most important one is her connection with the Free Thai. By just working the Free Thai on the radio, she will be able to tell us a lot about what's going on in Thailand. That's one of our priorities. Washington was convinced there was a resistance movement growing inside the country, but until we got Mango's comments, there was no way to confirm that. There's a lot of interest in this one. OSS is recruiting Thai students in the U.S. who will be trained and sent back into Thailand. The British SOE is doing the same in England. One thing you will have to keep in back of your mind: Sooner or later you will have to ask Mango if she is willing to go back to Bangkok." When he saw Harry getting ready to protest, he quickly added, "For now just think about it. It may never happen."

Harry relaxed, and Doyle went on. "Then, there's the ways in which you're using her against Tai Li. First, there is her reporting on what Tai Li is trying to do with the Thai resistance. The second is reflected in his comments on how China will expect Thailand to follow it once the war is won.

That has tremendous implications for our planners. It's one we really need to keep on top of.

"The other big thing Mango is doing now at your instigation is a deception operation. She's in a unique position as Tai Li's primary – and maybe only – trusted Thai speaker. If that is indeed the case, she can tell him whatever she wants about what the Thai resistance is reporting to her, and he won't be the wiser." Doyle stopped there, took a long look at Harry. "We have to be very careful with that."

Hearing Doyle say that made something click in Harry's mind. It was so obvious, and yet he had never thought of it. Doyle then said the thing that had just jumped into Harry's mind: "We have to make sure that Tai Li doesn't have any other Thai speakers who might get to see her exchanges with the Thai resistance. She says none of the Chinese she works with read Thai, but are there other Thais in Happy Valley that Tai Li could use as a check on her?"

Harry nodded; Doyle went on. "That's the one side of the Mango-Thai resistance equation: Without Tai Li being the wiser, she can give the Thai resistance what instructions she wants – instructions we will provide her.

"The Miss Mango operation is already quite complicated, and it will get even more so as time goes on – you can count on that, Harry. You have to watch it very closely. This is a big one. Don't screw it up. You're not ... ah... being intimate with this young lady, are you, Harry? She's your agent. If you were doing something you shouldn't be –and if we had enough people to do so – we would have to transfer her handling to some one else." Doyle looked away from Harry, examined his notes.

"Now let's see," he went on. "Getting away from your agents, let's take a look at your contacts."

"Wait a minute," Harry said. "I'd like to ask a question."

"Sure," Doyle said and looked up at him.

"What about the fact that Mango's a Communist?"

"Oh, that." Doyle squeezed his lips together in tight little smile. "That's a bit tricky." Harry waited. "Actually," Doyle went on, "I've asked for guidance from Washington. As I understand it, the official line is that we're supposed to stay away from the Communists. Because we support the Nationalists, dealing with the Communists at the same time gets to be very sensitive. But the prohibition seems to affect only Chinese Communists. The fact that Mango is a member of the Communist Party of Thailand may nullify the overall prohibition. I'll let you know as soon as I hear."

"Okay," Harry said. "It sure gets complicated."

"We'll sort it out. Okay, let's get back to your other contacts. The interesting one is John Birch. If Birch does what he says, he will belong to Chennault's new Army Air Corps organization, whatever that will be. But that's no reason you can't stay in touch with the man, get together with him once in a while, find out what's going on in the rice paddies. You might even get him to do a thing or two for us once in a while. We've got a lot to learn from him.

"Then there's Lucy, Sir Louie's daughter. I don't think there's anything we should do with her right now, except stay in touch. Stay on her good side. For God's sakes, don't get romantically involved with her. We want her to be there if anything ever happens to Sir Louie. She will come into her own one day, and then we'll have to look at her again, to see what we can do."

"It's starting to sound like you're running a meat market, Doyle."

Doyle ignored that. "There's the AVG. Stay in touch with the Old Man. He likes you. We can't say now what his role will be once the AVG is gone, but it will probably be a big one. So, stay on his good side. He'll be able to do things for us. The same goes for the pilots, like Ed Rector. If any of them stay on in China, they may not be able to do things for us directly, but they will get to know people. They will know things we don't. Stay in touch with those guys.

"Your war will be running intelligence collection operations here in China. That's the priority. Secondarily, you'll be cranking up operations with the Thai resistance. As time goes on, we'll use Sir Louie to get you fresh contacts here, and Miss Mango to get you worked into the Thai resistance. That's how things look to me for the foreseeable future. Any questions?"

"You sure have made me think. I can't disagree with anything you've said. You must have spent a lot of time with this. You've given me some perspective, a different point of view."

"A reality check is what it is, Harry. We all need that from time to time."

Doyle shut his notepad and put it aside. "Now, let me tell you what's been going on in Washington. We are now officially the OSS, the Office of Strategic Services. President Roosevelt has signed off on our creation."

"Does that mean we get a raise?"

"I don't know about a raise, but I can tell you what else is going to happen." Doyle looked at another piece of paper. "This cable talks about the OSS mission: 'to collect and analyze strategic intelligence, and to conduct special services.' 'Special services' means things like subversion, sabotage, and psychological warfare."

"Wow, a plateful."

"It is a plateful, even though there's one thing we don't do any more, regular propaganda. The COI did propaganda, but that's been put into an

'Office of War Information' back in the States. The OSS now has a group called Morale Operations. They have a responsibility for 'black propaganda'. Do you remember from your training what that is? It's information that can't be attributed to the OSS – or to the U.S. for that matter. It looks like the bad guys were the source of it."

"Give me an example."

"Well, let's see.... Say that you and I write a letter that looks like it was written by the Jap Commander in Shanghai to his wife in Yokohama. He tells her that despite all the victories Radio Tokyo talks about, Japan is really losing the war. The letter is put where other Japs see it, and it creates doubt, destroys their morale."

"That sounds neat, but it's not where you and I fit into the organization, is it?"

"As far as I can tell, you and I are part of the 'SI Section', that's SI for 'Secret Intelligence'. We're the guys who collect the information."

Harry shrugged. "Okay. And then what?"

"There's Research and Analysis, or R&A. They get the information from SI and other groups, and get it off to those who can use it, like MO, the Morale Operations people, or SO, Special Operations. SO will be doing the guerrilla warfare operations. Those are the main sections, I think. There are some other units, like the Commo, that handles all communications and cryptology."

"And how big will all this OSS be?"

"I don't know. A cast of thousands, I guess, maybe tens of thousands if the war goes on."

Doyle started collecting the various reports and cables scattered over the top of the table or that had slipped to the floor. The meeting was over. Doyle looked around the room. "I like this place," he said. "We'll get a lot of use out it. That reminds me. I'd like to meet here again a week from today, same time. I want to bring somebody, a man from Washington, an expert on Thailand. He was there just before the war started, and Donovan has used him as his Thai specialist. It's important that you talk with him."

"By the way," Doyle stopped at the door, "I guess you'll be at the big Fourth of July party. The Generalissimo will host it. Everybody will be there."

"I wouldn't miss it," Harry said.

CHAPTER 38

The twisting alleys of Chungking were a source of unending fascination for Harry. He had discovered the convenience of the rickshaw, that took him deep into an unknown neighborhood where he could dismount and explore. There were few areas of the city not touched by Japanese bombs, but there were many places where big sections of the old alleys remained.

He knew he might walk for an hour and see nothing but the blank walls that lined the narrow passageways, and that only a crack in a wooden gate would give a glimpse of the elegance or the squalor that the walls concealed. But he knew he could be lucky, and through a gate left open see a beautiful garden or the ornate façade of an elegant old house. Sometimes he boldly stepped inside.

A gate left open usually meant a commercial establishment, a workshop fabricating parts of some machine, or a ramshackle old house used only as a place for storage. If he chanced into a private residence, the worst he risked was a haughty look from a servant. Occasionally he would be offered cool water or hot tea, and rewarded with a satisfying look at a tiny piece of an old China that not many outsiders knew still existed. Once an old gentleman with white whiskers and mandarin robes led him into a library of old leather-bound books and then invited him to join in smoking a pipe or two of opium. Harry turned that down, and later would always regret it.

Harry knew there had to be wonderful restaurants hidden among the back alleys. He had heard visiting journalists talk about them, but had no idea where to look. But Sue would know. He asked her to pick one, where the food was exceptional and they would meet no one they knew.

Their rickshaw stopped at an unpainted wooden gate that hung half open. The garden inside was small. Most of the compound was taken up by a weary-looking wood and bamboo house. Places for the diners were set under the stars on two small round tables and two square ones, but it was too early for them to be occupied yet. They saw the kitchen in the garden's far corner, a fire pit and metal grill, terracotta ovens, a huge wok, blackened pots, and a light haze of blue smoke that hung over it all. A man and a boy sat on the ground cutting vegetables.

Sue said she had been there once, with an old man, a friend of her father, and the cuisine was special. Chungking was now a city of refugees from all parts of China, and little restaurants like this catered to those from distant places who still had a taste for their native foods. A small specialized restaurant like this would not be popular with the young mandarins who staffed the government bureaus like Tai Li's organization, and they would not meet anyone they knew.

There was no written menu. Sue discussed the choices with the proprietor, who looked more ox-cart driver than a chef. His three sons, young toughs, stood by to assist. The eldest, about 13, brought them cold beer in bottles with no labels. Harry and Sue sat at one of the round tables and drank their beer while their food was being prepared.

"How are your friends down south?" Harry asked, meaning Thailand.

"Well enough," she said. "They would like to visit here."

"Oh," Harry said. "Come here to Chungking?" He thought about that. "Not so easy, I would think. How would they come? By boat?"

"Walk," Sue said.

"Walk? That's a long way. They must want to see you badly."

"Not me," she said. "You."

"Me? They don't even know me...." Or did they? A thought came that created a sinking feeling in his chest. "Sue, you didn't...."

The smile lingered on her face just long enough to make his stomach twist. "Not you," she said. "They want to meet Americans, the real ones, the ones in the embassy. They have things to discuss with the American diplomats, they say."

"Does Tai Li know about this?"

"No." She sipped at her beer, and set her glass down carefully before continuing. "I had to tell him that Free Thai representatives want to come here, but I did not say why. He thinks they want to meet with Chinese officials, that they want help from China. He would like that. He wants them to come."

"Will they come here to meet with the Chinese?"

"They do not want a relationship with the Chinese, that much I know. I did not tell the Free Thai that the Chinese wanted to see them. I told them in Thai not to come to China now."

"You told them that in a radio message?" When she did not answer right away he said, "You have to be careful, Sue. One day Tai Li may have another Thai speaker read back over the messages you have written. He may catch you out."

"It's a small thing," she said. "What I wrote is… ambiguous, very vague. I never used a word for 'American'. I said yes, come to China. Then I added one small Thai word, three letters, that changes the meaning, makes the message say 'don't come.' Only a Thai will see that. Even then a Thai would not be sure. He would have to think that maybe I made a small mistake. Thai writing is very complicated. Thais always make mistakes when they write something."

Harry shook his head. "Jesus, Sue, let's hope so. Let's hope Tai Li never finds another Thai reader as smart as you."

"You worry too much, Harry," she said, as the eldest son of the proprietor slid a tray of sizzling morsels on their table. "Delicious," Harry said after he ate the first one. "What is it?"

Sue shrugged. "I don't know. These people come from a province where they cook anything that walks or crawls… and – what's that other word – slithers." Harry reached for his beer, took a big swallow, then another.

Another party of guests arrived. There were seven in all, all Chinese and all men: one old man, one middle-aged, and five younger ones in their early twenties. They were in high spirits and obviously known here. The proprietor's sons rushed out to push the two square tables together without being asked, while their father made deep respectful bows, then shouted at his sons to bring the drinks, beer for the youngsters and whisky for their elders.

The middle-aged man was the one in charge. He was a handsome, friendly-looking man. He shook hands with proprietor, nodded at the sons, and gestured with his hands as he spoke, obviously describing the dishes he wanted.

As the proprietor went back to his kitchen corner, the friendly man looked around, saw Harry and Sue. He smiled at them, and then bowed. They returned his bow, Sue rather respectfully, Harry thought. The old man of the group made some comment that drew laughs from the rest, and all of them were suddenly talking, quite loudly, and laughing and having a very good time.

"You know him, the man who bowed to us?" Harry asked. They were far enough from the group that they could not be overheard, even in the unlikely event that one of their number spoke English.

"You don't recognize him?" she asked.

He studied the man's face as he walked around the table pouring beer for the others. "He does have a familiar look, but I can't say I recognize him."

"He's famous," she said. "You must know him."

He shrugged. "Well I don't. Who is he?"

"Chou En-lai," she said. "He's a very important Communist."

"He sure is," Harry said. He recognized the man as soon as he heard the name. "No wonder he looked familiar," he said. "I've seen his photo many times. My God, Sue, isn't he risking his life by being here?"

Sue looked at him, and with a small smile said, "I thought you understood Chungking, Harry. All of those men are Communists. I don't know the old one's name, but I know his face. He was on the Long March. The others, the young ones, they work with Chou at the Communist liaison office here in the city. They deal with Chiang Kai-shek's government. The Communists and the Nationalists have a united front against the Japanese. Chou is the Communist ambassador to Chiang's Central Government, the official liaison with the government."

The evening went on pleasantly. The food was tasty enough, but Harry was wary of it. He was not always sure what he was eating, could not always tell if what he was putting in his mouth was meat or vegetable, or something in between. Sue would not always tell him. "It's good for you, Harry," she would say. "Eat it."

Just as one of the proprietor's sons was bringing out their final two dishes, one balanced in each hand, one of the young Communists, perhaps having drunk too much of the beer that Chou En-lai poured for him, got up from the table unsteadily and then lurched right into the boy. Both dishes went down, the food scattered on the ground.

"Oh, dear," Chou En-lai said. He was on his feet in an instant. "You're not hurt?" he asked the boy, patted him on the back. He turned to Harry and Sue. "You must forgive my young comrade. He moves with too much enthusiasm at times, and now he's destroyed a part of your dinner." He looked down at the spilled dishes that the boy was starting to clean up. "I see that one of the dishes is a famous Yangtze fish that we also have. Come, sit at our table, share this famous fish with us."

Harry protested at first, but his operational instinct won over, that and a look from Sue that told him to be gracious. "We would love to join you," he finally said.

"Please," Chou said to Harry, "Sit by me. Let me practice my English. If you can understand me."

"I can understand you all right. Your English is quite good. Where did you learn it?"

"In a missionary school here, later in Europe."

Harry thought it was worth the chance to acknowledge that he knew who Chou was. He worked up the courage to say so, while Chou spooned a large helping of the famous Yangtze fish into his dish, and then Sue's. Chou waited until they both tasted it and declared it delicious.

"You know," Harry said after Chou paused to drink some beer, "I didn't recognize you at first. But then I remembered. I first saw your photo in Edgar Snow's book."

"Ah, the book," he said. "You know it. It made us look too heroic, but it did some good." The way he spoke made it sound very matter-of-fact. "It introduced the Red Army and the struggle of the Chinese people to many who never heard of us. It helped us in Europe and America."

"I really liked the book," Harry said. "It was one of the things that made me want to come to China. Is there a Chinese translation?"

"Yes, of course. It was translated into Chinese in Shanghai in 1938. There are copies here and there. It is not so easy to get in Chungking now."

"I would imagine. I understand that you are the Communist liaison with the Nationalists. That's part of the united front with the Nationalists, I assume."

"There must be a united front to fight the Japanese invader. Chinese must not fight Chinese while the Japanese Army destroys our country. We must join our efforts in a unified national defense against the Japanese invaders."

"A lot of this is being done, isn't it?"

"We are fighting the Japanese, as the Nationalists are. The Red Army is strong in north and northeast China. We have the strong support of the masses there. In other areas the Red Army has popular support, but we do not get the help we need. Our efforts are not coordinated with the Nationalists. It is difficult without support. We need outside support as well, from America, from Europe, just as the Nationalists do. We are not getting it. For a while we thought Edgar Snow's book would bring us help, after bringing us so much attention. We have yet to see it. There are many people in Europe who would support us, but their governments will not."

Chou reached over to pour beer into Harry's glass. "It is too pleasant an evening to talk about politics," he said. "There are things more interesting. Tell me, what is your business in China? Are you with the American Embassy here?"

"I'm a journalist," Harry said. "I'm covering the war, like everybody else. I've spent most of my time here covering the American Volunteer Group."

"Ah, yes, the famous 'Flying Tigers'. What a good name that is. It must be a very good name for your propaganda."

Harry laughed. "I guess we don't think of it that way. We don't call it propaganda."

"Propaganda is what the West calls 'public relations,' I think. It's the same thing. As a journalist you must come one day to our liaison office. We will expose you to our 'propaganda.'"

They were all friends by the end of the evening. Harry liked Chou En-lai, an easy thing to do. He was a charming man and a practiced diplomat. They spoke for a long time, but there was nothing very substantive in what Chou said, which did not surprise Harry. He was an unknown to the Communists, although he had a feeling that Chou's office in Chungking, on a much smaller scale, was as thorough as Tai Li's. The Communists probably knew his name, had read some of his articles. But he was probably not important enough for the Communists to want to know more than that.

The surprise of the evening was Sue. She was very quiet, which was not at all the way she usually was in company. For the whole evening she was very much the proper Chinese young lady. She admitted she had studied abroad when one of Chou's young colleagues asked, but she seemed unwilling to talk about it. She answered questions simply, and spoke only of commonplace things, like the price of fancy goods in the market, and interspersed what she said with giggles, as Chinese ladies of the privileged class were wont to do. There was no suggestion in what she said that she was anything but the daughter of a middle class family. No one asked her where she worked, or if indeed she did work. She was so much the proper young Chinese lady that their Communist companions probably could not imagine that she did work.

Enroute back to his flat in their rickshaw, Harry asked her, "I assumed you didn't want to get into your background with Chou's chaps?"

"No," she said, "I didn't. Thank you for understanding that. If I become known to the Chinese Communists, my life would become even more complicated. Now, if Tai Li learns that I met Chou En-lai tonight, he will also know that I said little about anything and nothing about my past. It will be easy to blame you for meeting the Communists." She thought for a while and added, "And there are other reasons too."

She said no more. They rode on quietly for a while, until Harry, pressed by her silence, finally asked, "What other reasons?"

"When we get to the flat," she said. She was spending the night with him.

She took a bath and came out wearing one of his shirts. She looked preoccupied, sat on the bed and peeled some tangerines. Harry waited until she was ready.

"It is difficult for me to think about the Chinese Communists," she finally said. "I admire them, especially Chou En-lai and Mao Tse-tung, and the others on the Long March. They are brave men, they are wise men. The Communists are the ones who will make China one country."

She turned directly to him, held his eyes, looked almost fierce. "Not Tai Li, not Chiang kai-shek. I admire the Chinese Communist for what they did to survive, and what they are doing now to help China survive. They even helped us when the Thai communists needed help in Europe, and they helped in Thailand as well. They are Communists, but they are Chinese first. In the same way that the Free Thai must be careful when the Nationalist Chinese want to help them, I must be careful of the Chinese Communists.

She offered him a peeled tangerine. "That's what I was thinking about in the rickshaw when you asked."

He smiled. "I think I understand," he said. "Gee, maybe I'm starting to understand Asia. Do you think? "

Sue smiled a small smile.

* * *

The sky over Chungking was clear. It was still morning; the clouds would come later, full of rain to dump on the city. The monsoon was not yet finished with Chungking.

The sounds of the morning market around Harry were familiar, from the clanging of metal pots being beaten into traditional forms, to the cries of individual hawkers singing out the quality of their fish, radishes, or bloody chunks of meat. When something in the tenor of the sound changed, Harry looked up from the dried grasshoppers he was admiring. Around him, customers and the merchants both appeared tense, alert, looking and listening. The best ears were scanning the sky to the west.

In the next moment he saw them, six of them, two by two, low enough to make out the shark mouths on their long snouts. The six AVG P-40s crossed over the market like great sharks, then raised their noses and started to climb, banking gently in a wide turn. When they were high enough to be seen from every corner of the city, each pair went its own way, and moved into a separate sector of the sky. All at once, the airplanes started to twist and turn, roll and bank and dive, like a frenzied mating ritual of great birds. There was no other sound now, just the rising and falling wail of their engines. Around Harry, the Chinese watched in astonishment, eyes wide, mouths agape. They had never seen anything like this. An incredible show, much better even than moving pictures projected on a tall wall.

When it ended, the airplanes, much lower than before, joined up again in a wide turn over the city. Once they were all together, they flew toward the south, where Pei-shih-yi, their airfield, was located.

Only minutes later, another four P-40s went over the city low, in single file, one after the other. They flew with more purpose than the others, and also turned south toward Pei-shih-yi.

A few more minutes and another two P-40s went over, then two more, and two more after them. By Harry's count there had to be at least 16 P-40s at Pei-shih-yi, defending Chungking now. Or was it 16?

Some of the Chinese had counted as well. Everyone on the street was talking now, laughing, pointing at the sky, using hands to display the maneuvers they had just witnessed. Before this, what they knew of airplanes came from the Japanese bombers that flew over regularly with their loads of destruction and death. Knowing the P-40s were there to protect, not kill them, was a new experience.

Harry watched the Chinese around him for a time, and finally walked on, smiling to himself. It would make a great human interest article, but the censors would never let it through. What he had watched was the Old Man's doing, he knew that. The show had entertained the people in the city, but more importantly, it had made them feel secure. And not without reason. The Japs would think twice before sending their bombers against a force like that. Sixteen of the famous Flying Tigers were here now to defend Chungking.

A formidable force, 16 P-40s.... Or was it 16? Probably only six, Harry thought, the same six P-40s seen two and a half times. The Old Man's tactic was to bring the airplanes right over the city, let everyone see them. Then have them exit stage left and get down below the backdrop of buildings and other clutter and cross at the back of the stage. Then climb a bit and enter stage right. Repeat again if possible, give the impression of a lot of airplanes, but not too many. That would make it seem unreal. The Chinese audience would believe it, and the Jap spies in the audience would report to their masters that the city is now well-guarded by the Flying Tigers. Anyone would think a sizable force was guarding the city, even Harry – or he would have, had not Ed Rector told him once that this was something the Old Man did. Let them see your airplanes, the same ones several times. Make them believe there are a lot more than there really are.

Harry was to see Rector that evening. He would get the word from the horse's mouth.

* * *

"Yeah, that was the Old Man's idea," Ed Rector told him. "He wants us to do it every time we come or go. It makes Chungking look well-defended. It's good for Chinese morale and keeps the Japs off balance. You can bet your ass the Japs get regular reports of how many airplanes we have here, or how many their spies think are here. I sat in on a Chinese briefing once. Chiang Kai-shek's security guys run themselves silly just chasing the Jap spy radios around. We have to try to fool them. We just don't have enough airplanes left to scare the Japs. We have only four here in Chungking.

"What have I been up to? I've been down at Hengyang, one of our forward airfields. We have three airfields out in front, close to the Japs: Kweilin, Ling Ling and Hengyang. There's been a lot of rain and mucky weather, so we haven't been seeing so much of the Japs. We had some false alarms: the Japs are on the way, but they never got to us. Weather probably turned them back. Like us, the Japs are waiting for better weather.

"Not that I've been sitting on my hands. We've had a lot of new Army Air Corps pilots coming here. One bunch brought in a half-dozen B-25 bombers. That's just what the Old Man has been looking for. Every time it looked like the weather might clear, the Old Man would send them out to hit Jap supply bases. Then I'd have to send some of our P-40s out to escort them. Like the Japs, we didn't always get there. The weather would close in on us and we would turn back. Or the new B-25 pilots would just get lost. I had to take them to Hankow twice on the same mission. At the end they bombed some little village on the Yangtze. It's been a hassle.

"A couple of days ago, the Old Man came down to Hengyang. He wanted to know how many AVG would stay on for two more weeks after the Fourth of July, when we're officially disbanded. That would give the Army Air Corps a bit of a breather, let them get in shape to replace us. The Japs talk on their radio about wiping out the Army Air Corps after the AVG leaves. The Army Air Corps is all young, inexperienced pilots. The Old Man is really worried about that.

"I agreed to stay for the two weeks, and Tex did too, and so did some of our other pilots. Most of the AVG refused though, which is a goddamn shame. It's a hell of a way for the AVG to end."

CHAPTER 39

Jim Landry," the man from Washington introduced himself as he extended his hand to Harry.

"Harry," said Harry, seeing no reason to say more.

Harry watched as Landry watched him. Landry was a tall, thin man, with pale skin, little hair and thick glasses that gave the look of a startled owl. An analyst, Harry thought, not an operator.

Doyle finally spoke. "Jim is our visiting Thai expert. He worked as a diplomat there, knows the Thais well. He's with our office in Washington now. He knows all there is to know about the country. More important, he knows all about what Washington expects us to do about things there. I told Jim that you were the one who produced the reports on the Free Thai." Doyle winked at Harry then, signaling solidarity in the presence of a body from Washington. "Let's sit down and get started."

Landry sat across from Harry. "I understand you will be running operations into Thailand," he said, then studied Harry, as if to see whether he was worthy of that distinction.

"You know the background, I suppose," Landry went on finally, his voice growing stronger as he started to deal with things he understood. "Unlike the other countries of Southeast Asia, Thailand was never anyone's colony. It managed to remain independent even while it was being squeezed by the British in Burma and the French in Indochina. It's been a constitutional monarchy since 1932. The current king is still a boy, and so there's a regent.

"The country is run by a Prime Minister, a fellow named Pibul Songgram. A military man, of course, a Field Marshal. He was trained in Paris, learned about Mussolini and Hitler while he was there, became quite impressed with them, and with Fascism. He wants the Thai to call him 'The Leader.' He started cooperating with the Japanese when France fell in 1940. French Indochina came under Vichy rule then, and the Japs were given free rein.

"The Japs invaded Thailand the same day they attacked Pearl Harbor. The Field Marshal ordered the army not to resist. A few Thai units tried, but that didn't last very long. Within a matter of days the Japanese had a great force in Thailand. It was to be the staging ground for their invasions of Burma.

"Then something happened that could very well affect your ability to run operations into Thailand: The Thai government declared war on America and Britain. America took this in stride. The U.S. government position was that Thailand was invaded, that it was now an occupied nation. We did not declare war on Thailand, but called it an occupied nation.

"The British saw things differently. They had large interests in Thailand. Thailand was of strategic importance in defending their colonies. They felt betrayed. Despite American protests, the British declared war on Thailand. To the British, the Thai were now the enemy.

"This has immense ramifications for how the British will treat Thailand once the war has ended. It seems unlikely that they will support the continuation of an independent Thailand. Such a stand would, of course, support British imperial interests after the war."

"Wait a minute," Harry said. "You're suggesting an expansion of British imperialism?"

"Yes, I am. Many of us in Washington do not believe that England's imperial ambitions will end when the war ends. You may not be hearing this in China yet, but there is a chant starting to grow among Americans in India: 'The war in Asia is being fought to save England's colonies.' Are you surprised?"

"I'm not surprised. But I don't see how that might affect operations we run into Thailand."

Landry nodded. "Based on what we are seeing, the British are preparing operations that will put them in position to move politically after the war. Their primary goal is to replace whatever Thai government exists then with one of their choosing, a government favorable to British ambitions for the region. To succeed in that, the British will have to shut out OSS operations in Thailand."

Harry thought about that. "I'm not sure I follow your reasoning. The end of the war is a long way off. In the meantime we seem to be making an assumption that the Thai are not the enemy. When we deal with the Thai, I'm not sure we really know who we're supporting."

"A number of us have worked with the Thais for years. Since the war started, we see a lot of them in Washington. Consider the Thai Ambassador to the U.S., a chap named Seni Pramoj. When the Thai government declared war on us, Seni denounced it. He said the Thai alliance with the Japanese did not reflect what the Thai people wanted. The Thai have no use for the Japanese. He actually refused to deliver the Thai declaration of war to our Secretary of State. He's cooperating with our government very closely. He formed a Free Thai Council that most Thais in America have joined.

"Even before we were OSS, some of us were working with the Thai students. We've used them in our propaganda operations, and now twenty-odd have been selected to be trained as intelligence agents. Once they're ready, they will be inserted into Thailand. Presumably, you will be dealing with some of them.

"The other aspect of our views of the Thai is what's happening inside Thailand. A lot of us believed that an underground resistance would rise very quickly. Early on we heard that it had already happened, but details were sparse. Then we started to receive reports that there are Free Thai in radio contact with the Chinese. That confirmed that the Thai resistance exists." Landry took another long, hard look at Harry. "I understand those reports originated with you."

Harry said nothing. Landry went on. "At this point we need to learn as much as we can about the Free Thai. If the movement is viable, we must exploit it for intelligence. Information on the Japanese presence in Thailand will be increasingly important as the war goes on. That's primary, but when we get the opportunity we will train the Free Thai in guerrilla operations. Use them to bring the war to the Japanese. Those are our goals."

"And when the war ends?" Harry asked.

"As you say, the end of the war is a long way off. Anything I would have to say about that is pure speculation. It's better to stay with the present we know. I mentioned young Thais being trained as operatives. It's possible they will be sent here. There's some thinking that China should be the base for their overland infiltration. I mention this because that brings us to the Chinese factor. The Chinese are very possessive, of their country, and of the countries that border theirs. You may have already experienced some of the effects of that Chinese possessiveness."

Doyle interjected. "Actually, we've been very lucky. The Chinese don't really know who Harry is, and they don't care about me. I've seen it from a distance. I've tried to keep Harry informed."

"You are lucky then. Keep it that way. Don't let them know who you are. The Chinese perspective on Thailand is very basic. It's their land; Thailand is their backyard. In their eyes, the British, the French, and now the Americans have no business here. Thailand is their turf. They will find ways to defend it. This is especially true of any 'secret' moves we may try to make. They will go out of their way to block any intelligence operations aimed at Thailand. That goes for us as well as the British. We've seen Chinese reaction. The British Special Operations Executive has been driven out of the country; OSS Detachment 101 was never given permission to operate here.

"Americans have one advantage. The Chinese see us as different from the British. We're not a colonial power. Now, because of all the money we're pouring in, the Chinese feel they need to be nicer to us, at least give the appearance of being helpful. But, in fact, they will do what they can to assure that we do not succeed. Watch out for that."

Landry looked like he had exhausted himself. He sat back and drank some of his now cold tea. Harry relaxed.

Landry looked up. "There's nothing else I have to say. The whole reason Washington sent me out here is to give you this warning: Beware the British. Beware the Chinese. Beware their interference in our operations."

"Good reason to keep things to ourselves," Doyle said. "Not get involved in cooperative operations with the British, or the Chinese."

"That's why it's important to keep everything we do secret," Landry said. "Share nothing with the British and tell nothing to the Chinese. Well, there are exceptions, of course. When it could be to our advantage...but you know that."

"Oh, one other thing.... The chap who gave me my marching orders in Washington, said that if I meet a fellow named 'Harry', to tell him that 'Uncle Bill' is watching."

Landry leaned closer, smiled. "Good luck, Harry," he said. "We're all burdened with relatives. Can't get away from them, even in China. I have a distant cousin in the organization. She's a typist. Can't spell, and I hear about it. Well, I better be off."

They stood, shook hands. "Don't bother seeing me out," Landry said, "I asked my rickshaw to stand by. Don't worry, I won't go anywhere incriminating directly. I'll have the rickshaw chap take me down to the river, stroll a bit."

"Not a bad guy," Harry said after he left, "for a guy from Washington."

"I'll give him a few minutes to clear the area, then I'll be on my way," Doyle said. "Here, while I'm waiting you can read this." He handed an envelope to Harry.

Harry had not seen anything like this before. The envelope was stamped

"SECRET" in red ink, top and bottom, front and back. Centered on front of the envelope in black ink were the words: "EYES ONLY MARCO".

He turned the envelope over, looked at the back, examined the front again. "Eyes only Marco, what does that mean?"

"It's for only you to read."

"Marco?"

"Marco. It's your code name. It comes from Marco Polo."

"You're kidding."

"Marco Polo was the first of the big-nose foreigners into China. Someone in Washington thought that fits you."

"You're saying I have a big nose?" He was not going to let Doyle get off easy.

"I'm saying you're a foreigner. You were the first one of our bunch here. Read your message. I have a war to get back to." Doyle got up and walked to the bathroom.

Harry opened the envelope and started to read. "Dear MARCO," it started. He stared at that for moment. Not even his name, the one he had lived with all his life. Well, he thought, might as well get used to being somebody else. He started reading again from the beginning.

Dear Marco,

We have been watching your progress in Asia with great interest, and with considerable pride. You are among our first agents in the East, and one of our most successful. The reports you have sent to us fill important gaps in our knowledge of ongoing events, Your operational skills are reflected....

That was as far as his concentration took him. A personal note from some faceless bureaucrat in Washington who really had no idea who he was, who probably thought his name really was MARCO, in capital letters yet. His eyes drifted to the bottom, where some actual handwriting had been scrawled.

Harry,

I told your dad you're doing well, that he can be proud of you. He is chafing at the bit now, getting bored with the law in New York while all the excitement is in Washington – and China! I expect he will come to me soon – to find him a place with our organization. We'll be lucky to have him. Stay well. Keep up the good work and stay out of trouble.

Your Uncle Bill

Two real names! A big violation of operational security. And committed by the very top man in the OSS, the chief of their "Oh, So Secret" organization. There must be a lesson there somewhere.

Doyle returned from the bathroom. "Did you read it?"

"I did. What do you want me to do with it?"

Doyle shrugged. "It's yours. But you can't keep it. That would be bad security. Why don't you burn it the way they showed us?"

Harry folded the letter in the special secret way they had shown him in training, stood it up in the ash tray and lit it. He and Doyle watched with great interest; neither of them had done this before, at least not in an actual operational circumstance. The letter burned as it was supposed to. It left only a miniscule amount of ash. There was no smoke or smell.

"It actually works!" Doyle said, "Something we learned in Washington actually works."

CHAPTER 40

"Why does he want me to go along?"

"I don't know, Harry," Louie said. "Give you a chance to see more of China, I suppose."

"That's all?"

Louie shrugged.

"You're the one who said that Tai Li never does anything that doesn't forward his objectives. He must be up to something."

"I'm sure he is, something quite nefarious, probably." Louie shrugged again. "But I don't know what it is. Neither of us will, unless you go along."

"All right, I'll go. You just talked me into it. Tai Li told you that the purpose of the trip is to visit Chinese troops down near the Indo-China border? Isn't that curious? He doesn't deal with troops."

"He is a general."

"Sure, but not a general of soldiers. He's a general of bureaucrats and intrigue."

Harry and Louie looked at each other. They both shrugged.

"Let me make sure I have it all straight," Harry said. "The only ones going are you, me, Tai Li and Eddie Liu. And we're flying there?"

"Yes, we're going all the way to Kwangsi. It's a long way from here."

"I looked it up on a map. It borders Indo-China. It must be in range of a half dozen Jap airfields. Isn't it dangerous for us to be flying around down there?"

"Only if we have really bad luck. Usually, nobody has reason to fly into the area, so the Japanese Air Force doesn't pay much attention. The Japs might drop a bomb there now and then, but it's not likely we would meet any of their pursuit airplanes. Tai Li has all the facts and figures on who is flying where. We would not go there if the risk was not reasonable."

"Reasonable I like," Harry said.

"It will be a good trip. You'll enjoy it."

* * *

They flew due south from Chungking. There were only the four of them, and two Chinese pilots, but the airplane was small. Harry had his own window, and occupied himself by looking at rice paddies and watching distant hills drift by. When clouds appeared, he kept an eye on them and wondered if they could hide a Japanese airplane that might be stalking them. In time, the drone of the engines lulled him into a fitful sleep, only to be woken by Eddie Liu, with a great supply of tepid tea, which he kept offering and pouring. Harry knew there would be a fuel stop, but after the fourth cup, he put aside the tea and started praying for an airfield to appear.

The strip they landed on was small and all but invisible from the sky. As they circled the small clearing on their approach, he could see a troop of Chinese soldiers dragging logs and leafy debris off the runway, where it had been piled to discourage landings.

A meal had been prepared for them, set in an open-sided thatch-roof shed. While their airplane was being refueled, they were served by a staff of Chinese soldiers with ill-fitting uniforms and dirty hands. Tai Li seemed preoccupied. He had little to say at first, but as they ate, he spoke of where they were, described skirmishes that had happened there when Japanese units got lost and found themselves facing the local militia. Troops from the central government had finally been sent to guard the airfield, now that it was part of the early warning net that alerted Kunming and Chungking when Japanese bombers came out of Indochina.

Harry was surprised when, at the end of the meal, Tai Li summoned the local commander and graciously thanked him for the lunch. The commander seemed as surprised as Harry was. Eddie Liu had even brought a bottle of cognac. That cheered everyone. Tai Li toasted the commander and everyone shouted "*gambei!*" Harry knew he would be asleep as soon as their little airplane took off.

Their destination was a bigger version of the airfield they had just left. The runway was longer, and the area around it was wide and flat and clear of vegetation, a parade ground for the columns of troops that stood at the end of the runway.

A half dozen young officers were there to greet Tai Li. They crowded around him when he stepped off the plane. Harry was the last out the door.

Eddie Liu waited for him; he had something to say.

"General Tai Li told me to tell you this place is called Puerh. He asks that you not write anything, about this place or what you will see. The soldiers here are only Chinese, but they may be special soldiers in the future."

Harry nodded. He expected more, but Eddie Liu smiled and said nothing else.

The officers led them all to where the ranks of soldiers waited. The officers wore clean, unwrinkled uniforms that made them look fresh and well groomed. The men looked rough, like their uniforms. Tai Li trooped the line with the two senior officers, with Eddie Liu a few steps behind. Harry, Louie and the junior officers stood off to the side and watched.

Ceremonies finished, they were led to an open-sided hut where chairs had been set for them. The soldiers were marched by in crooked rows, not everyone in step. When all the troops had passed, a drill team of 20 came along to give a demonstration of close order drill. There were a few collisions, which everyone pretended not to notice. The drill team was followed by a squad of army acrobats. They juggled hand grenades, did cartwheels and headstands and then climbed on each other to form a human pyramid. They were tottering precariously when a dozen horsemen suddenly galloped up and caused the pyramid to collapse. The horsemen wheeled around and galloped right up to the guests in their chairs and skidded to a dust-raising stop.

Tai Li rose and walked the few steps to where the horses stood. He patted the horses, seemed quite interested in them, and exchanged a few words with the riders. He called one of the officers over and started asking questions. The man answered each at length, and Tai Li listened carefully, nodding from time to time. Finally, he called Louie over, and the two of them watched while the officer walked around one of the horses, and pointed out things on it. Louie watched and nodded, agreeing to something.

As Harry watched, Eddie Liu walked up and quietly asked, "The soldiers, do you think they are Chinese?"

Harry looked at the riders and started to say that they did look Chinese – the young officers certainly did, but then he hesitated. "When I think about it," he finally said, "most of the men we've seen here don't look Chinese. They're not as big as other Chinese, not as tall. Their skin is darker. They look more like people I saw in Burma. Somewhat like the Burmese, but not exactly."

"Well put, Mr. Harry," Eddie Liu said. He sounded pleased, which was peculiar enough to make Harry pause before adding, "China is a very big country. I guess you have all kinds of physical types."

Eddie looked a little concerned. "But you don't think the soldiers here look like Chinese?" he asked.

Harry shook his head. "If I had to say just yes or no, I would have to say no, they do not look like Chinese."

That seemed to satisfy Eddie Liu. He looked relieved. "Ah," he said, "very good. Thank you, Mr. Harry," and bowed as he backed away, which made everything more peculiar still. Harry watched as he joined Tai Li, and immediately started to tell the general something. Louie had been standing close enough to overhear Harry's exchange with Eddie Liu. He caught Harry's eye and winked.

It was time to go and Harry thought no more of this, until Louie stepped up to him as they stood by the airplane and waited to board. Tai Li and Eddie Liu were some distance off, saying their farewells. Louie looked around first, then raised his eyebrows at Harry and quietly said, "That was it."

"That was what?"

"That was the nefarious thing that Tai Li set out to accomplish today, the reason he invited you here."

"I feel a bit thick. Do you mean what Eddie asked? Do I think the soldiers look Chinese?"

Louie nodded. "That's it."

"You're kidding."

"I'm not," Louie said. "You will see."

And Harry did see, eventually. But it was not until the next day. Louie called him and they got together in the garden of a quiet tea shop. "I was right," Louie said. He continued only after looking around and assuring there was no one in earshot, "I was right about why Tai Li wanted you to come along. He needed to know if you thought the soldiers at Puerh looked Chinese."

"Those are the words to an old song," Harry said, borrowing the phrase of a Chinese acquaintance.

"Perhaps, but the words are correct. Tai Li and I spoke this morning. I know what is in his mind now." He held up his hand to stop what Harry was about to say. "Let me tell you the full story before you interrupt me. You will understand why your opinion was so necessary to Tai Li."

Louie waited to see if Harry had something to say anyway, and went on when he did not. "I didn't count how many troops we actually saw at Puerh, 500 perhaps? But as it turns out, that was the proverbial drop in the bucket. There are 10,000 troops at Puerh like the ones we saw, and all under the command of General Tai Li.

"Tai Li has a plan that requires 10,000 troops. The Generalissimo has approved the plan, but now Tai Li cannot proceed until he has something else he needs, 10,000…." Louie paused dramatically, raised his finger to assure Harry's complete attention,…

"Horses!"

"Horses?" Louie achieved the effect he intended. Harry looked thoroughly puzzled. He stared at Louie, not quite ready to believe what he had heard.

"Ten thousand horses!" Louie emphasized. "It's simple enough really, when you think about it. Tai Li has 10,000 troops. To make them mounted troops he needs 10,000 horses."

"Shades of Ghengis Khan," Harry said. He laughed. "That's crazy Louie, so crazy I know you couldn't have made it up. I have to believe you, but what does Tai Li need horsemen for?"

"For the invasion."

"Ah," Harry said, "yes, of course, the invasion. Well, let me just sit back and hear you out, Louie. Go on. I'll drink my tea and not say another word."

"Good. Once I explain Tai Li's plan, all will be clear to you. Tai Li needs 10,000 horsemen to invade Thailand. That's the optimum number. Once he has that many horses – a problem of no small magnitude that he expects me to solve – his horsemen will gallop out of Puerh, right into Indochina, and then gallop across it into northern Thailand. From there they will gallop into Bangkok. The effect of all these horsemen appearing at full gallop in Bangkok will be enough to make the Thai people arise and drive the Japanese invaders into the sea."

"That's even crazier than I thought," Harry said.

"Wait! You haven't heard it all. There is a kernel of brilliance in all of this. The arrival of the horsemen in Thailand will be preceded by a coup. The coup will be led by the Free Thai resistance. Tai Li has contact with them in Bangkok. He thinks there are royals among them who could revive the Thai monarchy.

"That's not all! Tai Li has also learned that the American OSS has recruited Thai university students in America to serve as Free Thai operatives. He will convince the OSS that these Free Thai should be sent here to China, from where they can be easily infiltrated into Thailand.

"Of course, the OSS doesn't know it yet, but their Free Thai will be infiltrated into Thailand at the head of Tai Li's horse force. It's very important to have real Thais leading Tai Li's 10,000 Chinese horsemen. The 10,000 must appear to be indigenous Thai, not Chinese. Tai Li's horse force must masquerade as Thai so that the real Thai, the Americans, the British and the rest of the world believe that the coming of the 10,000 horsemen is something that occurred spontaneously in Thailand and not an invasion by China."

"But the 10,000 horsemen, they are Chinese, aren't they?"

"They are Chinese. Ethnically, I suppose, they are tribal people of some sort. They probably shared common ancestors with the Thai a thousand years ago. Now they are Chinese, in their hearts and in their minds. They share some physical characteristics with the Thai, and that's all they need. Who will look at them closely if their officers are Free Thai who speak good English, who attended America's finest schools? That's why your opinion became important to Tai Li. He needed to see if a Western observer looking at these troops would say they are Chinese or not.

"Amazing," Harry said, shaking his head in disbelief.

"But there's a rub. Before his invasion can begin, Tai Li needs his 10,000 horses, and he's depending on me to get them."

That made Harry laugh. "That's a great job for you Louie. Where are you going to get 10,000 horses? I haven't seen many horses in China. There are six that I can recall."

"The six at Puerh, that's about as many as they have. There aren't 10,000 horses to be had in China. I'm going to have to go to Tibet to get them."

"That's great. You will buy horses in Tibet. That's a long way from Puerh. How will you get them there?"

"I'm not sure. That's what Tai Li talked to me about this morning. We talked about airplanes, but we just don't have that many. What we finally came up with is to do it the American way. We'll use cowboys, herd them across China…."

"You're kidding!"

"… or maybe the proper word is horse-boys. Do you know, Harry?"

* * *

"They thought it was a quite a satire, Tai Li's 'Horse Force', and very funny." Doyle shook his head and went on. "Your report got a lot of laughs back in Washington, Harry. It's a good thing you've established some credibility back there, or nobody would have taken it seriously."

"I hope somebody takes my reporting seriously. Ideas like that can cause big problems."

"Don't get me wrong, Harry. Everybody thinks the 'Horse Force' idea is crazy, but that doesn't mean that your report is not being taken seriously. Donovan certainly thinks so. He wrote on his copy of your report: 'A thoroughly serious business'. He thinks it reflects Tai Li's intention to take over OSS Thai operations. That would cut OSS right out of the Thai business. But, although everybody agrees that the 'Horse Force' idea is crazy, if by some improbable circumstance, the plan worked, it would give the Chinese exactly what they want – a very firm foothold in Thailand after the war."

Harry nodded. "So what do we do?"

"Nothing," Doyle said. "We don't have to do anything right now. We watch. Tai Li is a long way from carrying out his plan. He needs those 10,000 horses, and he's come to our man Louie to find them. I assume that if Tai Li gets serious about all those horses, you can probably get Louie to go slow, to run into obstacles. It could take him a long time to find 10,000 horses."

"I think you're right. Louie thinks the idea is crazy too. I don't think he would have any problem going slow if we wanted him to."

"Then we're in good shape. I don't have anything else Harry. Tomorrow is Four of July. Take the day off, go to the Generalissimo's big party."

"I won't miss it. It will be the last AVG get-together."

CHAPTER 41

July 4, 1942
Chungking

"Hey, Padre."

"Hey, Ross. I've been expecting you. The Old Man said you'd be coming out here today." "Got the numbers for me?"

"I think we have a good count. Subject to the Old Man's review, of course. He'll go over everything, confirm it all. I guess this will be the official record. My only concern is the total number of enemy aircraft destroyed." Frillman handed Harry the sheet of paper. "You can keep this one. It's your copy."

"Thanks. I'm sure it's close enough for newspaper work." Harry quickly ran his eyes over the numbers, then he went back to the top and started reading carefully.

"I want to make sure I have this right. The total number of Japanese aircraft the AVG destroyed is 297, right?"

"Destroyed and paid for," Frillman said. "It's why we have to be careful. Some pilot gets paid for each Jap airplane destroyed, at 500 bucks each. The number is as good as we can make it. I'm sure somebody will say it's too high, that we couldn't confirm each airplane destroyed, that many of the Jap airplanes went down over heavy jungle or into the sea where the remains could not be found."

"I'll let you guys argue over that." Harry looked at the next line. "The AVG lost 22 people…."

"Only four of those in aerial combat…."

"Only four killed in the war in the air." Harry thought about the swirling combats he had witnessed in the skies over Rangoon. So long ago now. "Only four," he repeated. "That's pretty amazing."

"That's four killed in the air, in actual combat with Jap airplanes. There were four other pilots killed in the air, but not by Jap airplanes. They got hit while strafing the Japs on the ground, or bombing them. That was probably the most dangerous thing our guys could do. And then there were three killed on the ground by Jap bombs."

Harry made a couple of notes. "I got that."

"And ten lost in accidents."

Harry nodded. "There are prisoners of war, too. What was that, four?"

"As far as we know.... Four pilots were known to be alive after they went down, but we can't be sure they still are. A couple of the guys saw Black Mac MacGarry waving at them from a clearing in the jungle after he got hit, but he was in a wild area, a long way from anywhere. He could easily have starved to death before the Japs found him. We know Charlie Mott is alive, or at least that he was. Jap radio told us they had him. They said he was badly injured, but then they said he asked them for a beer." Frillman shrugged. "Who knows how things turned out for those guys."

Harry nodded. "I see you even have all the AVG airplanes accounted for. The AVG started with a hundred P-40s and lost 73, but only 12 of those were lost actually fighting the Japs. Is that right?"

"Ninety-nine, " Frillman said, "We started with 99. They sent us a hundred P-40s, but one fell in the river when they were unloading it at Rangoon, so we started with 99."

"Okay, but what about the remaining 73? Only 12 were lost actually fighting the Japs?"

"That's right. The rest of them, 61, were destroyed on the ground, by the Japs or by us. We burned up 22 of them at Loi Wing to keep the Japs from grabbing them when they took the place."

"Looks like you have it all here. It's a good summary."

"Like I said, the Old Man has to go over the figures. I doubt he'll change anything. He has the same figures we have. Maybe he has something from the Chinese that we don't have, but there can't be much. So, what you have there should be close enough for the newspapers. Are you actually planning to publish these figures, Harry?"

"Maybe. I don't know if they'll let me. I'll have to talk to the Old Man." It was Donovan who Harry needed the figures for, but he could not tell Frillman that. Later he would do a story on the achievements of the AVG. "There's a higher power in the Office of War Censorship, Padre, that might see this as a revelation giving aid and comfort to the enemy. I personally can't believe the Japs would find much comfort in everybody knowing they lost 297 airplanes in the air to the AVG's 12. By the way, who pays the pilots for all those destroyed Jap airplanes?"

"The Chinese government, their contract is with them. Of course, the Chinese government gets the money from us. I guess in the end it's the American taxpayer who pays them for the dead Jap airplanes."

"Money well spent. Speaking of money well spent, are you going out to the farewell party?"

"I thought I'd pass it up. The nights have been hot lately, and they want us to wear our dress uniforms. I'm not up for that."

Harry had been enthusiastic about the party. He thought everybody would be. "But this is the last party the Generalissimo can give for the AVG before it splits up totally," he said. "It's the finale. It will be historic. Come with me, Padre, I have a car."

"Historic?" Frillman laughed. "Historic parties I have had. I've been to the historic parties the Generalissimo and the Madame throw. They're like a Chinese Methodist social: Chinese decorations on the wall and soft drinks and parlor games. I'd sooner stay out here and have a couple of beers with the guys."

Harry was surprised, and he said so.

"You have fun, Harry."

* * *

"It's the end of the beginning, Harry. That's what this is."

"Harry nodded. "That's a fine line. It would make a good headline. Can I use it?"

"Mine," Morris growled. "I already have the piece typed."

Harry looked down into his teacup where scotch whiskey glowed like gold. "And thanks for the whiskey," he said. "I never thought to bring any. I figured any party in Chungking would be flowing in it."

What was flowing was fruit punch, with no alcohol. In huge crystal bowls set on tables in the center of the large room. He and Morris stood by the back wall, trying not to be conspicuous.

It was to have been an outdoor barbecue – it was the Fourth of July after all – but rain had driven them inside. Their host was President of the Republic of China, an old man named Lin Sen, and the party had been moved into his mansion. Prominent Chinese guests were gathered around him now, probably waiting for the Generalissimo and Madam Chiang Kai-shek, who had not showed up yet.

Harry looked around the room to see who else was there. He had things to do here tonight, people to talk to. That was the proper use of a party.

"The end of the beginning," Morris said again. "But we were there at the actual beginning, do you remember that Harry, Rangoon and the Sittang Bridge?"

"I remember. It's all very distant now."

"Because of all that's happened. Think about it, Harry. The Japs bombed Pearl Harbor, took Singapore and Hong Kong. The Brits lost Malaya and Burma. The Dutch lost the East Indies. America lost the Philippines, Wake Island, God knows what else. And that was just the first month. And during that time only the AVG was able to beat the Nippers at their own game."

"A blazing flash of light," Harry said. "That's what somebody called the AVG in the Burma fight. A good phrase, that," one that he would have to work into his writing. The whiskey had relaxed him, opened his mind.

Morris twisted, craned his neck, looking for something. "There they are, over there. Look at them, sitting there, so well-behaved. They're drinking coke, for God's sake, not a drop of whiskey amongst them tonight. Can you believe that?"

"Highly unusual," Harry agreed as he looked to where the AVG was sitting together. They were exceptionally well-behaved tonight, and all neatly dressed. Most wore what served as an AVG dress uniform, a mix of Army Air Corps issue and Rangoon-tailored bush jackets. A sight not often seen.

"They're all being good, and the Old Man isn't even close," Harry said. "It must be fear of the Generalissimo that keeps them in place."

"Not the Generalissimo, Harry, the Madame."

"Fear of Madame Chiang?" Harry laughed aloud. "I'm sure you're right. We all learn that the fear of Asian woman is the beginning of wisdom."

"Just the Chinese ones," Morris said. "Chinese Methodist women are the worst. We must drink to that. Here, let me pour you more whiskey. Stand in front of me so nobody sees my bottle." The bottle was concealed in a dirty-looking paper bag that had already drawn looks from some of the Chinese.

They clicked teacups, then together said, "To Chinese Methodist women!" Each took a deep pull of whiskey.

"I've interviewed her," Morris said. "Madame Chiang. You should too, Harry. She's easy; she gives a good interview." Looking over Harry's shoulder he added, "Speaking of Madame Chiang, there's a good looking Chinese lady coming our way. Friend of yours, I think." Morris inclined his head in the lady's direction as Harry turned to see. It was Lucy. God, she looked beautiful, he thought, more beautiful than he remembered.

"Lucy! How good to see you. I didn't know you would be here."

"Louie ordered me. I dared not miss it."

"Well, it is the social highlight of Chungking's bombing season," Harry said. They shook hands, too self-conscious to do more. Morris stood back, waited for the appropriate moment. After introductions, he said, "Excuse me. I must wander." He bowed to Lucy; to Harry he said, "Here...," and tilted the bag toward Harry's teacup, "Should hold you a while."

"Thanks," Harry said to Morris's back as he wandered off. His teacup was full again.

"A good friend," Lucy said, "but where are the others?" She looked to where the AVG was sitting. "I don't see Ed Rector."

"Ed and others are out of town, at the forward airfields. They're holding the line, as friend Morris would say. The Japs always feel a need to attack something on a holiday. What have you been up to?"

"Working," she said. "Everyone in Kunming is working hard. The flights from India have opened the supply line again. They call them 'Hump flights', did you know that? Because they fly over the 'Hump', the Himalayas. It's very dangerous."

"You're back in the cargo business then?"

"Oh, very much so. Your Army Air Corps has started flying in military cargo. CNAC brings in goods for the Chinese market. Louie has us involved with both."

"You have helpers?"

"I do, but the delicate things I must do myself."

"Delicate things?" Harry raised an eyebrow.

"Off-invoice goods. Whiskey, medicines, fancy wristwatches."

"Ah, the smuggled goods."

"Yes, the smuggled goods. I thought I would need Louie's help with that, but I find I'm quite good at it. It's all in the negotiation, hearing what your agent says he wants, and knowing what he will settle for."

"Sounds like you're learning your job. Hope you can stay out of trouble."

"Speaking of trouble, Harry, have you seen Sue tonight?"

Harry looked around. "I wasn't expecting to see her here."

"Louie said she would come. Not with him, but with a Chinese officer, someone she works with." Harry waited for her to ask if he and Sue had been seeing each other. He was not sure what to tell her. But she did not ask.

The Chinese voices at the far end of the room got louder; something was going on. "Madame Chiang is here," Lucy said. "I must pay my respects. She will know if I don't." She held out her hand. "It was so good to see you, Harry. I'll be here a week. We can get together." They shook hands again. It seemed almost perfunctory to Harry. As he watched her walk away, he felt he had lost something. He would have to make time for her.

"I didn't want to interrupt your talk with the beautiful lady," someone said. Harry turned; John Birch stood alongside him. "John, how are you?"

"Splendid, Harry. I wanted to thank you for your fine words, your advice to me and the good words you said to General Chennault."

"The Old Man did not need good words from me. He has a very high opinion of you. Are you working with him now?"

"I am. I have become three-quarters intelligence officer and remain 50 percent a preacher."

"That doesn't add up to one, John."

"It's more than one. The Old Man has us all working more than full time. He's a hard-driving man. I must fulfill my duties to him before I can spend time preaching."

"Is he keeping you in the rice fields, sneaking behind Japanese lines?"

"Not yet, but I will be. The Old Man wants me to ferret out Japanese positions for the boys to bomb."

"We have to stay in touch then, John. There may come a time when I need...."

"Silence! Silence! Quiet, everyone please!" A voice of command.

The room went still. No sound, no movement, except for eyes turning to the senior Chinese army officer who had issued the order. He was a serious-looking fellow, probably the aide to some general, or to Madame Chiang Kai-shek herself, who now stepped up alongside him. Harry had not seen Madame Chiang before. He had heard she was an attractive woman, but he was surprised by how striking she looked, much younger than he expected, elegantly dressed and confident-looking. Just behind her stood the Generalissimo himself.

"Madame Chiang Kai-shek will now say a few words," the officer said.

Madame Chiang started by thanking everybody for coming and made a joke about the rain driving them into the President's residence. Her English was flawless, spoken with a drawl that came from the American south. Her voice turned serious when she thanked General Chennault and the American volunteers for their service and their sacrifices, and congratulated them for their victories over the Japanese Air Force. Her voice softened when she called the AVG "her boys." She was their honorary commander, after all. It was all very touching in a way.

She stopped, turned to where the AVG stood together. On her face was a gentle smile that could have been affection. It seemed a long time before she spoke again.

"The American Volunteers...the world press calls them the Flying

Tigers. Here in China, these bold Flying Tigers will always be Flying Angels. They may not look like it, but they are Flying Angels. A little naughty at times, some of them, but to us they are China's Flying Angels."

Oh my goodness, Harry thought, she was calling them angels. That was not a good sign. Somebody in the AVG must have just done something very bad. Rector had told him about her talk to the AVG when they first arrived in Kunming. She had learned of some of their "naughtiness" in Rangoon, and spoke to them of the need for discipline at some length. At the end of that lecture, she had called them her "little angels, with or without wings"

But that was all there was. She had nothing to say about discipline. The AVG was all but gone now; the "little angels" needed just a small reminder of past sins. Harry was disappointed. He felt he had missed something as the Madame brought her comments to a conventional close. Then he spotted Sue standing with the Chinese around the Generalissimo, and tried to catch her eye, discreetly, but he had no luck. She probably saw him, he thought, but did not dare to be 'naughty' while the Madame was speaking.

When the Madame finished, the Generalissimo stepped up. His comments were brief. He had no English, so his words were translated by one of his officers. He thanked Chennault and the AVG, said they would always be remembered by the Chinese people, that his own gratitude to the AVG was "infinite". The English for his words came from someone else, but to Harry they seemed genuine. The Generalissimo was sincere – or had a good knack for appearing so.

A senior Chinese officer stepped forward and presented a sword to Chennault, to great applause. Then two young Chinese officers marched up, carrying between them a large flat object. A cloth was drawn back to reveal an oil painting of the Old Man with the Generalissimo and the Madame. There was great applause from the Chinese and cheers from the AVG.

As things started to settle down again, John Birch said, "I haven't been to one of these before, but I'm told it will be very Christian now, like a Church social, all fruit punch and parlor games. Can I get you some punch, Harry?"

"No you may not, John. I dread to think what it would do to my digestion."

"Before the speeches, you said you might need something."

"Ah, yes, I most likely will. You get out to see the countryside, John. It's something I don't get the opportunity to do. If it's possible, I would like to talk with you now and then, about what you see when you're poking around behind the lines. Not about the Japanese targets the Air Corps is interested in, but what you see of the Chinese people and how they live with the war. I'll clear it with the Old Man."

"The general won't object." Birch looked directly at Harry then. "If he does, well, we can work something out."

"That's the spirit, John, thank you." Just then he saw Sue put down her glass and walk to the hallway. "Listen, John, I see another lady over there. I would like to speak with her before the parlor games begin."

"You better hurry, Harry. I think the Madame is gathering "her boys" for musical chairs."

The hallway was wide and well lit, lined with bowing servants indicating the route to the restrooms. There were no dark corners, but Sue, it seemed, had managed to disappear. Just as he was wondering where she might have gone, she stepped out of a room on the other side of the hall. "Oh, Harry," she said, with well-feigned surprise, "how good to see you." Then she explained . "I was looking for a window to see if it's still raining."

She turned to one of the servants, said something in rapid Chinese. He bowed toward the end of the hall. "How silly of me," she said to Harry. "There's a door there. Let's go see if it's still raining."

It was. They stepped out, under a small portico.

"I have things to ask," Harry said, "but we can't spend much time out here."

She pressed against him, turned her face up to his. "I can't come with you tonight," she said. "The boss from my unit…." She left it unfinished.

"I understand, but right now I need to know if Tai Li – or anyone – has spoken of tribal soldiers or 'special troops' in Sichang Province, if someone has talked of using such soldiers to invade Thailand."

"No," she said, "no one has ever spoken of anything like that."

"Have you heard of Free Thai operatives being trained in America who might be sent to China?"

"No."

"Do you know if Tai Li is training Thais to go back to Thailand as agents?"

"No, and I don't think he would. He does not need to do that. Tai Li has many agents in Thailand. But they are all like me, from Thai-Chinese families. He does not need the Thai, or trust them."

"One more thing, Sue, then we go back in. Would you be willing to go back to Thailand as an agent, not for Thai Li, but for the Americans?"

"You mean for you, Harry?"

"I mean for the Americans."

"I would go for you."

Harry nodded, started to say something, instead he said, "We better go back in."

Later he thought about it. She had pointed out the obvious: Tai Li must have Thailand thoroughly infiltrated. The Chinese community there was large and influential. His Chinese agents could get him whatever he wanted. He would not need to deal with the Thai.

But mainly he thought about Sue saying she would go back to Thailand "for him". It left him with feelings that were very mixed. He was gratified to discover that he could inspire that kind of loyalty – but that was not the way it was supposed to work. An agent was to be motivated by greed, by love of country, by ideology or revenge, but not by devotion to the handler. That was neither professional nor practical. In training he had been told that spying should be cut and dried and rational, that the right decision in planning an operation should always be clear. But it never was that way, never could be: Spying was too involved with people.

Those thoughts would have to wait for later, for the solitude of his room. As he and Sue stepped back into the hallway, he saw Louie ahead, turn down the corridor where the men's room was located. He said goodnight to Sue there, and hurried off to pursue Louie.

Louie was entertaining a half-dozen Chinese Army officers in the men's room. Everyone was laughing when Harry walked in. Louie had just finished one joke and started another. It was all in Chinese, so Harry took his time, washed his hands carefully, waited for the officers to leave.

"Ah, Harry, look here," Louie said as the last one stepped out. He held up two cigars, huge black ones. "Your favorite smoke. Come, let's step outside, enjoy these wonderful things." Harry had never smoked a cigar in his life.

They walked to the door by the portico that he and Sue had just vacated. Outside, Louie handed him one of the cigars. "You don't really have to smoke it. Hope you don't mind if I do. It kills the taste of fruit punch."

Louie lit his cigar, inhaled deeply, blew a stream of blue smoke toward the top of the portico. It hung over them like a small cloud. "Something I wanted to tell you," he said. "Your friend in Shanghai sent another letter. She plans to visit her uncle in Kunming next month. I assume she means you, or that she is letting you know that she will be coming out of Shanghai. She also sends a report. I'll have the translation for you tomorrow. It has counts of Japanese airplanes from her Chinese boss, and comments from her Japanese friends on damage the AVG caused. It's quite a good report. It could be useful to someone."

"That's great," Harry said. "I'll look forward to reading it. Will she have any problems getting out of Shanghai?"

"She shouldn't. It will require a good bit of cash, but we can arrange that. Tai Li's people need not get directly involved, but we can have them oversee the arrangements."

"I'll have a lot to do when she gets here."

"I'm sure you will." Louie tapped him in the ribs with his elbow, winked, blew a stream of smoke into the night.

"That too, but I meant mainly talking with her."

"Yes, of course, Harry, talking." Louie took another deep pull on his cigar. Harry stuck his in his shirt pocket. He yawned. "Long day," he said, "and too much whiskey. I'm bushed."

"Whiskey?" Louie said, "There's no whiskey here. Is there, Harry?"

"Not a drop," Harry said as he opened the door. "See you tomorrow, Louie."

Inside, there was music now, a piano that got louder as he walked down the hall. The Generalissimo, the Madame and the other senior Chinese had departed, and the AVG had rearranged themselves in the music room off the hallway. Most of them stood around the piano, singing British marching songs with impolite lyrics, something they had learned in Burma.

Harry went on into the main room that was almost empty. Many of the Chinese guests were gathered in the foyer, bunched near the door, waiting to say their formal goodbyes. Harry saw no point in joining them, stayed near the wall and edged around the crowd, and made it through the open door, inconspicuously, he thought. He paused at the top of the marble steps that led down to the drive and someone said his name. Chennault was right behind him.

"Glad you could come tonight, Ross," he said. They walked down the steps together.

The Old Man said, "I saw you and John Birch. He's with us now, you know. I wanted to thank you for helping with that."

Harry nodded. He did not have much to do with John Birch becoming one of the Old Man's intelligence officers, but the Old Man apparently thought so. And that was all right; it would not hurt to let the Old Man keep thinking that.

Chennault stopped at the bottom of the steps. "Listen, Ross," he said. "you tell your Uncle Bill that we will have more airplanes now, more men. We really will need to know where the Japs are, what their strength is. We can get some of that. Stilwell has no interest in what the Air Corps needs, but I have John Birch and a few others like him. I know you help us when you can. Uncle Bill will have to help us too. We can't destroy the enemy unless we know where he is."

Chennault's car pulled up and Harry held the door. "I'll tell him, sir. He liked the AVG. He will understand what you need."

"You give him my best." The Old Man climbed into the back of the Studebaker, looked back at Harry. "Your Uncle Bill has the whole world to worry about. We're at the end of the line. You take care now, Ross."

"Yes, sir," Harry said, and almost saluted. He watched the car drive off. Behind him a long line of cars waited to pick up departing guests. He looked back at the house. He had done everything he had come to do; it felt good. He started walking down the drive, to the parking area where the Americans had left their cars. Maybe he could find a ride back to town. It was drizzling, and although one car after another drove by, there was not another person to be seen.

"Hey, Marco Polo!" came out of the dark. "You, the guy with the big nose! Over here, I've got a jeep; I'll drive you into town."

Harry looked around. It had to be Doyle. Who else knew his code name? It was disconcerting to hear someone shout it like that. Not what he expected of Doyle. There were a lot of cars. Where was he, trying to hide behind a car? Harry shouted into the night:

"It's your nose you better worry about, Doyle. What are you doing lurking about? Have you been drinking?"

A jeep slowly rolled up alongside him. Doyle stuck his head out. "Well, there was this guy, generous chap, journalist, I think, very disreputable. Had a bottle of whiskey, bandied it about quite openly. No one else wanted to be seen with him. Felt it my duty. Come on, get in. I've been waiting for you. We can talk."

He got in under the flimsy canvas roof. It would not help much if it started to rain hard again. "Christ, Doyle," he said. "You shouldn't be shouting out my code name like that."

"There's no one to hear, Harry. Even if there were, Marco Polo is a very common name in China. A lot of kids are named after him."

They drove past the army of guards manning the gates, then down the road. Where it fronted the President's residence, the road was the best in Chungking. "I watched you working the floor in there," Doyle said. "You were going like a house afire. Was it productive?"

"Yes, it was. I got at everybody I wanted. Here, you can send this to Donovan." He handed Doyle the sheet he got from the Padre. "It's a summary of the AVG's record in combat. He asked for it."

"Let me give you the short version of the rest." he said. He told Doyle what Sue had said about Tai Li's use of Thai agents.

"Makes perfect sense," Doyle said. "If he's only trying to collect intelligence. But if Tai Li also wants to manipulate the Thai political system, now or after the war, he will need Thais. According to our visiting Thai expert, Landry, the Thai-Chinese may have great influence in the economy, but they stay out of Thai politics. They leave that to the Thais. It's a lot healthier for them that way."

Harry nodded. "Good point, something to remember." He told Doyle that Sue was willing to return to Thailand, but said nothing of why she was willing to go.

"Excellent," Doyle said, "We'll have to start planning."

Harry told him about John Birch, and what Louie told him about their Shanghai girl. "Wow!" Doyle said at the end. "You were busy in there."

"Isn't that what cocktail parties are for?"

"You're making a lot of work for us, you know. This will keep us busy for months. Meanwhile, your friends in the AVG today reached 'The End,' as they say in the cinema."

"The 'end of the beginning', actually." Harry could not resist saying that, but Doyle was too quick for him.

"What does that mean, 'the end of the beginning' of what?"

"The 'end of the beginning of the rest of our war,' I suppose," Harry said. The whiskey was wearing off. He was feeling tired. "The AVG was the one successful thing that happened out here. Everything else crumbled."

"We've done okay, you and I. By the way, I meant to ask you, where was Olga tonight, the beauteous Madame Greenlaw?"

"Delhi, I think. That's what someone said."

"Delhi, huh?" Doyle sighed. "So Olga's gone too. Is she coming back?" He shrugged, did not wait for answer. "I was ready to propose to her tonight, did you know that?" His voice turned sad then. "You're right, everything out here has crumbled, Harry. Life was more fulfilling in Burma, wasn't it? It was much simpler there."

"You miss our garden? Makes me wonder what happened to the old woman."

"She speaks Japanese now, serves green tea. Rangoon was you and me, Harry, and things that were easy to understand. The Japs were the enemy, and sometimes the British. Here you can't trust anyone. The Chinese are our friends, but they're the enemy too. The Thai have declared war on us, but they're really our friends. How do you fight a war like that?"

"By reading the wind," Harry said. "We'll learn as we go. It's what we've been doing."

"Learn as we go. What a way to fight a war."

"It's the spy way. There's no precedent."

"It's our way, and "Oh, So Secret." Doyle pulled something from under the seat and passed it to Harry. "Here, you go first, he said. It was a bottle of whiskey in a dirty bag.

"To you, Doyle," Harry said, and held the bottle high. He put it to his lips and heard Doyle say:

"Listen, Harry, in the darkness, the sound of hooves!"

CHAPTER 42

July 8, 1942
Chungking

Ed Rector signed out a jeep from the Army Air Corps motor pool. He was a squadron commander now, and could do things like that. He picked up Harry in town, and they drove to a quiet spot on the riverbank at the edge of the city, high above the Yangtze. There was a small restaurant there, run by a family with three pretty daughters. When the AVG found it, they kept it in eggs, and meat and other things that were hard to find. Ed brought along two bottles of scotch. He presented one to the proprietor. "That will assure us an excellent meal," he told Harry as he filled their glasses from the second.

"So you're staying on in China, Ed?"

"I am. The Old Man talked to Tex, and Tex talked to me. The Old Man needed some experienced pilots. Tex and I agreed to stay, and three other AVG pilots did too, and a handful of ground crew. Now I'm a major in the Army Air Corps and the commander of the 76th Fighter Squadron."

"You've come a long way for a Navy dive bomber pilot."

"I sure have. Hey, I don't know if you remember this, Harry, but back in December, when this hassle all started, old Ace Rector here got credit for bagging the first Jap airplane that the AVG shot down."

"How could I forget something like that? It was at Kunming, and you got lost coming back."

"That's right. Well, guess who is being credited with the last airplane the AVG shot down?"

"Not Ace Rector!"

"Bet your ass it's Ace Rector! I got the last Jap on the Fourth of July. Want to hear about it?"

"Bet your ass I want to hear."

"Well, it's basic stuff really. The Old Man was expecting trouble on the Fourth. He sent me down to Hengyang. It's one of our forward bases close to the Nippers. I had this ragtag outfit, 14 pilots, new replacements just in from the States. I kept them up till midnight teaching them the Old Man's tactics.

"Early next morning, our warning net alerted us. The Japs were coming. We got up high, saw a dozen Nates diving on another flights. And we dove on the Nates. I got one in a diving turn.

"Then I climbed back up to make more passes. One Nate came at me, forced me into a dive. On the way down I got in a head-on burst at two others. One spewed out a big cloud of smoke.

"Anyway, in the end I got credited with one of the Nates…which just happened to be the last Jap airplane to go down on the Fourth of July!"

"Well, how about that! You got the first Jap, and you got the last. That's one for the record books."

"So it seems. And now the AVG is gone. A big part of my life, Harry. Yours too."

The rest of lunch was pretty quiet as they ate and thought. The food was excellent, as Ed said it would be. Afterwards, they walked along the riverbank, looked down at the Yangtze far below. A mist came rolling in, filtering through the branches of the big old willow trees that lined the bank.

"The mist makes it look like an old scroll painting, doesn't it?" Rector said. "I guess I'm glad I'm staying in China, even though I'm back in the military now. It's not something I've been looking forward to. The AVG was an easygoing outfit. It was tough and it was effective, but it was easygoing. A lot of us started to think like the Old Man, and concentrate on things that mattered. But now the AVG is gone and a big part of my life is over. Maybe it was the best part."

"Hey! Hey!"

The cry startled them. They looked around. An old Chinese man was crouched under the overhanging limb of one of the willows.

"You! You!" He pointed at Rector.

They stopped. Rector smiled, shoved a hand in a pocket for a coin. The old man suddenly stood up. He had no teeth, not a wisp of hair. He looked agitated now, started to shout: "Fei Hu! Fei Hu!" And pointed at Rector all the while. "Fei Hu! Fei Hu!"

"He's calling you a Flying Tiger," Harry said. "It's your leather jacket.

Fei Hu means Flying Tiger."

"Is that right?" Rector said, and smiled. He walked over to the man, held out his hand. The old man looked uncertain, reached for it tentatively, then finally grasped it in his. Rector shook the old man's hand vigorously. It put a surprised look on the old man's face, that slowly turned to a smile of pleasure.

"Fei Hu," Rector said, "AVG." He pointed at himself.

The old man took a step back. His smile faded. He regarded Rector and Harry for a few moments, pointed a finger at Rector again. He spoke, but it was quieter than before, and barely comprehensible. It was an attempt at English words that they both understood:

"AVG, AVG," the old man said. "American Very Good."

"Is that right?" Rector said again. He laughed. The old Chinese man laughed too.

"It's your legacy," Harry said. "American Very Good. That's how the Chinese will remember the AVG."

Rector shrugged. "It could be worse," he said. "Come on, Harry, let's go before it rains again."

They started walking. After a few steps, Rector stopped. He turned back to the old man, squared his shoulders, and snapped off a salute.

"You take care, grandfather," he said.

The End

WHAT BECAME OF THEM?

Harry survived the war – as did most of his friends. Ed Rector stayed on in China as a squadron leader and later as commander of the 23rd Fighter Group. He became a double ace. He stayed in the Air Force after the war and was sent to Taiwan to help build a modern Air Force for the Chinese Nationalist Government.

Tex Hill also spent much of the war in China. He would be called the most outstanding fighter pilot and combat leader of the air war. Olga Greenlaw and husband Harvey left China when the AVG was disbanded. Olga wrote one of the first books about the AVG, "The Lady and the Tigers", split up with Harvey and dropped out of sight. Olga's defender, Greg Boyington, returned to the Marines, was sent to the South Pacific, where they called him "Pappy" and gave him the Medal of Honor.

John Birch spent most of his war as an intelligence operative behind Japanese lines, first for Chennault and later for the OSS, and did an exceptional job. On a mission at the end of the war his temper got him in a scuffle with a young Chinese Communist soldier. He was shot to death, the first American killed by the Communists in China. In the U.S. a society was named for him.

Just months before the war ended, General Chennault was eased out of his command by the Air Force leadership in Washington. By then, he and his "Flying Tigers" were the stuff of legend. Tai Li survived the war as head of the largest espionage organization of its time. When he was killed in plane crash not long afterwards, many believed he faked his own death, others that OSS did it. President Truman disbanded the OSS a month after the war ended and General Donovan went back to practicing law.

Harry's lady friends fared well. Sue managed to balance conflicting loyalties between Harry, the OSS and Tai Li, and between the Free Thai and the Thai Communist Party – and to stay in everyone's good graces. She returned to Thailand after the war, but left when political conditions became unfavorable for both the Free Thai and the Thai communists. It was said that she went back to China then, and perhaps she did for a time. Lucy saw her in London in the early 1950s. Harry tried to find her, but lost her trail in Paris. Someone said she married a Frenchman with business interests in Vietnam.

The Shanghai girl had a good war. She stayed close to her Japanese friends to the end – and reported faithfully on them to OSS. Once the war ended, her relations with the Japanese would have been a problem had not OSS provided her with a new identity and helped her start an art business, in Kunming and later in Taipei. Her business prospered with branches in Hong Kong, Singapore, and eventually, Shanghai. When old Chinese advertising posters started being treated as works of art, there was one she refused to sell – where she was posed demurely with a bottle of whiskey at her feet. She never married, but had a happy life. .

Louie was wealthy when the war started, and even wealthier when it ended. He moved to Taiwan with the Chiang Kai-shek government and helped create the island's prosperity. He was offered cabinet positions in Chiang's government, but preferred to stay behind the scenes. He maintained ties with American intelligence and had a passing acquaintance with the intelligence services of a dozen Asian and European countries. The only spies he would not lunch with were those from the KGB – or at least that was what he told the Americans.

Lucy followed Louie to Taiwan as a partner in his businesses. She saw the possibilities of computers early on, got into the industry and grew wealthy in her own right. She married an Englishman with some minor title, divorced him and married another. She met with Harry often during her frequent travels. They remained great friends, had morning coffee together when they could, but were never lovers. Lucy never understood why – nor did Harry.

Doyle learned a lot during the war, about intelligence and bureaucracy. He returned to Washington and when the CIA was formed in 1947, he was among the first to join. He became a powerful bureaucrat, but left intelligence work – quietly – sometime after the Bay of Pigs affair. Over the years he thought often of Harry and their meetings in the scraggly garden in Rangoon, where they had learned to become spies.

Harry seemed a bit lost after the war. He wrote for newspapers and magazines, always about Asia, and became known as a minor expert. Then he was called on to write "think-pieces" for the learned journals and became "an authority". He traveled much, mostly to the hot-spots in Asia: Burma in the late 1940s, Hanoi in early 1950s, then Indonesia, and finally Saigon. Because of his peripatetic life style he was accused regularly of being a "spy" - and passed it off with a laugh.

ACKNOWLEDGEMENTS

I have tried to be accurate in my descriptions of the historical events portrayed in "Spies in the Garden". The many written accounts of the times served me well, but to get a real feel for that era, I went to those who were there.

For a sense of the first desperate days of the ground war in Burma, I am indebted to Major E R B "Roy" Hudson, of the Royal Bombay Sappers and Miners. He managed to stay ahead of the Japanese Army as it marched on Rangoon, and was there when the tide of war turned and it was the Japanese who tried to stay ahead of the pursing British. Among other distinctions, he set the charges that dropped the Sittang Bridge into the river.

For a sense of the good life and how it ended in Rangoon, and for what it was like to be high above the city, diving on the Japanese bomber formations, I must thank the AVG Flying Tigers. Ed Rector, Charlie Mott and Tex Hill shared their recollections over many years and much fine scotch. Dick Rossi, Bob Layher, Peter Wright, Robert Keeton, Ken Jernstedt, and Charlie Bond also told me their stories during AVG reunions and when we traveled to Thailand and China together. AVG nurse, Red Hanks, one of the few Flying Tiger ladies, gave me a unique perspective on life in the AVG. Her husband, Fletcher Hanks, was an inspiration. He flew the Hump during the war, and 50 years later climbed Chinese mountains to find the wreckage of a friend's airplane.

There are many things about the war in Asia I would not have fully understood without the insights of my friends there. Among them, Free Thai officers, Wimon Wirayawit, Piya Chakkaphak, Pisoot "Pete" Sudasna, and "the youngest operative" of them all, Orachun Tanaphong. His aunt, Kronthong Chutima, is a remarkable lady and was a Free Thai from the very start. Another old friend in Thailand witnessed the AVG raid on Chiang Mai and was inspired to become a pilot: Royal Thai Air Force (RTAF) Air Marshal (retired) Boonzong Suphanan helped me in countless ways over the years – and still does. And very special thanks are owed to my friend "Tang", RTAF Group Captain (retired) Veerayuth Didyasarin, who recovered the wreckage of an AVG P-40 – the only one ever found – and made possible the adventures we shared with the Flying Tigers.

Among those who helped me understand the China of World War II was Renji Hua, who also helped me understand the China of today. For special insights I owe thanks to Madame Gao Li Liang, whose father, Gao Chi Hang was the first Chinese Air Force pilot to score a victory over a Japanese bomber and a hero to all Chinese. The veteran airmen of the Aviators

Associations in Beijing, Nanking and Kunming, were always welcoming and eager to help. My interpreter Zhao Gang of Yunnan University, helped me see Kunming through fresh eyes. An American friend, Robert Lee, who served in China during the war and still visits there regularly brought perspective to an era he knew well.

Over the years I spoke with a number of OSS officers – long before I thought of writing a book. Regrettably, I now remember their stories better than I remember their names. Two in particular stand out: Elizabeth P. McIntosh, who served in India and China, and later got to know "Wild Bill" Donovan. She gave me wonderful insights into the OSS organization and its people. Major General John Singlaub, who went to China after serving in occupied France, related his experiences and answered many of my questions.

To all those who helped me understand the era, the people and the places about which I wrote – and to Monique, my wife, for her encouragement, knowledge of Asian history, and constructive readings of my drafts – I am most grateful.